"AIR DEFENSE ALERT!"

The officer screamed his warning into the wind, as if the sheer volume of his words could drive back what was coming out of the night. It had broad wings and was black all over, but it was the thing slung under the middle of its wings that filled him with terror.

Some people heard him. Some of them had weapons, and some of those used them. The officer himself was firing when the stealth drone reached its programmed altitude and the radar-activated fuse detonated the bomb under its belly.

Where there'd been darkness and shadows, now there was only light. And there was nowhere to hide as the fireball reached out to envelop them. . . .

☆ ☆ ☆

STARCRUISER SHENANDOAH #3

The Sum of Things

by
Roland J. Green

A ROC BOOK

And with special thanks to Larry Nichols, for this contribution to the characters of Lucretia, Mickey and Herman Franke.

ROC
Published by the Penguin Group
Penguin Books USA Inc., 375 Hudson Street,
New York, New York 10014, U.S.A.
Penguin Books Ltd, 27 Wrights Lane,
London W8 5TZ, England
Penguin Books Australia Ltd, Ringwood,
Victoria, Australia
Penguin Books Canada Ltd, 2801 John Street,
Markham, Ontario, Canada L3R 1B4
Penguin Books (N.Z.) Ltd, 182-190 Wairau Road,
Auckland 10, New Zealand

Penguin Books Ltd, Registered Offices:
Harmondsworth, Middlesex, England

First published by Roc, an imprint of New American Library,
a division of Penguin Books USA Inc.

First Printing, May, 1991
10 9 8 7 6 5 4 3 2 1

 Roc is a trademark of New American Library,
a division of Penguin Books USA Inc.

PRINTED IN THE UNITED STATES OF AMERICA

To the memory of Lurton Blassingame, the best agent a new writer could have had—or any other kind of writer, for that matter.

And with special thanks to Larry Nichols, for his contribution to the characters of Lucretia Morley and Herman Franke.

Principal Characters

A. Human

Major Nathan ABELSOHN: Federation Army commandant, Camp Aounda.

Lieutenant Colonel Peter BISSELL: Associated States Forces Intelligence.

Captain Madeleine BLOCH: C.O., Federation Ranger Team on Victoria.

Captain Pavel BOGDANOV, U.F.N.: Executive officer, *Shenandoah*.

Father Elijah BROTHERTONGUE: Member, House of Delegates and Military Council, Associated States of Victoria.

Colonel Indira CHATTERJE: Chief medical officer, Victoria Command.

Captain Lucco DiVRIES: Administrative officer, Medical Corps, A.S.F.

Captain Raimondo DiVRIES: Officer in First Battalion, Freedom Legion; brother of Lucco DiVries.

Sergeant Juan ESTEVA: Scout Company HQ and operative for Federation Intelligence.

Brigadier Domenic FEGELI: C.O., Alliance ground forces on Victoria.

Ronald FITZPATRICK: Prime Minister, Associated States of Victoria.

Acting Commander Herman FRANKE, U.F.N.: Staff officer, Intelligence, and representative of the Kishi Institute.

Jeremiah GIST: Former Governor-General, Dominion of Victoria.

Judith GLICKSOHN: President, Associated States of Victoria.

Martin HOLLINGS: Governor, Freeworld States Alliance Territory of Seven Rivers, on Victoria.

Philip KARRAS: Senator, Associated States of Victoria, and Chairman of the Military Council.

Major General Mikhail KORNILOV: Commanding general, Federation Victoria Command.

Acting Vice Admiral Sho KUWAHARA, U.F.N.: Admiral commanding Federation Victoria Task Force.

Brigadier General Marcus LANGSTON: Commanding general, Federation Victoria Brigade.

Captain Rose LIDDELL, U.F.N.: C.O., Federation battlecruiser *Shenandoah*.

"LIONHEART": Code name for data–processing technician, acting as agent for Colonel Pak. Given name Ramdur.

Second Lieutenant Charles LONGMAN, U.F.N.: Attached to naval ground party, Camp Aounda.

Admiral Marya LOPATINA, F.S.N.: Senior Alliance naval officer on Victoria.

First Lieutenant Brian MAHONEY, U.F.N.: Communications Department, *Shenandoah*, and adviser to Victoria Militia.

Commander Joanna MARDER, F.S.N.: Former executive officer, heavy cruiser *Audacious*, now agent for Colonel Pak.

Acting Major Lucretia MORLEY: Military Police officer, attached to Provost Marshal's office, Victoria Command.

Lieutenant Colonel Liew NIEG: Intelligence, Victoria Command.

Colonel Somtow NOSAVAN, M.D.: Associated States Forces Medical Corps.

Colonel Sun Ji PAK: C.O., Alliance 96th Independent Regiment.

Major General Alys PARKINSON: Former commanding general, Victoria Militia, now commander-in-chief, Associated States Forces.

Acting Major Candice SHORES: C.O., Scout Company, Victoria Brigade.

Second Lieutenant Brigitte TACHIN, U.F.N.: Weapons Department, *Shenandoah*, and adviser to Victoria Militia.

Commodore Tazuo UEHARA, U.F.N.: Second in command, Federation Victoria Task Force.

Rear Admiral Mordecai UZEL, F.S.N.: Former chief of staff to Admiral Lopatina, now acting commander of Alliance naval forces off Victoria.

Colonel Ludmilla VESEY: Chief of staff, Federation Victoria Command.

Commodore Carlotta YAGUE, U.F.N.: Chief of staff, Federation Victoria Task Force.

First Lieutenant Elayne ZHENG, U.F.N.: Electronic warfare officer, 879th Squadron.

Sergeant Major Raoul ZIMMER: Company sergeant major, Scout Company.

B. Baernoi

Eimo SU-ANKRAI: Fleet Commander of the Seventh Training Force off Victoria.

Ship Commander First Class Brokeh SU-IRZIM: Inquiry staff commander, Seventh Training Force.

Ship Commander First Class Zhapso SU-LAL: Chief Inquirer, Seventh Training Force.

Ship Commander First Class Rahbad SARLIN: Observer, Special Projects, Office of Inquiry.

F'Mita IHR SULAR: Commander, chartered merchant vessel *Perfumed Wind*.

C. Merishi

Councillor Payaral NA'AN: Leader of Merishi merchant refugees.

Essteb Y'EEL: Proprietor, Web of Hrar restaurant and hotel, Silvermouth.

Glossary

Act of Union: Agreement between Bushranger Republic and Dominion of Victoria forming the Associated States of Victoria (see *Division of the Spoils*).

AD: Air Defense.

AG: Attacker Group.

AI: Artificial Intelligence.

A.I.: Action for Independence.

Antahli: Leading minority nationality in the Khudrigate of Baer.

AO: Area of Operations.

A.S.F.: Associated States Forces.

ASP: Advanced Surgical Post.

Associated States of Victoria: See "Act of Union."

Baernoi: Sapient humanoid race, highly militarized, whose remote ancestors resembled Terran pigs.

BBA: "Blabbers Boiled Alive," legendary, ultimate level of security classification.

Bushranger Republic: Short-lived political unit formed from both Federation and Alliance territory by the first Victorian rebellion (see *Squadron Alert*).

CA: Combat Assault.

CAG: Commander, Attacker Group.

CC/ACC: Combat Center/Auxiliary Combat Center.

C-cubed: Command, control, communications.

C.O.: Commanding Officer.

CG: Commanding General.

CP: Command Post.

ECM: Electronic Countermeasures.

EDP: Equivalent Duty Performed.

EI: Electronic Intercept/Intelligence.

ETA: Estimated Time of Arrival.

EVA: Extravehicular Activity.

EW/EWO: Electronic Warfare/Electronic Warfare Officer.

FAE: Fuel-Air Explosive.

F.I./F.I.O.: Field Intelligence (Operations), the covert-operations specialists of the Freeworld States Alliance.

Freedom Legion: Paramilitary force organized by the Freedom Party for the invasion of Seven Rivers Territory.

F.S.N.: Freeworld States Navy.

Great Khudr: Military leader who united the planet Baer under Syrodhi leadership.

Guidance: Baernoi term for navigation.

HE: High Explosive.

HQ: Headquarters.

IFF: Identification, Friend or Foe.

Inquiry: Baernoi term for Intelligence.

IR: Infra-red.

JAG: Judge Advocate General.

(J.) O.O.W.: (Junior) Officer of the Watch.

KIA/WIA: Killed in Action/Wounded in Action.

Kishi Institute: Leading research institute of the United Federation of Starworlds, founded by the Federation's first President.

K'thressh: Sapient octopoidal sea-dwelling race, never leaving their home planet but defending it with powerful projective telepathy.

LI: Light Infantry.

LZ: Landing Zone.

Merishi: Humanoid sapient race, evolved from climbing omnivorous reptiles; ruthless and far-flung traders.

MP: Military Police.

NCO: Non-commissioned Officer.

OP: Observation Post.

OTC: Officers' Training Course *or* Officer in Tactical Command.

Petzas: Nearest major Baernoi planet and Fleet base to Victoria.

POW: Prisoner of War.

Pterch'a: The "Catmen" or "Catpeople," a felinoid sapient race formerly serving as mercenaries for the Merishi.

QRF: Quick Reaction Force.

RHIP: Rank Hath Its Privileges.

Scaleskins: Derogatory term used by both Baernoi and humans for the Merishi.

SFC/SFO: Supporting Fires Controller/Observer.

skrin: Small, voracious predator, native to mountainous regions of Baer.

SOP(S): Senior Officer Present (in Space) *or* Standard Operating Procedure.

Special Projects: Baernoi term for covert operations; under the Office of Inquiry.

SSW: Squad Support Weapon.

Syrodhi: Dominant nationality among the Baernoi, empowered by its leadership in uniting the planet.

TD: Temporary Duty.

T.O. & E.: Table of Organization and Equipment.

Tuskers: Derogatory human term for the Baernoi, who have visible and non-vestigial tusks.

U.F.N.: United Federation Navy.

UI: Urgent Immediate (communications priority).

Watch: Baernoi unit of time, equivalent to 5.2 hours. The Baernoi day is divided into five watches.

X.O.: Executive Officer.

Prologue

Astronomer-Academician Martina Kovacs wondered if her life was caught in a playback loop. It seemed that way since she came to the Nicola Chennault Observatory in the Victoria System in the middle of the planet's war.

Again she was part of a group of six astronomers. Again she was listening to a briefing by a naval officer. And again the naval officer was summarizing the history of Victoria's first round of fighting.

"So the Alliance's recognizing the Bushranger Republic forced the Federation's hand. We also recognized it, and everyone expected that once the Armistice Commission tied up the loose ends peace would break out. At least that was what people of goodwill thought.

"Unfortunately, there were too many people who either didn't have goodwill, or weren't thinking, or both."

Kovacs decided that the playback wasn't perfect. She was in the conference room of Director Kuttelwascher's office suite at the observatory, not aboard a ship in Victoria orbit. The other astronomers included Kuttelwascher herself and several senior members of the staff, instead of Kovacs's fellow passengers on the liner to Victoria.

Finally, it was a different naval officer briefing the astronomers on a different situation. Nightmarishly different.

"There are lots of theories floating around about responsibility for the first few incidents, like the shooting down of *Mahmoud Sa'id*. Too many theories, and not enough facts.

"But we know that the tensions produced by these incidents led to a rebellion against the government of the Bushranger Republic. With Federation support, this rebellion was suppressed.

"However, it left some of the people of ill will desperate. They launched an invasion of Seven Rivers Territory. At

1

the same time they or people friendly to them made a suicidal attack with fusion weapons on the Alliance squadron defending Seven Rivers.

"At the moment Federation policy is to cooperate with Alliance and the Victorians to prevent any further incidents and learn who was responsible for the previous ones.

"Any questions? There are some that I'm not allowed to answer and some I can't. I'll do my best with all the others."

Kuttelwascher frowned. "Surely you don't need to maintain security restrictions with this group?"

The briefer smiled. That was another difference, Kovacs realized. The lieutenant who gave the first briefing, the Brian Mahoney who did so well as an adviser in the first Bushranger Rebellion, was tall and lanky and looked almost cadaverous even when he smiled.

Lieutenant Commander Herman Franke was shorter, broader, rounder, and looked almost cherubic even when he wasn't smiling. Kovacs wondered what he would look like without clothes, other than probably rather hairy. She also wondered about the rumor that Franke had some connections with both Intelligence and the Kishi Institute.

Franke shrugged. "I can't give you BBA ratings, and a lot is classified that high. I still think it would have been a better idea to have me brief the whole staff, in one or two sittings."

"You don't trust us to disseminate your intelligence correctly." Kuttelwascher was politely making a statement, not asking a question. Kovacs wondered how long the politeness would last.

"I trust the Standing Administrative Committee to do as well as any committee. But the failings of committees tend to be greater than their individual members'."

Kovacs wondered if the director would ask Franke about his orders, with an eye to challenging Admiral Kuwahara over them. So far Kuttelwascher and the commander of the Victoria Squadron had avoided head-on collisions. But being stonewalled in her own observatory, even in her own office, might push the director past the bounds of good judgment.

Instead Kuttelwascher leaned back in her chair and swept the table with her eyes. The others now had her permission to ask questions, as well as Commander Franke's.

"Is the Alliance cooperating with us?" Kovacs asked.

"At the moment they don't have much choice. They lost more than half their naval strength in the attack. We outnumber them two to one now. It will be four to one when Commodore Uehara's task force is fully deployed around Victoria. If anybody is going to prevent a suicide run on the 96th Regiment while it fights off the invasion, it won't be Admiral Lopatina's ships."

"How is Admiral Lopatina?" That was Dr. Dao Yung, the chief of administrative services.

"Rear Admiral Uzel is acting commander of the Alliance naval forces. Lopatina is reported in serious but stable condition. We have sent medical supplies and personnel and are negotiating over technical assistance and spare parts."

Those negotiations might take a while, Kovacs knew. By all reports Uzel was almost a caricature of the Bar Kochban—gifted, prickly, and proud. He wouldn't deliberately endanger his ships or his admiral by refusing Federation assistance, but he would exhaust every other resource before accepting it.

Academician Fleischer, the head of physics, frowned. "Then we might be able to assist the Alliance forces ourselves, without Federation interference?"

Franke looked bemused for a second, then nodded. "But remember, I can speak only for the Federation. There may be other armed and dangerous parties lurking out there, as we were so unpleasantly reminded a week ago."

Ice clinked in Kuttelwascher's voice. "Are you questioning our courage?"

Franke's disarming smile returned. "If I did, I'd be throwing the first stone. Personally, I'd rather be several hundred light years from Victoria. But I have orders to stay here. You don't.

"Also, whoever took out the Alliance squadron clearly thinks they're the main enemy. These may be the same people who tried to hijack *Leon Brautigan*, with no regard for the safety of observatory people. If they learn that observatory people are helping the Alliance, do you want to bet that they're out of bombs and ships?"

"Isn't the Navy planning on guarding the observatory?" Kuttelwascher asked. She sounded almost plaintive.

"We are. *Rasmussen* will remain on patrol off the observatory, while I shift to *Cavour* for the last leg to Victoria. But suicide attacks can usually get past one ship. Something could happen to force us to withdraw *Rasmussen*. And—I wish I didn't have to bring this up, but—"

Before Kuttelwascher could dissect Franke for his hesitancy, the com chime sounded. Kovacs watched her screen light up, to show the sensor administrator's sweating dark face. Then the screen went blank, and Kovacs saw the director insert an audio plug into her left ear.

Whatever she heard, it was short and unpleasant. Kovacs didn't want to meet the director's eyes when she pulled the plug. To his credit, Commander Franke could.

"Commander Franke. Our safety radar has just picked up a large force of unidentified ships. Course and velocity data are only preliminary, but compatible with Victoria as a destination.

"Commander Franke, I have also been informed that the radar on both light cruisers has been active. Its range is sufficient to have picked up those ships.

"From what you have said, these cannot be Federation ships. Who are they, and why has the Federation withheld information about them?"

Kovacs looked at Franke as intently as the director did. It was now up to the commander to prevent the observatory declaring war on the Navy. That would be as futile as a mouse declaring war on a cat. Or maybe not, when the cat already had other and bigger wars on its paws. . . .

"Well, Commander Franke?"

In Battle Command of *Night Warrior*, Ship Commander First Class Brokeh su-Irzim thumbed data onto the screens in front of him. Then he reclined and contemplated it. Finally he raised and swiveled his couch and faced Fleet Commander Eimo su-Ankrai.

"Two radars, Commander. One is the observatory's old S-218. An exact match for our data. The other is an S-311, probably a Mark V at least. Also a good match for our data on Marks V and VI."

The old commander bared his tusks briefly. "A Federation capital ship at the observatory. What of their neutrality now?"

Su-Irzim had never been sure if Inquiry had a patron lord

or even deserved one. So he wasted no time in prayers or rites of aversion. He merely returned the fleet commander's hard look, to the limits of respect.

"You disagree?"

"The late models of the S-311 are compact enough to be fitted to ships down to light cruisers or even scouts, if they are disarmed. We know that the Victoria Squadron has been using light cruisers as tenders to the observatory, to avoid another *Leon Brautigan* incident.

"Also, the reinforcements might be carrying out-system supplies for the observatory. The Victoria system is hardly the safest place for unarmed merchant vessels. It would be within reason for the supply vessel to be conducting a radar scan, without any hostile intent."

"At least not hostile to us," su-Ankrai said. His tusks had returned to normal. He looked ready to smile.

Su-Irzim knew he could erase that smile and bare those tusks again by asking what this said about the People's human allies. Were those who destroyed the Alliance squadron really friends of the People? And were they friends worth winning over, if they were not?

Su-Ankrai coughed, giving su-Irzim the sensation of having his thoughts read. But the Fleet Commander only said mildly, "Very well, Inquirer. Advise me as such."

Asking what advice the commander wanted, or suggesting a call to the fleet's senior Inquirer would produce bared tusks at best. At worst, it would end su-Irzim's effectiveness aboard *Night Warrior* before the mission to Victoria had reached its most critical phase.

"My advice is not to treat this as a breach of the observatory's neutrality. If we attack it at once, we will be at war with the Federation immediately afterward. If we merely threaten it, the Federation will evacuate the staff and leave as hostages only some expensive but replaceable equipment.

"Indeed, I suggest that we prevent the Federation radar operators from panicking by identifying ourselves."

"Why not wait until we receive their IFF signal?"

"Federation Navy and civilian IFFs are distinctive. Naval ships might not wish to reveal their presence. The observatory's own IFF is less capable, and the director is less than willing to become involved with the Navy."

"One wonders how the Smallteeth became so advanced

when their scientists know no discipline," su-Ankrai said. "But that is not a question we can ask today."

He reclined. "Call Signals and tell them to identify us. Add to our description as a training squadron that we picked up signals suggesting a crisis while in the outer system. Instead of another Passage, we are approaching to offer compassionate assistance."

"I—we—suspect that the ships will turn out to be either Baernoi or Merishi," Franke said.

"Wonderful!" Kuttelwascher said. "I am even more ecstatic than before over being left ignorant of this."

Franke shook his head. "You're in good company. I—"

"I do not care what the company is. I want to know why the observatory is part of it!"

"You'll learn a damned sight faster if I'm not interrupted every other sentence."

Kuttelwascher took a deep breath and Kovacs shifted in her chair, ready to divert the director's wrath if she lost her temper completely. One of the twenty or so most distinguished living human astronomers, Academician Birgitta Kuttelwascher was not accustomed to being told to shut up.

To Kovacs's unashamed relief, the director let the breath out and nodded. "Continue, then, Commander. But please be brief."

Franke succeeded. The only previous evidence of anybody else being in the Victoria System was an unidentifiable Emergence detected two days before the attack on the Alliance Navy. It had been near the limit of detectability from Victoria, below that limit from the observatory or the incoming Federation reinforcements, both on the opposite side of the Victoria System.

"So all anybody in the Victoria Squadron had was a guess. We in Uehara's squadron didn't even have that until we got within tight-beam range. Kuwahara wasn't about to risk telling our visitors that they'd been spotted."

"But he ordered you into tactical formation, didn't he?" the director asked.

"That was after the attack on the Alliance. We couldn't be sure if the same people were going to come after us next, or with what. I was authorized to discuss the Emergence two hours before I transferred to *Rasmussen* to pay you people a call.

"We've concealed some guesses, from you and a lot of other people, for good and sufficient reasons. We haven't concealed any hard data. If you disagree, take it up with Admiral Kuwahara. I'll even take your request to him myself."

Kuttelwascher still looked forbidding, but Kovacs knew that this was partly an act. She would not apologize, but she also wouldn't press the matter. She would try to leave Franke in doubt and even fear as long as possible.

"I hope that won't become necessary," the director said. "At the worst, what seems to have happened is an honest mistake by people coping with an unexpectedly demanding situation. If the observatory is not endangered . . ."

Franke's face twisted and Kovacs knew that he'd understood what the director implied. *If the observatory is safe, everybody else can squabble over Victoria until the heat death of the universe.*

"There's one thing you can do to help, as I started to say before our visitors crashed the party," Franke added. "Don't send that aid mission to the Alliance. We have reason to believe that there's a security leak in the observatory's support staff on Victoria. Intelligence hasn't had much time to track it down, so we have to assume it's still open. Anything you sent to the Alliance would become known to the same people who tried to hijack *Brautigan* and succeeded in destroying the Alliance squadron."

Kovacs suspected Commander Franke knew more than he was saying, even that some of the observatory staff was suspect. But he could hardly say that without snatching the director's olive branch from her hand and slapping her in the face with it. Kuttelwascher was a tree tiger with one cub when it came to defending her staff from outside attacks, whatever she might do to them herself.

Before anyone could react, the com chimed again. It was the sensor desk again. "Message from the unidentified squadron, ma'am. They say they're Baernoi."

Kuttelwascher didn't cut in anybody else's screen, but signaled Franke to come and look over her shoulder at her own. Kovacs saw the officer's bushy eyebrows rise and stay up, then heard a long whistle.

"Trouble, Commander—" the director began, but Franke cut her off with a sharp gesture. She actually obeyed, and Kovacs would have sworn she licked her lips.

The printer whined. Franke tore off the sheet of paper and handed one copy to the director, stuffing the other in his tunic pocket.

"This could be trouble," he said. "The Baernoi have identified themselves as the Seventh Training Force, under Fleet Commander Eimo su-Ankrai. He's one of their oldest and best, and a hard-core Syrodhi aristocrat to boot.

"His ships include a carrier, two battleships the size of *Shenandoah*, and a flagship as big as *Valhalla*. Fewer attackers, but they have three light cruiser squadrons and their lights can work better in atmosphere than ours. They also don't have a dockyard, but their ships are more damage resistant than ours.

"Generally, I still don't think we have an immediate threat. The Baernoi do run training forces this deep into Federation space, although they usually give notice when they do. Also—and please, this doesn't go outside the room—the people we've found involved with the rebels on Victoria have so far been either Merishi or humans working for the Merishi. Baernoi-made weapons have turned up, plenty of them, but the Baernoi arms dealers will sell to anyone with trade goods or usable currency."

Kuttelwascher looked as if she wished all arms dealers aboard a ship falling into a black hole. For once Kovacs agreed with the director.

Kuttelwascher nodded. "I certainly cannot imagine the Baernoi being so barbarous as to threaten a scientific institution of our stature. But—do you have any specific suggestions?" The last sentence sounded forced out, like congealed syrup from a tube.

"Strict neutrality. Ration supplies and make sure the life-support systems are on the top line. If you want, we can evacuate any nonessential staff if they're ready to go within four hours."

"That soon?"

Franke shrugged. "I could be wrong. But I suspect *Rasmussen* will be heading out in a few minutes, to shadow the Baernoi. *Cavour* may be ordered to remain on station to protect you. She may also be ordered in to Victoria. If she is, she'll be the last ship out of the observatory for a while. We don't want to put isolated ships in places where 'accidents' can be arranged."

"I understand and appreciate the offer," Kuttelwascher said. "I will speak for my staff, though, in saying that none of us wishes to abandon post."

"As you wish, ma'am. But any sort of secure communications may be chancy for a few weeks. It might secure the interests of the observatory if you could send an observer down to Victoria aboard *Cavour*. Just one, but preferably somebody who would be listened to."

Kuttelwascher nodded. "I have no problem with that, either. Now, is there anything further we need to discuss?"

There being nothing, Kovacs was first out the door, for all the good that did her. Fleischer caught up with her before she reached the elevator.

"The director wants to talk to you."

"About my taking over your projects while you go to Victoria?"

"You're not passing the graveyard yet, Marty. You don't have to whistle."

"No, just passing my own grave."

Fleischer hugged her. "I'll keep it in flowers, if it comes to that."

"Glory to God," Kovacs said, and turned back.

Kovacs found Kuttelwascher in her private office, with her chair turned away from her desk and a brandy bottle with two glasses set out on a side table.

"You wanted me?"

"Pour yourself a drink, if you wish."

Kovacs wished it. She also wished not to appear nervous. "Thank you, but not on an empty stomach."

"Or while you're waiting for bad news? Never mind. I will ask you: Can you be our observer?" Kovacs nodded. "You're sure about your projects?"

"Between Pedzko and any help he can bribe out of Fleischer, none of them should wind up orphaned. At least not for the next three months. I have all of them except 767 past the initial stages. Any decent senior tech can do 767 blind drunk and in bed with three partners."

"We can hope the crisis won't last more than three months. That should be enough time for you to develop a picture of most of the people we'll be dealing with. Under the right influence, Commander Franke may help you."

"And then again, he may report me to his superiors, and where does that leave us?"

"Us, Academician?"

"Us, Madame Director. If I go down there to play spy and get caught, I won't keep quiet about who told me to do it."

"You can't risk that! Everybody will be so nervous about spies—"

"That I shouldn't become one in the first place."

"I thought you had your eye on Commander Franke."

"If I did, my affairs are not your affair."

"When they may breach observatory security—"

"What security, if the Navy becomes angry enough to take control of the observatory?"

"Do you question my loyalty?" Kuttelwascher's indignation seemed to be genuine. She also seemed ready to scream.

"No, I don't. But you're asking me to do things that might cause the Navy or Intelligence to do so. Are they worth that danger?"

Kuttelwascher swallowed her scream and looked down at the floor. "Will you at least keep your eyes and ears open?"

"That's part of the job, if I take it at all."

"Will you take it?" The director seemed to be almost pleading. Sympathy stirred in Kovacs, for a fellow astronomer nearing the end of a long and distinguished career that she'd hoped to finish in peace and quiet. It was no great surprise that she was thrashing about wildly to find some way out of the situation.

"Yes."

"Bless you. Now, is there anything you need?"

"Let me ring you back from my room. I'll know in twenty minutes."

One

Captain Rose Liddell respected the infantryman, who did most of the down-and-dirty fighting. She also had to admit that infantry combat must be more interesting to the people involved than to observers aboard *Shenandoah* five hundred kilometers upstairs.

The display in the C.O.'s conference room showed only cartoon figures darting from one misshapen gray rock to another equally ugly red one. Some reached safety. Others fell, touched by lines of fire that might be tracers or lasers, knocked flat by golden explosions, or flung into the air by invisible hands.

Three explosions close together enveloped a red rock. A strong wind must have been blowing last night; dust and smoke vanished in an eyeblink. The rock reappeared, uglier than before, with half a dozen bodies sprawled around it. Some of the bodies began moving as other, standing figures closed in on them.

What happened after that faded into a blur of movement; then the movement itself faded into the desert. The satellite was moving on along its orbit around Victoria. A live observer on the craft could have held position until the fight was over, or until it attracted the attention of shipkilling weapons.

The desertscape flickered, then vanished. The image of Victoria Command's chief of staff, Colonel Ludmilla Vesey, replaced it.

"That firefight you just saw was spread over an area of about ten square kilometers, to the southwest of Mount Aramis. It's part of an area of small farms, where there were several incidents with the police before the invasion.

"Analysis of the tapes indicates that many of the troops attacking Gamma/Third/96th wear no uniforms, have only

11

personal weapons, and are generally even more irregular
than the Freedom Legion. We have correlated this with EI
evidence that the invasion force now includes at least seven
companies.

"Our conclusion is that civilian support for the invasion
in the Border Counties area is becoming more active. Civilians are actually being issued arms and fighting Alliance
troops beside the Freedom Legion. This clearly gives the
Alliance's ground security problem a whole new dimension.
Mount Aramis is only seventy kilometers from the limits of
the Border Counties Administration. Beyond that limit, the
Freedom Legion will be in what has been Alliance territory
since the recognition of Victoria as a dual-sovereignty
planet.

"Victoria Command is preparing contingency plans for
this situation. We are also requesting an update on naval
capabilities for supporting Victoria Command ground operations in the Border Counties area of Seven Rivers
Territory.

"Thank you."

Vesey saluted and the screen went blank. The starscape
outside *Shenandoah* replaced it, a considerable improvement in Liddell's opinion.

Re ctantly she turned her eyes to Vice Admiral Sho
Kuw; ara, sitting across the little breakfast table. "Admiral?"

"A little more breakfast, please; then we can court indigestion." Kuwahara poured himself another cup of tea,
plucked a croissant from the basket, and handed the basket
down the table to Pavel Bogdanov. *Shenandoah*'s executive
officer took it as gravely as a priest picking up a chalice,
but it was empty when he set it down.

Liddell wasn't hungry. It had been seven days since she
was. She'd watched the sky catch fire with fusion explosions
and saw those explosions eat five ships and two thousand
men. Whenever her appetite tried to recover, something
else happened to knock it flat again, like Colonel Vesey's
news.

She still haggled and gnawed her way through the rest
of the omelette and half the croissant. With Commodore
Uehara's ships and men riding the skies of Victoria, *Shenandoah* was no longer the heart of Federation strength. But

Rose Liddell was still *Shenandoah*'s captain, with as many responsibilities as ever to five hundred officers and crew. Like a pregnant woman, she had to keep herself fit for the sake of others. Her own impulses were so much wastewater.

Kuwahara set down his cup. "I'd like to defer a detailed discussion until I've conferred with my new staff. Uehara is sending them over from *Baikhal* today, ETA 1300. Schedule the maneuvers accordingly."

Rose Liddell gaped helplessly. It was not done, to leap across a table and hug your commanding admiral. Bogdanov was less self-restrained. He dropped his last croissant, then smiled gravely.

Liddell was the first to speak. "Thank you, sir."

"Not curious about why?"

"Yes, but—"

"Not your business?"

"I would think so."

"Well, I disagree, and I am the admiral. Besides, this will be the last of our *Shenandoah* family breakfasts for a while. My staff will insist on my being walled off behind them, like a proper admiral. Sometimes I think *staff* should be spelled *s-t-a-p-h*."

Kuwahara poured his fifth cup of tea and leaned back in his chair, muscular hands cradling the cup. "*Baikhal* is already Commodore Uehara's flagship. Two flags on one capital ship strain tempers and communications.

"As for *Valhalla*, *Shen*'s command facilities are just as good, when you deduct what a carrier's attacker group uses. The carrier also has one major drawback."

Nobody said "Captain Prange," but Kuwahara nodded. "His previous squadron commanders usually didn't have anyone to replace him. Either that, or they were afraid he would end up senior to them and remember every time they'd sat on him."

More nods. Gustavus Vasa Prange had reached four stripes at the age of thirty-two, the youngest captain in the Federation Navy since the Hive Wars. Everyone expected he would go on to be an equally youthful admiral, and eventually look down from the lofty pinnacle of four stars on many of the people who had served with him.

"His turning *Valhalla* into a feudal estate is his affair for

now. It's an estate that breeds good warriors, and we need
them.

"But if he sulks over my not flying my flag from his
castle—he gets one warning. After that, Captain Bogdanov,
you get *Valhalla*."

"Admiral, blood feuds have started over less," Liddell
said.

"You are referring to losing Captain Bogdanov?"

"Yes. Also, if I recall correctly, both Prange's exec and
CAG are senior to Pavel."

"The exec, yes, but not the CAG. And the exec doesn't
have a current attacker rating. That's one of the regulations
Prange has been allowed to ignore. His friends may learn
that was a mistake."

Bogdanov frowned. "Admiral, with all due respect, I
would rather go to the original Valhalla, Christian that I
am."

"I am sure you would. It has no small-group politics and
you would be dead. But in this world we can't afford to
pick and choose. If Captain Prange understands that minor
point, you can see this affair out aboard *Shenandoah*."

"I will pray that reason will prevail," Bogdanov said. "I
also have to ask how large your staff will be."

"Didn't I send you—no, I must not have. A chief of staff,
nine other officers, and four warrants are coming aboard
this afternoon. They'll need one warrant and three petty
officers from *Shen* for support.

"We also get Herman Franke, when he's finished soothing the astronomers. He may spend most of his time down
on Victoria, on the Combined Intelligence Committee."

"Thank you," Bogdanov said. "I'll talk to Commander
Charbon as soon as she gets off watch."

Liddell prayed even more fervently that Captain Prange
would see how the wind blew and keep his command. Dealing with the abrasively efficient first lieutenant jumped up
to exec would be a headache she didn't need.

A severely handsome woman's face replaced the starscape. "I'm sorry to interrupt, but we have a message from
Rasmussen."

Speak of the devil, and she appears, thought Liddell. Then
she was clutching her napkin, as the Baernoi suddenly

turned from a vague possibility into a looming menace on the screen.

"Well done to *Rasmussen*," Kuwahara said. "Have her shadow the Baernoi as long as they don't regard this as a hostile act. *Cavour* is to be under way by 1230, and stay within radio distance of *Rasmussen*, out of sensor range of the Baernoi."

"Aye-aye, sir. Permission to continue maneuver program?"

"Of course."

The starscape returned, then cartwheeled slowly across the screen. *Shenandoah* and her escorting light cruisers and attackers were shifting course and speed and would do so for the next five minutes. Then they'd settle down to a new combination for anything from fifty to sixty-seven minutes.

The Victoria Squadron had been doing this since two hours after the Alliance ships died. Once the larger chunks of orbital debris had been tracked, there was no need to be an easier target than necessary.

Continuous manuevering would have been ideal, but too exhausting to the watchstanders. Also, the squadron was taking aboard supplies and personnel, most of them less exalted than an admiral's staff but even more essential, and sending assistance to the battered Alliance ships. Shuttles and attackers had to rendezvous and dock.

So random vector changes at random intervals became SOP. Orbital debris was still a problem if a chunk of starship came along while a Federation vessel was maneuvering with drive up and shield down, but was nothing compared to megaton-range fusers. One damaging hit on a transport, with one dead and two wounded, and an attacker from *Valhalla* lost with all hands, was the sky-junk toll so far.

The stars cartwheeled for three minutes, except when Victoria's cloud-streaked grayness swept across the screen. Then Charbon's voice returned.

"Orders transmitted, Admiral. Evasive manuevers completed. New base course and speed—"

Liddell listened with half an ear. When Charbon signed off, she saw Kuwahara rising.

"If anyone has an hour to spare for kendo this morning, it will save me having to work out alone. Otherwise, I want the flag suite completely clear by 1200, and a reception for the department heads to meet my staff at 1730."

"Aye-aye, sir," came as a duet. "What shall we tell the crew?" Bogdanov continued.

Kuwahara smiled. "Just announce the arrival of my staff, and let everyone draw their own conclusions."

Elayne Zheng lay naked on a comfortable couch in a warm room. In the past this had led to agreeable experiences, but not this time.

She was alone in the room, except for a Med tech who was neither interested nor interesting. She had body-function monitors all around her, plus a few glued on and the usual nanoware sneaking a really close-up look from the inside.

The medical scanners in the couch and above her went *bweeeemmmmpppp*! The restraints crossing her rib cage and thighs loosened, then fell free. The tech applied himself to dismantling the entire apparatus, including yanking out the nanoware. At least it felt like yanking, even if he was trying to be gentle.

Eventually Zheng was sitting on the edge of the couch, feet dangling, when Commander Mori walked in.

"Feel faint?" the surgeon asked.

"No."

"Really?"

"Ma'am, how many times can you call me a liar to my face?"

"As often as I think you are one." The surgeon tossed Zheng a robe and pushed a chair toward her. "Sit down, Lieutenant."

The robe scraped skin still delicate from both injuries and examinations. Zheng finally tied it around her waist like a sarong, then sat down.

"So?" she asked.

"If I was as afraid of you as you seem to want me to be, I'd clear you for flight duty."

"But since you obviously fear neither God nor man nor lieutenant—"

"I still may clear you for flight duty. But frankly, I'd recommend that you stay off flight status for another ten days. You can go back on duty, allow time for an exercise

program, and if there's no trouble at the end of ten days—
liberty hall."

"What happens if I go back right away?"

"Your endurance may be down. That could affect your
alertness in a high-stress situation. High-threat environ-
ments mean high stress loads. Figure it out for yourself."

"I already have. The 879th still needs me aboard an
attacker, not pushing papers."

"The 879th has fifteen out of the seventy-two attackers
currently operational on Victoria. Neither it nor you are
indispensable."

"Most of the other attackers are from *Valhalla*. They
don't know the Roskills from the Lizardspines and they'd
rather run into either one than admit it. They have to protect Prange's precious pride!"

"Don't say that where *Valhalla* crews can hear you."

"If I put five or six of them in the hospital, will you call
me fit?"

"Oh, yes, fit to stand trial for inciting to riot. Pushing
papers wins no medals, but isn't it better than—"

Zheng said obscene things in Tagalog and Mandarin.
Mori blinked.

"You don't like being called a medal hunter?"

"Maybe I'd rather be called a liar."

"All right. I assume you've used your best judgment.
Assume I've used mine, and listen. Low endurance could
put your crew in danger, as well as yourself. Then where's
the profit? Up the anti-matter feed, as far as I can tell."

Zheng nodded slowly. She wanted blood, for too many
good men and ships gone, and not all of them Federation.
She would gladly trade her own for it. But she didn't have
the right to ask a crew to die with her.

"All right. If Roisman needs a TD in Intelligence or
Material, I'll do it."

"Ah-ah. No squadron assignment. Next thing I know,
you'll be sneaking missions."

Zheng mimed a kick at Mori's kneecap. "Then where?"

"Plans and Operations at Fort Stafford. They need an
experienced EWO to design EW plans for operations
against the rebels. Or so the beervine told me."

"Fort Stafford!"

"It's not a circle of hell, Lieutenant. And one more thing—you're trained in tae kwon do?"

"It's my favorite conditioner."

"So if you had a regular partner, you'd shape up faster?"

"More than likely."

"Fine. There's a young doctor at Fort Stafford Base Hospital, just out from Riftwelll. Rafael Zenac. He's second degree black belt. Good enough?"

I'll be damned. Brigitte Tachin's old bedfriend. Maybe I can arrange for some extra exercises.

"Fine."

"Good morning. I'm Second Lieutenant Gower, reporting for duty with the W-4 Division."

Brigitte Tachin looked up at the gangling young man half stooping over her desk, then rose. "I'm Lieutenant Tachin, the junior division officer. Or—what's your date of commissioning?"

"Yesterday."

Tachin frowned. "I'm not in a mood for jokes."

"I'm not joking. I was pulled out of the Riftwell OTC to make up the complement of *Stepan Pucinski*, just before I took the exams. Captain Steckler put in an EDP chit for me during the Armistice. Approval only came in with Commodore Uehara. His com people rated transmitting it as 'nonessential.' So it wasn't until yesterday that Wolfie handed me the paper and the pips."

"I see. That gives me about a Standard year's seniority on you. Sit down, give me your files, and pour yourself a cup of tea."

Gower seemed about to bump into something while he did all this. He was graceless enough, at least physically, but also oddly attractive.

Tachin finally realized that he looked rather like a younger Brian Mahoney. *And if he is becoming my ideal of male beauty . . .*

She spread out Gower's files and bumped into a cup of tea that seemed to have sprouted from her desk.

"I thought I'd pour you one while I was at the urn."

"Thank you."

The file showed nothing unusual or spectacular, either good or bad, except a notation that Gower's enlisted service had been extended one Standard year because he was Essential Personnel for work on the WC-65 Upgrade.

Tachin cast her mind back over the weapons specs. "WC-65. That's the bus with the baffle problems, right? They finally classified it nonstandard about the time I left Alcuin Arsenal."

"Yes. Uehara brought out a few of them, or so I heard. I think Steckler sent me over here so that I wouldn't be snatched up for *Baikhal*. I requested assignment to *Shen*, I admit, but you know how much that can mean."

"I do indeed. But a warning. If you're qualified on bus maintenance, Chief Nakamura is going to leap on you like a glider-snake on a fresh worm."

"The Sumo? Oh, lord—" Gower looked genuinely frightened.

Tachin smiled. "Don't worry—much. Some of the stories about Nakamura are true, I admit. But I've been working with him for half a year, and I don't show any bite scars, do I?"

"No—" Gower broke off and flushed.

"Yes?"

"Not with your clothes on. But then I remembered that you're sort of paired off with Lieutenant Mahoney, aren't you?"

Tachin smiled again. The interest had been flattering. Had being attractive to Brian made her more attractive to other men? Definitely an off-duty question, regardless.

"Yes, but I won't hold what you said against you, on one condition. Do you have your baggage with you?"

"It was supposed to go straight to my bunkroom, when they assigned one. Right now it's in Receiving Division, I hope."

"*Peste*. Well, we have a few spare coveralls for occasions like this. You'll find them in a closet in the head. Down the passage straight ahead, second door on the left."

"All right." Gower sounded bemused, and Tachin took pity on him. He would be jumping through enough hoops and losing enough sleep without her talking in riddles.

"It's just that the first person in Weapons you'll be seeing is the Sumo. He likes young officers to be ready to go to work."

"But Commander Zhubova, and the division officer—"

"Zhubova and Majeski are in conference, and they may be able to fit you in before lunch. If not, you can guarantee yourself a warm reception by putting in a day's work on anything Nakamura gives you. If he leaves anything out of your orientation, I'll finish it off before dinner. Fair enough?"

"Fine."

Tachin handed Gower back his file and watched him nearly trip over the hatch coaming on the way out. *To think that only a Standard year separates me from the Gowers!*

A Standard year, aboard Shenandoah, *not to mention the fighting and frostbite on Victoria. Not every new lieutenant is so lucky.*

Brian Mahoney looked at his watch. Twenty more minutes, and his four hours as Communications J.O.O.W. would be over. Then lunch, maybe with Brigitte or Elayne, and a departmental conference to review Communications' personnel needs.

With Baernoi in-system, doctrine would mean evacuating personnel and spares from Dockyard. They'd be distributed among the ships of the Victoria Task Force (Victoria Squadron, until half an hour ago) where they might be needed and at least wouldn't be aboard a large immobile target. Dockyards could take a lot of punishment, but people and supplies were another matter.

And speaking of orbital debris—

Mahoney began the end-of-the watch scan of the message log. Four attackers from *Valhalla* had spent the last three hours tagging large chunks of debris with radar beacons. The job was nowhere near done, but most pieces of the Alliance squadron big enough to kill a ship had been tagged, fragged, or pushed to escape velocity toward Victoria's primary.

If it had been up to Mahoney, he would have assigned *Valhalla*'s entire AG to garbage disposal. He hated the idea of fighting the Tuskers in a patch of man-made junk space. Worse, the more damage resistant construction of Baernoi heavy ships let them use that kind of space deliberately—

"Lieutenant, I've got an Army intercept, calling for a recon. From the coordinates, right up on the border."

"Call sign?"

"Huntress."

Candy! "Push it over here."

Mahoney watched Scout Company's request for aerial reconnaissance of a chunk of the Roskill Mountains unroll on his screen. "Right up on the border" was an understatement.

Worse, it was the border with Seven Rivers. The Bushranger Republic and the Dominion of Victoria were nominally under a single government. The Bushrangers in Kellysburg might grumble about Federation overflights; they couldn't do more if they wanted to. The Alliance had the crack 96th Independent Regiment available, if they wanted to claim a border violation.

Not to mention that sooner or later the Alliance would send reinforcements. When they showed up, the Federation did not want them in a mood to retaliate so thoroughly that the Victoria Task Force would have to bail the Associated States out of their own mess. And if the Baernoi decided to join the party—

Unless the Baernoi already had, by bankrolling that half-assed "Freedom Legion" invasion of Seven Rivers. Then the best thing for the Feds might be to let the Tuskers and the Alliance go for each other's throats.

No. That would kill men and ships, in ways Mahoney didn't want to live with afterward.

The message-completed signal tinkled. Mahoney activated his throat mike. "Record in File Gardenia, print, copy to department head, and transmit to Combat Center, Urgent Immediate Priority."

The operator looked at him quizzically. It would be his tail in the crack if he'd used UI Priority for a routine matter that the Army was already taking in hand.

But Mahoney knew Candice Shores, the C.O. of Victoria Brigade's Scout Company. She didn't have a panic button. If she was putting through that kind of a request for recon in that area, it wasn't routine. It might be something where a look from space could learn more faster than any methods the Army had available.

"Command sequence executed," the computer reported. Then the intercom screen lit up for an all-hands announcement.

"Now hear this. Now hear this. The staff of Admiral

Kuwahara, Commander Victoria Task Force, will be boarding at approximately 1305. Repeat, the staff of Admiral
Kuwahara will board *Shenandoah* at approximately 1305.

"The boarding will be broadcast live to all hands. All
housekeeping and quarters assignments for staff personnel
should be completed by 1215. That is all."

"Hot damn!" the operator shouted. She jumped out of
her chair and danced around, waving her arms over her
head. Mahoney felt like doing the same, but remembered
Lieutenant Rosza's by-the-numbers attitude.

Mahoney started to ask the operator to sit down, when
Lieutenant Rosza stepped through, a jaw-dislocating grin all
over his face. From the corridor outside, Mahoney heard
cheers and more than one "Banzai!"

"I knew the Shogun had his head screwed on eyes to the
front!" Rosza shouted. Consoles and bulkheads bounced
echoes back. Mahoney winced.

"What's with you, Mahoney?" Rosza growled. "Think we
should have kissed Prange's bum like everybody else?"

"Lieutenant, I may be dumb, but I'm not crazy!" Mahoney said. Then the operator was pulling him out of his seat,
and they were dancing under Lieutenant Rosza's tolerant
gaze.

Two

The Scout Company lifter floated free, letting the wind carry it to the border of the landing pad. Then the drive fans cut in, until their blades vanished and a faint drone of disturbed air reached Candice Shores.

Then the pilot fed power to both lift and drive. The flattened box shape rose a hundred meters, then darted away toward Hill 1674. Candice Shores's eyes followed it until it merged with the twilight and the dun-colored rock. When the drone faded into the icy wind, she turned toward HQ.

The last daylight glimmered on polished metal, hanging above the hilltops against the bloody orange sky. One of the patrolling attackers was making a random change of station while scanning the ground below. Nothing less well armored than an attacker lifted above the hilltops around Camp Aounda, not since the Alliance squadron died.

The rebel outposts around the camp might be only observation teams, with no orders to attack Federation forces or even orders *not* to attack them. They also might have no heavy weapons. No Federation commander was betting lives on either assumption.

The Camp Aounda task force had enough on its hands patrolling the borders. Providing targets for hotheaded rebels wasn't in its job description.

Shores returned nods as she strode through the heatlock and down the hall to her office. One good thing about being based out of the old Armistice Commission buildings: They had plenty of room. Her office and quarters were actually separate, each of them at least two meters on a side, and her quarters had a private toilet!

Her message board was lit up and Sergeant Esteva standing beside her desk when she reached the office. He took one look at her as she stripped off headgear, then handed her a glass.

"Yours or mine?"

"Would I be crude enough to offer you your own whiskey? Besides, it's rum."

It was, too sweet for Shores's taste, but she wasn't fussy. It got the dust out of her throat. Now for enough hot water to get it off her skin, and she'd feel up to reading the message board.

"Ah, Major, I think you'd better lift over to the C.O.'s office."

"Abelsohn won't mind waiting."

"Ah, it's not Major Abelsohn. Colonel Shamil's in and wants to see you."

Shores looked at the message board. Unfortunately, Esteva was right.

Well, the fun had to end sooner or later.

The task force's original C.O., the X.O. of Second/215, had lasted exactly twenty-two hours after the space battle. Then his lifter slammed into a valley wall, hard enough to put him in the hospital. Since Shores was senior company commander, she inherited the task force.

She kept it for five more days. Victoria Command had suddenly gone from having three field-grade officers for every job to having three jobs for every field-grade. Nobody objected to Shores leading the task force in searching the area for rebels who turned out not to be there.

Nate Abelsohn had his hands full organizing the base to support whatever turned out to be its share of the 6,000 fresh troops about to hit dirt and would have stayed out of her hair even if he'd had time on his hands. He'd commanded Scout Company before she did, and his was one of the recommendations that let her keep it when he was knocked on the head by a flying rock in an early terrorist incident.

However, Camp Aounda's share of the new troops would certainly have somebody with them senior to a junior captain/acting major. Somebody senior in rank but without local knowledge. So the coming of a local field grade had been inevitable.

It might have been otherwise if the original plan to base the task force up near the Seven Rivers border was still in effect. But apparently the brass had made an informal agreement to soothe Bushranger nerves: unlimited overflight rights, but no actual bases in what had been Bushranger territory other than Camp Aounda.

Shore tried to remember what she knew about Shamil the Camel. Plans and Operations at Fort Stafford, hard-nosed, hard-working, and supposed to be hard to work for. Also—

"I thought Shamil was a major."

"Acting promotion, to sweeten him. At least that's what I heard."

"Shamil needs sweetening about as much as this rum." Shores set her glass down.

"I've got Bee Golubeva guarding the shower, and your clean uniform's ready."

Shores wished that Esteva had conjured up a few demons as well, to keep Shamil busy while she unwound from two days in the field. She frowned.

"Shamil's that kind?"

"If I were betting, I'd say yes."

Shores used a Ptercha'a phrase. Esteva looked a question.

"That means, 'May his claws rot from his body, one at a time.' "

"More rum, Major?"

Shores shook her head. Esteva hauled her spare bathrobe out of the closet as she stripped off her clothes.

A chemical-powered weapon coughed. From the dust it kicked up, Raimondo DiVries thought it might be a shotgun. To either side of him, several pulsers and a couple of light sporting rifles replied. More dust rose at the mouth of the alley behind the police station. Rock chips flew from the buildings on either side.

"Hold your fire!" he shouted. To be heard all along the firing line, he had to shout loud enough for the police to hear. But that might tempt the police into a rush for freedom. A few more casualties, and they might see reason and surrender.

DiVries still hoped the next supply shipment would give him radios down to squad level. Lack of secure communications wasn't always going to be an advantage.

Most of the platoon obeyed. One pulser got off a final burst, chopping the letter E off the POLICE sign over the station door. DiVries ducked behind a well-perforated groundcar and crawled toward his left flank.

"We need observation on that alley," he whispered to the squad leader. "Can you send up the grenade launcher with the observer?"

The squad leader jerked his head. "Sure, but what if the police buggers counterattack while it's movin'? Or the only place for the OP's where the grenades might hit us?"

"All right. The launcher stays here. But the observers take frags as well as illums, and extra ammo."

"If there is any."

"I'll have the other squads kick in, if you're short."

"We'll manage."

DiVries hoped that was the truth, not just an evasion to get rid of the C.O. The squad leader was the most experienced soldier in the platoon, a former militia lance corporal who thought he should have been a sergeant. He knew he should have had the platoon, instead of a politically appointed old lag of a lieutenant who hadn't pulled on a uniform since Boy Scouts.

I'd gladly swap his problems for mine, if I dared let anyone know what they are. But if I don't get back to face my brother, I want my wounds in front.

Setting up the OP went fast enough. Four Company had been in the field now for nearly ten days and in combat for a week. That was long enough to sort out the lazy and the slow, and bury a good many of them.

The observers were on their way before DiVries remembered to make sure that they could communicate what they observed. He thought of sending a runner after them; then heard a lifter approaching. If it overflew them, a runner in the open would be a helpless target.

To judge from the sound, the lifter grounded about two hundred meters behind the police station. A half minute of silence, then the police SSW opened up, rapid fire from the rear of the station.

Whatever the lifter was, the police certainly thought it was hostile. Then an illum popped, lighting up the whole alley, and DiVries heard a wild shout.

"They're coming out."

The squad leader was on his feet before the first illum faded. As a second blazed, he led his squad toward the right. DiVries hastily slammed a fresh magazine into his pulser and brought up the rear. He reached the squad's new position as the leader opened fire, right over the heads of the former right-flank squad.

Slugs and bullets poured down the alley, ricocheting from stone and puncturing or gouging metal and plastic. Another illum, then the frags came down. Regulation Alliance battledress made the fragments and concussion painful rather than lethal. The four policemen who staggered out of the alley had bloody faces and hands, but their hands were high over their heads.

The squad leader raised his pulser. DiVries gripped the barrel and pulled it aside. The squad leader's eyes seemed to glow with kill-hunger. DiVries groped for his pistol, hoping that he'd remembered to unlock the feed.

Then a pulser droned from the far end of the alley. Heads and chests erupted bloodily, as high-velocity slugs punched through battledress. The four surrendering policemen collapsed like dolls thrown down in a tantrum.

"Who the Hades did that?" DiVries screamed. "Who?"

"Saved us some trouble, they did," the squad leader muttered.

DiVries wanted to smash the man's face with the butt of his own pulser, or even ram the muzzle up between his teeth and empty the magazine.

"Damn you, they were prisoners!"

"They were police!"

"They had their hands up."

"Don't bloody care, Mr. DiVries. And the ones down the alley, they don't either. Want to go and dump a load on them?"

"You're coming with me if I do."

"Who's to keep the platoon—?"

DiVries's pistol was in his hand and its muzzle in the squad leader's ribs before he realized what he intended to do. The man actually had turned pale.

"No offense meant, Lieutenant. But does the talk-talk need both of us?"

"Yes. And you walk in front of me."

The squad leader could still signal to a friend, and then DiVries would be as dead as the policemen. But there was

no risk-free alternative except staying here and letting the
new arrivals come forward in their own good time.

Even that would just change the risks and put them off.
DiVries wanted to curse fate. He'd volunteered for field
duty, to get away from the men who'd killed his brother's
fiancée, Sophie Bergeron. So what did he find in the field?
More kill-crazy bastards!

DiVries pulled himself to his feet. Lungs and legs seemed
to work; he hoped bowels and bladder would wait their
turn.

Lieutenant Colonel Shamil might have been of any
Semitic descent and any age between thirty and fifty Standard. He certainly believed in immaculate uniforms, but
even on Victoria that was only a mistake, not a crime.

Shamil rose from behind his desk and put down a file
folder. His face was hardening when Shores realized that
she was expected to salute.

Her snapping-to won no prizes, the way it had in OTC,
but it did win a slight softening of Shamil's expression.

"Sit down, Captain—ah, Major Shores." The correction
was a pure verbal noise. Reluctantly, Shores sat.

"I wanted to discuss your report on the mysterious
ground and air sightings this afternoon."

"*Mysterious* is too strong a word, sir. I'd use *unidentified*
myself."

"Even though you requested air reconnaissance, in or
close to Alliance territory? I would call that mysterious, in
an officer of your caliber."

"Thank you, sir." *Now, what does he want in return for
the flattery?*

"I don't need thanks. I need to clarify what happened
out there."

*A request for clarification from a superior officer does not
mean that she or he thinks you're lying,* an OTC instructor
had said. *It means exactly what the word implies—something
isn't clear. Two minds are usually better than one, to sift the
same body of data for the truth.*

The instructor, Candice Shores decided, had never met
Colonel Shamil, or a few other superiors she had encountered in the years since she stopped being an officer cadet.

"Very well, sir. If I might have a map of the area . . ."

The desk screen lit up. Shores stood beside it and fell into her best lecture-room style. She took the colonel through the first reports of ground movement, the deployment of her platoon-strength patrol in standard formation, and the airborne radar contacts reported by the overwatch lifter. She was starting to detail the ground search when Shamil interrupted.

"You have recordings of the radar contact?"

"Not with me, sir. But I'm sure the files of the lifter's on-board systems still have it. Also, the Navy should."

"The Navy!" Shamil looked as if Shores had confessed to molesting his daughter.

"Sir, the Navy intercepted my request for air reconnaissance. They then requested full data, by authority of the admiral commanding Victoria Task Force. Obeying that order, I sent everything via tight-beam relay to attacker Crimson Four, which was supposed to relay it to *Shenandoah*."

"When was this?"

"The data should have been received aboard *Shenandoah* not more than half an hour after I completed the ground search of the site. That would have been not later than noon local time."

"I see. I will request copies of the data from both the Navy and the lifter files. But you were saying, about the ground search?"

"Definite signs of people on foot, apparently heavily loaded. Probability of one or more lifter landings, and some lift-pallet activity. On the basis of my experience in the area—"

She caught herself when she noticed Shamil's go-ahead-and-hang-yourself expression. Instead she shook her head. "Whoever was there, I doubt if they're friendly."

"I agree. But they're the Alliance's problem, not ours." Shamil leaned back in his chair. "Our job here is to keep the Alliance from using the right of hot pursuit to justify violating *our* borders. Chasing ghosts into Seven Rivers won't help."

"Sir, I've read the standing orders for this task force."

"Then why in Satan's name did you risk causing a border incident? The last I heard, the 96th had only two battalions engaging the Freedom Legion. The other three were free to move anywhere along the border. That's more than a platoon can take on, even a platoon of Scouts with a red-hot C.O.!"

Shores decided that Zen techniques for calming wouldn't help now. They mostly started with taking off your clothes. What she really wanted to do was armor up. Then bear-hug Shamil until his eyes popped and she had his undivided attention.

"I asked you a question, Major."

"My answer, sir, is that if you are going to prefer charges against me, I will call witnesses for the rest of this discussion."

"I am not planning on doing any such thing. Don't be paranoid, Major."

"Yes, sir."

"Anything else?"

Tact, Candy. It is an officerlike quality, or so the books say, and not all of them are just good doorstops.

"The truth is, sir, that after you've been patrolling the border for as long as I have, you begin to have extra eyes and ears for troublemakers. I don't think you would disagree there."

"I also don't doubt that these people are likely to be hostile to the Alliance. We're only responsible for preventing their use of Associated States territory."

"That's supposed to be the job of the Associated States Forces. They assumed the responsibility when they declared the Union."

"If they are incapable of exercising the normal powers of a sovereign state over their own territory—but you know the relevant clauses."

Shores did. She also knew that the entire situation was fuzzy enough to admit both her interpretation and Shamil's. About the only unfuzzy thing was her gut feeling that she was on the trail of at least some of the people who saw mass murder as the equivalent of a soccer game. Her guts, however, would not be evidence, even if the old custom of reading entrails was revived for Intelligence use—

Shamil rose. "Major, I thank you for your time and tolerance. I suggest you go and catch up on your sleep. I am sure that if there's anything more to discuss, we can do it better when we're both rested and complete data are available."

Raimondo DiVries put one squad into the police station to search it for intelligence material and holdouts. He sent a second squad to overwatch position, joining the OP on the roof and taking an SSW.

The rest he kept with him, as he confronted the people who had shot the surrendering policemen. At least there would be witnesses to any more nonsense.

Three men and two women came up the alley, paused to count the police bodies, then approached DiVries.

"My name's Gilly," the woman in the lead said.

"Lieutenant DiVries, Second Platoon, Four Company, First Battalion, Freedom Legion." That was more information than she'd given him, but not more than she could find out herself in two minutes. Then she would waste time resenting him for holding out on her.

"Do you have any weapons?" Gilly asked.

DiVries raised his carbine. "Does this look like a whiskey bottle?" He felt a touch warmer at seeing somebody who was probably an Action for Independence stormtrooper not quite as calm as she pretended.

"Sorry, I mean weapons to spare. We're here with one lifter, an SSW, and personal weapons with maybe fifty rounds apiece."

Not even enough for one good firefight. But then, 4 Company and in fact the whole battalion wasn't much better off.

"We can spare enough for you people, if you're going to stay with us."

"And if we don't?"

"You'd better stay. Independent allies in a night action can wind up hurting each other worse than the enemy. Besides, I don't really like having people who'll shoot surrendering prisoners at my back."

"Let me tell you about what those policemen did, before you melt down. Or better yet, let some of the people I've got waiting in the bush tell you. That's why they were in the bush, most of them."

"Where?"

"When you deliver the weapons, I'll tell you."

DiVries tried to rub dust out of red eyes and push a

thought or two through his thirst and exhaustion. Since the Freedom Legion crossed the border, it had been obvious that a lot of Alliance citizens weren't going to put up a fight against being "liberated." Many gave what little they could spare, in the way of food, clothing, and medical supplies. Quite a few offered to join the Legion, although they could seldom bring more than water, clothing, and personal weapons.

An organized body of Seven Rivers citizens ready to join up was rare. It wouldn't hurt, either, if they could give hard evidence of police or military atrocities, instead of just "A friend told me that something too bad to talk about happened to the wife of a friend of his cousin. . . ."

"What caliber do you use?"

"You name it, we've got it."

DiVries groaned. "All right. The most common caliber, then?"

"Six-millimeter."

"Wonderful. I don't think there's a round of that in the company." Gilly looked ready to spit in DiVries's face.

"All right. This has to be approved by the company C.O. and maybe Battalion, if we can get a secure link to them. But I'll throw in an SSW with a thousand rounds, all the grenades we can spare, and all the loot from the police station. Weapons, medical supplies, electronics—if it's there it's yours.

"I'll fly out in one of our lifters to deliver the goods and talk to some of your people. If any of them are willing to come in and testify to police atrocities, so much the better. That'll probably sweeten Battalion, and you'll get another load when we get resupplied."

"When will that be?"

DiVries frowned at the sharpness in her voice. Then he decided that it was more likely desperation and fatigue than fishing for intelligence.

"We'd like to know ourselves. If I can get a secure link to Battalion, I'll ask. Otherwise, I don't recommend we wait for the answer, let alone the resupply!"

Cracked lips actually smiled for the first time. "Won't argue that." She turned to her people. "All right. We've got first claim in the police station. Move it!"

*   *   *

Candice Shores flexed her shoulders, but the aches Shamil the Camel had put there and elsewhere didn't go away.

From a side hall a soft voice spoke.

"Hey, pretty lady, wanna come have a drink with me and my fran'?"

Shores whirled around and was half into karate stance when she recognized the street accent Esteva could drop into at will. "Pour 'em out."

Esteva took her at her word. Two drinks sat on Major Abelsohn's desk when Shores arrived, and Abelsohn himself was doing one-armed push-ups on a square of tattered rug. He bounced to his feet as Shores entered, gripped shoulders, and threw Esteva a "lift out" look. The sergeant grinned and vanished.

Abelsohn pushed a glass toward Shores. She lifted it and sniffed.

"More sweet rum?"

"Shamil came out with a load of Gurkha juice and nothing else. Or at least not enough of anything else that it wouldn't be missed. Juan's not going to use up all his favors with Shamil's secretary just to keep us in whiskey."

"Ugh." But she drank, and the sweetened rum didn't taste so bad this time. Or maybe after Shamil the Camel anything with alcohol in it would be an improvement.

"Are we going to have as hairy a time with Shamil as I think we are?" she asked, when the glass was empty.

"Tell me why you think so." She did, and when she was finished, Abelsohn shook his head. "That's worse than I expected, but I think I can guess the reason."

"So tell me, and we'll both know." She thrust out her glass.

Abelsohn poured. "If somebody is seriously up to something in the border mountains, they'll put half of 215 down our way. Shamil will be maybe fifth or sixth in seniority, instead of SOP. He may even be back to Plans and Operations, instead of commanding."

"So he's going to pretend that nothing's happening, so he can play with the task force all by himself?"

The moment Shores said that, she realized it was the rum and fatigue talking. She didn't need Abelsohn's frown.

"The Camel didn't object to ringing up the Navy, or so

you said," Abelsohn pointed out. "I also agree with him, that you need some sleep, and then a couple of days in camp."

"Who's going to—"

"Give Shamil his orientation? You and I can split the lectures, and your X.O. or Captain Bohlen can fly him around."

Abelsohn gave her a brotherly hug. "Candy, you're a damned good leader from in front. But when you're doing a field-grade job, you have to think about your rear as well."

"When I need to think about my rear, I call a proctologist."

"No, seriously. I have a confession to make. We've had two field-grades with enough work for three or four. I twisted a few arms at Fort Stafford to get someone sent up here. I didn't know how much longer you were going to last, the way you were pushing yourself. Everybody in Scout Company was on a good sleep schedule except you."

Fatigue washed back and forth in Shores like a tide, making it impossible for her to lie, difficult to speak. Finally she nodded.

"Okay. But—you didn't ask for Shamil, I hope?"

"I hope to spit in your mess kit, I did not."

"Good. Otherwise you'd find I'm not too tired to wring your neck." Shores sat up. "I'm going to take everybody's advice and get that sleep. But wake me when the recordings of that radar contact come through.

"I didn't tell Shamil everything. I'm only guessing. But I think those aerial contacts weren't just diving for the rocks when they went off our screen. I think they had wide-spectrum sensor jamming coming on."

"That doesn't sound like rebel sky junk," Abelsohn said.

"No. It sounds like some of those gunships they had the first time around. At least."

Abelsohn started to speak, then poured her more rum and steered her toward the couch. She fell asleep while he was pulling off her boots.

Three

The fleet commander's briefing room aboard *Night Warrior* had room for eight in comfort or twelve in hardship. It now held fifteen.

Brokeh su-Irzim wondered if this was deliberate on the part of Fleet Commander Eimo su-Ankrai, to make everyone so eager to leave that they would speak briefly. The stratagem had not worked with Chief Inquirer Zhapso su-Lal. He had now been lecturing on the strength of the three forces off Victoria now for the best part of a tenth-watch. So far, he had said very little that most of those sweating at the cramped table did not already know.

All the elaborate details in any case added up to a few simple sums:

The Alliance squadron would be a light meal for the Federation, a heavier one for the People. It could support its own ground forces, as long as no one interfered.

The People's squadron could face the Alliance with ease. It could badly hurt the Federation, if it was prepared to die in doing so. It had no ground forces to distract it from its opponents in space.

The Federation task force could face the other two squadrons combined. It would be stretched to the limit in doing so, unless it abandoned the support of its ground troops. It might do this once they were landed, as they would be strong enough to face anyone except the Alliance's 96th Regiment.

"In ship-to-ship combat between the heavy vessels, we will have a larger advantage," the Inquirer continued. "The human carriers are weak in ship-to-ship weapons. However, unorthodox tactics may compensate for some of that weakness. Both Kuwahara and Prange have a reputation for these, and Liddell is developing one."

35

"This," Eimo su-Ankrai said, "is not unknown to me."

Su-Irzim smiled. From the chill in the fleet commander's voice, this lapse of memory was going to cost the Inquirer. Su-Ankrai had commanded a squadron in the battle where Prange won his Federation Star.

"Yes, lord," the Inquirer said. "I have now presented the capabilities of those who share the space around Victoria. For the intentions of the humans, I would defer to Commander Brokeh su-Irzim."

Su-Irzim's smile faded. Su-Lal had not been slow to strike back, and had chosen his target well.

"In a complex situation like this, our own information is limited through no one's fault," su-Irzim said. "So anything I say will contain many guesses."

"You have no intentions estimate prepared?" su-Lal asked. He almost bared his tusks.

"Of course Commander su-Irzim has one," su-Ankrai replied. "He is known for his thoroughness. For the same reason, I will ask him only for a summary."

All the High Lords bless your death feast and your kin. Su-Irzim began to believe that he could win if he simply kept talking until his brain caught up with his mouth.

Never in his life had he tried to reduce so much material to so few sentences on so little notice. In less than a hundredth-watch he was approaching his conclusion.

"The Federation's actions are most crucial, for now. They have the force to impose almost any solution they wish.

"So far, we can believe they do not wish war with the Alliance. So they will continue to refrain from encouraging the invasion of Seven Rivers. Because the Alliance may view Federation neutrality as a hostile act, the Federation may even actively discourage it.

"They certainly have the ground troops and air support to enter Seven Rivers and destroy the rebel troops. However, this would mean a breach with the Associated States of Victoria formed by the Act of Union."

"I, too, can see the Alliance objecting," the commander of *Thunder Flower* put in. "I wouldn't want to risk accidental encounters between my soldiers and the Federation's 'police.' Besides, the Federation might learn too much about what the Seven Rivers people think of Alliance rule.

The Alliance is a naked man, who has to pretend to be clothed while hoping it will become the truth."

"I agree," su-Irzim said. "Ruling out direct action, however, still leaves the Federation with as many choices as reasonable warriors can ask for. If you wish—"

"We do, but as part of your final intentions estimate," su-Ankrai said. The gray eyes in the wrinkled face did not leave su-Irzim. The younger commander felt that not only his face but his thoughts were under scrutiny.

"Let that be your next duty," the fleet commander concluded. "Now let it be our pleasure to drink to the victory of the People."

How the People could win anything worth the price here on Victoria, the Lords only knew. But perhaps they would answer, if enough good beer went down throats. *A dry throat certainly never made for a swift mind.*

Major General Mikhail Kornilov kicked off his boots and lay back on the bed. Colonel Indira Chatterje remained standing beside it.

Kornilov contemplated his chief medical officer and bedfriend—no, more than that now, and for some time. Since before she acquired that eyepatch, from an explosive bullet meant for him, but how long before?

Chatterje wore a sari-like garment made of surplus Medical Corps cloth. The bland green did not suit her complexion, but Kornilov doubted she would wear the sari much longer. She had already kicked off her sandals.

"Cutting off the rebels' supplies is your plan?" she asked, hand on the waist of the skirt.

"I wish there was something that would work faster," Kornilov admitted. "But we've already wasted enough time, being sure the Associated States won't actively oppose us. If the Alliance was willing to cooperate, I would be happy to listen to them. The supply cutoff will be the best we can do without their help."

"What kind of supplies?" It was not his imagination that Indira's voice had hardened.

"Everything from lifters down to ID disks, if the Legion's bothered with those."

"Everything?" Now he could have sworn that Indira, who

weighed about fifty kilos in a fig leaf, bulked as large as he
did.

"Everything we can get our hands on. We'll salvage what
we can, destroy what we can't lift out, and put the Rangers
to work—"

"Including medical supplies?"

Kornilov blinked. He had to look twice, to assure himself
that one of the more bloodthirsty Hindu goddesses wasn't
standing beside the bed, holding a curved sacrificial knife
over his chest, or perhaps lower down—

"Food and medical supplies?" Chatterje repeated.

You object? was what nearly came out. Kornilov caught
himself in time to avoid seeming stupid. He couldn't hide
being confused.

"Your Hippocratic Oath?"

That turned the Hindu goddess back into something like
his Indira. She nodded. "We couldn't allow a cutoff in medical supplies, for the same reason we can't let medical treatment be withheld to make POWs talk."

Kornilov frowned. For the first time in half a Victoria
year, he doubted the wisdom of his personal relationship
with Indira. It had grown deep enough to make him unwill-
ing to simply override her.

Except that overriding her would be incredibly stupid, if
one thought it over. If the relationship kept him from it,
more blessings on it. Victoria Command did not need to
pick a fight with its medical services. It already had enough
enemies it couldn't get out of fighting.

"What bothers you, beyond the oath?"

"Am I that transparent?"

"That sari is, almost." He rested a hand on hers, where
it touched the waistband of the skirt.

"Do you love me for my body or my advice?"

"Are they mutually exclusive?"

She shook her head, but backed out of reach before
speaking.

"If we cut off food and medical supplies, the Lord only
knows what may happen in the Freedom Legion's AO.
They aren't going to collapse soon. There's too much support for union and independence. So the 96th won't win a
quick victory. If it does win, you know how Hollings is
likely to treat the locals."

"Pak will try to stop him," Kornilov pointed out.

"Even if he succeeds, will he have the supplies to help? Meanwhile, civilians will die. Not just the wounded, but babies, the sick, the elderly, the just plain unlucky."

"So the only food and medicine the invaded area is likely to get during the fighting comes through the rebels?"

"Exactly. If we cut it off . . ."

She didn't need to finish. Both Kornilov and Kuwahara had rejected simply moving in on the Freedom Legion and blowing them off the map. Even after 215 Brigade was fully landed and deployed, half of Victoria Command's ground troops would still have divided loyalties. They might favor the Associated States if the Federation started chopping their friends and relatives to bits.

Add in that the Association government didn't seem to like the Freedom Party and its private army, but refused to to move strongly against them. Prime Minister Fitzpatrick and his improvised cabinet probably shared the Federation commanders' fear of turning neutrals into rebels.

Added together, the two factors made brute force impossible. Now Indira was making a case that starvation would be almost as bad. She was probably right. But sitting on his arse would be worst of all! He had maybe two more days for doing that, before Kuwahara would light a fire under it. In another four days, the Baernoi might throw in a log or two. And the madmen who'd wrecked the Alliance squadron might pop up again at any moment.

Kornilov tried to rise and felt small hands pressing on his forehead, holding him down with more strength than he'd imagined they had in them. Without the familiar touch, he'd have suspected the goddess was back.

He turned his head, and it was only Indira, unencumbered by anything except her eyepatch. She smiled at the look on his face.

"This isn't an apology or a bribe. But I know when you need a massage. It comes from being so stiff-necked all the time."

Kornilov's aches vanished quickly enough. He'd even stopped worrying about the rebels before the therapeutic massage turned into an erotic one.

* * *

The messenger from Fleet Commander su-Ankrai reached
Brokeh su-Irzim's cabin just after the change of watch. The
Inquiry officer fought his way up out of sleep and was pull-
ing on a uniform before that battle was done.

He looked at his watch as he tucked the intentions estimate under his arm. Enough time since the staff conference
for the other commanders to be asleep, on watch, or else
preparing the training exercises su-Ankrai had ordered for
the next two days. Enough time for there to be few prying
eyes at large in the corridors of Gold Deck.

*Not enough for me to heal my wits with a full watch of
sleep, but no one promised me a special miracle merely for
doing my duty!*

Su-Ankrai had an array of glasses, bottles, and vegetable
snacks on a side table and a tape of unfamiliar music playing
when su-Irzim entered. He returned the Inquirer's honors
cursorily and waved him to a couch.

Su-Irzim found that he was hungry enough to do justice
to the commander's hospitality. While he ate, su-Ankrai
flipped his way through the intentions estimate. It seemed
impossible that he could be understanding anything, but his
questions when he was done were searching and perceptive.

"If you had a wager to make, where would you put it?"
the old warrior lord said.

"On Victoria Command's trying to cut off the rebels'
supplies."

"With or without the cooperation of the Alliance and the
Victorians?"

"The Alliance is already doing everything its strength per-
mits. As for the Victorians, Kornilov will not need their
help to confiscate supply dumps and lifters. At least not as
much as he would for more active measures."

"What if he faces their active opposition?"

"Then he may have to resort to destroying supplies indis-
criminately. But the Victorians cannot stop him. Not if the
Victoria Task Force supports him, as it surely will."

Su-Irzim knew from the other's face that his voice and
face had let out more than was wise. Unless that was
another reason for having him here now. . . .

"Brokeh su-Irzim. I am not pleased with the games
Zhapso su-Lal has chosen to play. They are aimed at you,

but like an ill-made sunbomb, they cast poison on me as well.

"I may judge you qualified to replace su-Lal."

"I—that is great honor—"

"It also saves me the trouble of having to summon a replacement all the way from Petzas. But before I choose to save myself that trouble—what makes you uneasy about our plans for Victoria?"

Su-Irzim had not imagined that anyone could sit so erect, or that his ears could rise and flare so splendidly. "Do not hide the unease," the fleet commander added. "I respect you enough to believe that you have reasons that seem good. What are they?"

At least this time su-Irzim could remain silent until wits and tongue worked together. "The sunbombs were a bold step. Too bold, I think."

"Perhaps. But had we offered less, would we have won the young Merishi commanders to our side?"

"If we have won them to our side, it may be only as long as they need to shift the balance of space power against the humans."

"That will take longer than my lifetime, perhaps longer than yours. Is fifty years of having humans and Merishi keeping each other out of our space so small a prize?"

It was not. The People taking their rightful place among the spacefaring powers—that was not a small prize. It was a vast and noble one. Worth some risks—indeed, many risks—*if* they helped win the prize.

"If we can help bring the warrior Merishi to power, so much the better," su-Irzim said. "But what I fear is bringing the Alliance and the Federation together. The Alliance will not forget or forgive us if they learn that we put the sunbombs in the hands of people who used them against the Alliance Navy."

"After great provocation from the Federation."

"Dung bury the provocation!" su-Irzim stormed. "It was our sunbombs and a rebel ship. The Federation lost warriors trying to *stop* them!"

"Yes. I wish the humans had our tradition of song. Commander Gesell would make a worthy subject."

One did not throw one's glass at a fleet commander. Su-

Irzim's grip only tightened. He was surprised when he heard
a *pop* and felt shards tear his skin.

Su-Ankrai watched dispassionately as the younger commander bound up his bloody hand. Then he smiled. "I can
forgive more than you have said, or even forget it, on one
condition."

"What, sir?"

"Tell me how to keep the Alliance from learning. If they
do not, our defenses are intact."

*I thought I was well off because I did not expect a miracle.
Now it seems I am to perform one.*

"Review all the material we have, for any clues on where
Alliance suspicions lie. Use as much computer time as we
need, or at least as much as we can spare from the exercises.
Evaluate the security of every contact we have on
Victoria. . . ."

Su-Irzim had never found his mind producing so many
ideas on so little sleep. Good ones, too, from the look on
su-Ankrai's face.

Finally the fleet commander nodded. "I put you in complete command of this operation, speaking with my authority. I only forbid you one thing: You may not go down to
Victoria yourself."

Su-Irzim started to protest, then saw the wisdom of the
order. He knew too much to risk capture, and if the operation remained secret, no one would know that he had not
gone planetside. If it did not remain secret, he would have
much worse to face than accusations of cowardice.

"I hear and obey, my lord."

"Very good. Then you will hear and obey a command to
have another drink, then catch up on your sleep."

"Mahoney, what the Hades are you doing?"

Brian Mahoney didn't need to turn around to know who
was standing behind his chair. "Lieutenant Rosza, I'm eval-
uating this sighting record for ECM traces."

"Who authorized you to use the computer?"

Mahoney decided that regulations was a game two could
play. He stood to attention and saluted.

"Sir. I am authorized to operate this equipment with a
qualified technical rating present." He pointed to his assis-

tant. "I am not on watch or other essential duty. No orders have been recorded prohibiting this evaluation."

Rosza's voice turned peevish. "Right as far as you go. But didn't you hear that the transmission of the recording and other data was unauthorized by the C.O. of Camp Aounda?"

Mahoney's disgust was taken for genuine surprise. "Sir, if you'll forgive me, I don't know when that message came through. If it came through since I was on watch—"

"You didn't check the message log?"

"Sir, not being on watch, I wasn't required to. Also, I wanted to complete this evaluation with minimum use of computer time."

"I see being a hero hasn't completely wiped out your judgment. The message log, please." The last was addressed to the technician.

The message log scrolled, with the technician quietly crossing her fingers. "See," Rosza said, pointing. He looked mildly disappointed, and Mahoney knew why. Tampering with any log aboard ship was a general court-martial offense.

"I understand, sir. But since I'm halfway through the evaluation—"

"Are you going to spend as much time with unauthorized messages as with real business?"

"Only if I think they may be important."

"I was wrong about your judgment," Rosza said. "Being a hero seems to make you think you know everything."

"No, sir. Not everything. Just three things. One is that the source of the recording is Major Candice Shores. She's an exceptional officer.

"Second is that a lot of funny stuff has been going on in and around these mountains. All the way back to the *Eriksen Gamma* incident and the *Mahmoud Sa'id* shootdown. If somebody we don't know about has an ECM capability and is operating in that area—maybe it's time we found out.

"Third, if the Army is going to sit on intelligence that doesn't conform to some local C.O.'s prejudices—that's another thing we'd better learn fast."

Rosza gripped the back of a vacant chair and stared at the blacked-down console in front of him. Anticipation slowly replaced disappointment on his face. Mahoney could almost read the slow march of his thoughts.

If we catch the Army with a finger in, the Navy will look good. So will the officers who helped catch the Army. Mahoney doesn't need much of the credit; he's already a hero.

"All right. Go ahead and finish. But work fast. Our Baernoi friends are in a hurry. There's going to be a partial com blackdown in about eight hours."

"If it takes more than half an hour, I'll eat the tape."

"I'll bring the barbecue sauce. Carry on."

As Rosza vanished, it occurred to Mahoney that he really wouldn't mind if Candy was wrong for once. There were too many things already going bump in the night on Victoria; one more would not be good news. But ignoring bad news just made it worse when it finally got through.

"I think I begin to understand why we need Rahbad Sarlin down on Victoria," F'Mita ihr Sular said. Brokeh su-Irzim heard the anger rumbling low in her voice. "But I'll be rotted if I understand why we need to use *my* ship."

Su-Irzim hesitated a moment too long in replying, as he considered the commander's need to know. When she spoke again, the anger no longer rumbled, it crackled.

"I'm under strict orders not to put this ship where the Smallteeth can pick it over. Those orders come from Fleet Command, seconded by the Office of Inquiry *and* Special Projects. Now you're asking me to throw those orders out the wastelock.

"I will do no such thing. *Perfumed Wind* will not be your toy just because you woke up this morning with your tusk nerves inflamed!"

Perfumed Wind's commander and the Inquirer glared at each other, tusks bared, until Rahbad Sarlin slammed his mug down on the table. Beer fountained from his mug and slopped from the others'.

"That's wasting good drink," ihr Sular said in a more subdued tone.

"We have plenty on board, and I am sure we can buy more on Victoria."

"If we have to ride off Victoria that long, I may defect," ihr Sular muttered.

Su-Irzim's expression turned back into a glare. "You make a joke—"

"You're going to make a joke of this whole operation if you go on fighting, and not a funny one either," Sarlin said. Listening to his tone, one might have thought he hardly cared. Watching him said otherwise.

In the silence, Sarlin, the Special Projects commander continued. "*Perfumed Wind* has all the assets needed to operate off Victoria as a civilian ship. This includes not being associated with the training force or any other unit of the People's Fleet."

"It also includes having aboard a good deal of material on *Fireflower*'s history," ihr Sular pointed out.

"Computers can be wiped. Physical evidence can be destroyed."

"Given time, yes. Where will we find that time? We'll be off Victoria in three days."

"Correction," su-Irzim put in. "The Seventh Training Force will be off Victoria in three days. The chartered merchant vessel *Perfumed Wind* will be somewhat behind that. Say two days, or even three or four."

"That won't allow for us to come in from a different direction," ihr Sular said. At least she now sounded interested in solving the problem, not in keeping her ship out of danger.

"No. All we need is to drop back, starting not later than two watches from now." Su-Irzim flipped open the cover of the desk terminal and began doing calculations. "Two and a half is possible, but two would give us a margin of safety against any ship the humans send out to meet the force."

"It won't give us much of a margin against anyone already trailing the force," the commander said.

"No. But what they can learn without revealing their presence with active sensors will be limited."

"The whole idea seems right on the edge of feasibility," ihr Sular said. "But I like that kind of idea. It's what I came to space for.

"We still have the problem of a resupply, though. If we're going to be off Victoria as a merchant vessel, we'll have to be independent of the Fleet for longer than I'd planned."

Sarlin nodded. "There are a few things I will need that I haven't found aboard *Wind*, in spite of diligent searching."

"Was it you who turned over all the hair oils?" Sular snapped.

"I confess."

"The Lords be praised. I thought it was someone with an addiction."

"I think you do have a problem of that kind aboard," Sarlin began. "It is—"

"Not urgent," su-Irzim interrupted. Ihr Sular only frowned. "Supplies are no problem. Remember, we came out from Petzas ready to support operations like this. If the Fleet has it, it's somewhere aboard *Night Warrior*. Do you have a shuttle?"

Ihr Sular nodded. "A Prad 89-II."

"Fine. Let me borrow it and a shuttle pilot and head over to *Night Warrior*. If we transmit our requirements in advance, they may have it waiting for me in the dock. Even if they have to hunt a bit, the shuttle can still be back in half a watch under our safe time."

"And if we're being trailed?"

"If the Smallteeth can pick out one shuttle among twenty maneuvering ships from beyond our sensor range, then perhaps they're as good as they think they are. I would suggest that you go to passive-sensor mode for a watch or two after you drop back, even chill the power."

"You have a point," ihr Sular said. "If the Smalltooth trailer thinks we're just a patch of empty space, they may come close enough to tell us something worth knowing." She looked at the clock. "How soon do you need to leave?"

"A tenth-watch or less."

"I won't stop you," ihr Sular said. She drew on her gloves and rose. "I'll send the pilot and the supply requirements down here as soon as they're ready."

"Bless you," su-Irzim said with feeling.

Alone with Rahbad Sarlin, he found the Special Projects commander staring at him with unmistakable amusement.

"What's the joke?"

"'Are you planning on staying aboard *Wind*?"

"If this would keep you from seducing Captain ihr Sular—"

Sarlin's laugh was harsh. "If she was interested, you would not influence matters. Since she is not, six fleet commanders could not deprive me of what I will not have. Or indeed, particularly want. She is not the most even-tempered woman I have known."

"You have a habit of understatement," su-Irzim said. "I hope this does not affect the accuracy of your reports."

"When I am in a position to make them, no," Sarlin said. "As long as you and F'Mita do your part, I can produce cover identities that should let me do mine."

Sarlin divided the last of the beer. As he lifted his mug, he said. "You aren't staying on board *Wind*, are you?"

"Not for the time being. You and the commander hardly need me looking over your shoulders. Commander su-Ankrai does need me aboard *Night Warrior*."

"As a possible replacement for su-Lal?"

Fortunately su-Irzim's mug did not have far to fall. Very little beer spilled. He frowned. "I would not wish us to quarrel again—"

"We won't, if you'll just confirm or deny. No details needed."

"I can confirm. But even if I don't move up, there's enough Inquiry work for six senior commanders, let alone two!"

Four

On Admiral Kuwahara's screen, *Night Warrior* looked like a child's giant silver top. Appearances were more than usually deceiving.

That "top" was a starship with more cubic volume inside her outer hull than the carrier *Valhalla*, Victoria Task Force's largest ship. Inside that hull was ample vacuum storage for a year's supplies and a dozen spheres' worth of habitable space, each sphere thicker than one of *Shen*'s.

Smaller and heavier habitation spheres made Baernoi ships more damage-resistant but less comfortable. Neither quality made much difference now. Kuwahara had no intention of either outshooting or outsitting the Baernoi. He would do his best to outwit them.

Of course, the Baernoi might really be a training force, here entirely by coincidence on completely legitimate business which the Federation had no right to protest. And the next incarnation of God would appear any day now.

A knock on the door proved to be a staff messenger, with an ADMIRALS EYES ONLY message. Kuwahara signed for the message and again asked himself if a staff's main purpose wasn't increasing the commander's paperwork.

A couple of the staff officers would need a quick tightening up. They had the habit of forwarding items without a recommendation. They were going to find either the courage to make recommendations or other jobs.

Kuwahara let the message wait long enough to pour a cup of tea, then pulled the tab.

TO: VICE ADMIRAL SHO KUWAHARA, COMMANDING FEDERATION VICTORIA TASK FORCE.

FROM: FLEET COMMANDER EIMO SU-ANKRAI, COMMANDING SEVENTH TRAINING FORCE, KHUDRIGATE FLEET.

SUBJECT: SAFETY AGREEMENT.

IT IS PROPOSED THAT THE THREE NAVAL COMMANDERS AND OTHER APPROPRIATE INDIVIDUALS MEET AS SOON AS POSSIBLE TO SETTLE ALL QUESTIONS CONCERNING SAFETY IN SPACE WHILE THE TRAINING FORCE IS PRESENT IN THE VICTORIA SYSTEM.

THIS MEETING MAY TAKE PLACE AT THE CONVENIENCE OF THE PARTIES CONCERNED, AT ANY MUTUALLY ACCEPTABLE LOCATION. ACCEPTABLE LOCATIONS FOR THIS COMMAND INCLUDE *NIGHT WARRIOR, SHENANDOAH,* VICTORIA DOCKYARD, ANY HABITABLE SHIP OF THE ALLIANCE FORCE, OR A SECURE LOCATION ON THE PLANET ITSELF.

THE FAVOR OF A REPLY AT ADMIRAL KUWAHARA'S EARLIEST CONVENIENCE IS REQUESTED.

COPY TO REAR ADMIRAL MORDECAI UZEL, ACTING COMMANDER, ALLIANCE VICTORIA TASK FORCE

Kuwahara read the message twice without finding a translation code. That meant Eimo su-Ankrai knew Anglic. No surprise there; the conceptual framework and vocal anatomy of the two races allowed them to learn each other's languages fairly well. No ambitious and far-sighted Syrodhi aristocrat like su-Ankrai would miss learning at least one "Smalltooth" language.

It would be Dockyard, Kuwahara decided, unless Uzel objected. Since the Baernoi had appeared, the Victoria Task Force had been industriously adding armament and

removing nonessential personnel and stores from the
Dockyard. It was now a large, comparatively stationary,
but well-defended and hard target. It could soak up
hostile firepower and even ships without the Federation's
losing anything vital when its defenses did collapse.

*Better check with Wolfie Steckler, to make sure he didn't
strip himself of security people and that he's got a meeting
room that can be humidified to Baernoi standards.*

"Message," he said, and *Night Warrior* vanished as the
screen switched to RECORD/TRANSMIT.

For Fleet Commander Eimo su-Ankrai, the meeting
with the other commanders began well.

He marched deep into Dockyard, along corridors and
passages posted with armed guards, through compartments
filled with shrouded equipment. It amused him to think
that the Smallteeth still believed they had secrets from
the People.

He found his colleagues in a meeting room well-fur-
nished with carafes of water and couches as well as
reclining chairs. The air was even moistened to the comfort level of the People, although su-Ankrai knew this
was less comfortable for humans.

Admiral Uzel was small for a human, rather ill-dressed,
and showing every sign of not bearing well a heavy
burden. Admiral Kuwahara was average in height, but in
no other way.

Kuwahara was said to be descended from the *Haponi*,
a formidable warrior people, and certainly looked it. His
stance resembled the deployment of his ships: deceptively harmless, but in fact allowing swift strikes in all
directions.

It occurred to su-Ankrai that perhaps it was time to
abandon the insulting term "Smalltooth" for the humans.
Their teeth might be small, but they had effectively
gripped the necks of several other races, the People
among them.

Eimo su-Ankrai vowed that Kuwahara's teeth would
stay out of his neck and those of the folk under him.
What he could do for the People's friends on Victoria
he would also do—but he would wait for Rahbad Sarlin
to go to work before deciding how much that might be.

From this promising beginning, the meeting slid rapidly down into a putrid muck, thanks largely to Admiral Uzel.

"I don't see why this cattle call is needed in the first place," Uzel said, when it was his turn to speak. "The Kirov Agreement really covers about everything we need to discuss. I assume you're familiar with its terms?" he asked su-Ankrai.

The fleet commander was tempted to expose his knowledge of Anglic simply to avenge that insult, but refrained. The translation computer took the anger out of his voice and said in tones of mellifluous moderation:

"It is required knowledge of all Fleet commanders of the People, as it is in human Fleets."

"Good. Then why the Hades do we have to discuss what we all know and what all of our governments agreed on before we were born?"

Kuwahara smiled. "Some of the standard provisions may not be applicable to this situation. Why enforce them if they are not? We may also need special provisions because of the military operations on Victoria. I am sure that all parties have the kind of security interests that do not exist under more peaceful circumstances."

The truth did not soothe Uzel. At least he did not oppose any of the standard provisions, but he seemed to be waiting like a mountain *skrin*, to leap on any variations.

"I also think we should form a tripartite inspection team, strong enough to have six inspectors and two ships available at all times," Kuwahara concluded.

"For inspecting what?" Uzel barked.

"All new ships entering the Victoria System, civil or military. I think we wish to avoid any more surprises like *Fireflower*."

It was a surprise in itself to su-Ankrai that the humans had learned the death ship's name. No doubt some minor material had been overlooked in the evacuation of *Imre Farkas*. A pity that the overload setting on the drive had failed—or perhaps not, since it might have exploded when the human boarding party was aboard *Farkas*.

"I have no authority to agree to any such provision," Uzel said.

"Will you consult with those who do have the authority?"

That request fell just short of an order. For a moment su-Ankrai thought that Kuwahara had overreached himself. Then Uzel shrugged.

"I can consult until the heat death of the universe, but I don't expect anyone will agree. I certainly don't, and I'll recommend that."

"Could I ask you to consult now? A secure circuit will be made available."

"Certainly."

Uzel drew out an old-fashioned notepad and withdrew to a far corner of the room to compose his message. This left su-Ankrai and Kuwahara facing each other across the translator terminal.

"Was Admiral Uzel wounded when *Fei-huang* was struck?" su-Ankrai asked.

He had the pleasure of seeing Kuwahara at last uneasy. Clearly the wish to talk to the People's admiral warred with suspicion. A human admiral trapped into making common cause with the People against another human, even a hostile one, would be a civilian before he could draw a deep breath.

"He suffered from concussion, smoke, and shock," Kuwahara said. "I cannot make his medical records available, of course."

"I was not asking for them. Would he also perhaps suffer from the loss of so many comrades?"

Kuwahara was silent, but his eyes spoke for him. *We have both been where Uzel is now. Do you need to ask?*

Su-Ankrai decided that he did not. Not when he remembered listening to a friend who had brought home a cruiser with half its crew vacuum-dried mummies in empty compartments, and among those mummies a brother and a niece.

"I also think that Admiral Uzel is not as much master of his own ships as he could wish," su-Ankrai went on. "That is an additional burden. Let us hope that those with whom he must consult are wise enough to recognize his gifts and his need to be free to use them."

Again Kuwahara's eyes gave the answer. So Uzel was bound more closely than he should be, by fear of the

Alliance's Field Intelligence? This was not unknown, and su-Ankrai did not know if he was disgusted or delighted at the prospect.

It was disgusting that any commander had to draw lips to any Inquirers with exaggerated notions of their own importance. It would also be delightful if the division of authority in the Alliance forces allowed the friends of the People to operate with greater freedom and less risk of exposure.

A tenth-watch passed in silence until Uzel handed over the printed reply from Silvermouth.

NO REPEAT NO VARIATIONS FROM KIROV STANDARD ACCEPTABLE. NO COOPERA-TION OF ALLIANCE FORCES WITH ANY VARIANT PROVISIONS PERMITTED.
FEGELI/HOLLINGS

"You will, of course, cooperate with all the standard provisions, I trust?" su-Ankrai asked.

"Do I look like a fool?" Uzel snarled, and gathered his outerwear.

Su-Ankrai wondered if Uzel truly wished an answer to that question.

Admiral Kuwahara listened to his chief of staff report on the unexplained sightings in the border area. He was listening with half his attention, the rest on the migraine headache that Uzel and su-Ankrai had deployed.

Deployment finished, the headache was now setting an ambush. Kuwahara knew the ambush would be sprung inside of half an hour. If he withdrew from the field now, it would take no longer than that to be fit for action again. If he pushed on, he might have to lie down for two or three hours.

The chief of staff finished the briefing and handed Kuwahara the printout. He would not imply that he hadn't been listening by leafing through it. Besides, she had to have a good deal going for her. She had, after all, reached flag rank with an unpleasantly nasal voice, a weight problem, and a name like Carlotta Yague.

"Thank you, Commodore," Kuwahara said. "How

much additional intelligence do you think we need from the Army?"

Yague looked vexed rather than surprised. One point to her. "I'm sorry, Admiral. I didn't run a continuity check on the Army's reports."

"Do it. If it turns up—"

The desk terminal chimed, and the flag secretary came on the screen.

"Messenger from *Cavour*, sir. He's asking to see you personally."

Kuwahara nodded. "Send him in." If neither the man nor the message justified that effort, the messenger would regret the day he'd joined the Navy.

The door opened, revealing Lieutenant Commander Herman Franke. Franke, Kuwahara decided, had much in common with Colonel Vesey, Kornilov's chief of staff. He wore clothes only for warmth or propriety and uniforms only to avoid being mistaken for a civilian.

The salute was brisk enough, and so was the gesture that handed Kuwahara a sealed packet. "Captain Moneghan knew this had to come over by messenger. Since I was transferring to *Shendanoah* he picked me."

This made three ADMIRAL'S EYES ONLY messages today. Kuwahara hoped he would not have to smoke out anyone abusing that category. If he did, though, it was unlikely to be Captain Moneghan, with his reputation for a level head.

Kuwahara read the message twice, then handed it to Yague for receipt and filing. He leaned back and stared at Franke, who had remained at what he no doubt considered attention.

"Who ran the comparisons between this unidentified Baernoi trailer and *Fireflower*? And how recent was the data on *Fireflower*?"

"Captain Moneghan did it himself, Admiral. He was using the update on *Fireflower* he received just before he left for the observatory."

So Moneghan had everything known about the killer ship from her first appearance on *Shen*'s sensors back before the shooting started, up through the moment of her death. The data from *Imre Farkas* had been useful, but didn't add anything on *Fireflower*'s sensor signature.

"So the trailer is probably Baernoi, but not a sister to our friend *Fireflower*."

"Yes, sir. I would say, almost certainly Baernoi, and probably a chartered auxiliary."

"Power and sensor signatures are fairly high for a freighter."

"Not necessarily, sir. The Baernoi tramp captains are like ours. They like to tinker with their equipment for nonspec performance. They sometimes get nearly warship configurations that way. Also, a merchant vessel would have one advantage. She could appear to be coming in by coincidence and then used to protect 'friendly' civilians."

"Merishi?"

Franke nodded. "And anybody else su-Ankrai was told to call a friend. A merchant ship could maintain contact with the ground much more freely than any Fleet vessel."

"A lot of guesswork, Commander."

"Yes, sir. But we didn't want to use our active sensors. That would have meant signals the training force could pick up. We didn't think—"

"Point taken. Only don't use *we* so freely, Commander. I assume Captain Moneghan commands *Cavour* according to regulations, not with the aid of a soviet of officers."

"Yes, sir. Oh, one more thing before I go."

"You'll go when I dismiss you. Why shouldn't that be right now?"

"Astronomer-Academician Martina Kovacs made efforts to obtain confidential information about the Navy's plans while we were aboard *Cavour*. I believe she was acting on instructions of Director Kuttelwascher."

Yague muttered something rude in Hispanic. Kuwahara was glad he hadn't dismissed Franke. He was less happy that he couldn't declare a Space Emergency and bring the observatory directly under Navy control.

Unfortunately he had no senior officers to spare for beating astronomers into submission. Apart from that, throwing away the neutrality of the observatory while the Baernoi were in-system could do more harm than good. A long-term precedent that might let the Baernoi harass scientific installations was too dangerous.

"How far did she go?" he asked Franke.

"I think she had orders, or at least strong suggestions, to seduce me. I felt then and feel now that she was obeying that one very reluctantly. I think she is too professional and too sensible to believe that would influence me."

"You seem to have unbounded faith in your own judgment, Commander."

"More a combination of faith in Academician Kovacs's and mine together, sir."

"All right. Thank you for the warning. Report to Personnel and Orientation, and I'll see that you have an A-2 Priority for everything you need from them.

"Get some sleep, shower, shave, put on a clean uniform, and be ready to go dirtside when you've done all that. Incidentally, when you go, you will have the acting rank of Commander."

"Aye-aye, sir."

Yague muttered another Hispanic crudity as the door slid shut. "Now, now, Commodore," Kuwahara said. "Let's not say that sort of thing about a candidate scholar of the Kishi Institute."

"He still needs a few lessons in military courtesy," Yague said.

"No, what he needs is an introduction to Captain Morley."

"Who?"

"MP Captain, assistant Provost Marshal of Thorntonsburg. Formidable young Afroam lady, one of the Monticello Morleys, I think. She treats flag officers like disorderly drunks, so nothing would save a mere lieutenant commander."

"Yes, sir, but has it occurred to you that they might join forces against all their seniors?"

Kuwahara pretended to be appalled. The headache was firing ranging shots now. Real emotion was too tiring.

"Run that sighting list through as I said. If it turns up as many holes as I suspect, I'm going to burn a few holes in the Army. That, or ask Kornilov to shoot his own dogs before I lose my temper and do it for him."

"Yes, sir. Ah—since Franke is associated with the Kishi Institute—might I suggest we use him against Kuttelwascher?"

The headache's fire was growing heavier. Kuwahara pressed his fingers to his temples. The throbbing receded slightly, but he knew it would be back.

"How?"

"The observatory's director has to be approved by the board of the Benford Institute. The Benford is virtually a clone of the Kishi's Astrophysics Department. If word goes from the Kishi to the Benford and from the Benford to Kuttelwascher about what she's doing to scientific-military relations, she may take the hint."

Kuwahara nodded. It was amazing how pleasant Yague's voice sounded when she was making sense, which she did most of the time. In a week or two, he might even stop wishing she was Rose Liddell.

That had happened too often in the past ten days. Kuwahara knew that he'd failed to remain as detached from his flagship and flag captain as an admiral should. Once or twice he'd even thought he'd made a mistake, not shifting the flag to *Valhalla*. It would have been easy enough to remain detached from Gus Prange and his spacefaring feudal fief.

That thought erased the benefits of the temple massage. Kuwahara rose unsteadily to his feet.

"Commodore, I'm going to lie down for an hour or two. Don't disturb me unless *Night Warrior* is about to ram us."

Joanna Marder felt Colonel Pak's eyes looking both at her and at things inside and beyond her. It was an unnerving sensation and an ability she wished the C.O. of the 96th didn't have.

Particularly since he can't see a way out of this situation, much short of what is effectively treason. But then, neither can I.

A wind from the sea whipped the drifted snow around their legs and laid fresh snow on the hills above Barnard's Crossing behind them. This was a cold, bleak place to meet, but it matched Marder's spirits and it had other advantages as well.

No one would be able to recognize them in their cold-weather clothing, or hear what they said above the wind.

If anyone had trailed them, he would have nothing but frostbite for his efforts.

"You think no one suspects why you're curious about submarines?" Pak said.

"Everyone is buying the story about needing extra radar pickets. Or seems to. Without a lie detector—"

Pak held up a hand. "I know. But—Uzel has just refused joint inspection teams. That, or any other variations from the standard—"

Pak broke off as Marder swayed from more than cold, wind, and fatigue. Rage churned her stomach until she was afraid she would vomit.

Pak reached for her, but she struck his hand away and whirled, stamping off until she hit a knee-deep drift. Her legs quivered under her, and she nearly fell.

She wouldn't have minded too much either. Fall into the snow, let the cold pull her the rest of the way down as it surrounded her, blot out everything for as long as necessary, and if that turned out to be forever—

Two strong hands jerked her to her feet. *Paul was so gentle when I stumbled. Pak is as gentle as a heavy-assembly robot.*

Why do I prefer Pak?

"Withdrawal, Commander?" The voice wasn't gentle either.

"No, I—well, maybe, but not more than I can handle." *I think.*

Marder wanted that first drink. Wanted it desperately, and all the drinks that would follow it even more desperately.

She also knew where it would end, now that she didn't have Paul. *Naked, filthy, and facedown in my own vomit, with my problem certain to become official at long last.* She'd been that way before, all except for the official mark on her record. She knew she would go that way again, if she fought one nightmare with another. Her stomach would spew out the alcohol long before it clubbed her brain into forgetfulness.

"You be the judge. But I have to warn you. With the joint inspection teams shot down, we'll have to think of another way to pass intelligence. I'll concentrate on that.

You finish off the submarines, but—be careful, Commander."

"Things are a lot looser in Barnard's Crossing now that Schapiro's in the field."

"Yes. That's one reason why I shifted him. He's also a good infantry officer, as disagreeable as he is."

"Was that wise? If I step over the line and they notice I did it after you moved Schapiro—"

"General Marder, I can run the 96th without your advice, thank you."

Pak was actually smiling. Legend in the 96th ran that on any day when Pak smiled, you should either make your will or break out the best liquor. Marder knew she would have to celebrate or die after she finished her submarine investigation.

The missile that damaged *Eriksen Gamma* and began the present crisis had to be submarine-launched. Barnard's Crossing was the logical place to start looking for the submarine, since it had its own fleet of half a dozen minis and one larger deep-diver. It also had records on all the other submarines in Seven Rivers Territory.

And if nothing turned up?

If it didn't, she could stop thinking that her own people had murdered the Bonsai Squadron. She could resign her commission with a clear conscience and go on to something new.

The thought didn't warm her. Her world was cold without Paul; without the Navy it would be like the core of a gas giant, hard, dark, and eternally frozen. But it would be hers.

"All right. I'll stick to counting submarines and keeping my head down and my rear covered. This weather is no inducement to nudism, in any case."

Going home, Pak didn't help her through the drifts even when she could have used it, which again was an unexpected relief. Paul had hovered—like a guardian angel, she'd once thought. But walking alone was a privilege and it might soon become a pleasure.

After that, in time it might even be a habit.

Five

Captain Raimondo DiVries, C.O. of Four Company, First Battalion, Victoria Freedom Legion, braced himself for a rough landing. The pilot of his command lifter was a ham-fisted sort at the best of times, which a CA into a hot LZ wasn't.

DiVries couldn't see out of a window without shifting position, so he held on to the straps and tried to form a mental picture of his company's situation. Three lifters were coming down in a standard triangle formation, rear hatches toward the middle of the triangle, bow and top gunners ready to cover the unloading.

They were supposed to ground two hundred meters west of the bridge across Kiley Canyon, connecting the town of Bengshan with its landing pad and light-industrial park. Sixty-five troopers with lifter-mounted heavy weapons should be enough to control the bridge.

A crunching bump as the lifter grounded, then a dying whine as the pilot cut power to the fans. One fan faded with an angry hiss; DiVries smelled ozone. Electrical failure, and he'd smelled too many this last week. The Freedom Legion was still expanding its territory, but also expending its lift vehicles.

At least a lifter with no more than one or two fans out would still fly. Not fast enough for CA'ing, maybe, but for supply runs and refugee lifts, where the Alliance usually didn't interfere to avoid civilian casualties—

DiVries stopped musing as he realized the rest of the platoon had stopped waiting for him. The rear ramp and side doors were down; sandwich panels boomed and crinked as laden troopers' boots hit them. DiVries turned to look out the cockpit window and cursed.

The lifter at the point of the triangle farthest from the

bridge was at least fifty meters out of position. That left a wide gap, exposing the rears of the two lifters at the base of the triangle.

DiVries wasn't the only one to see the gap. From the darkness beyond the pad fence, rocket trails flared, rose, then plummeted toward the lifters. Overhead the ring-mounted SSW droned as the lifter's gunner let fly. Tracer arced into the darkness; white light flared as the slugs hit something explosive.

But the incoming rockets were on fire-and-forget mode; whatever happened to the men who launched them no longer mattered. One plunged too far, hit the top of the pad boundary fence, tumbled, then exploded harmlessly on the pad. A second flew straight into a warehouse door; the explosion blew in the door, blew out windows, and started a fire, but didn't hurt any Legionnaires.

The third rocket hit squarely among the men of 1st Platoon. DiVries saw an SSW fly through the air, with the arm of its gunner still gripping it. He saw grenades pop like firecrackers, killing the dead. The gunner in the hatch above ducked but not fast enough. When he fell on top of DiVries, fragments had ruined half his face and carried away most of one hand. He didn't start screaming until DiVries was on his way out the rear hatch.

As his feet hit the gravel, he started shouting orders. "Four Company, execute the planned mission. 2nd Platoon, cover the bridge. 3rd Platoon, suppressive fire against the rocket launchers. 1st Platoon, set up an aid station and act as company reserve."

Some people had kept moving right through the rocket hits. Others began to move under the whiplash of DiVries's voice. By the time the second rocket salvo came in, nearly everybody still alive and fighting was out of the target area. The blasts missed all three lifters, and the fragments only tore the dead or dying.

DiVries did a quick visual check of his company's position, then called Battalion. Instead he got the reserve company.

"This is Four Boss. We need a hit on some launchers, now!"

"Negative, Four Boss. That's the gunship's job. We go

swanning around out there, the gunship may think we're
hostiles."

Tactical prudence could be masking cowardice and disobedience, but what was a man to do? A man with no
military experience more than three weeks old and no way
of enforcing an order somebody didn't want to obey except
by putting a gun—

Guns opened up from two lifters, and the gunship came
on the air. "We've got lifter and personnel targets. Engaging with fire. Any objections?"

DiVries listened to the coordinates. They matched the
rocket launchers. "Execute."

Heavier vehicle weapons outranged the troopers' personal
weapons, both pulsers and grenade launchers. The platoons
had their own SSWs, but they damned well ought to be
covering the bridge!

Tracer and incendiary rounds blazed off into the night,
until DiVries began to worry about the ammunition expen-
diture. He was about to order a cease-fire when the night
erupted again in two explosions. One came from across the
bridge, on the edge of Bengshan. The other was airborne,
and DiVries saw flaming bits trail down from it.

Before his ears stopped ringing or his voice formed questions, 2nd Platoon's SSW opened fire. Small-arms and grenades joined in a moment later.

"Four Boss to Cobber Four. What the Hades—"

"Big bang in town, Boss. Flipped a ground truck trying
to get across the bridge. Somebody's holed up behind the
truck, trying to shoot their way out. We're shooting back."

"Any chance they're friendly?" The Freedom Legion had
lost the equivalent of half a company from friendly fire since
it crossed the border. DiVries prayed not to increase the
figure.

"Negative. I can see police and regular uniforms."

In spite of the cold, DiVries was sweating. He lifted his
hood to wipe forehead and neck, then nodded.

"Permission to continue engagement?" That was Cobber
Four, who seemed to have a reasonably accurate notion of
what to do.

"Go ahead. I'll try to reach Battalion again and find out
who blew up what."

Second Platoon beat down the fire from the wrecked

vehicle, then took it by assault with only three WIA. Cobber Four was the same corporal, now a sergeant, who'd been such a pain in the police-station fight. Maybe running a platoon was keeping him too busy to argue with superiors, or giving him enough subordinates to work off his bad temper.

One of the policemen jumped off the bridge rather than surrender, but two policemen and two regular corporals surrendered. DiVries made sure they got both first-aid and blindfolds before he let them out of his sight. By then the aid station was beginning to catch up on all the casualties it could help, and DiVries was wondering what had happened in the town. No more explosions didn't quite balance out not knowing what the first two were.

DiVries was about ready to leave his CP (the foreman's office in one of the warehouses) when Battalion finally came through.

"Four Boss, this is Woomera Chief. Situation report?"

DiVries summarized the past fifteen minutes. That's what his watch said, unbelievable as it seemed. He'd been expecting sunrise any minute.

"Casualties?"

"Seven KIA, nineteen WIA, four enemy prisoners, two police and two regular."

"No civilian hostiles?"

"No live ones, anyway."

"Good." The relief in the voice from Battalion made DiVries want to ask more about "civilian hostiles," but first things first.

"What blew?"

"We think your regulars were a stay-behind demo party. They blew a ton or so of ammo, police and Army stuff both, before heading for the bridge. The gunship was missiled from the ground."

That last had to be something other than the complete truth, from DiVries's reading of the voice. The gunship was one of the three that Federation Intelligence had brought over during the first rebellion. Its crew had abandoned it when the Freedom Legion crossed the border, but had they done this out of fear or on orders? If they'd done it on orders, could they have left something behind, like a time-fused charge or a booby trap?

"If the town's secure, we can search the crash area."

"Clear on that," Woomera Chief told him. "Make sure your people have their IFFs ready, though."

DiVries took the patrol out beyond the pad himself, two rifle squads and an SSW. They found plenty of wreckage from the gunship and crew remains that made a couple of the troopers vomit. One light Army lifter was burned out— score to somebody's gunner. Otherwise no sign of hostile casualties or even much sign that hostiles had ever been there.

"Prints of both police and regular boots on the ground," DiVries reported back. "I think they had enough lift for either one but not both. Looks like the police hauled out on foot. Want us to trail?"

"Negative. The gov types could be praying for that, so they can set an ambush. We need to hold Bengshan until we inventory supplies and count civilian casualties. Pull back and hold the park and pad until further orders."

DiVries was relieved that he wasn't going to be leading a patrol out into that frigid darkness, where the darkness and the terrain could hide a battalion of Baernoi Death Commandos until he was in the middle of them. Nothing else was a relief.

They had Bengshan, but no ammunition to replace what they'd used capturing it. They had a civilian population that might not be friendly, and would need food and medical care whether they were or not. If the town didn't have its own stockpile, there'd be another evacuation to lay on.

Meanwhile, except for maybe a dozen slow or unlucky, the government forces had gotten clean away. Clean away, after inflicting more casualties than they suffered, and leaving the Freedom Legion with a victory it couldn't exploit and people needing supplies and protection it couldn't provide. Not without dipping into its own reserves, anyway— and how long could those reserves supply both the Legion and liberated civilians if the border snapped shut behind them?

DiVries cursed Colonel Pak. It had to be him. Nobody else on the Alliance side would have the wits to let the Freedom Legion go on winning, until it collapsed from an overdose of victories!

*   *   *

The wind hit Lucco DiVries harder than usual as he left the hut. It even hit him with a few tiny dry snowflakes.

It was a big storm pattern, if it was producing snow this far inland. Every plan that depended on good flying weather might wind up on hold for a few days.

He hurried downhill toward MedCorps HQ. The call from Dr. Nosavan had said URGENT, and besides, he wanted to get out of the wind. At least there were few people out at this hour, so he didn't have to ignore refusals to salute or even outright glares.

It was getting easier to do that, and maybe it wasn't just imagination that there was less of it. He wasn't the only one who'd thought well of Sophie Bergeron, or thought the Freedom Party had stepped in it by killing her.

He'd just been the only one who was going to marry Sophie and start a new life with her, maybe on Victoria, maybe somewhere else, maybe with children or maybe without. A lot of maybes now ended in one cold never, his own life back to its usual ragged formless state.

The storm front had covered half the sky with clouds before DiVries signed in at the hospital gate. He then got lost three times before he reached the door of the office block. Blackouts made no sense anymore, not when any serious attack would be guided by all the nonvisual sensors known to man or Merishi, but Brigade had spoken and the normal percentage of the Bushranger forces were obeying.

Dr. Nosavan was at his desk but in scrub gear when DiVries arrived. The MedCorps colonel also wasn't alone.

"Colonel Bissell," DiVries said. He neither saluted nor extended his hand to the Intelligence officer. "Suspicious of my loyalty again?"

The two senior officers exchanged looks. Nosavan's was his unmistakable I-told-you-so frown. "Sit down, Lucco," he said.

"If that's not an order, I'd rather stand until I hear what Colonel Bissell has to say."

"If you want to be uncomfortable, I won't order you," Bissell said. "But I suggest you get yourself a cup of tea, unless it's warmed up considerably since I arrived."

DiVries decided that meeting politeness with sullenness helped nothing. He drew the tea, added milk, and sat down.

"Fine," Bissell said, so smugly that it drew a warning

look from Nosavan. "I came through as a messenger, to tell
Dr. Nosavan that he's been appointed head of the Medical
Observation Team for neutralizing the Freedom Legion.
Your role in this, however, is something on which—"

Nosavan cleared his throat. "Colonel, perhaps you should
start at the beginning."

Bissell, DiVries noted, took the reproof with good grace.
He even managed to deliver his briefing in less than two
minutes.

The Federation and Associated States had agreed to
tighten the screws on the Freedom Legion. The Federation
would go on holding those areas of the border where its
firepower might be needed, or where it wouldn't risk a
direct confrontation with the Legion. Such a Federation
presence should soothe the Alliance's nerves, while leaving
a ground reserve for emergencies.

The actual down-and-dirty work against the Freedom
Legion would be a matter of cutting off its supplies, by
"inspecting" to death everything crossing the border. Medical supplies and food would pass; everything else would be
stopped.

"The inspection teams will be Associated States, probably
with Federation advisers, but not many of them and keeping
a low profile. Also, it'll be mostly the ones who were down
during the rebellion and who know how to be polite to
Victorians."

All this would generate pressure slowly but steadily.
Everyone hoped it would avoid Associated States forces and
the Freedom Legion ending up shooting at each other.

"It would avoid leaving the Freedom Legion at the mercy
of the 96th, too," DiVries put in.

Bissell frowned. "That sounds like you support the invasion, or—"

"Crap, sir. I think the invasion's the worst idea since the
Battle of Sierras Verdes. But if the Freedom Legion winds
up desperate— The last time somebody around here got
desperate, they blew up five ships and two thousand people.
Case closed, as far as I can see."

"I don't know whether you ought to be a lawyer or a
staff officer when this is over," Bissell said. "You'd do well
as either. But it isn't over, which means finding a job for
you now."

Nosavan took over. "When I go north, I'd like to have you as my administrative chief of staff. But that would put you close to the fighting. You'd have to go armed, and you might be seen armed by Federation advisers.

"On the other hand, MedCorps administration also needs a cadre chief to stay behind. You'd do well at that too, and not be open to any charges that you were violating your Change of Allegiance agreement."

Both offers were tempting. Both meant responsible positions, where he could help put things back together or at least keep them from falling any farther apart. But there was something else in Nosavan's voice—and come to think of it, on Bissell's face.

"Sir, who else is scheduled to stay behind as cadre?"

"I'm making up a list now. If you want to defer the decision until you've seen it—"

Bissell started to interrupt, which left DiVries an opening. "Is it going to be all the people you suspect of being Freedom Party and Action for Independence supporters? And I'm to keep an eye on them—for Associated States Intelligence, among other people?"

Bissell had both the grace to wince and the courage to reply. "Yes to the first question. No to the second. I assume you'll take action if any of them steals drugs or tries to shoot you, but that's only assuming you're not a damned fool. Please return the courtesy."

It took long enough to draw another cup of tea before DiVries was sure he could control his voice. "All right. I'm sorry I thought the worst of you, Colonel.

"But I'd rather go north. I'm a combat veteran, which may turn out to be useful even for a medical administration type. I'm also probably not too safe in charge of a bunch of once and future rebels. You're right about some of them trying to shoot me. Of course I'd shoot back, but they might not give me the chance.

"The people up north, Feddies and all, won't be so trigger-happy. As for legal trouble—if the Federation needs Associated States cooperation in preventing a war with the Alliance, why the Hades should they make a fuss over one allegiance-changer packing a sidearm? Unless the Shogun comes down with terminal stupidity before this is over—"

Nosavan held up a hand and Bissell nodded. Both senior officers were clearly trying not to laugh.

"Staff officer, definitely," Bissell said. "All right, Dr. Nosavan, he's all yours."

"Thank you," Nosavan said. The doctor reached into a drawer and handed over a belt and holster. The holster held a loaded Police Model Steurmann 76; the belt held six five-round magazines of frangible sleep doses.

"You'll probably be around crowds most of the time," Nosavan said. "This way any misses won't do permanent damage. Also, you won't end up at feud with the relatives of anybody who deserves shooting."

"Thanks."

DiVries really was grateful. He didn't want to add anyone to the casualty list, except the man who'd gut-shot Sophie. But that bastard might already be dead, and if he wasn't, the chances of finding him were pitiful.

DiVries now understood the reasoning behind the passage from the Bible: "Vengeance is mine, saith the Lord." God presumably knew everything, was everywhere, and had all the time in the universe.

"So long, Judy. Give my best to Ken."

On Prime Minister Fitzpatrick's screen, President Judith Glicksohn waved good-bye. Then the screen went gray, and the secretarial computer's voice came on politely.

"The special visitors are here, sir."

"Two minutes, please."

"Yes, sir."

Fitzpatrick leaned back in his chair and stretched. Muscles screamed, then subsided to murmuring darkly. Some of it was being up at this Christless hour of the night to see his "special visitors." Most of it was the strain of one crisis after another.

"Crisis without end, amen," Fitzpatrick muttered. Eighty wasn't old, or so he'd told himself until his job turned from a farewell present into a nightmare. What would he do without Elijah Brothertongue, and Judy—yes, and the people in the Fed services who had their heads screwed on the right way, like the Shogun and Captain Rosie. . . . ?

What would he do? Probably start looking like Judy, a physical wreck. Probably also give those special visitors a much warmer reception than he intended, if they came from where he suspected they did.

Suspicions procured no supplies, or anything but more headaches. Time to dive in, and hope they hadn't drained the bloody pool overnight!

"Come in, please."

The two special visitors were a man and a woman, both middle-aged, with unmemorable faces of no particularly evident ethnic origin. Fitzpatrick suspected that the woman had a skin dye and the man's beard was artificial, and was sure that minor alterations in their appearance would make them hard to recognize.

He glanced at the clock, both to check the time and to make sure the recorder was operating. He hadn't much liked installing an all-modes recorder in his office, but he'd liked the alternative even less. If he didn't install one under his control, Federation Intelligence would install one under theirs. He'd taken the chance to volunteer before he was conscripted.

"Is time short, Your Excellency?" the woman said. The accent might have been Madrassi, but that covered a multitude of sins, not to mention planets.

"Short enough that I don't want to play games. If you have a serious offer, I'd like to hear it."

The man nodded. "Supplies. Military supplies for the Freedom Legion."

Fitzpatrick smiled. The courtesy deserved that much. "What makes you think we need any? Look at that map, if you need to, and then tell me who's winning in Seven Rivers." He pointed at the wall display, which gave what he suspected was a highly edited version of the situation map at Fort Stafford.

The woman took her turn.. "We are not unfamiliar with the situation. But it only appears favorable. The logistical problem is already serious. It will be insoluble if the border is closed."

"What makes you expect that will happen?"

"Are we correct in assuming that discussions have taken place concerning a border closing?"

Under most circumstances, that knowledge would have been incriminating enough to justify calling the bodyguards. However, security in the present crisis concealed about as much as a pair of those sheer briefs Judy wore so many years ago. Fitzpatrick suspected that the two hadn't learned about the inspection plan innocently. But that wasn't evidence.

"You are."

"Have you made any commitments?" the woman began. The man put a hand on her arm.

"Better to put it—has the Associated States government made any commitments?"

"No."

First direct lie, and if they climb the walls over it, they don't get out of this building.

The two looked genuinely relieved. The man even smiled. "Would you consider putting the Associated States government in a position to ignore any border closings, if it turned out to be in its interests to do so?"

"I can think of a number of circumstances in which that might be in our interests," Fitzpatrick said. "None of these were likely to arise, but why not give them a little more rope?"

"I'm glad we see that much," the woman said. "In fact, we may not need to see any more."

"You may not," Fitzpatrick said. "But I would need to see—"

"Not the supplies themselves," the woman said. "Your movements would be too easily traced—"

"Balls," Fitzpatrick said evenly. "I was a public prosecutor for sixteen years. I haven't forgotten how to hide a trail." Both visitors looked the next thing to alarmed. *That was the stick. Now for the carrot.*

"But I would be satisfied with knowing where the supplies are. If they're dirtside, I would have to delay the border closing in order to see them across. That would put us directly into confrontation with the Feddies."

Who were warming up two more rifle brigades for Victoria, so that in another thirty days they would be able to close the border without asking for Association help.

"So far, it has been in the interests of the Freedom Legion to avoid such a confrontation," the man said.

"It had damned well better stay in the interests of the Freedom Legion," Fitzpatrick said. "Otherwise the Freedom Legion and the Associated States may not end up as friendly as we'd all like."

The look the woman gave Fitzpatrick made the Prime Minister wonder if she had alternate orders, to blow him away if he wouldn't cooperate. *Hard yakka if so, but you've been learning the job was dangerous ever since you took it!*

Neither bombs, bullets, nor gas came out, although the temperature in the office dropped about five degrees. "Well," Fitzpatrick prodded. "Where is the stuff?"

"Off-planet."

"In orbit?"

"Yes." The man's answer was reluctant and drew a frown from the woman.

"I see." What Fitzpatrick saw in his mind's eye was the storerooms and cargo pods of the Baernoi ships, bulging with weapons, ammunition, explosives, electronics, knocked-down vehicles, medical supplies, field rations—a small army's worth of goodies for the asking.

If they could be landed safely. No doubt these people had ways they thought would work. Probably they involved that Tusker "merchant ship" that had come into orbit last week to "supervise the evacuation" of Merishi and other friendly non-People who had no binding claim on the Fleet for assistance.

A ship that size could hold quite a lot, then transship it to Merishi-chartered shuttles that would not be easily subject to Alliance inspection. As for Uzel or Hollings or even Pak letting the Federation inspect Merishi vessels operating in Alliance territory, the Great Khudr would rise from his tomb first!

It was almost a pity that the supplies would have to come down that way. They would go straight into the hands of Freedom Party sympathizers in the rear of the 96th and set the whole territory ablaze. At that point, the Alliance's strategy of trading territory for time would turn around and bite them in the arse!

An entertaining picture, for all of two seconds. A desperate Alliance would be just as dangerous as those crazies who fuser-bombed Baba Lopatina's ships. The Federation would no doubt defend the Associated States, but at the price of their independence, as long as the fighting lasted and maybe longer. The war might also spread, giving the Baernoi or Merishi hotheads their chance.

Fitzpatrick had never wished the Baernoi well in their duel with the human race, and he wasn't going to start now.

"I wish I could say an unqualified yes," Fitzpatrick said. He shifted one foot, so it could hit the alarm faster than the people could draw a weapon.

"But I don't see any safe way of taking on additional supplies during this war. I would be more than happy to deal with the interests you represent after the war. At that point, Victoria or at least the Associated States will be wanting to strengthen its armed forces. We'll probably have to do it without much help from the Federation or the Alliance, and without much money either.

"So please don't go away angry. Just go away, and come back when I can talk to everybody and their second cousin from Asok without the Feddies whining and pissing!"

The two people recognized dismissal. "Thank you for your time," the man said, and led the woman out with a firm grip on her arm.

Fitzpatrick loosened his collar and punched up a beer. *Imported Swan, maybe two or three of them. Christ, is double-crossing people thirsty work!*

Six

The lights above the screen showed all scrambling and security on-line. General Kornilov nodded at Captain Morley. She vanished, and the recording of Prime Minister Fitzpatrick's late-night secret meeting began to play.

It was not as agreeable a sight as Captain Morley, although learning that Fitzpatrick was probably loyal and certainly sensible was good news any way one looked at it. When the recording ended, Kornilov allowed himself a moment of contemplating Captain Morley before he spoke.

"Analysis, please?"

"He does not want to cooperate with the Baernoi or the Merishi now. He is leaving open the option of dealing with the Merishi, to supply the armed forces of a united and independent Victoria after hostilities end."

Morley referred to something off-screen. "We did the standard nine-mode analysis three times. I can play that back for you if you—"

Kornilov's growl was wolflike. "Thank you. I can appreciate your concern for adequate evidence. But believe me, I know by now how thorough you are. I will take your word on the analysis."

Kornilov played key scenes of the meeting back in his mind, then straightened. "The recording was remarkably clear. I would have thought the agents would try to scramble any recording equipment."

"Not necessarily, sir. That would have been admitting that they were offering something illegal. Also, there is a rumor going around that anyone trying to tamper with official recordings is liable to immediate arrest and shipment off-planet for trial. *Official* includes both Federation and Associated States."

"Really? I hadn't heard that one."

"I'm sorry, sir. I should have asked your permission or at least informed you before I started circulating it." Kornilov decided that what he'd heard was what Morley had actually said. After a moment he laughed.

"Don't apologize. It was a good idea, and I'll say that for the record. I also think I'll appoint you a local major."

"Local or acting?"

"It will be both as soon as the Sho—as Admiral Kuwahara agrees, and that will be a Standard day at most."

"Thank you, sir. I'll send the whole file on the recording over with Commander Franke this afternoon. He's spent the morning meeting the provost marshal's Intelligence people, and I was able to persuade him to stay for lunch."

"Complete with bodyguards, I hope."

"Of course, sir." The face didn't quite match the tone, but then Kornilov hadn't expected it to. Morley was cultivating Commander Franke with the same directness that she used in everything else, duty or not. The general didn't expect her to have any trouble wooing him away from Academician Kovacs, if indeed he needed any wooing.

What happened afterward might be interesting. When the heiress to one of the great Monticello families and a scholar well regarded by both the Kishi Institute and Federation Intelligence met, who was the irresistible force and who the immovable obstacle? Finding out would be entertaining, possibly even for people besides Morley and Franke.

However, one minor load was off Kornilov's mind. Morley did not have to be ordered to take a professional's care for her own safety, even when she might have to sacrifice privacy for it.

"Try to release Commander Franke by 1300, if you can. Otherwise, well done, Major."

"Thank you, sir."

The screen blanked. Kornilov yawned and contemplated a nap against reinforcing his caffeine load. If Franke left Thortonsburg by 1300, he would be at Fort Stafford by 1500 and on his way back to *Shenandoah* by 1730.

That would be long before a report on the Ranger operation reached Kornilov. It might even be before it took place, if Captain Bloch decided to wait until dark.

Except that Franke would probably have some good ideas about how to handle the news of the operation. He might even be able to suggest a secure way of telling Colonel Pak that the Federation was beginning operations against the Freedom Legion's supplies. If Franke could be persuaded—even ordered—to spend the night—

No. Kuwahara needed the man more than Kornilov did. That didn't rule out getting his advice. Franke had security clearances coming out of every orifice; he could be put completely into the picture. A little vodka, the last of the Dynamo, and a plate of *zakuski* would help; Franke was a man to be won with the carrot, not beaten with the stick. . . .

"Flag Mess, please," Kornilov told his terminal, and leaned back to wait for the inventory of hospitality supplies to come up.

From the hill beyond the farm, a laser blinked. Madeleine Bloch counted the blinks.

"*Ça va,*" she muttered with satisfaction. Then she slapped Abdul on the rump. "Time, *mon vieux.*"

Bloch and her partner crawled from behind a boulder onto the open slope. At the same time the other pair of the four-man Ranger section crept out of the foot of a ravine to the left.

All four Rangers froze, waiting for some indication that they'd been spotted. The Freedom Legion was slack as usual—only one ground-mounted SSW and that clearly visible. But it could still sweep the slope if its crew had a chance.

Fire trails sprang to life in midair, then plummeted toward the farm and the six lifters parked in its yard. Abdul raised his pulser and switched on its targeting laser. To the sensors in the heads of the five cold-launched rockets, the SSW now stood out like a bonfire on a beach.

Four of the five rounds plummeted on to their target. The SSW and its crew flew into the air as a cloud of smoke and fragments, organic and otherwise.

Pity, when our orders are to hold down the casualties, Bloch thought. *But what to do, when neither gas nor tanglers nor flashbangs will work fast enough in the open?*

The Rangers leaped to their feet and sprinted down the slope. Bloch felt the ground falling out from under her feet,

tucked herself into a roll as she went over the drop, and
landed already coming back up.

"All right?" Abdul asked.

"Certainly," Bloch replied. "I've fallen harder than that
on—"

A sudden explosion among the lifters interrupted her.
From the smoke color, it was the fifth rocket, by accident
or intent a delayed-action burst. Several people scrambling
out of one of the lifters stopped looking around wildly and
started running. Bloch let them go.

Then the Rangers were past the wrecked SSW, leaping
over the remains of its crew, and coming up among the
lifters. One of each pair hunted down openings in the lifters
and tossed in the demo charges, while the other provided
cover.

They'd loaded charges into four of the six lifters when a
gaggle of people in shirtsleeves scampered out of the farmhouse. Another half dozen ran from the organics plant.
Most had pistols or rifles; one seemed to be carrying
grenades.

"Merde!"

Bloch had timed the assault carefully, to be sure no local
civilians were at the farm picking up weapons and rations.
Either her timing was off or those lifters had heavier crews
than she'd been briefed.

In the next moment Bloch's launcher crew on the hill
earned another bonus. A flare burst over the farm. The
second and third rounds were tanglers, one dropped practically on the farmhouse steps, the other between the lifters
and the point man of the counterattack.

Two tangler rounds were enough for half a dozen pairs
of feet. Bloch fired a burst, aiming high, to encourage the
other people to join their friends on the ground. Most of
them took the hint.

This ended the counterattack from the farmhouse, but
the organics-plant people were stouter or luckier. They
skirted the tangler area and came on, firing as they came.
Bloch swore again, drew down on the apparent leader, and
shot him.

Kimberly, leader of the second pair, sprang up onto the
top of a lifter. She swiveled the ring-mounted SSW and
pumped a long burst into the ground at the feet of the

organics people. The leader's body jerked and writhed as the slugs tore it. Two of his people fell into the burst and died with him, apparently pushed by the people behind them. The rest ran. Another SSW burst chewed the rocky ground at their heels, to keep them running.

Kimberly pointed at the plant and made the interrogative signal. Bloch gave a negative reply. The organics plant might hold more Freedom Legionnaires or their supplies, but it was also private property. "Minimum casualties, minimum damage to private property," were the orders; boiling alive was probably the penalty for disobedience or even carelessness.

Bloch shoved a fresh magazine in her pulser and pumped it up and down over her head. *"Marchons."*

The four Rangers were halfway up the hill when the demo charges started blowing. One lifter completely disintegrated; a second flipped over and began to burn. The other four merely jumped slightly, then settled back, hatches sprung and windows shattered. No doubt they had already been unloaded, but they would carry no more supplies for the Freedom Legion.

Once back out of sight of the farm, the four Rangers checked and evened out their loads, then headed for the rendezvous with the launcher section. They'd had a forty-kilometer approach march since dawn, and the march out would be longer and probably slower.

Now that the enemy knew they were in the area, all the people who'd been issued weapons would turn out after them. Some of them might have lift with IR detectors or even more sophisticated sensors. Enough amateurs could make life short and exciting even for eight Rangers.

As they marched, Bloch dictated her action report. "Position 26 attacked successfully. All lift and lift-housed supplies destroyed. No friendly casualties, regrettably heavy hostile ones."

"Regrettably?" Abdul frowned.

"Just send it the way I put it, as a favor."

"God does not favor such fools as the Freedom Legion."

"Nobody ordered us to favor them, Abdul. Just to be careful about how many we killed."

"God is great, but Kornilov is closer."

"Bien sûr, and remember that."

"I obey," Abdul said, and started coding the message for a squirt signal to a satellite.

General Kornilov looked at Captain Bloch's message on his screen.

"Well done. Photos?"

"Squirt on the next pass, and we'll have them straight up to you," came Colonel Vesey's voice.

"Good. Double-check the satellite readings for any sign the Freedom Legion's on Bloch's tail. We may be able to arrange a faster pickup if they need it."

"In Alliance territory, sir?"

Kornilov did not call down curses on legalistic chiefs of staff. "In territory currently not under any effective legal authority, and therefore open to anyone who is trying to preserve peace on Victoria. I doubt the Alliance will argue that our blowing up the supplies of people who are shooting at them is a hostile act."

"No, sir. We have the abstract and printouts of Commander Franke's combined data base ready."

"Fine. If you bring them yourself—do you have time for a cup of tea?"

"I can arrange it, sir."

"Good."

Kornilov ran his hand over his brush-cut hair. A good thing he hadn't started pulling it out, as much as this mess justified the habit. Otherwise he'd be as bald as a pearl melon by now.

He was looking forward to what Commander Franke had done with the combined Navy and Army data on the Freedom Legion's supplies. The man had a rare combination of an analytical head for details and the ability to make intuitive leaps. Not that this was surprising, in somebody the Kishi Institute was grooming, but it also made him nearly the ideal Intelligence officer.

Could Kuwahara be persuaded to put Franke on permanent Intelligence liaison with the Army? He was certainly the best man for the job. He could also keep an eye on Kovacs while Morley keeps an eye on him.

A moment's reflection brought Colonel Vesey with the tea and a reluctant decision. Kuwahara was managing twice the general's workload with fewer than half the staff. If

Kornilov even suggested stealing Navy people, he would not help interservice relations.

"Sit down, Colonel Vesey. No lemon in mine, thank you."

The water in the covered dock was scummy and dark. Joanna Marder didn't want to look at it; she had the sense of things best not seen or even thought about lurking down there.

She told herself that this was only nerves, that nothing could lurk in ten meters of water surrounded on three sides by concrete. Victoria's oceans didn't hold any vast lethal predators like Farsi's Blue Deaths, and even on Farsi they didn't come into shallow bays.

"I wouldn't go to the trouble of keeping this place up if it was warmer around here," the dock manager said. He wore a sleeveless sweater over coveralls, but the handkerchief in his breast pocket was still sodden. "But with the harbor icebound a third of the year, it helps to have a place where the smaller subs can dive right at the dock."

"How much did it cost?"

"Cost me, or the government? The government built it during the Hive Wars—Second, I think—and my grandfather bought it from them. How much he paid is somewhere in the files, if you want to know."

"Thanks. I'm just here to check out the local submarines."

One of the local submarines, an eight-meter mini, interrupted conversation as the lifter crane hauled it up into the workshop. From the whining and grinding of the crane, it was overdue for maintenance.

"Old 64's going to be down for a couple of days while they fit a new shroud to the prop," the manager said, pointing at the newly landed sub. "Otherwise, what we've got or can get is yours."

"Thanks." Marder looked at the prestressed beams of the roof and realized now where she'd seen something like this before. A historical film about twentieth-century submarines, with the Swedes or the Germans—somebody who produced a lot of blondes, anyway—keeping their submarines in underground caves to protect them from air raids.

Now that she remembered the film, she also remembered

the ending—an air raid that blew open the door and sank the submarines at dockside. She shivered and wished her memory would be a little more selective.

They walked up the stairs from the dock, through the workshop, and into the manager's office. Marder accepted a chair with relief. Half her fatigue was tension, but it was as real as the rest.

"I'll want to check—no, study—the specs on all your submarines and any others that have been through here. I'll also want to look over maintenance files, to see what you can do to modify the boats."

"No problem with any of that, unless . . ." The manager frowned, then went on in a near-whisper. "You aren't going to use the boats against the Freedom Legion, are you?"

"What do you mean, against? They don't have a seagoing fleet, so we certainly won't be fitting the boats with torpedoes."

"Commander, I'd take a serious answer kindly, if you could manage one. I'm a loyal citizen myself, but some of the lads and girls—they're thinking about independence. Just thinking, so far, but if they had a chance to do something foolish . . ."

"Like sabotaging the subs?"

"Well, I wouldn't put it quite that way—"

"But it's close enough, isn't it?"

The manager nodded. Marder grinned. "Everybody can rest easy. We're going to need subs for two jobs. Neither is complicated or secret.

"One is salvaging fallen orbital debris from the continental shelf. The other is monitoring the gulf, so we won't have any more *Eriksen Gamma* incidents. I assume you and your people agree that sort of garbage doesn't help anybody?"

"I don't hire bloody fools!"

Not knowingly. He probably didn't knowingly hire Field Intelligence people either. But if he didn't have some of both, Marder would swear to celibacy as well as sobriety.

"Fine. You can explain what we're doing in general. Anybody wants details, send them to me. We may even wind up airlifting some miniboats in from up the coast and having them modified here."

The look in the manager's eyes was hard to ignore and impossible to mistake. A bribe to his own pocket would

offend him. But a promise of more work for his people—
that had him. His loyalty was to them, probably more than
to any government.

The manager opened a cupboard behind his desk and
pulled out a bottle. "Drink to our association?"

"Light for me, thanks."

One drink shouldn't hurt. It should even help, if it kept
the reverse psychology she'd used on the manager working.
If he'd been told to keep the project a secret, he'd have
certainly babbled, or at least warned those people he
thought might be troublesome. With the project as open as
the sky, his suspicions would stay asleep and his tongue
quiet.

Marder sipped from the glass, and nearly choked. *If this
is his idea of a light one, remind me never to take a strong
one on this job!*

General Kornilov put the last sheet of the supply-intelli-
gence data on the stack, tidied up the stack, and rang for
Colonel Vesey.

"A well done to Commander Franke, and have fifty copies of the abstract ready for tomorrow."

"The conference?"

"What conference?"

"You, Gist, Fitzpatrick, Parkinson—anybody I left out?"
Kornilov glared. "Where did you hear this?"

"Ah—around and about. I didn't confirm anything I
heard, sir."

"*Sookin sin!*" Kornilov growled. "No, you're not a son
of a bitch. Not his mother either. But loose tongues on
this—"

"I said as much, sir."

"Well, the next time somebody's tongue wags, remind
them of two things. I can start enforcing security by court-
martial, and one well-placed bomb at that meeting could
leave the four of us dead and the rest of you in a mess I
wouldn't wish on the devil's grandmother!"

"Yes, sir."

"Seriously, if everybody shuts up now, I won't have to
chop off heads later. But if they don't, it may be either me
or the Freedom Party. Anybody who thinks the Federation

is immune from attack should remember what happened to
the Bonsai Squadron."

Vesey took Kornilov's handing her the papers as dismissal
and vanished with more speed than dignity. Kornilov emptied the teapot, saw only dregs in his cup, and tossed everything in the trash slot.

Fresh tea and a satellite report on Bloch's progress
arrived at the same time. Kornilov studied the report, noticing that the Freedom Legion was reacting but that their
airborne sensors were pitiful. No reason yet to change the
pickup plans for the Rangers.

Well, not quite. A quicker pickup would spare the Rangers some hiking and get the best Ranger officer on Victoria
back in hand that much sooner. It would also warn the
Freedom Legion and maybe the Alliance that the Federation could easily penetrate Legion-held airspace.

Several tactical options would be easier to use, if nobody
on the other side learned that right now.

Colonel Pak folded and unfolded Brigadier Fegeli's request
for an evaluation of the incident in Freedom Legion territory. It was more of a nervous gesture than he usually
allowed himself, but then he was more nervous than usual.

Fegeli (and behind him, Hollings) would surely want the
incident assessed as Ranger work. They were probably
right. Pak could give them that assessment with a clear conscience, if he knew what they would do with it.

Since he didn't . . .

Pak tore the paper in two, then shredded each half. It
was time to sit down with Fegeli and lay all his cards on
the table.

The colonel had kept his personal life simple by not mar-
rying. He did not understand why Fegeli had chosen to let
his become incredibly complicated, with a wife on Nuova
Sicilia and a mistress on Victoria. But Sharon Farber was
undoubtedly Fegeli's mistress of long standing, and she was
just as undoubtedly in danger from Field Intelligence.

At least Pak had no doubts. If he could convince Fegeli
as well—life would certainly be simpler. It might even
become less dangerous for quite a few people, beginning
with Sharon Farber and Joanna Marder. Both women had

committed themselves as far as being F.I. targets, but at least Marder was an officer and a volunteer.

Fegeli's support would even make Pak's situation safer. Danger to himself had not been a major concern until recently. But with the 96th engaged in ground combat, his own life was now to some extent the property of his soldiers. He could not throw it away when that might mean some of them joining him prematurely.

There were two points where he might be feeling the pinch, and Fegeli could help him with both of them. One was the tactical situation in the invaded territory. So far the Freedom Legion seemed convinced that he was sucking them in deeper as part of some shrewd strategic plan. When they guessed that he wasn't defending Seven Rivers town by town because he didn't trust the population and refused to risk the civilian casualties, he would need a shrewd plan. He could develop one more easily with Fegeli's help.

The other was the code-named computer technician who'd dropped out of sight two days ago. It could be a routine reassignment with the paperwork a little behind schedule; Support Group had been stripped of too many people to be on top of even basic recordkeeping. It could be a special reassignment, which Pak would learn about if they decided he had a need to know.

Or it could be the F.I. people discovering that under the code name Lionheart, Ramdur was one of Pak's best private agents. If so, he had gone somewhere for a thorough interrogation. Followed by termination.

If Lionheart was blown, involving Fegeli might only drag the brigadier down with Pak. But the colonel could hope that Uzel, if nobody else, would veto Hollings leading the 96th in a combat situation. If everybody on the Alliance side failed, Pak was ready to trust the Federation to save his regiment from misguided superiors.

Seven

General Kornilov regretted bringing Commander Franke to the meeting in the prime minister's office as soon as they walked in the door. Every face except President Glicksohn's showed surprise, and hers didn't because she was too tired. Governor-General Gist looked suspicious, Karras looked outright hostile, and Father Brothertongue seemed reluctant to meet Kornilov's eyes. Only General Parkinson recovered quickly, and her unnaturally bland face was almost as suspicious as Karras's glare. It looked as if rumors of Franke's affiliations with the Kishi Institute had once more run ahead of him.

"Commander Franke is acting as naval liaison officer to the Ground HQ of Victoria Command, with special responsibilities in Intelligence," Kornilov said. "I insist on his presence at this meeting at least. I am willing to hear arguments about other meetings."

Kornilov hoped he wouldn't hear any. He could settle them by an appeal to Admiral Kuwahara, but that was a tactic of desperation. If the general showed he was not master in his own house, he would face endless arguments, appeals, and delays that would waste time they did not have.

Commander Franke cleared his throat. "With your permission, sir?"

"If anyone objects to my presence here, I will be ready to leave, to maintain good civil-military relations. But I was ordered here for a reason. Also, I remind you that the charter of the Kishi Institute specifically forbids it to give any orders to its people, while they are on active duty, that conflict with the orders of their appointed superiors."

It took a moment for both Kornilov and the Emergency

84

War Council to sort out that sentence. President Glicksohn was the first to reply.

"I understand. But what orders have you received?"

"This council has to keep a Command Secret classification. Otherwise it's useless. Admiral Kuwahara made this very clear before he assigned me to this position."

"What about after you leave the Navy?" Karras said.

The answer came from Gist. "A Command Secret classification would bind Commander Franke as long as he lived, unless he was specifically released by the Joint Commanders-in-Chief. I'd wager the war will be long over before they could act on that appeal, even if the institute asks them.

"If we win, it won't matter who learns about little mistakes. If we lose, we'll all be in the holding tank anyway."

"Are you saying we should buy off the Navy at the expense of our—" Karras began.

Gist snapped an obscenity. "I'm not buying anything. But what are you selling?"

Karras half rose, and Kornilov saw for the first time that the senator was armed. Well, he himself and Franke were wearing sidearms and light armor, and Karras did hold a militia commission, but—

"Sit down, Philip," Glicksohn snapped. She was strong enough for her anger to bite. "Jerry, you were out of line. We need an apology."

"Sorry, people," Gist muttered. "But I just want to say one more thing. A Command Secret classification won't keep Franke from telling Kuwahara that we wanted to flush him down the loo. Do we want that?"

Parkinson shook her head. So did Brothertongue. After a moment, the prime minister added, "No, we don't. Senator Karras, I'll consider that you've registered a protest and been outvoted. Now can we get on with the meeting? Or has the agenda been changed too?"

"No, Your Excellency," Kornilov said. "We're still going to review how to deal with the Freedom Legion's invasion of Seven Rivers. I know General Parkinson would agree with me that the faster we move, the more work can be done by local forces without Federation help."

That was as tactful as he could be about Victorian loyalty. He thought he had his reasons for doubting when the Fourth Battalion of the Victoria Brigade had openly mutinied in the Bushranger Rebellion. Not to mention the several hundred militia who were neither present nor accounted for and the several dozen who'd actually turned up in the ranks of one or another rebel army.

The longer the Victorians had to think over their loyalties, the more doubts they might have. Also, the stronger the rebels grew, the harder the fight against them. The harder the fight, the greater the chance that the Victorians might decide to pull out.

Then Kornilov would have to choose: direct Federal intervention against the Freedom Legion or letting the Alliance smash them. Either would be bloody in the short run and catastrophic for Federation-Victorian relations in any other run.

He'd given the Victorians all the time they were going to get. Now they were going to shut up, even if they didn't put up.

"AO and deployment maps, please," he told the computer. The display wall lit up, showing both the area of the fighting and a map of the whole inhabited area of Victoria.

"Pointer, please," he added. A beam of light began to cross the planet in thousand-kilometer strides, as the general explained who was where and why.

"The Alliance's 96th Independent Regiment is fully deployed to oppose the invasion. This means they share our interest in containing it before it causes security problems in their rear. There have been rumors of such already.

"Our own deployment puts three battalions of the Victoria Militia Brigade into the critical area, the 'Freedom Legion's' rear. One of these battalions will act as a reserve and also garrison Mount Houton and Kellysburg. The last battalion will cover the Blanchard Canyon area, and act as an additional reserve to both the northern and southern forces.

"The Victoria Brigade now has only three active battalions. The Second will garrison Thorntonsburg, the Third Port Harriet. First will be in the field, along with three battalions of 215 Brigade. The odd battalion of 215 will be Command Reserve at Fort Stafford.

"We plan to put one battalion of 215 up at Loch Prima, one plus the existing task force at Camp Aounda, and one down on the southern end of the frontier. That's the best choice of positions for responding to the widest variety of threats."

Parkinson's eyes met Kornilov's. He mentally dared her to discuss the worst threat: open Alliance intervention against the Associated States. In that case the three battalions in the southwest would have a clear path either through the mountains or over the ocean, into Seven Rivers. Into the rear of the 96th, and in fact all the way into Silvermouth if that proved necessary. But if Fegeli and Uzel could read maps as well as Pak, it probably wouldn't be necessary.

"These deployments can be completed within the next Victorian day. Once they are, the main militia force will cut off all supplies to the Freedom Legion, except medicine and food. At the same time, the Alliance authorities will be requested to turn over all Freedom Legion POWs to the Associated States authorities."

"Not Federation?" Brothertongue asked. Kornilov shook his head. He thought he saw the other's shoulders slump in relief.

"With no more luck than we can reasonably expect, we should have the invasion controlled within seven Victoria days. We can then open negotiations with the Alliance for an armistice, an amnesty for any of their citizens who joined the invasion, and other matters that can be settled locally.

"It will also be the joint recommendation of all senior officers in Victoria Command that the Federation, Associated States of Victoria, and Alliance open negotiations for the compensated cession of Seven Rivers Territory to the Associated States."

Brothertongue swallowed and seemed ready to weep. Glicksohn was wiping her eyes. Fitzpatrick was trying to look at both Karras and Kornilov at the same time, a feat that would have needed eyestalks like a K'thressh.

"Don't carry me around on your shoulders yet," Kornilov said. "We haven't won, the Baernoi are still here, and no battle plan ever survives contact with the enemy. But when we have won, what the devil else did you expect? Anything but an independent, united Victoria will be a permanent pain in the tail to both Federation and Alliance."

"Also a permanent opportunity for the Tuskers," Parkinson put in. "I gather they're the Navy's job?"

"Yes. Kuwahara intends to know every time su-Ankrai

or Uzel move their bowels, let alone their ships. Anything
that looks like intervening in the ground situation will be
interfered with in turn, politely if possible."

Kornilov turned off the pointer and sat down. "Just in
case somebody does start slinging around heavy firepower,
I'd like the Emergency War Council to move to Fort Stafford—"

This time it was Glicksohn who snapped out the obscenity. Fitzpatrick and Karras were almost as fast and as rude.

The prime minister shook his head. "That would look
like running away from our own people and hiding behind
the Federation's walls. Everybody would doubt our courage. Nobody would believe we weren't Federation puppets.
I'm sorry, General, but we can't smash our authority overnight. You'd be the loser too."

"I know I would," Kornilov growled. "But we'll all lose
even more if somebody blows us away. It wouldn't even
take a suitcase fuser. Half a dozen suicide commandos could
do the work, with HE and small arms."

"That's just a possibility," Brothertongue said. "The loss
of authority is a certainty. We can't trade off the one for
the other."

Impasse was written in the air between the Victorians and
the general, in glowing letters. Then Commander Franke
cleared his throat.

"Ladies and gentlemen, if I might make a suggestion?
Why not split the council? The prime minister and the other
civilians can stay in Thortonsburg. Governor-General Gist
and General Parkinson can move to Fort Stafford. The governor-general is a legal representative of the Federation,
and General Parkinson is CG of an allied army."

"Allied?" It was at least a trio, if not a chorus.

"Any armed force conducting operations in cooperation
with the Federation receives most of the legal status of an
allied force even without a treaty. I can look up the prece-
dents if—"

Kornilov broke in before somebody asked Franke to do
so. He would do such a thorough job that the meeting
would last until evening.

"All right," Gist said. He seemed to be measuring Franke
for his potential as either friend or foe. In fact, the two men
had much in common, with their alarmingly quick minds in

deceptively slow bodies. "I can manage that. Can you put in a communications detachment in Thorntonsburg, so we aren't dependent on commercial links?"

"Certainly. It will need a small security force, of course, but I'm sure we can find the people for that. Also, we can make Navy transportation available any time you want a face-to-face."

The communications detachment would have a 'security force' of fifty picked troopers and MPs. The civilians would be guarded to the eyebrows, whether they liked it or not.

Parkinson was nodding but not smiling. "I'll agree under one condition. The militia reserve battalion moves into Fort Stafford with me."

"*Sookin sin!*" Kornilov growled.

Parkinson smiled. "No, the bitch herself, not the son. I can't be separated from all my troops. Not and still have any authority over them."

"You don't trust your commanders?"

"When I'll look like a Federation prisoner or a coward? No."

"Which ones?"

"Don't I trust? I'm damned if I'll give anybody but God a list. Certainly not a bloody Feddie general."

"If Alys doesn't go to Fort Stafford, I won't either," Gist put in.

Kornilov carried a sidearm for personal security, not for assassinating the government of the Associated States. He kept his hand off the pistol butt and drew a deep breath.

"Will you communicate through Federation links?"

"Except within the battalion, which will have its own system, yes."

This time Commander Franke didn't clear his throat. "I'd like to point out that Fort Stafford will provide better base facilities for the reserves. It's close enough to Blanchard Canyon—"

"Commander, I have not forgotten how to read a map." Kornilov also hadn't forgotten how many times this particular trick had been used to infiltrate an enemy's strongholds. Some of the times had led to nuclear terrorism or even exchanges.

Kornilov fixed his gaze on Parkinson.

"What will you do if we refuse?"

"I'll have to move my HQ into the field, with the two battalions of the main force," Parkinson said.

Where she would be harder to control if the Federation needed it, and have less control over her commanders if she needed it.

"I can't promise a general security clearance for your people."

"We won't need it," Parkinson said. Her smile stopped short of being triumphant. "There's plenty of room in Fort Stafford."

"And we'd also like you to take charge of local civilians we're reassigning."

Fort Stafford normally employed about five hundred Victorian locals on assorted housekeeping chores. By tomorrow Kornilov intended that number to be zero.

"You're dismissing them?" Brothertongue said, frowning.

"Call it an indefinite leave of absence, with pay continuing unless they actually resign," Kornilov replied. "We don't want to tempt the few unreliable ones among them to make trouble. On the other hand, we don't want to just throw the loyal ones out onto the streets where we can't protect them. Your sector of Fort Stafford seems like a good compromise."

"This whole situation seems like one big compromise!" Glicksohn said.

"Welcome to the real world, Judy," Gist said. "Now, I don't know about anybody else needing to keep a clear head. But *I* think it's time for a small drink."

Kornilov had gone abstinent for the duration of the crisis. Otherwise he would have joined the rest for the Caledonian whiskey Gist poured out.

Rahbad Sarlin knew that Essteb Y'eel had done him as much courtesy as a Merishi could contrive. The little room at the back of the Web of Hrar was not only private, it had been humidified almost to the comfort standard of the People. That, Sarlin knew, was unpleasant for the Scaleskins, who liked their heat dry.

Citizen Y'eel had also permitted Sarlin to bring his portable scrambler to the conference. It was the most sophisticated such device the People had, supposedly able to make anything said in the room unintelligible to human and Merishi spies alike.

Why, then, did Sarlin feel the alertness of one at the edge of a bottomless canyon? Y'eel was saying nothing that needed more attention than good manners dictated. Sarlin began probing his recent memories for clues.

Some of it was doubtless instinct sharpened on a dozen war-scarred planets. Where sapient beings sought each other's lives, wisdom said to expect the unexpected.

More of it came from his walk through Silvermouth to the Tangled Web. Since he had no hope of concealing his race, he merely dressed warmly and walked openly to his destination.

The usual number of humans seemed either surprised or hostile. But others smiled at him, and still others seemed to pay him no more attention than a piece of windblown trash.

Did they know—or rather, had they heard—something he had not? Had they been promised that the People were sending down more than a merchant vessel's commercial agent, to do more than watch over neutral interests?

Sarlin also remembered his coming to the door of the Web, and the two Scaleskins who met him there. The T'aarm brothers, Raukis and Phisthor, were larger than most of their race, apart from the weapons they both displayed openly. Sarlin was no expert on Merishi body language, but he judged the brothers to be alert, fit, loyal to their employer, and totally ruthless with his enemies.

Turning his back on such folk was not much to Rahbad Sarlin's taste. That went very much against what the romances said of Special Projects agents, but any agent who lived down to the romances would have died on his first mission. A wise agent contrived, with the favor of the High Lords, to keep potential enemies where he could see them.

Sarlin realized that Y'eel's tone had changed, and set aside further speculation for later. "Excuse me, my host. But that last point was not quite clear."

Y'eel appeared to accept the question as honest inquiry. "I was concerned about police attention, if the Web becomes the meeting place for those whom you wish to take off-planet."

"Are you engaged in anything you do not wish the police to learn?"

Y'eel laughed mirthlessly. "Can anyone be a proper host on another race's world and never cross the bounds of the law? No one but a god, and that I am not."

Sarlin wanted to remind Y'eel not to waste time by stating the obvious. "I grant that. But consider the need of both your fellow Merishi and those of other races caught in this war. Consider also that you have empty rooms, a reasonable amount of hoarded food—"

"*Hoarding* is a harsh term, my friend."

"Let us then call it food laid aside with prudent foresight, for a crisis which is now upon us."

"How so? The nearest fighting is still more than a thousand kilometers from Silvermouth. The city's population remains both loyal and peaceful, even though not a fighter of the 96th remains in town."

"You've noticed that too?"

Y'eel's face and tone turned sour. "Why otherwise would I have so many empty rooms and . . . as much food as I have?"

"You do not find enough customers among your own folk?"

"I fear that half of my customers took ship during the Bushranger Rebellion. Of the other half, many have retired to their properties."

"And some, I imagine, are among those Merishi presently enjoying the Federation's hospitality?"

Y'eel spread his hands. The vestigial webs between the fingers were turning yellow; he was older than he appeared. Considering who he was, this was hardly surprising.

"I fear so. Neither they nor their friends will ever be my customers again."

"On that, my host, I beg to differ." Sarlin rested his scrambler on the arm of his chair and thumbed the activation plate in a complex pattern. A small screen unfolded from the top, and on the screen—

Y'eel clapped both hands over his eyes and at the same time tried to stand. The two gestures proved incompatible. He stumbled over his chair and fell, dragging the chair over on top of him.

Sarlin heaved the table out of his way, spilling ornaments

and papers. He grappled Y'eel, pinning him to the rug with superior weight, gripping both of the Merishi's hands in one of his. With the other he drew a small red injector.

"If you call for help, you'll be dead of an apparent heart rupture before it arrives."

"The autopsy—"

"May not be conducted by Merishi surgeons. Even if it is, this is a new generation of S6. It becomes undetectable within two hours."

"You're lying."

Sarlin thrust a thumb up under Y'eel's jaw, against a sensitive nerve. "Don't say that again. Or at least don't wager on it."

Y'eel gasped something wordless but full of meaning. "Repeat that, please."

"Leave me alone. I swore then it was an accident. It was, please."

The nictitating membranes were down over the yellow eyes now. They also were showing age. If he had been human or of the People, Essteb Y'eel would have been weeping.

"Too bloody for an accident, my friend. And you fled afterward."

"I had powerful enemies."

"You still do. One of them is right here. But you can turn him into a friend very quickly."

"How?"

"Are you so stupid that I need to spell it out for you?"

Y'eel wriggled, then seemed to decide for preserving the little dignity he had left. He nodded. "Release me and I will talk. I do not know much—"

"I have reason to believe otherwise."

Y'eel tried to pull loose. He might as well have tried to pull free of a heavy-duty clamp. The People had a stronger grip than the Merishi, and Sarlin had strength-trained his hands and arms as well.

"One more bit of nonsense like that and I load you with truth drug." Y'eel's face crinkled in horror. "Ah, have you had one of those anti-interrogation treatments? The one that makes truth drugs lethal?"

Y'eel's expression made words superfluous. "Knowing who you are tells me much of what I know," Sarlin said.

"So I have no reason to keep you alive. Perhaps you can give me one. Gratitude is not a common virtue in my profession, but it is not quite unknown."

Y'eel was too shaken to speak for a hundredth-watch, but when someone came on the intercom he told them he was engaged. After that the prospect of keeping life and reputation as well as property seemed to loosen his tongue.

It took no more than a tenth-watch for Sarlin to learn as much as he could reasonably expect. Some of it, after voice analysis, would doubtless prove to be lies. Also, Y'eel had refused to give Sarlin more than a handful of names.

Sarlin could let that pass. He had enough additional clues to direct the search for at least two hands of suspects. Sooner or later, he would find someone who was willing to talk—or could be made so at leisure.

When he was finished, Sarlin pulled out a purple injector. "Does your treatment extend to amnesiacs?"

"N-no."

"Good. It will be better for both of us if you forget about the past half-watch." The injector punched its needle through the wine-colored scales on Y'eel's throat, into the great vein there. The Merishi stiffened, then slumped over his chair.

"Help!" Sarlin shouted in Merishi. "Help! A doctor for Essteb Y'eel! He has had a seizure." Sarlin crossed the room and popped the two injectors into the waste disposal. Frantic knocking drowned out the faint *pop* of their distingration.

"Help!" Sarlin shouted again, and from beyond the door Raukis T'aarm replied, "Open the door, you scaleless fool!"

Sarlin fumbled the door open, practically fell past the brothers, tucked his scrambler under his coat, and hurried off down the hall. His last sight of Essteb Y'eel was the brothers bending over him, waving more injectors.

This was the first large conference Captain Liddell had attended in *Shenandoah*'s flag quarters since they'd been home to more than Admiral Kuwahara himself. (Bunfights like the party to introduce the staff didn't count.)

She couldn't detect any changes, but then she needed all her attention for General Kornilov's briefing. He'd come himself, wearing battledress and leaving both Colonel Vesey and Commander Franke behind.

The general was also talking faster than usual, and he looked as if he had a permanent case of indigestion or maybe the early stages of an ulcer. Liddell suspected he wasn't the only senior officer of Victoria Command with that problem. Her own mirror had not been kind this morning, and for several mornings past.

Kornilov finished explaining the deployments about the time Liddell finished her tea. "Any questions?" the general asked.

"Yes," Kuwahara said. His voice was flat to just this side of hostility. "Why?"

"Why what?"

"Why this particular deployment?"

"It gives us the best chance of supporting the Vics in their actions against the Freedom Legion. It does the same for meeting the 96th, if it intervenes. It does both of these with the minimum of on-station Navy support."

"Don't call you, you'll call us?" Kuwahara's voice was more normal, but he didn't smile.

"Exactly. We have complete confidence in the Navy's ability to support us if we need it. When we don't need it, we'd rather not distract them from watching the Baernoi."

"And the Alliance?"

"Is Uzel feeling suicidal?"

Kuwahara now managed a thin smile. "Thanks for the vote of confidence, Mikhail. I can see your compliments are sincere. Maybe they're even deserved. But you're missing the main point."

"Which is?"

Kornilov looked ready to stonewall. Liddell prayed that he would think twice before he actually tried it. Victoria wasn't oversupplied with generals, but these days Kuwahara was even shorter of patience.

Kuwahara massaged his temples. "What other contingencies are you considering?"

Liddell contemplated doing anything short of dancing on the display cube to prevent the confrontation. Then she saw Kornilov's shoulders slump.

"Not a contingency. More of a hunch, and more Commander Franke's than mine, originally. But after he presented it, he convinced me."

"I wish he'd convinced you to include it in the initial briefing. Hunch or contingency, *what is it?*"

Liddell was almost out of her chair before Kornilov replied. "Trouble in the south. Anything from individual assassination attempts to a full-scale uprising. Probably but not certainly at the lower end of the scale."

"That explains the lower positioning of the Victorians in Fort Stafford and garrisoning their southern cities. But why not even more muscle?"

"In the urban areas? Several reasons." Kornilov ticked them off on thick fingers.

"One, the Alliance and the Freedom Legion are known problems. Trouble in the south is only a possibility.

"Second, we can't prevent an uprising by garrisoning the cities with troops who don't know the Vics. We'll more likely offer targets and provoke incidents that could lead to the most dangerous kind of uprising. A low-level urban guerrilla war, forcing us to either retake the cities house-to-house or abandon them."

"We couldn't do the second," Commodore Yague said. "That would give the rebels a claim for Baernoi recognition that we couldn't dispute without blowing the Seventh Training Force out of the sky."

"Stop telling me things I already know!" Kornilov growled, like an animal giving its final warning before the attack.

"Excuse me," Captain Liddell said, "but I think General Kornilov is trying to draw these contingent rebels into massing in the open field. They may not have enough support in the cities to take them from inside. But if they can march on Port Harriet, like the Freedom Legion did on Buschton . . ."

"Did you ever think of transferring to the Army, Captain?" Kornilov said. The cornered-animal look and tone were gone.

Blessed are the peacemakers, for they shall get all the ulcers the warriors don't. "Not yet."

Kornilov shrugged. "I never intended to ambush you with this. But low-order probabilities—if one tries to cover all of them—"

"One risks leaving out a high-order one. I know. It may

be true, and certainly it's a line of argument as old as the Assyrian Army. Or did the Neolithic civilizations have a chain of command?" Kuwahara's fingers were at his temples.

"Never mind," Kuwahara continued. "I agree with your risk assessment. What exactly did you have in mind for the Navy, if we do have trouble in the south?"

Kornilov handed over a stack of printed sheets. "That's an extra annex to my report that Commander Franke prepared. Personally, I thought it was ass-covering—"

"It was," Kuwahara said. "But yours, not his." He flipped through the stack, then handed everything except two pages to the other Navy people. "Nicely condensed, too."

With only two pages to read, Liddell didn't bother skimming. Carlotta Yague finished first. "Nice work all around," she said. "It pretty much matches our Contingency L Plan. There's only one thing I'd suggest we actually do in advance, and that's pre-position most of the nonlethals."

"What about the security problem?" Commodore Uehara asked.

Liddell rocked a hand back and forth. "Balancing risks. It's a security problem only if the hotheads are determined to rebel no matter what we do. Then we do want to provoke them as the general says, and be ready with the nonlethals the minute they do.

"But if they're still making up whatever they use for minds . . . a little warning that we're ready for them may not be a wholly bad thing. Even the slowest minds can be changed."

"Agreed," Kuwahara said. "Sorry, Mikhail, but Rose stays in the Navy. Can we draw on Army transport for the pre-positioning?"

"Yes. How much, I'll check with Milla."

"Good. Then I think we can call the steward and drink to pulling our cakes out of the fire."

The intercom alarm squealed. Kuwahara voice-switched the display to intercom, and Captain Bogdanov appeared.

"Sorry to interrupt, sir, but we thought you'd like to see this."

An enhanced planetscape replaced Bogdanov's face, a satellite view of the southern part of Seven Rivers. A bright

orange dot flared against the white-streaked gray of the
south coast, faded, but didn't vanish entirely.

"We have a signature and location. That was an explosion
and fire, both big, in Silvermouth."

"Industrial accident?"

"It's a commercial-residential area. The signature is also
chemical-explosive."

"They're hitting Silvermouth, then."

"It looks like it, sir."

"Thank you, Captain. Put a magnified visual through as
soon as you have one." The deployment map returned, and
for a moment Kuwahara held his head in both hands.

The explosion at the Web of Hrar didn't knock Rahbad
Sarlin off his feet. That came a moment later, as what
seemed like several hundred humans rushed past him
toward the corner for a better view. Heavy clothing and the
massive bone structure of the People saved him from more
than loss of dignity, although he was walked on as well as
over.

When an ebb in the tide of bodies allowed it, he staggered
to his feet and joined the crowd at the corner. One wing of
the Web had completely collapsed, and smoke was pouring
up from the wreckage. The central part that housed the
atrium restaurant was heavily on fire, and the flames
seemed to be spreading to at least one other wing.

Cutting through an alley and across a small park with all
its flower beds shrouded for the winter, Sarlin headed for
the Web. He would be conspicuous as the only one of the
People on hand, maybe conspicuous enough to attract the
attention of the police. They were already present in force,
airdropping barriers, hustling spectators behind them, and
setting up emergency lighting to guide the firefighters.

If he didn't appear, though, his cover story of being concerned about Merishi and other neutral merchants might
lose some weight. After all, half the people he was supposedly here to help might be buried in the ruins or trapped
by the flames.

In the corner of the garden, he found a place where he
could climb on the wall behind a dwarfed tree with inward-
curving branches and reddish bark. He didn't know its

name, but it offered reasonable concealment without hiding the Web.

Sarlin activated the camera in his hat and let it record the scene. A spectroscopic analysis of the flames would help. A chemical analysis of the smoke would have helped more, but that was something he wasn't equipped to take himself. A judicious bribe to someone in the fire department might help.

Not that there could be much doubt that the explosion and fire were no accident. The only question was who had done it, and why. There Sarlin had enough suspicions to fill a report the size of *Land of the Lords;* what he wanted was evidence.

The fire department arrived, five lifters skimming the rooftops in loose formation. One made an even lower pass over the intact part of the Web, dropping foam bombs on each roof. A moment later the bombs erupted, hurling gray-white clouds in all directions.

Two others hovered over the foam-drenched roofs, dropping humans turned almost as massive as the People by their firefighting gear, Sarlin was watching the pumpers land and start deploying their hose towers when new siren wails and blazing lights warned of the ambulances.

The last of the three had markings in both Merishi and Anglic and carried both the red cross and the green trefoil. It turned as it passed over the Web, stopped just above Sarlin, then floated down into the garden. Plant shrouds crunched as it settled; the Merishi Emergency Service was going to have a nice bill to settle with the city's Parks Administration.

Sarlin turned, saw two Merishi at the controls of the ambulance—and an unmistakable human behind them, pointing at him. Sarlin lunged for one of the tree's branches, to swing himself over the wall and down the other side. But the short arms of the People defeated an escape that a Smalltooth could have made with ease.

Sarlin had just given up trying for a branch and was ready to leap blindly when something smashed into the back of his left knee. The leg buckled under him, throwing him off balance. Arms flailing, he fell backward, dropping a body length to the frozen ground.

His head struck a plant shroud as he landed. For a

moment none of his limbs seemed attached to his body or
to anything else. He worked his jaws, trying to bring pressure on the poison-loaded tooth that he'd carried for most
of his life.

But his jaws also seemed detached from his body, or at
least his brain. He could think about biting down on the
tooth, imagine the poison spreading through his body,
dream of the frustration of the human as it bent over his
corpse.

His thoughts could run, but his muscles were locked.
Frustration seemed to slow his thoughts, until they too
stopped dead, or at least went around in futile circles.

Captured. Who? Captured. Who—

Until finally he stopped thinking or feeling at all.

Eight

"Time to initial launch, one hundred fifty seconds. Repeat, one five zero seconds." Commander Charbon's voice came over the intercom with its usual precision.

Admiral Kuwahara leaned back in his chair, willed out of his awareness the Auxiliary Combat Center that now served as Flag Plot, and considered the case of General Kornilov. Roughly ninety seconds to decide whether to relieve him of command, and if so, when.

Ten seconds. Points in his favor: He knew Victoria, his work had been good, he had the loyalty of Victoria Command, and his plan for baiting the rebels into a tactical blunder was good.

Thirty seconds. Points against him: He'd thought the Navy didn't have to be told about the plan, or else forgotten that they might notice he'd left something out. A deliberate move, or a mistake?

Fifty seconds. If deliberate, relieve. That kind of game was intolerable. If a mistake—why? Probably fatigue and strain.

Sixty seconds. Query Colonel Vesey, General Langston, and Colonel Chatterje. Emphasize strictly medical nature of query. (Also emphasize possibility of reducing Kornilov's workload as alternative to relief.)

Seventy-five seconds. Make that a formal proposal, to Kornilov himself. Treat him as a wise and honest man, even if a tired and stress-ridden one.

Ninety seconds. Kornilov stays, if he can stop working fifteen-hour days.

Kuwahara felt the decision sweep away the early stages of another migraine. They were in midstream, the current was fast, and the horse might stay on his feet just a little longer.

"Twenty seconds to initial launch. Two-zero seconds and counting."

Kuwahara watched the display tank, listened to Charbon, and held his breath. In the tank the three capital ships formed a squat V, with two squadrons of cruisers turning it into an almost equally squat X. All weapons and sensors covering the space around *Valhalla* were linked through *Shenandoah* and under Kuwahara's control.

"Launch initiated!"

Aboard *Valhalla,* the tube-mounted launchers would be slamming the first four attackers out into space, far enough from the carrier to avoid drive interference. In thirty seconds—

"Second launch initiated. Launching at Alert One-Plus rate."

"Show-off," Kuwahara muttered. Sixteen attackers would be plunging out of their tubes every minute. That was a rate normally used only when a carrier was trying to clear her AG before power failed or a missile impacted. Drive-field interference and outright collisions were a distinct risk.

But if anything happened, it would be his responsibility, not only legally but morally. He'd put it in the orders for the exercise himself: "Launch AG at maximum safe rate," and by precedent and custom that gave Prange total discretion.

Now in the tank *Valhalla* seemed to be in the middle of an expanding globe of amber dots. As the outer rim of the globe reached critical distance from *Baikhal* and *Shenandoah*, dots began breaking away from it and streaming toward the edge of the display.

In three minutes *Valhalla* had launched her entire Attacker Group, fifty-two attackers and the CAG's command ship. More dots streamed toward the edge of the display, dancing like mating lanternbugs into pairs and then into fours.

By the time the AG hit Victoria's atmosphere, they'd be formed into standard finger-fours. Only a large-yield weapon could take out more than one attacker in that formation, but they could easily support one another with weapons, ECM, and if all else failed the Mark I Eyeball.

The display shifted, to show the surface of Victoria. Silver lines superimposed a triangle, with its points at Mount Houton, Fort Stafford, and the main base of 215 Brigade.

Kuwahara signaled for a cup of tea. With 20,000 kilometers to cover, even attackers would take a while to reach that triangle. When they did, they would demonstrate just how thoroughly the Navy could cover the area, to seek, strike, and destroy hostile forces with weapons and at ranges of their choice.

Along with the movement of the nonlethal munitions, this exercise would be a warning to the hotheads. If they didn't cool down somewhat after this, Kuwahara was prepared to weed them out of the gene pool with a clear conscience and a firm hand.

Actually, they would be the hands of *Valhalla*'s AG 11/9, and Kuwahara was prepared to forgive Captain Prange a good deal for the skill he'd taught those hands. "You can't live with him and you can't live without him" was the popular view of Prange.

The tea appeared. As Kuwahara sipped, the intercom reminded everybody that Prime Minister Fitzpatrick's appeal for peace would be broadcast live to all hands beginning in forty-five minutes.

The stick was in place, or on its way. Now it was time for Fitzpatrick to wave the carrot.

"Who gave *them* the jeweled tools?" Ehmed met-Lakaito grumbled.

Brokeh su-Irzim ignored *Perfumed Wind*'s First Guidance. The man grumbled most of the time when he was in a good mood, and all the time when he was not. For the past two days, nobody aboard *Wind* had been in a good mood, even those who did not know about Rahbad Sarlin's disappearance. It was enough for them to know that a secret was eating their superiors from the guts outward.

F'Mita ihr Sular couldn't afford to be so detached from anything that might affect the safety of her ship. She swiveled her chair, then flinched as four more Federation attackers flashed across the near-ship display.

"How long are those children of poisoners going to be parting our hair?" she snapped.

"Is that a request for a message?" su-Irzim asked. He could now handle several of *Wind*'s consoles. Most of them were standard Fleet models, although old enough to have been bought at surplus sales.

"If His Lordship knows his tusks from his tail—" ihr Sular began.

"A little respect, please."

"If His Lordship doesn't know everything about the Smallteeth, he'll have all channels and sensors concentrating on learning the rest. They usually don't show off around the People this way, do they?"

"No." Su-Irzim felt blood rushing to his skin at forgetting such an elementary detail of Fleet procedures. He had been away from ship duty too long, and while he was aboard *Night Warrior* he was not part of its operational crew. He was relearning what he'd once known much faster aboard *Perfumed Wind* than aboard the command ship.

In rapid succession, three more four-attacker formations raced past *Perfumed Wind*. Two were so tight that the individual attackers barely registered separately on the screen.

In spite of interference from the number of radars activated once, met-Lakaito tracked the mass of attackers to the edge of Victoria's atmosphere. As he switched *Wind*'s detectors back to area surveillance, the close-approach alarm sounded.

Ihr Sular and su-Irzim sounded the maneuvering alarm and sought a visual lock on the approaching object. The commander swore and sighed with relief at the same time as the screen showed a large Federation Navy shuttle cutting past no more than twenty marches away. Two attackers rode in formation with it.

"Somebody down there ordered a hot dinner, and the Smallteeth are wetting themselves to deliver it," met-Lakaito muttered. "Or maybe a hot partner?"

Ihr Sular rose. "Call us when the Prime Minister's about to come on," she said. "Switch to translate/record mode when he does."

"I wasn't born last year," the First Guidance said, although su-Irzim thought he heard a less polite tail to the remark. He rose to join *Wind*'s commander as she led the way to her cabin.

Once there, she opened the hospitality cabinet, contemplated the gauges on the beer and strongwater tanks, and grunted. Then she poured herself a mugful.

"How many watches now?"

"Seven." She couldn't be referring to anything but the time since Rahbad Sarlin's disappearance.

"He's probably dead."

"We don't know that."

"But how can we find out, without giving people who want him dead a clue about his identity?"

It was about the fourth or fifth time they'd had this exchange, and the dilemma was as many-tusked as ever. A full-scale search for Rahbad Sarlin would reveal his presence on Victoria to the enemies of the People, even if the Alliance authorities were not among them. Since they might be, a full-scale search was impossible.

But so was simply sitting on their tails and doing nothing while one of the great Special Projects commanders of their era might be dead or dying. Or worse, in the hands of people who either knew who he was and would at best hope to use him as a hostage, or who didn't and would kill him, perhaps not even bothering with an interrogation—

Ihr Sular slammed her mug down on the table. Beer slopped over the rim. "He always was a gambler, and this time he lost. Must the People lose too?"

Su-Irzim didn't see how anyone could take Sarlin's place in Special Operations, but that was for the future. For now he and F'Mita had a good deal to do, to prove themselves worthy even to attend Sarlin's memorial songfest!

A gamble. Contact with enemies who might talk was one they couldn't afford. Were there any other kind?

"F'Mita. I'm going back to *Warrior* as soon as the traffic thins out. I want to pull the whole file on Federation Intelligence operations in Victoria."

"Can't it be squirted?"

"Not some of what I'll be looking for, with this many Federation ears listening."

He knew that his ears must be blooded and his neck sweating, from the way F'Mita was looking at him. She rested a hand on his.

"Then the High Lords go with you." She thumbed the communicator. "Shuttle bay—"

The First Guidance broke in. "The Prime Minister Fitzpatrick is about to speak."

Ihr Sular consigned Fitzpatrick to the ripest level of a

compost heap, then poured two more mugs of beer. This time a dry-throated su-Irzim did not refuse.

The flat screen flickered, then Prime Minister Fitzpatrick's oddly People-like features flowed together into a firm shape.

"My fellow Victorians—"

On the screen at the forward end of the shuttle's cabin, Fitzpatrick's face wavered, blurred, then solidified again.

His rough voice kept right on.

"—this is a dangerous time for our homeworld. It will be dangerous no matter what we do. But we can make it less dangerous, or at least some of us can.

"I call on the Freedom Party and its allies, including Action For Independence, to abandon their rebellious and illegal actions against Seven Rivers Territory of the United Planetary Alliance. I also call on them to disband the Freedom Legion and turn over all its weapons and communications equipment to the legal forces of the Associated States of Victoria.

"In return for this, I offer the Freedom Party and its supporters a conditional amnesty. All persons guilty only of participation in the invasion will be set free on one Victoria year's probation. All persons who participated in the first rebellion as well as the invasion will be subject to trial, by the authorities of the Associated States of Victoria.

"All persons who have committed crimes against the Federation or the Alliance will be held for trial on Victoria by the authorities of the United Federation of Starworlds, with observers from the Alliance and the Associated States.

"All citizens of the Associated States who have been taken prisoner by the forces of the Alliance are to be released immediately. The Associated States will do the same for any Alliance citizens currently held by the Freedom Legion.

"I do not have words to express my grief that I must threaten punishment instead of merely appealing to reason. But it seems that reason has fled from a small minority of my fellow Victorians, and nothing but fear of punishment will bring it back.

"The Freedom Party and its illegal military forces have three Victoria days to surrender under these conditions. During this period, the action of the forces of the Associated States and the Federation will be limited to confiscating military supplies destined for the invasion force. The shipment of medicine and food will be allowed, as we do not wish the civilian population in the invaded area to suffer.

"At the end of this period, the Associated States and the Federation reserve the right to take any other appropriate action to end the rebellion, the invasion, and the suffering and death they were causing to Victoria."

Fitzpatrick swallowed. "I have appealed first to the Freedom Party, its allies, and their illegal army, because they are most directly responsible for the present crisis. But I hope that others listening will also be guided by my words.

"To the loyal citizens of the Associated States: The best way to protect any family or friends among the rebels is to remain loyal and see that the rebellion is ended and the rebels are given justice. Victoria must in the end be free and united. It will be neither if the folly of its people forces off-planet authorities to endlessly burden us with garrisons in the name of 'security'—or because we have made them suspect that we cannot manage our own affairs.

"To the authorities of the Federation and the Alliance: Victorians are of one mind on the subject of independence and union. Do not think that, because only a foolish minority has turned to military adventurism, the rest will sit still indefinitely.

"To the citizens of the Khudrigate of Baer, the Anisfar of Merish, and any other groups who may seek influence over events on Victoria: Think on what you are doing. If you treat us as pawns, the truth will come out sooner or later. Then you will have a planet of implacable enemies, where you might have had one of friends.

"I will not point accusing fingers. There is enough blame for this situation to go around, and enough blood shed for all of us to bear the stain.

"I will only ask that the killing end and peace begin, now and forever, for the future of this our homeworld."

Toward the end Fitzpatrick was speaking slowly, and when "Waltzing Matilda" began, Brian Mahoney thought he saw tears on the Prime Minister's cheeks. He knew he saw them on Brigitte Tachin's.

"Does anyone want to listen to the commentary?" the pilot's voice asked.

"Bugger the commentary!" shouted a voice with a Southern Cross accent. In the chorus of assent that followed, Mahoney looked for the speaker but couldn't pick anyone out of the cabinful of advisers.

Sixty-odd advisers and other people with urgent business on Victoria were riding the shuttle down from *Shenandoah.* Brian Mahoney would have resented the assignment, except that he knew that the "old Victoria hands" were the best possible choice. It also didn't hurt that this time he thought he knew what he was doing and would be X.O. of the Communications team on the adviser force.

If the Communications C.O. stayed healthy and Brigitte didn't have to play SFC again, it would all be chowder and beer. At least compared to last time—

The screen went kaleidoscopic and the pilot's voice came on again. "We will be taking about twenty minutes longer than usual to reach Fort Stafford. We want to stay below the radar horizon of both rebel and Alliance territory after we hit atmosphere.

"There will be a fifteen-minute stop at Fort Stafford for people leaving us there. After that we will be proceeding to Camp Aounda at low altitude. People continuing with us, please stay in your seats and keep your safety harnesses locked."

Mahoney looked at the back of the seat in front of him. He was relieved to see the sickbag where he'd expected it. He'd never been spacesick or airsick, but a rough ride surrounded by unlucky stomachs could be too much even for him.

In fact, he felt a little queasy already, but the motion of the shuttle had nothing to do with it. Running a shuttle directly to the advisers' base meant one of two things. Either Victoria Command was very sure it knew where the rebels were, or else it was in the devil's own hurry to get the advisers on the ground and in action.

Candice Shores was on her way to the shower with nothing on her mind but a shower cap. This novel condition was the result of a sudden influx of officers senior to Shamil the Camel and a continued stand-down of Scout Company while the Navy maneuvered over the whole potential AO.

She even hoped that this condition might continue. The

Scout Company of 215 Brigade was with the battalions holding down the southern end of the border. Her Scouts were part of the reserve for Task Force Borha, now operating out of Camp Aounda in support of the Vics trying to cut off Freedom Legion supplies.

The whole layering of forces in the Victoria AO was beginning to remind Shores of a torte she'd once encountered in a German restaurant run by a Turk with an Armenian cook. It had eight layers, fell apart the minute she stuck a fork into it, and gave her the worst case of diarrhea she'd ever had.

She didn't quarrel with the principle behind this complicated layering. Keeping Federation and Freedom Legion troopers out of shooting distance of each other was good politics.

It might not be such good tactics. In every "peacekeeping" operation that Shores had heard of, sooner or later the time came to kick ass and take names. It helped if you didn't have to ask several friendly asses to move out of the way before you had a clear kick at the unfriendly ones.

Shores rounded the last corner and stopped as if she'd stepped into a mantrap. The shower room door was open and an anonymous kitbag squatted on the visible end of the bench. Or rather, a kitbag that would have been anonymous to anyone except Candice Shores.

Candice Shores, and three other people who'd been saved from a thousand-meter fall off the north face of Fortinbras Peak, when Madeleine Bloch dug in her ice ax, her free hand, her toes, and for all anyone knew her nose, chin, and teeth. The ice ax now sat on top of the kitbag, with a few more scratches that Shores didn't remember but otherwise very much the same as it had been when she crawled up the couloir past Maddie, on to firm ice.

She hadn't kissed the ax, or Maddie (who would have been sure to misinterpret the gesture even under such circumstances). But the ax had sunk into her memory as firmly as it had into the crack, and anywhere it appeared, Maddie might as well have left a holoportrait.

Shores sat down on the bench and picked up the ax. It was an ordinary Eisenkopf 21, and she balanced it, testing its throwing qualities.

"Kiyaaaah!"

Shores dropped the ax instead of throwing it, came off
the bench into a roll, and lashed up and out at the knee of
the woman who'd leaped out of the shower. The woman's
knee seemed to displace half a meter sideways and up without the rest of her moving, then she was leaping high, to
come down on Shore's rib cage or throat.

Shores was out of the way before the woman landed, but
found that she'd rolled herself into a corner. Never mind—
one leg bent under her let the other lash out and back. Her
opponent rode the kick up on one hip bone, chopped down
with both hands at a leg that was nowhere in reach, then
jumped back and bowed.

"You'd still make a good Ranger, Candy."

"You're still a better one, Maddie. So who needs me?"

Then the two women were hugging each other. Shores
felt herself being lifted right off her feet, as usual. Madeleine Bloch packed the same weight as Shores into ten centimeters less height, thanks to massive bones and muscles.

Also as usual, the hug went on about two heartbeats
longer than Shores really enjoyed. Another thing about
Maddie that hadn't changed. Fortunately Bloch had never
yet spoiled a friendship she valued that way.

Shores flexed her knees as she landed, then pulled off
her bathrobe. "What brings you here, Maddie? The usual
Ranger business that will be classified BBA until three days
after the heat death of the universe?"

"No."

"What part of the question does that answer?"

"All of it."

In an unsecured room, where uncleared people might
wander in at any moment, Shores wasn't going to ask more.
Instead she tossed her bathrobe on the bench and stepped
into the shower. It was a shipboard shower—wet down,
soap up, then rinse off—since the wells and purifiers were
at full stretch with the expanded garrison.

When Shores came out, Bloch was fully dressed except
for socks and boots, and was trimming her toenails. Maddie,
Shores decided, still looked better bare than clothed. She
was so close to being chunky that anything more than a fig
leaf took her over the edge.

Bloch stuck her cutter in a pocket and pulled on her boots.
Retrieving their cold-weather gear, the two officers climbed

the stairs and stepped out of the heatlock onto the barracks roof. Powder snow caught in the cracks of the appliqué armor squeaked underfoot as they walked to the edge of the roof.

"So," Shores said. "What's the business, and when does it go on the map? Interfering with the Freedom Legion's supplies?"

"Don't say I told you."

Shores grinned at Maddie's usual formula for confirming a guess. "Makes sense. The militia wouldn't be much good, and we've agreed not to openly use our own troops inside Seven Rivers."

Maddie's reply wasn't a grin, only a brief nod. Shores frowned. "Am I supposed to guess when you'll be de-classified?"

"You can guess. But you don't need to. I think some-body's going to tell you, when Intelligence has finished sort-ing some new data."

If that somebody was Major—no, they'd spotted him up to light colonel—Nieg, she just might go and ask. But Nieg couldn't tell her what he didn't know himself, and he'd learn that she'd been talking with Maddie.

"All right. I'll wait. But—does Scout Company wait too?"

Maddie nodded. Shores wasn't surprised. Scout Company had been on light duty the past five days, only one platoon at a time deployed outside the camp perimeter. That could simply mean that 215's Scouts were now acclimatized and oriented. More likely it meant a special assignment coming up for her company.

One that just might prove that Shamil the Camel really had been full of it. . . .

"Think we'll need special equipment?"

"No, but if you have any shortages, I'll bet you can get them filled in record time."

"What are you betting?"

"Any Armagnac on this grapeless planet?"

"Shall we call it the best that Esteva or—Abdul's still with you?" Bloch nodded. "The best that they can come up with. Although I never did understand why you send a devout Moslem to scare up liquor."

"He takes advice, and I never need to worry about his drinking the stuff on the way home."

An orbital shuttle slid down an invisible slope in the sky, wobbling slightly in the random gusts of frigid wind. It grounded on the pad, the navigation lights died, and ground lights showed its markings and a hatch unfolding.

"*Shenandoah*," Bloch said. "That must be the first contingent of advisers. Want me to fade while you greet old friends?"

"Thanks, Maddie."

Personally, Shores thought that using the old Victoria hands for another round of advising was flogging willing horses. But deciding that wasn't her job. Hers was to tune up Scout Company, to take the field with Maddie's Rangers.

Like any other portable computer, Joanna Marder's Soltam 88+ worked more slowly in "black" mode, invisible to eye, ear, and all but the most sensitive electronic detection. She could have drunk half a bottle without gulping while the little machine made its definitive sorting of the data she'd accumulated in Barnard's Crossing.

Finally the telltale came on. The data was secured against unauthorized acquisition, if not against physical destruction. She stuck her UniCharge into the transmission slit and the telltale went off, then on. Now the data was also recorded along with her financial data in her main financial card.

Recorded, and so thoroughly mixed that only a particular access code could unmix it. An access code known only to Pak and a couple of his most trusted people. Once her data reached them, Marder knew it would be "mission accomplished" for her—the mission of weaving another length of rope for the necks of the people who'd killed her comrades.

It added up. A submarine fitted with external racks (specifications and pictures included) for ZP sequence containers (capable of holding the type of missile that hit *Eriksen Gamma*). A three-day trip, at exactly the right time. And a crew that the workers said didn't look like your regular sub hands (with descriptions of all three).

Marder wished she could have recorded her talks with the workers. But they wouldn't talk to her outside the sub yard, and when she tried to play back the conversations she understood why. They'd somehow rigged up a crude scrambler array that covered the whole work area.

She'd wondered if they suspected the crew. But that was a question she hadn't cared to risk asking, assuming somebody was prepared to answer!

It was more likely that the workers were just as their boss had said—loyal but sympathetic enough to the independence movement to be reluctant to talk freely except among themselves. Marder envied them that much freedom and knew that this had to be her first and last spy mission.

Just this one had pushed her too close to that edge marked by a litter of empty bottles. Pak had used her just like everybody else, because he knew she'd snap at the bait of avenging *Audacious*.

He'd been right, too. But if he dangled any more bait for her, she'd spit it back in his face. No, something even better. *I'll get stinking drunk in his HQ. Won't that make Colonel Neat-and-Tidy unhappy?*

Marder shivered, more from the twisting of her thoughts than from the chill of the room. She shut down the Soltam and bagged it, then started tidying up the room. No fingerprints, and nothing suspicious about wearing gloves. No body fluids, hair, or other odd bits that she could see, but she would go on looking for them until her nerves settled down a bit.

Then back to her hotel, for her last night in Barnard's Crossing. She'd spend another day in town, because there was a submersible diving platform and a newly repaired minisub coming out of the shop tomorrow. Not looking them over might chip her cover.

Besides, she still hoped to find someone who'd seen the missiles themselves being loaded. Maybe they'd done it far out, from a wave-skimming lifter invisible in sea effect. And maybe somebody had been looking the right way at the wrong time for the troublemakers.

Marder pressed her coat shut, pulled her hood across her face, and let herself out of the office. As she descended the stairs, her footsteps echoed in the bare stairwell. The first time she'd heard those echoes, she'd been sure somebody was following her.

Fleet Commander Eimo su-Ankrai hadn't moved from his couch all during Brokeh su-Irzim's presentation. The somnolence was only an appearance, though. Su-Irzim had been watching the old commander's eyes every moment. This kept him from watching the Fleet Inquirer, but he doubted if Zhapso su-Lal could surprise him anymore.

"Quicken my memory," su-Ankrai said. "How many died in the Agamemnon incident?"

"Fourteen humans. Thirty-five Ptercha'a. Eight Merishi."

"So all three races seek the person whose negligence caused the incident and would be grateful to those who brought him to justice?"

"That is my assumption, yes," su-Irzim said.

"Not an unreasonable assumption," su-Lal said. "Nor does it seem unreasonable that Essteb Y'eel was in fact the guilty party. Beyond that, I begin to differ with my fellow Inquirer."

"How?"

"He appears to think that Federation Intelligence will consider Y'eel's identity a valuable piece of information. I think they may already have it, from the Scaleskins who fled during the first rebellion.

"Even if they do not have it, they may not be able or willing to bargain for it. It also seems likely enough that Y'eel died in the destruction of the Web of Hrar and is beyond anyone's judgment save that of the High Lords of his own folk."

Su-Lal had offered no surprises but made a persuasive case. Su-Irzim set out to refute it with as much determination as hope.

"We do not know that Y'eel is dead. The Alliance authorities have said nothing either way. Even if he is dead, Rahbad Sarlin may not be. Or his intelligence may have survived him.

"If it has, it may well identify those who helped Y'eel leave Agamemnon and reach Victoria. We have all heard the rumors of Merishi smuggling operations in this part of space. Perhaps Sarlin could help turn the rumors into something more solid."

"And what if those smuggling operations are supported by our own Special Projects?"

"I am sure that if they exist they are used to some degree," su-Irzim replied. "But I am also sure that Special Projects will not forget or forgive the death of Rahbad Sarlin. Whatever relations they have with the smugglers may become ashes when he does."

"So you believe Special Projects will take no action if we embarrass the smugglers?" Su-Lal's voice rumbled like boulders rolling toward the jaws of a rock crusher.

"I believe they will not. And I believe that the humans will be grateful. Enough to give us—"

"You seem very eager to earn the gratitude of our enemies. Or perhaps I should say, of the People's enemies—"

Both Inquirers had their tusks bared and hands curved into battle-grip before su-Ankrai could open his mouth. When he did, it let out a roar worthy of a warrior a quarter of his age.

It won the Inquirers' attention. Su-Irzim suspected that it won the attention of everybody on the Gold Deck. He drew his lips over his tusks and forced his hands into his lap.

"Enough! Both of you apologize or leave."

The two Inquirers used the most formal declarations of guilt and requests for forgiveness. Su-Ankrai at least stopped glaring.

"I am glad you have more sense than it appeared, although still less than you need. Both of you are right, and neither of you is imagining dangers.

"Unfortunately, the person who knows the most about Special Projects' connections with the Scaleskins is Rahbad Sarlin himself. His next superior is too far away to tell us anything soon enough.

"The same thing can be said of Nieg's superiors. Anything known only on Charlemagne or even Riftwell is as useless to us as if it were not known at all."

Su-Ankrai sat up, with careful movements that revealed more of his age than the thunderous voice. He pulled his screen toward him and began calling up files.

"I think the best person to approach the Federation is not either of you, but myself. Su-Irzim, I want a summary of your findings and Sarlin's. Su-Lal, I want you to correlate your comrade's data with some that I shall provide."

Su-Lal's mouth opened, but what came out was more of a squeak than a roar. At last it turned into words.

"What grade of secrecy is—"

"Gold Grade, of course. Which is why I must take the responsibility for offering the data myself. It will be authentic. Neither of you will have it on your records that you received a special authorization for Gold Grade material. That is not as much of a blessing as you seem to think, su-Lal."

"I defer to your experience, my lord."

"And not a heartbeat too soon. Finally, if I put the data in the hands of either of you, it makes you valuable targets. I will know even more, of course—but I think our worst enemies will pause before attacking a fleet commander at a formal conference."

Su-Lal was quicker to find words this time.

"But a formal conference means Admiral Uzel as well as Admiral Kuwahara!"

"Of course," su-Ankrai said blandly. "How otherwise?"

"But do we wish the Alliance to know how much we know about what is going on in their territory?" su-Irzim said. He had crossed ground in the sight of armed enemies with less chill in his belly, but the question had to be asked.

"It will do us no great harm," su-Ankrai said in a tone that slammed the hatch on all discussion. Then he relented. "No harm, and even some good. If it forces Uzel to either open hostility or greater cooperation, we will be the better for it."

The only way su-Irzim could see Uzel's hostility helping was if it made the Federation more cooperative. It probably would, and that cooperation might even help the People. But su-Irzim thanked every Lord that he had heard of that it was the fleet commander taking the responsibility for this entire proposal!

Nine

Raimondo DiVries saw the pad controller waving the lifter to a landing with a lighted wand instead of hands or a flashlight. One more of the items that distinguished armies from mobs must have arrived.

The lifter touched down, its fans whined to a stop, and doors and hatches opened. A mixture of armed and unarmed civilians tumbled out. A woman screamed as a child ran across the hard-packed ground toward the edge of the pad.

One of the armed civilians ran after the child, slinging her pulser as she ran. DiVries recognized Gilly and remembered that she'd taken her squad out for security on this evac mission.

The child zigged when it should have zagged and Gilly caught up with it. She knelt and hugged it, consoling and restraining it at the same time.

"All right," she called. "This is Buschton, our civilian collecting point. Actually it's the military pad for Buschton. The town itself's on the other side of Kang's Gap. You'll have to walk it, but we have guides posted. Evacuees, line up over there with your personal baggage. Civilian recruits, line up over here beside Captain DiVries."

DiVries let himself serve as a landmark for five minutes until the civilians were on their way up the Gap and the recruits were lined up behind him. Then he turned and tried to ignore the icy wind blowing dust into his eyes.

"Welcome to the Freedom Legion. I'm the duty officer, Captain DiVries of Four Company, First Battalion. Our reception center is in the warehouse at the end of the pad. Citizen Gillingham will guide you there."

He looked them over, five men and two women, armed with a motley collection of hunting rifles, shotguns, and one target pistol. Their clothes looked warm, at least, and they all had bulging pockets.

"I hope you all brought at least one day's food and some medical supplies, as well as ammunition for your weapons. We've discovered that every new squad has to be self-sufficient for at least that long."

Most of them nodded. Some opened pockets to show first-aid kits and packages of survival rations. One man raised a hand.

"Yes?"

"No medicine, Lieutenant. The child, he have cold, so wife need take it all."

"I'm sure someone will share with you, Citizen—"

"Cho."

"And I'll see that your child has priority for sick call if he hasn't been treated by morning."

"You have doctor?" The man sounded as if he'd been granted a glimpse of Paradise.

"Yes." The Freedom Legion had one doctor and an assortment of paramedics, nurses, and volunteers who claimed they knew first aid, for two thousand civilians and a thousand soldiers. If that was Paradise, DiVries didn't even want to think about the Inferno.

"Thank you."

"You're welcome. Okay, Gilly, move 'em out."

The recruits shuffled into a line facing toward the reception center. As they stepped off, DiVries saw a shadow flicker in the north, low over the desert. Another lifter coming in at rocktop height, probably because the pilot wasn't sure if the generator would hold and wanted to crash as gently as possible—

Then the shadow was climbing, and DiVries saw that it wasn't a lifter. It was something with broad wings, black all over, and a cylindrical shape slung under the middle of the wings—

"Air Defense Alert!" DiVries shouted into the wind, as if sheer volume could drive back what was coming out of the night.

Some people heard him, including Gilly. Some of them had weapons, and some of those used them. Again, Gilly was one. Both she and DiVries were firing when the stealth drone reached its programmed altitude and the radar-activated fuse detonated the bomb under its belly.

Where there'd been darkness and shadows, now there was only light. Then there was darkness again, as DiVries's eyeballs melted. He felt heat on his skin, but it didn't have time to reach the level of pain before the fusion fireball enveloped him and Gilly.

Poor communications security, concentrating most of the First Battalion outside Buschton, and no AD capability worth the name all added up to an irresistible temptation for the bomb launchers. The only radars and weapons capable of acting against the drone were either over the horizon or in orbit, and a six-minute flight time didn't give the orbital ones much time to do their work.

The ten-kiloton fuser was aimed to take out First Battalion with a minimum of "collateral damage" to Buschton. Good intentions, however, count for even less in war than in most activities.

At least fifty civilians were on the pad when the bomb went off. They died with the Freedom Legionnaires. The bomb also went off directly opposite the mouth of Kang's Gap.

Heat and shock wave roared down the Gap. Everyone in the Gap or on the main street of Buschton might have been in the muzzle of a shotgun. Heat, blast, and fragments hammered at the town, and an ammunition store for the Buschton volunteers detonated. The double shock dropped the roof of the town meeting hall on the refugees and volunteers there.

The first thing survivors heard, if they heard anything at all, was screams.

It wasn't quite as bad as it might have been. The ridge on either side of Kang's Gap intercepted much of the hard radiation. The bomb was not only clean but went off downwind from the town. Heavy-walled Victorian buildings gave additional radiation protection. Most radiation casualties fell into two categories: the minor and the doomed.

But of more than eleven hundred casualties, less than seven hundred were from the Freedom Legion. Most of the dead were soldiers, but most of the medical people were among the soldiers.

The senior Freedom Legion survivor, a lifter-pilot lieutenant, gave two orders. One was to cordon off the Gap and shoot to kill anybody who tried to reach ground zero. The other was to broadcast a general appeal for medical aid.

The lieutenant then collapsed and died from internal injuries and a radiation overdose. It might have consoled him to know that the rest of the world already knew about Buschton.

Rose Liddell slept and dreamed of *Shenandoah* maneuvering violently, fusion explosions tearing space around her. Both alarms and wounded crewmen screamed as the explosions came closer.

She awoke sweating and was stripping off her pajamas when the Alert One alarm did scream. She didn't bother cutting off the visual as the intercom showed Bogdanov's face.

"Bridge, Captain. Combat Center's reported a nudet in the Freedom Legion AO. Somewhere around Buschton, low-kiloton range. We're getting more parameters—"

"Right." Liddell started jerking on clothes. "Pavel, hold on to the bridge. Put Jackie in the ACC, to roll out the red carpet for the Shogun when he shows."

"I'm already on the way," Kuwahara's voice broke in. "Captain, I'm taking my staff in with me. I'd like you to be part of the conference. We need your feel for Victoria."

That was flattering, even probably true. She still had a priority duty: commanding her ship. *Well, the head doctors did once say you had parallel mental processes. Let's see if there is anything to it.*

"Can I join in on intercom from the CC?"

"Fine, if you use the security hood. I'll make Uehara OTC until we're done." Liddell nodded, swept up her survival gear under one arm, and killed the screen with the free hand.

Five minutes later she was in the captain's chair in the CC, after a harrowing journey through the passageways of a ship that suddenly seemed to be crewed entirely by Olympic runners. Liddell had never seen so many of her people relying so completely on their collision-avoidance instincts.

She settled into the chair, pulled the hood toward her, then paused.

"Scherbakova."

"Ma'am?"

"Have somebody bring my toilet kit and a change of uniform up to the dorm."

The "dorm" was an eight-bunk cabin just off the CC, with a private cubicle at one end for the C.O. It let half a full CC team rest next door to their posts, so they could survive days on Alert One.

"Aye-aye, ma'am."

Liddell pulled the hood over her head and voice-ordered a link with the ACC.

The main display in the War Room at Fort Stafford showed General Kornilov much less than he needed, let alone wanted, to know. It did show him that Victoria Command was carrying out nuclear-alert dispersal and protective measures.

All the dispersing units were heading away from the frontier. It wouldn't make any difference if the fuser was an Alliance attack; retaliation, if any, would not be with ground forces. If it was somebody else who'd burned Buschton and the First/Freedom Legion, keeping Federation forces away from the frontier would soothe the Alliance.

Personally, Kornilov's money was on somebody besides the Alliance military. Uzel was the toughest of the bunch, and even he wasn't crazy enough to pop a fuser where it would burn civilians. Pak would sooner star in a porno holo, ditto Fegeli, and Hollings didn't control the fusers.

Or did he? The thought wouldn't go away, and neither would the queasiness it gave Kornilov. But suspicions and stomachs could wait; Alys Parkinson couldn't.

Kornilov pulled the security hood over his screen and watched the Victorian general's face appear.

"Greenwillow to Monitor. I am protesting the orders to ground Flight Blue." Flight Blue was half of Parkinson's Fourth Battalion, more than three hundred troopers on their way to join the rest of the battalion at Fort Stafford.

"Greenwillow, your protest is rejected. Your vehicles have no air-to-air, IFF, or ECM capabilities. They will be maneuvering in a nuclear-alert environment just loaded with friendlies ready to shoot first and identify afterward. We don't want another Flight Six."

"Monitor, that was a low blow."

Kornilov realized that he had been talking to Parkinson as if she were a politically appointed ignoramus, like some of the other militia commanders. She wasn't, but she was still wrong.

"Greenwillow, a compromise. You ground Flight Blue at a location of your own choosing, within ten minutes of our signing off. Squirt a location signal, and we'll have Navy attackers overhead in another twenty. You organize your people for a hasty defense, then come on—"

"Negative on the last, Monitor. I stay with them." Kornilov wanted to ask if she didn't trust her commanders or was reneging on her agreement to move her HQ to Fort Stafford. Even over a secure circuit that big an insult would leak out, and meanwhile Alys would have to be tied down to keep her from biting people.

"Greenwillow, the last time I looked at your T.O., you didn't have C-cubed for running your brigade from out in the middle of the Naukatos Plain."

"How long are we going to be out there?"

"In this kind of a fluid situation, it could be too long."

"I'm not leaving my people with their arses hanging out."

Kornilov wanted to suggest that theirs wouldn't be the only arses in peril if she disobeyed a direct order. But reason told him that firing Parkinson would destroy the usefulness of the militia brigade and impose the tactically feasible and politically stupid alternative of using Federation forces directly at every point.

Reason also suggested a middle ground. "Greenwillow, you have permission to remain with Flight Blue, on one condition. We will send out an adviser team, including SFOs and everything else needed to coordinate with your air cover. We'll also get tac air assets out to you as soon as possible."

Including enough Federation troops to handle everything from mutiny to nervous sentries.

"That's acceptable, Monitor. I'll tight-beam my C.O.s and we'll be on the ground inside your limit. Greenwillow over and out."

When Kornilov opened the hood, a printout lay beside the screen. It was a list of naval personnel on ground duty who could be reassigned to Army units if necessary. Kornilov didn't need to see the signature to know it was Commander Franke's work. Franke might be a staff type rather than a field commander, but he was the kind of staff officer who considered that his job was just as around-the-clock as any groundpounder's.

On the main display, Kornilov saw that one battalion of the 96th Regiment was moving. If the data were being correctly interpreted, it was mounted up and airborne, heading back toward Silvermouth.

For Kornilov, that settled the question of Alliance military responsibility for the Buschton bomb. If they'd barely been able to hold the invasion with the whole 96th, the last thing they would do now was weaken it. The Freedom Legion might have lost most of a battalion, but they'd be gaining a lot of civilian support. If Pak was planning to follow up the bomb with a counterattack he'd have every trooper in hand for it.

"So you don't think it was the Alliance getting desperate?"

That was Kuwahara. The reply came from the Intelligence officer, Commander Golikov, after a moment's hesitation.

"No, sir. At least not the Alliance military."

Rose Liddell breathed more easily. Following Kuwahara's staff meeting with nothing but voices to go on was annoying. But the alternative would have been a split screen that shrank both faces and situation display until neither told her much.

Golikov still went into more detail than necessary—Liddell had wanted to scream halfway through his description of the bomb's characteristics—but he would now come to conclusions when asked. He'd begun as one of the officers reluctant to make recommendations, but Kuwahara had spoken to him—rumors abounded about what he'd said—and cured that particular vice.

"All right," the admiral said. "Carlotta, start drawing up a message, addresses to include su-Ankrai, Uzel, Hollings, Fegeli, Pak, and the CG of the Freedom Legion if we can find him. Information copies to Kornilov, all brigade commanders, and all commodores.

"Basically I want to say that because we don't believe the

Alliance responsible for this criminal act, we will take no action against Alliance territory or forces. However, we expect that those same forces will take no action to exploit the tactical situation of the Freedom Legion, or interfere with our efforts to peacefully control the invasion.

"If they do, they risk a confrontation for which we will not accept the responsibility. If they cross into the territory of the Associated States of Victoria, it will be regarded as a hostile act and met with appropriate force."

"Do you want it condescending or one professional to another, Admiral?" Yague asked.

Liddell decided that there were advantages to being a ghost at the feast. She could laugh without anyone noticing, even if she couldn't see Kuwahara's face.

"Did I sound condescending?"

Yague was eloquently silent.

"All right," Kuwahara said. "I do feel that the Alliance has, if you'll pardon the expression, pissed in the beer. But they may know some things that we don't."

"I'll have a draft in ten minutes, sir."

"Good. Now, our priority objective is supporting the Army, particularly Flight Blue and the medical relief effort. Colonel Chatterje has asked for attacker assets to transport key personnel and supplies to the jumpoff point for the relief flight. Skinner, get on the horn to Captain Prange and his CAG and start setting that up."

"On the way, sir," replied the ops chief.

"Good. Any comments, questions, suggestions, reasons to believe that I'm losing my grip?"

"Suggestion, sir," Liddell broke in. "Can we provide remote attacker cover for the med flight? Above the hundred-klom limit, they'll be legal."

"They'll also be able to track the whole 96th except for the battalion that's lifted for Silvermouth. Do you think Uzel and Pak will overlook that?"

"I wasn't proposing to do it without their permission, sir."

"Carlotta, add the request to the message. Bao, squirt the recording of this meeting over to Uehara immediately and wait for his evaluation." The chief of communications must have nodded; Liddell heard nothing.

"The squadron will remain on Alert One at least until all

the recipients of our message have acknowledged it. Thank you all, good luck—and if it comes to that, good hunting."

Liddell heard the scrape of chairs pushed back and the *clik-purrrr* of terminals shutting down. On the screen a new unit had appeared, moving out of Fort Stafford. No, two units, one in Kellysburg and the one on the move, both of them with MedCorps signs.

The relief effort was on the way. Liddell knew that neither she nor anybody in Victoria Command would really be happy until the bomb throwers were dead. But saving as many of their victims as possible would be a good second best.

A hollow feeling amidships reminded her of a minor matter of ship's administration.

"CC to Exec."

"Captain?"

"The admiral and his staff are on the way down. One of them will brief you as soon as they're settled in. Meanwhile, we need to feed people."

"I checked that, Captain. I thought of unsealing the emergency lockers, but Charbon and Kemper had worked out a way of providing at least one hot meal at stations. It will mean drawing volunteers from the damage-control parties to distribute the food, but—"

"I authorize it. And 'well done' to both of them." She would have expected something like that from the paternal and efficient supply officer, but from the efficient and utterly nonparental first lieutenant? Not all of today's surprises were going to be unpleasant, it seemed.

Meanwhile, RHIP, and one of those was getting something for herself right now.

"Scherbakova."

"Ma'am?"

"A sandwich and a cup—no, make that a pot—of tea."

Commander Franke seemed to sprout from the floor in front of Kornilov's desk.

"Satellite report, sir. One element of the retiring Alliance battalion has pulled out in front of the rest. Estimated speed is eighteen hundred kilometers per hour, on the deck."

"Somebody's in a hurry."

"So we concluded. Our estimate—"

"Did somebody else help you?"

"Ah—no."

"Then drop the *we* until they elect you czar."

"I don't think I'm eligible, sir."

"A pity. That's not a joke, either. Anyway, someone's in a hurry. My guess is Pak. My second guess is that the fast lift will be coming back as soon as they drop him off. Probably with an Alliance relief effort."

"You read my mind, sir."

"No, just assumed that when the Alliance people see a road-hurt dog, they'll try to get it to a vet."

"Aye-aye—yes, sir. Anything else?"

"Well done, on that list of Navy deployables."

Franke saluted and left, as Kornilov's terminal registered an incoming call.

"Hi, Indira." Colonel Chatterje seemed to have shrunk in the last hour. She still carried herself like a color sergeant, but Kornilov had the feeling that he could now pick her up between thumb and forefinger.

"Med Flight One is on its way out of Kellysburg. It's combined Federation and Associated States, with an Associated States security force. Med Flight Two has left Fort Stafford. I understand the Navy will provide security until it crosses into the Freedom Legion AO. What happens then?"

"We're mounting up a company from Fourth/215 at Loch Prima. The transports that dropped the nonlethals there will lift the company down to provide security for the combined relief force."

"What about the attackers for high-priority lift?"

"They're on the way. Have your people and their loads ready to go by 0730. Also, the Navy's planning on providing attacker high cover all the way to Buschton."

"Isn't that a little provocative?"

"Provocative to who? The Alliance probably didn't do this, but they're not in a strong position to complain unless they tell us who did. The Freedom Legion isn't going to object to anything that may save its troopers and the people they were trying to liberate.

"And if the sons of bitches who burned Buschton lose their tempers and shoot at us, we are going to shoot back and go on shooting until we've burned *them!*"

"Yes, sir." Kornilov recognized the tone: Indira trying

desperately to keep from using their personal relationship to influence him.

"Sometimes I wonder if we doctors didn't make matters worse, finding ways of handling so many fuser casualties. It didn't help in the Hive Wars, and people sometimes seem to toss the smaller bombs around more freely than they might otherwise."

"You know that's not true, Indira. The stupid, the vicious, and the careless we always have with us. The only thing we can do is stop them before they move if we can, and clean up after them if we can't.

"Indira. We've both got leave piled up to our—never mind. Anyway, once we've done our duty by our families, what about taking the rest of the leave together? Someplace where I won't have to do anything more violent than swat a fly, and you won't have to treat anything worse than an ingrown toenail. Someplace where we won't have to wear uniform, or anything else."

"I—yes, on one condition. I want you to visit Asok with me."

Is she contemplating our actually getting married? *When I've been afraid to raise the question for nearly a Standard year?*

The female of the species, Kornilov decided, might not be deadlier than the male. But she seemed to take less time to implement major decisions.

Colonel Pak had a bet with himself about how long it would take Brigadier Fegeli to notice the results of one of Pak's orders and come to confront the colonel about it.

In fact, Pak had barely sat down behind the desk in his office in the Silvermouth Armory when the intercom beeped.

"Brigadier Fegeli presents his compliments, and does the colonel have a few minutes?"

"As much time as we need."

Pak's eyes chased the orderly out while he reached under the desk and tested the scrambler, to make sure that it was there, working, and hadn't been turned into a snooper itself. It passed all three tests.

"Please come in, sir."

Fegeli was obviously a man walking when he wanted to

stride or even stamp. He waited until the door closed before
he leaned over Pak and glared.

"What's the meaning of the guards around Sharon
Farber?"

"I'm not interfering in your personal life, sir, if that's
what you're worried about."

"Sharon's not under suspicion?"

"Not by me."

"But the guards are from the 96th."

"Sir, you ordered the whole Third Battalion back to Silvermouth, I believe at the governor's request—"

"That's not your concern."

"Sir, I believe I can convince you that it is. In any case,
having reliable men from the advanced party of the battalion available, I assigned them to an immediate and known
security problem."

"I thought you said Sharon wasn't under suspicion."

"That is not the same as not being in danger."

"Danger?" Fegeli sounded skeptical but not incredulous.
"From whom?"

"Sir, if I can totally trust your discretion, I can provide
that information."

"Who don't you want me to tell?"

"Everybody, but starting with the governor, Admiral
Uzel, and anybody you suspect of ties with Field
Intelligence."

"At this point I'm not sure I'd trust my right testicle not
to squeal on the left one. Shall we leave it between us for
the moment?"

"Quite satisfactory." Pak unlocked his desk terminal.
"Access code is Zanzibar Toscanini Ursula. Spell out each
word, then add a number sign."

Pak heard the keys click and turned his back. He did
not want to watch Fegeli's face, and when he heard the
"Gesumaria!" he knew he didn't need to.

"The bastards," Fegeli said after a long silence.

"At least," Pak replied. "The only question is, what are
we going to do about it?"

"That depends mostly on you."

This time Pak watched, and the silence was even longer.
At last Fegeli shrugged. "If it was anybody but Sharon—or
Sophia and the kids," he added hastily.

"Mistresses are an open invitation to trouble. Wives, our friends usually leave alone." Not that Sophia Fegeli would have been in danger this time anyway. The cover Field Intelligence was going to use for the attack on Sharon Farber was the Pure Soul Movement, and they were devoutly anti-Semitic.

"I thought you weren't going to criticize my personal life."

"Stating something fairly obvious that you seem to have overlooked is hardly a criticism."

"The devil it—oh, forget it." Fegeli sighed. "How long are you going to be in Silvermouth?"

"That depends on what happens in the field. If I can stay long enough to deploy the battalion for maximum effect—"

"And brief it on which orders to obey and which to ignore?"

"You have a suspicious mind, Brigadier."

"That is the pot calling the kettle black—and thank God. Well, do we have at least a few hours to pool our suspicions?"

"Yes. Coffee, tea, chocolate, or something stronger?"

"Coffee, but if there's a drop of something to put in it, I won't complain."

Ten

"Huntress moving," Candice Shores said. "Current position twelve north Point Sigma."

That meant eight kloms west of the highest point of Akabla Ridge, for anyone on the Federation side. Probably there was somebody on some other side with a radar to tell them where Scout Company really was. Shores wished she knew which side, and whether it was friendly, unfriendly, or unable to make up its mind.

Sergeant Esteva produced a cup of hot chocolate. It lasted her until the command lifter passed over the Wagga Wagga Valley and grounded on the north side. The rest of Scout Company and its attached Rangers, SFOs, and medical team grounded in a nuclear-dispersal formation that gave them overwatch both to the north of the valley and a good ways up and down the river.

They weren't going to be easily approached from the ground. They were too dispersed for a low-yield fuser to do much damage. For anything big, they had the Navy overhead, from their dedicated attacker all the way up to *Shenandoah*, staying 20,000 kilometers out in order to be free to manuever.

Shores scanned the display. "You look nice on the screen, people. SOP in effect—three, two, one, *mark*."

Two-thirds of the load of each lifter would now be sealing up, checking weapons and masks (in winter on Victoria, unwarmed dry air took up where the mites left off as a menace to sinuses, throats, and lungs) and climbing out into a dismal late-winter morning. The remaining one-third would crew vehicle-mounted sensors and weapons and start preparing a hot meal for the rest.

Once they'd dispersed in perimeters, the outside people would pair off to cut fighting positions. At six-hour intervals half the people in the fighting positions would come in, warm up, eat a hot meal, and sleep if they could.

The only people exempt from this rotation were the medics. The C.O. could use her own judgment. Shores judged that she would go crazy if she didn't spend at least enough time outside to inspect the nearer positions. She stood up and signaled to Maddie Bloch.

"I'm going to make an eyeball recon. Want to join me?"

Bloch pulled her mask up and stuck her ice ax in her belt. "Lead on."

Shores had thought the ice ax was simply habit, but two hundred meters of slipping and sliding over the mixture of rock, ice, and snow underfoot changed her mind. They finally climbed almost to the summit of a low ridge and sat down in its lee. The sun was beginning to at least struggle against the clouds instead of wearily letting them swathe it, and the wind had dropped.

"I'd like to go climbing in the Lizardspines once this is over," Bloch said. "Would you like to join me?"

"Separate tents?"

"Candy, you don't trust me?"

"No."

"Where you're concerned, maybe I don't trust myself. Ah, well, first things first."

"Such as telling me why your Rangers came out with the Scouts?"

"We may be working together on a special operation."

"It doesn't take much insight to conclude that." Rangers backing up Light Infantry operations or vice versa had been SOP since Sam Briggs was alive. "Any particular kind of operation?"

"Here we go to suspicions," Bloch said.

"Whose?"

"Mine, based on what Intelligence has told me."

"Are they trying to cover their asses or—?" Shores inquired.

"Colonel Nieg said their data was still limited."

"Oh." Nieg had, in fact, a quite reasonable ass, along with other parts of his superbly conditioned body. Covering it, in the unethical sense of the term, was not in him.

"I probably shouldn't have named him."

"I disagree. He's one of the minority of Intelligence types that I trust."

"Thanks to pillow talk?"

"Maddie, do you want to see if I can force a kidney transplant?"

"We'd both be court-martialed while we were still in the hospital."

"They need us that badly?"

Bloch nodded. "All jokes aside, I think they will. So—if we are out here long enough, I would suggest platoon exercises with Ranger teams. Every combination the terrain allows, including caves if we can find any."

"That will eat into our supplies. Are we going to get more?"

"I don't know."

"Well, try to find out. And also find out about air support. We can simulate some with the lifters, but a little nonsimulated help from tac air or the Navy wouldn't hurt."

"The operation may not allow for that."

"Maddie, if they're going to be using Scouts on this— whatever they're cooking up—it won't be a deniable operation. Or they'll figure out some way to make air support deniable. You Rangers can put your bare arses out on the line if you want, but that's not Scouting."

Bloch made a parody bow. "I defer to your superior wisdom."

Shores stood up. "Will you also defer to my inferior tolerance for sitting on cold rock?"

The combined medical relief force was staggered in a layered formation, 3,000 meters deep and 10,000 meters square.

Lowest were four gunships, each loaded with ECM and sensor pods. They kept the terrain below and ahead under an all-modes sensor scan.

Next came the unpressurized civilian lifters carrying the bulk of the medical personnel and supplies. All around them were the armed lifters of the "security force"—which Lucco DiVries knew was really a reinforced rifle company from the Fourth/215.

With its air support, the company could probably gut the rest of the Freedom Legion, if the Federation thought that was a good idea. If it did, DiVries knew that he would finally shift from merely preferring his homeworld to the Federation, to actively hating the Federation.

So now he knew how the people who'd murdered Sophie Bergeron and done so much else might have come to believe they were right. He still didn't agree, but only philosophers said that understanding brought tolerance. The soldiers' experience was that it more often made you absolutely certain you had to take out the other guy before he did it to you.

DiVries craned his neck, to look up through the roof window. More military lifters rode a thousand meters above, including a couple of big command vehicles, and DiVries thought he saw more gunships. The high cover of attackers that the Alliance authorities had reluctantly allowed into their territory was lost in the sun.

Dr. Nosavan pulled off a com headset and rubbed a chafed neck. But he was closer to a smile than DiVries had seen him since they had the news about Buschton.

"The advanced team has clearance to proceed. They'll be jumping in about fifteen minutes."

The advanced team was six doctors and twenty paramedics, riding in attackers along with a couple of tons of medical supplies. It wasn't that making DiVries stare at Nosovan.

"Jump?"

"The Navy wouldn't be responsible for bringing attackers down and hovering while the team unloaded. But they agreed to a pass-and-cover while the team jumped."

"I hope they're jump-qualified."

"Some of them probably are. Anyway, it's always been true that you're in more danger from a complete jump course than from one cold jump."

"So they told me in crew training. Am I going to get a chance to find out on this mission?"

"I can't see why." Nosavan stood up. Unlike DiVries, he was short enough not to crack his skull on the cabin roof. "If it's a hot LZ, the security force C.O. is supposed to arrange to coordinate the gunships, the attackers, and the Freedom Legion to suppress the opposition."

Coordinating three different arms from two different and substantially hostile forces sounded like a prescription for confusion. "I wish him luck."

"Ah, ah, defeatism."

"No, just wondering which side we're on."

"Against the people who bombed Buschton. Isn't that enough?"

"Not if I have to be ready to shoot."

Nosavan looked at the carbine slung across DiVries's chest and the magazines hooked to his belt. "Do you want to disarm? I suspect the regular company will be doing most of the security work."

"All it takes is a couple of madmen with guns, and we lose a whole tentful of patients." *That's all it took for Sophie, and she wasn't helpless.* "Thanks. I'll take my chances on telling the good guys from the bad guys."

"Good. Believe me, I wasn't doubting your courage."

No. I was doing enough of that for both of us.

"Hang on, people," the pilot said. He shifted his aromatic from one corner of his mouth to the other and studied the navigation display. "Yeah, coming up on our turning point in about a minute. Even better than hanging on, why don't you sit down?"

Nosavan and DiVries took the hint. The lifter tilted into its turn. Through a sand-scarred window they watched a valley blotched with snow patches pass below. Far off to the east DiVries saw snowcapped peaks. The Lizardspines? No, it must be the tag end of the Jenkins Range, with Jenkins's Jaws somewhere off below the horizon.

"Course two seven five true, airspeed two hundred kilometers per hour, altitude twenty-eight hundred meters, ETA Buschton 1300," the pilot recited.

DiVries's mind, legs, and bladder all protested at the figures. At least he could do something about the bladder.

"Where's the relief?"

"Left rear, and go slow. I mean, go back slow. This old bird's loaded right up to the limit. You start waltzing around and we start going unbalanced. That can ruin your whole day."

Elayne Zheng was feeling so good she almost felt guilty about it. An officer and a lady did not feel like dancing when she was on duty and people were lying in improvised emergency wards, suffering torments that none of the old religions had imagined for their damned.

Oh, the doctors could do miracles, if they got there in time, had the proper facilities and medicines, and weren't swamped by the sheer number of casualties. They could pack burns in gel, use life-support cocoons to substitute for ruined organs, load people up with immune-system boosters and anti-radiation drugs to just this side of cardiac arrest.

They had done this often enough, so that over the years millions of people who had been too close to fuser blasts had lived instead of dying. They would probably do it here, because there looked to be about one med helper for every treatable casualty by the time all the relief forces arrived.

Meanwhile, the pain was real, the fear was worse, and for some all the help in the world would still be too late. Being back on duty (and finally tripping Rafael last night, with much mutual pleasure) was an explanation for ignoring that fact. It was not an excuse.

"Burgundy Leader to Control Five. We have a little problem here."

Zheng pulled on the headset. "Control Five here. What kind of problem?"

"Flight Blue doesn't want to move out. They say they've spotted unidentified ground movements within missile range."

"What?" The Victorian militia had been a headache all day. If they sat around bouncing one another much longer, a line would form to hang them in a rope of the guts they didn't have.

"Repeat, unidentified ground movements. They want more tac air support before they'll move."

"Is Greenwillow still in the area?" General Parkinson had taken off half an hour before, heading for Fort Stafford.

"We've been in contact with Greenwillow. She refuses to override the C.O. of Flight Blue."

"Oh, wonderful." Although that was probably not what General Kornilov was saying. "All right, Burgundy Leader. How long can you remain on station?"

"As long as these turds need us to hold their hands and ten minutes longer."

A large hand reached over Zheng's shoulder and took the second headset. "Grumbler to Burgundy Leader, that last remark was uncalled for. What is your status?"

Zheng looked up to see Commander Franke. His eyes were now as red as his cheeks normally were, his hair was rumpled, and he actually seemed to have lost weight since the last time she'd seen him.

Burgundy Leader gave a crisp report on his four attackers from *Valhalla*. "Acknowledged, Burgundy Leader. Request that you remain on station until you hear from us."

"Or somebody," Burgundy Leader said. "That's a roger. Burgundy Leader out."

Zheng split her screen. Half now showed the area around Flight Blue, the other half the status of the attacker and tac air assets available to Victoria Command.

"We can put light attackers or gunships out there easy," Zheng said. "But they wouldn't have the on-station time or the firepower of the heavies. Something tells me the Vics are too nervous to be satisfied with anything less."

"You know them better than I do, Lieutenant," Franke said. "But what about Brandy Three—oh, I see."

Brandy Three was four attackers from the 879th. They were currently uncommitted, but that was because they were being rearmed for air-to-air and ECM. In a few hours, they would be escorting the converted liftliners loaded with the Buschton casualties to the hospital at Fort Stafford.

It made sense not to haul seriously hurt people in slow, unpressurized, sometimes unheated, and generally uncomfortable utility or carrier lifters. The converted liners could each handle up to a hundred stretcher patients or half again as many ambulatory ones, with enough room left over for a dozen medical attendants and a portable operating room.

But they would also be big, tempting targets at altitude, and couldn't rockhop like the smaller lifters. So they needed escorts practically joining hands around them, just in case somebody with a missile yielded to temptation.

"Let's not give up too easily—sorry, Commander," Zheng said. Her fingers flew, calling up data on Brandy Three's present and prospective armament.

"Good. They've all got working guns, and their Tulwars are Mark VI's. Pretty expensive to use for air-to-ground, but they can do it."

"Leaving the Vics bare-assed—or thinking they've been left that way—could be even more so."

"Right. And while I don't want to blow the horn for my squadron, the 879th is the veteran outfit around here. They know Victoria. They can tell a rock from a rockheaded rebel a lot better than the carpetbaggers from *Valhalla*."

"A little respect for superior officers, please."

"I have never failed to show a little respect, sir."

"Arguing manners supports no Vics. Lieutenant, get on the horn to Brandy Three and suggest that they get ready for an early liftoff and a side trip to the Naukatos Plain. I'll start shepherding our hunch up the chain command. If we're lucky, it will go just fast enough to get there after Kornilov and Parkinson have stopped arguing and calmed down enough to listen to practical suggestions."

Zheng nodded and started setting up her console. She was going to enjoy working with Franke, who had the same lack of reverence for rank that she did. Just as long as he didn't step over the line and become ground zero for Victoria's next nuclear incident—

The screen showed the face of the 879th's weapons officer.

"Hello, Lainie. What can we do to you today?"

The deeper valleys in the Pfingsten Mountains were already in shadow as Colonel Pak's courier swept toward them. He was not returning to the field as fast or as high as he'd left it, because the courier was now part of a convoy.

In the lifters of that convoy rode several riot-control experts from the Silvermouth and Territorial Police and half the riot-control gear in Seven Rivers. That was the main result of his new alliance with Brigadier Fegeli, and it might be the only one they needed to make public.

With three days to issue the gear and refresh four battalions' training in riot control, the 96th would be ready to take advantage of the Buschton strike in a way that wouldn't offend the Federation. The Freedom Legion had lost a third of its strength to the bomb. Another third was scattered garrisoning "liberated" towns.

The remaining third was new recruits, mostly unarmed and likely to remain that way if the Federation was at all serious about cutting off the invaders' supplies. They might gain a few hundred more desperate or angry supporters, but without weapons, how much was their support worth?

Even if the rebels still managed to send weapons across

the border, there was the Federation "relief force" at Buschton sitting squarely in the middle of their AO. All Freedom Legion troop movements would have to be steered clear of Buschton.

Meanwhile, the 96th could organize a battalion-strength task force to move on one "liberated" town at a time. Offered martyrdom or surrender, people could be unpredictable, and if they chose martyrdom, deadly dangerous. Offered embarrassment (from giggle gas, tanglers, and so on) or surrender, the reasonable people and the fanatics might be too busy fighting each other to fight the 96th.

Do that to half a dozen towns, one at a time, and the Freedom Legion would begin to look like a loser instead of a winner. Psychological dominance would shift to the 96th, and that counted for as much on the battlefield as in the dojo.

The courier was entering one of the valleys now, above the shadow line but below the crests. In the shadows the lights of hunting lodges and wilderness conservation posts twinkled. Pak called up the rearview and saw the rest of the convoy riding in acceptably tight formation. High up, where it was still full daylight, the sun glinted on the top cover of attackers.

Too many things could go wrong with this scenario, of course, and the Federation vetoing any movements at all by the 96th was only one of them. (Although possibly not the worst; that would speed up ground as well as Navy reinforcements to Victoria, and somebody senior to both Hollings and Uzel might arrive with eyes and ears open and brain properly programmed.)

Coup attempt in Silvermouth? Unlikely, with a full battalion of the 96th settling in there. Successful attempt on Sharon Farber's life? If so, she wouldn't be the only corpse—and if that led to martial law, Fegeli would be running Seven Hills and too busy to mourn.

Unless real Pure Souls were after Sharon Farber, instead of Field Intelligence people using the movement as a disguise? That possibility hadn't occurred to Pak, but now that it did he couldn't rule it out.

Certainly the hard core of the Pure Souls had been refugees, conservative Moslems and Protestant Christians, from Alliance planets. They'd fled because they feared "Zionist tyranny"—a government in which the Bar Kochbans had a major voice.

They would no doubt happily spy or murder against the Alliance, if anyone was willing to hire them. So far the Federation hadn't been that stupid, at least at the top. But what about station chiefs getting carried away?

Pak decided he'd better warn Fegeli of this new twist. That would keep the brigadier cooperative even if Pak had to approach Federation Intelligence.

The colonel cursed softly. The reasonable people on Victoria outnumbered the others by an overwhelming margin. If they could just mass against a single enemy, victory would be easy. But they were having to watch every insect in a swarm at once and look back over their shoulders at the Baernoi and the Merishi every so often as well!

Silvermouth glowed in the middle of the night hemisphere of Victoria, centered on Fleet Commander su-Ankrai's screen. As Force Inquirer su-Lal finished his presentation, su-Ankrai murmured a command and the screen went blank.

"Commander su-Irzim. You may call up any data you require."

Su-Lal knew the consequences of baring tusks at his rival now. He only frowned. Su-Irzim let the silence last a moment longer than necessary, to let the other Inquirer taste the fear of a full-scale rebuttal.

Then:

"I have little to add to what Inquirer su-Lal has said. With Admiral Kuwahara unable to meet with the Force Commander, we have no secure method of approaching Federation Intelligence. Insecure methods would be worse than none.

"In short, among them the Federation, the Alliance, and the various rebel and terrorist groups have fairly thoroughly tied our hands as far as tracking Rahbad Sarlin."

"Are you implying that we can do nothing?" su-Lal said. His tone was that of a warrior sensing an opponent's weak spot.

Su-Irzim deftly closed his guard. "You implied that yourself. I was merely stating the same thing explicitly."

The worse *defeatism* hovered on su-Lal's lips but the

Inquirer knew how su-Ankrai would react. He only shrugged. "We seem to be at the mercy of the Smallteeth's ability to solve their own problems."

"Or inability," su-Irzim said. "Has it occurred to you that the confusion on Victoria may be doing everything we could have hoped to do ourselves? Human-Merishi and Federation-Alliance relations can hardly benefit from all of the incidents since the crisis began. Nothing has been proved against us, but we will reap the harvest without sowing a single seed."

"I respect your poetic images but question your optimism," su-Ankrai cut in. "You have not, I trust, forgotten the problem of being sure that we had nothing to do with the destruction of the Bonsai Squadron. Or if we did, that the humans never learn."

"I have not forgotten," su-Irzim said. "Indeed, I would like to make a suggestion. I would like to be formally relieved of ordinary Inquiry duties to study this problem. If nothing else, it will show our concern about the matter. This may soothe the humans and improve the Force Commander's negotiating position when he and Admiral Kuwahara can meet."

Su-Ankrai smiled. "I think you overestimate the ease of soothing Admiral Kuwahara and underestimate his tenacity in negotiations. But I see no reason not to grant your request.

"However, I think you will have to transfer back to *Perfumed Wind*. Tomorrow I am taking the rest of the force out to a mutually agreeable distance and spending two days on maneuvers. Su-Lal, if you will provide su-Irzim with anything he may need to function aboard *Wind* for three days at least—"

"Certainly, my lord. But might I suggest that *Wind* not be left unescorted? We do not know who many learn what in three days. You know *Wind*'s powers better than I, su-Irzim. What would you call sufficient escort?"

Su-Irzim was slow to answer, because he had to be sure he was not hallucinating before he spoke. Then he said, "Two light cruisers will be sufficient. One would be enough, but accidents can always happen."

"Indeed," su-Ankrai said. "I will order the two cruisers

assigned to *Wind*. Otherwise I will leave you to divide the Inquiry work as seems necessary."

If su-Ankrai had been the Khudr himself, su-Irzim could hardly have bowed longer or deeper. By the time he stood again, he was alone with su-Lal, who was smiling for the first time since the force made its final Passage to Victoria.

"What is so cursed amusing?"

"Your face, when I suggested the cruisers."

"I hope you don't think I'm ungrateful—"

"Hardly that." Su-Lal extended a hand. "Indeed, it is I who should be grateful. You laid our rivalry to rest, in a way that su-Ankrai could hardly protest."

"I did not see that he was encouraging it."

"Perhaps not. But it was no secret that one of the Fleet's great Syrodhi commanders was seriously contemplating making an Antahl of unorthodox views the Force Inquirer."

"If you had failed in your duty—"

"We can waste time trading quotations, my . . . soon-to-be friend? Or we can order some beer and turn to the work su-Ankrai has set us."

"Some food with the beer, I think." Su-Irzim realized that it was past dinner, and lunch had been early. Beer now would make him drunk almost as fast as it would a human.

"Easily done," su-Lal said, swiveling his couch to face a console. Su-Irzim lay back on his own couch and stared at the overhead.

Su-Lal had not mentioned that the Inquirer who learned what had actually happened on Victoria would carry away the lord's share of the glory from this mission. Perhaps he had not realized it?

No, he was not that stupid. Indifferent to his share of the glory? Also unlikely. Convinced that there would be enough to go around? Not impossible, and he might be correct. If the People could cover their tracks and recover Rahbad Sarlin, the crisis on Victoria could hardly be other than a victory for them.

Perhaps Rahbad Sarlin was the real key to su-Lal's change of heart. No one became a high-ranking Inquirer without knowing what Special Projects could do to a career if it chose.

Eleven

In the last rebellion, Federation advisers were scattered like sweetbush pods wherever anybody thought they might be needed. This time the generals wanted to seem as if they knew where the advisers would be needed and had them organized into self-contained teams.

One team for each militia battalion and one in reserve made five teams. An extra batch of advisers for Brigade HQ and Parkinson herself ran the warm-body count up to over two hundred. Between casualties and essential assignments elsewhere, the Federation's old Victoria hands weren't enough. A few slots could be filled with reliable Victorians, even from the former Army of the Bushranger Republic.

But at least half the two hundred bodies had to come from Federation newcomers to Victoria. So Brian Mahoney didn't resent his and Brigitte's assignment to an adviser team this time. They knew the job, and it not only had to be done but taught fast to newlies.

One look at the landscape as he climbed out of the lifter had him praying for the absence of enemy forces until he and the other advisers had oriented themselves. The Vic Militia's Second Battalion was perched on a bare hillside that offered excellent visibility as far as the foot of the hill.

Beyond the foot of the hill, the ground had twisted itself into a tangle of ravines, small monoliths, patches of boulders, and occasional stands of winter-dormant lazyboy. It might have been terrain designed specifically to hide snipers or even more lethal forms of attack.

Brigitte was looking at the land with the same expression Mahoney suspected he was wearing. "I wonder if it's as bad on the other side of the hill?"

"I don't know. I was too hungry to notice as we came in."

"I told you not to skip breakfast."

"Brigitte, when they wake us up at 0400, you can't get me to take more than a cup of tea if you point a pulser at me."

"Let's take a look at the other side of the hill, then find the mess."

Just below the crest of the hill, a militia sentry challenged them.

"Halt! Who is there?"

"Lieutenants Brian Mahoney and Brigitte Tachin—"

"Oh, Feddie advisers. Sorry, can't let you pass. Nothing personal, you understand, but the story goes they want to brief you first."

"Who's they?"

"Damned if I know. All they did was stick me and my chums up here and tell us to keep you from swanning around before the briefing."

Mahoney recognized Victorian notions of military courtesy and blinked wind-started tears out of his eyes. "Suppose we brought you up some tea—"

The sentry grinned but shook his head. "If I thought you'd have time, I might be tempted. But they were just setting up the advisers' mess tent when I went on duty. If they've got anything yet, it'll be a bloody miracle."

"So what are we supposed to do, wander around until we either freeze solid or get called to the briefing?" Brigitte's voice was harder than the stones underfoot.

The sentry pointed along the crest to a cluster of field shelters huddled just below it. "That's the warming center for this side of the hill. If they're not using it to work on some electronic fancies, I don't suppose anybody will notice."

"That's worth the tea, if we can ever get any."

"Oh, don't worry about that. Just don't make bets on *when*."

They started toward the shelters. Brigitte, more sure-footed on rough ground, had to drop back several times to let Mahoney catch up.

"Do you get the feeling we're not exactly welcome here?" she said at one halt.

"Maybe, but I get the feeling that it's nothing sinister. Either they're worried about our getting killed and being blamed for it, or they aren't as combat-ready as they wanted us to think. Remember Flight Blue."

"They might really have seen something. You could hide almost anything near where they grounded, if you could avoid giving a heat pulse." She looked downhill and shivered. "Or around here, for that matter."

"I wish they'd distributed their combat veterans over all four battalions, or borrowed some people from the Bushrangers," Mahoney said. "Either way they'd have better cadre. Oh, well, lieutenants don't get paid to worry about that sort of thing. Let's stick to communications and weapons and leave the big picture to the big payslips."

"Amen," Brigitte said. She'd just slipped a hand through his arm when they saw someone waving from the door of the shelter.

Mahoney cupped his hands. "What is it?" he shouted.

"All Federation advisers are to report to Battalion HQ," was the reply.

Mahoney looked around the hillside for something that looked large enough to house a battalion headquarters. He saw nothing. The—woman, he thought—went on waving her arms. Then she pointed.

With her help, Mahoney spotted a dark slit in the rock, about halfway down the slope. "A cave?" he shouted. The woman nodded.

Brigitte led the way downhill. As Mahoney studied the hillside again, he saw camouflaged fighting positions that he hadn't noticed before. What had looked like rocks now looked more like sensor arrays posted to cover each approach to the hillside. He even thought he saw a patrol crouched in the shadow of one of the monoliths.

The man who answered to the name Ramdur but was recorded in Colonel Pak's files as Lionheart looked both ways down the corridor, then locked his door. That wouldn't defeat electronic eavesdroppers, but what he was about to do was silent.

Under the blanket on the camp cot, he pulled the microslip out of his belt buckle and inserted it in the scanner. The scanner was the size of a fist, not easily concealed, but the beauty of it was that he didn't need to conceal it. He'd been issued it quite according to regulations when they pulled him out of Barnard's Crossing and sent him to this underground base in the Roskills.

At least he *thought* he was in the Roskills. He couldn't be sure, and he wouldn't have asked even if it hadn't been made clear that the question would attract notice. He'd come here on a completely windowless lifter flying low and slow, and debarked already underground in a cave lit only by IR, when he had no IR goggles. He would be quite happy to leave the same way, as long as he left alive—and as long as the information he was collecting could not only leave but reach the right hands. Specifically, the hands of Colonel Pak.

The scanner's ready light came on and Ramdur opened the screen. Very good. He had a recognizable, reproducible picture of the Baernoi prisoner. That might have to be passed on beyond Pak, but it if got as far as the colonel the agent's job was done.

The agent pulled out a second slip and inserted it. Some of these scanners were equipped to record any slip inserted in them. But the recording could be scrambled if you "accidentally" recorded the second slip over the first.

The images of the second slip came up on the screen, rolling over the Baernoi features, blurring them almost past recognition. It seemed to take forever before the second slip was recorded, and Ramdur knew that this was not entirely nerves. He liked his women plump and dark, and while the second micro was explicit enough to be distracting, the pale, emaciated women in it were boring. The agent unloaded both slips, returned them to his hiding places, logged his finishing with the scanner, then dropped it through the slot in his door into the basket outside. One of the housekeeping robots would collect it before the lights dimmed for the sleep hours.

Ramdur lay back on the bed, adding up the pieces of data he'd collected in the last five days. Once Pak had them, he would have much of what he needed—probably all of it, with the Baernoi. That was something Ramdur had not believed when he first saw the prisoner, and something that Pak would probably not believe without the picture.

Ramdur, however, was a perfectionist, and the last two pieces he wanted could be obtained with little risk. All he had to do was listen and remember what he heard on two points. One was the location of General Liu, who had clearly played some critical role in the events surrounding the attack on the Alliance squadron.

The other was the origin of the sixty to a hundred mercenaries who did most of the base's dirty field work. That had a lower priority than General Liu. Mercenaries for this kind of work could be bought by the shipload and terminated or memory-wiped when their work was done. No planet was ever short of the adventurous, the desperate, or the merely irresponsible.

Battalion HQ lay at the end of three hundred meters of winding tunnels and occasional caverns, with two apparently bottomless pits thrown in to season the mixture. Brigitte Tachin, who had no head for heights, carefully hugged the wall as they passed the pits.

The HQ was just beyond the second pit, in a cavern whose walls were lined with tenting. Tunnels that looked newly cut led off in several directions. Ground sheets and inflatable benches covered most of the floor of the cave.

"Be seated, please." The speaker beside the display on one wall was Colonel Luvic, who'd been senior adviser at the time of the rebellion against the Bushranger Republic. Tachin remembered Brian's description of her the day the Victorians proclaimed their Act of Union, looking ready to strangle them with her bare hands.

"Thank you. I would like to introduce Lieutenant Colonel Peter Bissell, Associated States Armed Forces Intelligence."

Tachin wondered when he'd stopped calling himself Intelligence liaison from the Bushranger Republic to the Victorian Militia. It hardly mattered, though, as long as he knew his business.

"Thank you," Bissell said. His beard was turning shaggy and his clothes aimed at warmth rather than a military appearance. "I'll try to keep this short.

A map came up on the display. "As you can see, this is the highest ground in an area that provides excellent cover for ground movement and lots of caves for storage of supplies. We have a high-probability estimate that much of the Freedom Party's remaining supplies are in this area."

This meant searching the area and keeping it under sur-

haven't had any more lunch than you have, and I smell an open mess cave."

Luvic nodded. "Dismissed!" she called, and joined the flow of advisers toward the yellow-marked cave that now exhaled the smell of cooking food.

Half of Admiral Kuwahara's private display showed the dispositions of the various squadrons around Victoria. The other half was scrolling the last chapter of *Hawk of Twilight,* Yorck's famous novel about the First Hive War.

This was the fourth time he'd read it, but right now it was more interesting than the activities of the ships. With the crucial troop movements on Victoria completed, everything else connected with defusing the situation there would take place in atmosphere.

The only activity in orbit right now was the Federation and Alliance finishing off the orbital debris and the Baernoi going through squadron exercises. Orbital-debris clearance, while essential, was about as inherently fascinating as watching grass grow.

The Baernoi were exercising both intensively and extensively; the whole force was involved and they'd been maneuvering at close quarters, high speed, or sometimes both for six hours now. But *Baikhal* and her group were in sensor contact with the Tuskers whenever *Shenandoah* wasn't. Anything the Baernoi did would be recorded, whether it was novel or not.

Kuwahara doubted that the recordings would show much except that the Baernoi were first-class practical spacehands. This was something known to everyone who dealt with the Tuskers since ten days after first contact, and was hardly worth the space it would take up even in *Shenandoah*'s capacious computer memory.

The flag secretary's face replaced *Hawk of Twilight.* "Commander Franke presents his compliments, and he has General Kornilov's message and an intelligence supplement to deliver."

"Send him in."

Kornilov's message had been expected since this morning, but the warning hadn't said anything about an intelligence supplement. Possibly Franke—or even Colonel Nieg—had caught the rough side of Golikov's tongue when he expected them to produce a miracle and they didn't.

Everything was in both micro and print. Clipped to the print of the intelligence supplement was a hand-scribbled note from Kornilov.

Dear Admiral,

Nieg and Franke got their heads and data together and produced this. I endorse passing it on to you without necessarily endorsing their conclusions.

Mikhail Kornilov

Kuwahara skimmed the supplement, ordered tea for himself and coffee for Franke, then settled down to read the supplement in detail. Twenty minutes and two cups later, he raised his head to stare at the commander.

"Are you sure you and Nieg aren't letting your impatience lead you into wishful thinking?"

"Sir, with all due respect—"

"Why do I have the feeling that I am about to be tactfully informed that I've stepped in it?"

"Sorry, sir. You may be right. But it's also wishful thinking that we can just quietly strangle the Freedom Legion and call it a day. They may not go quietly. Even if they do, they may take so long that somebody else will have time to act."

"And you think the Merishi who claimed asylum may be able to tell us who?"

"They certainly know more than they've told anybody. It hasn't helped, our not being able to bug either their quarters or the Association Intelligence people who *have* bugged them."

"No, but that kind of a violation of the rules for political asylum wouldn't have helped either. There wasn't any way we could have kept it secret, so it would have been spread from here to Merish by now. Also, once we have something to trade, we can sit down with the Association and discuss it."

Kuwahara stacked the pages of the printout with fussy neatness, then stared at Franke again. "Two questions. You assume that the bombing at the Web of Hrar was the act of genuine anti-Merishi terrorists. What if it was a Field Intelligence provocation?"

"Then the Merishi in Seven Rivers are in even more danger than they think," Franke replied promptly. "Hollings is in the pocket of Field Intelligence, or so everyone says. That reduces police protection for the Merishi. All they'll have left is whatever the Third/96th can spare."

"So our refugees will be even more nervous for their friends' safety, and even more willing to talk in return for our promising it?"

"That seems logical, doesn't it?

"My notions of what constitutes logic have been considerably extended by this crisis," Kuwahara said. "So have your notions of the powers of a local commander to negotiate with foreign political bodies."

"Ah—well, it seemed to me that none of these Merishi had any sort of diplomatic standing. Also, I thought the limitation was only on threats, not rewards."

Kuwahara grinned. "On the second point, you're simply flat wrong. On the first point, there is no reason we can't give some of the Merishi the status of representatives of the local Merishi community. That increases their diplomatic immunity and general status. It should help get them to talk."

Kuwahara's grin faded. It was not really an honorable pleasure, catching a Kishi Institute expert in a factual error. But pleasures of any kind had been few since the Alliance squadron died. Desperation might be warping his judgment.

"Anyway, my orders do give me discretion to protect the Merishi or any other group on Victoria. To make the protection most effective, I would need the cooperation of all other Federation authorities and the Associated States of Victoria. That of course gives de facto recognition to the Act of Union, but I hope nobody will whine about that at this late date."

Franke was obviously doing mental arithmetic. "That means Gist, Glicksohn, Fitzpatrick, Kornilov, somebody from the Bushranger Republic, and ideally the Alliance and the Baernoi. Quite a lot of signatures and not much time to get them."

"Oh, I think it's not so many signatures that we can't get them fast, if I have a messenger hand-carry my proposal to each of the signatories. At least the ones on our side," he added, as Franke seemed to realize what he'd just let himself in for.

Kuwahara poured the commander another cup of coffee. "Relax, Commander. I won't have the proposal drafted for at least a couple of hours. Just remember, the next time your bright idea means a great deal of leg work, that the legs working may be yours."

"Aye-aye, sir." Franke gulped his coffee as if it were the one thing between him and instant demise, then rose.

"With your permission, sir?"

"Dismissed."

Two hours was at least an hour and three-quarters more than Kuwahara intended to take. Franke and Nieg had practically written the proposal for their admiral. He hoped Franke would take the extra time to relax.

Kuwahara skimmed the proposal again, then realized he'd overlooked something. What about that Baernoi merchant ship, still on station over Silvermouth with a couple of light cruisers riding shotgun? The light cruisers were only common sense, but what were the Tuskers up to with that trader?

The admiral realized that he would have been in a better position if the second admirals' conference had taken place. The people who'd burned Buschton had also burned what might have been a major intelligence breakthrough.

But "might have been" was a dirty phrase, even if the tactics instructors said so, and there was no time to set up another meeting. Waiting for complete intelligence was fine in theory. In practice it meant you always lost to somebody who went ahead and acted on the intelligence they had plus educated guesswork.

Joanna Marder walked openly aboard the lifter from Barnard's Crossing to Silvermouth. She had no reason to conceal either her identity or her destination. Given that her mission was what everyone thought it was, it was logical for her to report to a superior officer. Colonel Pak was in the field; Brigadier Fegeli was both available and senior.

Was he reliable? Marder knew that her life hung on the accuracy of Pak's estimate. His average reliability had been high in the past, but averages weren't perfect predictors. If Pak wasn't one, she was probably dead.

Sooner than she wanted, too. Nobody lived forever, but she wanted more of life than she'd had, whether drunk or sober. She also didn't want to die without striking back, for Paul and the Bonsai Squadron.

More for the Bonsai Squadron than Paul, now. She knew now that Paul had made it easier for her to stay drunk when he'd intended to keep her sober. She wasn't angry, because anger couldn't affect the behavior of a dead man any more than the dead man's behavior could have affected her drinking.

Paul had still taken second place in her survivor guilt, her nightmares, and any other psychological baggage she might be carting. Maybe he would come back, as persistent in death as he'd been in life, but she hoped not until after this mission was done. Between them, Paul and the bottles had killed too much; they would not have this mission.

It was an hour and a half to Silvermouth, with the lifter keeping low and just offshore. There it would be lost against the land if looked for from the sea, and lost in wave clutter from the land or the air.

Snow was swirling across the Silvermouth field when the flight landed. Marder saw it draw a curtain across the mouth of the passenger hangar as she scurried toward the terminal.

Nobody was waiting for her, so she deposited her carry-on bag, with a copy of the data and a suitable selection of booby traps, in a rented locker. By the time she'd retrieved her checked baggage, she noticed a Navy petty officer and an Army corporal watching her.

"Commander Marder?" the petty officer asked. "We're to escort you to Government House. Standing orders, for all officers traveling on official business."

Marder doubted that Hollings would describe her business as "official," but didn't mind the escort. Twilight was joining lowering gray sky and the snowstorm to make Silvermouth look even more dismal than usual in winter.

"Security that big a headache?"

"We're trying to keep it from getting that big, more like it," the corporal said. He lowered his voice. "Rumor is, some big Tusker spook got caught when the Web went up. Don't know what he was doing down here, but the Tuskers are supposed to be buying up everybody who thinks they might have seen—"

"I think the commander needs a ride, not a gossip update," the petty officer said.

They exchanged IDs. Everybody's seemed to be as legitimate as a Puritan's heir, and the order about officer escorts was signed by Fegeli, Pak, and Colonel Cronin of the Third Battalion.

Marder climbed into the backseat and let the warmth of the groundcar soothe her. It soothed her so thoroughly that the other groundcar was up alongside them before she knew it.

She sat up, then flew to one side as the corporal threw the wheel over. It wasn't enough; with a metallic *chunnnggg* the other car grappled theirs. The driver tried to fling himself out of his door, but the petty officer somehow had control of the door locks.

The Marder was clawing for her pistol as the petty officer shot the corporal in the side. She had the satisfaction of shooting the petty officer in the face, then the entire right side of the car collapsed on her.

She could move, so she tried to raise her gun again. But something invisible and intangible seemed to be slowing her movements. The pistol weighed too much to hold steady. It clattered to the floor, and Marder's head sagged onto her chest.

Before her eyes closed, she flogged her brain to form and hold two thoughts.

They'd used gas.

Some of them were Merishi.

Twelve

Like a conservative bathing suit, Brigadier Fegeli's report on Joanna Marder's disappearance covered the essentials.

Commander Marder had been involved in a terrorist incident when the car she was taking to HQ was bombed, and was believed dead. The petty officer escort was also believed dead, and the driver was seriously wounded and not expected to live. It was not clear whether the petty officer had been cooperating with the terrorists or not.

The report reached Colonel Pak in New Xianglun, the first town to be recaptured from the Freedom Legion. It was a dismal little place that lived off hydroponics, fish from a small lake, and the cash income from a small titanium deposit. Its occupation by the Freedom Legion hadn't improved it. Neither had the departure of most of its three hundred people along with the platoon of the legion "garrisoning" it.

Pak had just finished reading the report when the com center called. "Message from Siren Leader. They have visual contact with the convoy from the town. They report four armed vehicles but no way to engage them without risk of hitting the civilian transport."

"So what else is new?"

"Sir?"

"Siren Flight is to maintain contact with the convoy until it either reaches its destination or the armed vehicles can be safely engaged. If they are engaged by AD weapons they may return fire as appropriate."

"Yes, sir."

It didn't matter whether the Xianglun people got away unscathed or not. They would be another load of largely useless mouths for some town already short of supplies. Their protecting platoon might delude themselves that they'd scored a victory by joining some other Legion force, but Pak intended to disillusion them at his earliest convenience.

If the Freedom legion concentrated its entire force of two short (one might almost say dwarf) battalions in one place, all it would do is give the 96th a chance to end the Legion and the invasion at a blow. Pak hoped that the Legion's soviet of C.O.s would overlook this until he was ready to drive home the lesson.

For now, priority went to the reply to Fegeli: analyze the DNA of the human remains in the vehicle, guard the driver as closely as Sharon Farber, and record anything he said. As an afterthought, Pak added that he was sending this message by a trusted courier, who also had orders to retrieve Commander Marder's intelligence data from its drop.

That would mean stripping himself of all but two of his reliable people, but Pak knew he had no choice. Marder's drop would self-destruct quietly if it wasn't retrieved in two days by someone with the proper codes, not so quietly if anyone else played with it. That would be the end of data that Marder had risked (and probably lost) her life to obtain.

It also might be counted as another "terrorist incident" and make the atmosphere in Silvermouth even tenser. Colonel Cronin of Third Battalion had been reporting numerous brawls and other minor incidents and a general lack of cooperation almost amounting to civil disobedience. A "terrorist" locker bomb could put the city over the edge and turn civil disobedience into uncivil harassment, if not outright urban guerrilla warfare.

Pak did not hope that Marder was dead. Such a selfish wish went against principles hammered into him from boyhood. One did not wish for a friend's death, simply to reduce danger to oneself.

Besides, Marder's secrets could only destroy him and Fegeli when Hollings had somebody to replace them. Uzel would tell the governor plainly that he did not; whatever kept the admiral cooperating with Hollings would draw the line at such criminal folly as the governor playing general.

Reinforcements were finally on the way, though; a composite squadron including heavy ships and a naval landing force supposed to include at least two rifle battalions. They would have commanders senior to Fegeli and Pak; they might also have commanders willing to listen to Hollings.

Unless Admiral Lopatina could talk to them first—and she was not only alive but recovering faster than anybody had dared expect. Including Hollings, Pak thought—and he revised the message to Fegeli to add a request to provide guards for the Baba along with everybody else.

Gregory Cronin was going to hit the ceiling if Pak went on parceling out his battalion as bodyguards for everybody and his cousin. He couldn't tell the colonel why, either.

But they were in a race, Hollings and Field Intelligence running against Fegeli and Pak, with peace or chaos depending on who won, and never mind the Federation, the Baernoi, and the Victorians themselves!

"Tiller to Spark, we have a little problem."

Brigitte Tachin's voice was fuzzed by the amount of rock between her radio and Brian Mahoney's, but recognizable.

"Spark here. What kind of problem?"

"Maybe not so little. The third cave is floor-to-ceiling crates. The outside rows all have medical markings, but that's maybe one-tenth of the whole pile."

"So start moving the crates."

"What with? I've got three advisers besides myself. The rest of the people in here are 3rd Platoon, Red Company."

"That should be enough."

"If they cooperate."

Mahoney decided that this was as far as the discussion should go on the radio. "Spark to Tiller, I'm coming in. Send one of your people out to act as a guide."

"That's a roger, Spark. Tiller out."

Mahoney stood up and started buckling on his harness. "Herb, take over. Tell Huong that I've gone to investigate a suspicious cache and evaluate its communications equipment."

"That's not all, is it?" Lieutenant Darlington asked.

"No way, but it's all Huong needs to know right now. Our team exec has a heavy finger on the panic button, in case you hadn't noticed."

"I have somehow achieved cognizance of the fact. I'll cover for you."

"Thanks."

Five minutes later Mahoney was airborne in a liftscooter; ten minutes later he was greeting his guide at the cave entrance. He didn't know how long it took him to half slither, half trot into the cave, but when he arrived he saw Federation advisers standing at one end of the pile and most of the militia platoon at the other.

He pulled Brigitte aside.

"What's the problem?"

"The platoon won't start hauling crates, and their leader won't order them to. He also pulled rank on me when I suggested that he call for some lift pallets."

Mahoney grunted in disgust. This was only the most serious such incident, not the first. Some of the militiamen had worked like slaves, using a very narrow definition of food and medical supplies to justify confiscating almost everything that wasn't nailed down or actually on fire when they found it. (Mahoney suspected that some of these zealots were dealing on the growing black market, but had no evidence.)

Others seemed to be dragging their feet and anything else they could drag without directly disobeying orders or provoking incidents. Mahoney thought most of them were not so much supporters of the Freedom Party as not wanting to be blamed for its impending collapse. That was stupid, but so far it hadn't been dangerous.

"Lieutenant—" Mahoney called.

"Langwell," the platoon leader replied. He walked over with a slouch that made Mahoney feel like a 101 Light color sergeant, and his clothes matched his posture.

"All right, Lieutenant Langwell. I'm an adviser of equivalent rank, unlike Lieutenant Tachin."

"Date of rank?

They exchanged dates, and Mahoney emerged comfortably the senior. In fact, Langwell had been a second lieutenant until last week, when he became part of a big batch of company-grade promotions the Associated States had pushed through. The official story was providing cadre for the expanding Associated States Forces; Mahoney suspected it was to reward the politically loyal (especially Bushrangers) and make trouble for Federation advisers.

"All right. I'm senior. So I suggest we stop playing games and arrange to check out this dump."

"I'm not going to order my people to shift all those crates by hand, for Christ's sake!"

"Who said anything about handwork? What I suggest is that we put out security, a squad or so, in case the bad guys are close enough to notice what we're doing. Then we can call in some lift and maybe another dozen or so warm bodies. We might even get a couple of pallets in here."

"The cave mouth's too narrow."

"Not if we haul the pallets in here before we assemble them. Surely your people are up to hefting a lightweight lift generator?"

"I suppose so."

"They'd damned well better be," Mahoney said without raising his voice. He went on in a near whisper. "Look, you sound like you're running scared of your own platoon. If you are, the sooner we know it the better we can guard your back.

"If you're doing this on your own, you're skating right on the edge of noncooperation. General Parkinson has been relieving people of command for that. If you don't want me to report—"

"I get your point. All right, but we'll have to scrounge some food and bedding from that pile if we're going to stay here. My blokes didn't come out with heavy packs, if you get my meaning."

"I do." *Which is that you may be just incompetent instead of uncooperative.* "Tell your people to go ahead and make themselves comfortable. There's enough in that dump to keep a company going for a week, let alone a platoon for a day."

Langwell returned to his men, while Tachin and Mahoney exchanged expressive looks.

His said, *Something smells here.*

Hers replied, *Yes, but until we can be sure what it is, shouldn't we walk softly?*

Which, Mahoney decided, would leave them exactly where they had started, if some lift didn't show up reasonably soon. At least he could call for it without having to deal with Lieutenant Langwell or his platoon!

*   *   *

A buffet for seven people in quarters the size of General Berkson's might have been laziness. But the commander of the Eleventh Army didn't like robot waiters and the room was knee-deep in secrets that no loyal steward would *want* to know even if he were allowed to.

Admiral John Schatz was staring at the branch outside as he forked stuffed shrimp into his mouth. A week ago the berries on the branch had been a vaguely tainted green. Then Riftwell's summer leaped down from the sky onto the land, and everything seemed to turn summer-hued overnight.

A reflected face superimposed itself over the branch and the gardens beyond. Schatz turned to greet Lieutenant General Korbus, deputy commander of Eleventh Army's I Corps and C.G.-designate of the Victoria Corps.

"How goes it, Georgi?"

Korbus spread his hands. "I don't want to make an enemy of Ginnie Sonderberg, but she's not being too nice about losing the job."

Sonderberg, Schatz knew, had her heart set on Victoria as her last chance for a combat command before her next promotion evaluation. She also had her heart set on an evaluation that would give her that fourth star.

"How unnice?"

"Sober, she's fine. After the second one, though . . ." Again, spread hands.

"I'll keep an eye on her. Meanwhile, just be glad Our Lady of the Saber didn't grab the job herself."

Korbus started to look indignant. Schatz got ready to apologize for forgetting the fierce loyalty most of the Hentschmen had to the I Corps C.G. Then Korbus grinned.

"I don't think anybody here realizes just what Frieda's up to. She's getting more than half the Hentschmen involved on Victoria, starting with me. When she takes over Eleventh Army—"

"If."

"Let's be realistic, Admiral. Who the hell else is there, when Berkson goes?"

"Short of bringing somebody in from out of the Zone, I admit the Pocket Pistol is way out in front. But let's also not tempt fate while we're being realistic."

"All right. *If* Frieda takes over, I'll probably get I Corps.

Then we can split the Victoria-trained Hentschmen, and both I Corps and Eleventh Army will stay up to their previous standard."

"You really wanted to say 'Surpass their previous standard,' didn't you?"

Korbus looked over his shoulder to see if Berkson was in hearing. "Maybe the Army. No way I Corps. That's one reason I want Victoria. Without a combat command, the Pocket Pistol's going to be a damned hard act to follow."

There was nothing to say to that, except what would be unreasonably tactless for even a four-star fleet commander to say to a three-star general. Which was that he hoped they never had to send out two more brigades and activate Victoria Corps, because the people on the spot had settled the crisis.

Instead Schatz said, "Mind some advice?"

Again the spread hands. It was legal for General Korbus to ignore advice from the commander of the Eleventh Fleet. It might not be wise.

"You've got a good team already in place, so don't shift either one unless it's absolutely impossible to deal with them."

"I wasn't worried about Kornilov. He doesn't seem to be having any trouble with the Hentschmen already on the spot. I wouldn't call him an original thinker, but he seems to have the confidence of the Victoria Command."

Schatz noted Korbus had left out more than he said. If the general was ready to have trouble with Kuwahara, whom he would outrank—

"How well do you know the Shogun?"

"I haven't served with him since we were both field-grade gophers for Plans. I also haven't heard anything bad about him."

Schatz nodded. With no more than 400,000 active-duty people, Eleventh Zone was still large enough that people could reach quite high rank without ever meeting one another. He groped for a concise summary of Kuwahara.

"He's one of those people who make you think that the old Imperial Japanese Navy never died. Or rather, it died, went to Yasukuni, and hung around drinking sake and playing with geishas until the time came for it to be reincarnated as a damned high percentage of our best officers."

"I know the type. I did two years with Uehara on the Joint Mobilization Committee, then two Thundercloud exercises with my battalion embarked under him."

"Kuwahara's head and shoulders above Uehara, except as a tactician. He's wonderfully methodical and apparently quite orthodox, most of the time. Then all of a sudden the situation explodes, the Shogun does a complete transformation, and he's pulling the weirdest damned ideas you never want to argue with out of God knows where."

"Sounds like he and Kornilov cover each other's blind spots."

"You said it, I didn't."

"No, but—what's the old Navy phrase? 'Don't change the set of the sails when you first come on watch.' "

"Will wonders never cease? An Army man knowing Navy tradition!"

"Wait until you see my next wonder. An Army man leaving the Navy commander on the spot to get on with the job."

"Is that a promise?"

"I never make that kind of promise without a glass in my hand."

"The bar's still open."

"Nothing," Brokeh su-Irzim said.

Zhapso su-Lal looked around his cabin as if the answer his deputy could not give might crawl out of the walls. Then he bared his tusks.

"No, my anger is not at you," he said. "It is at the situation." He sighed. "You are absolutely sure we have no prospect of making an informal approach to the Smallteeth Inquirers?"

"Not in Seven Rivers," su-Irzim said. His reluctance was no more an act than su-Lal's anger. "The Fleet Commander may have to renew his proposal to Admiral Kuwahara."

"Which is to not only hide tusks but go on all fours to the Smalltooth, when they are already defeating our friends on Victoria!"

"I agree that this would encourage the humans to believe that we are abandoning those friends. But I do not think that they would be turned from their course in dealing with the Freedom Party by anything short of our declaring open war. This, I imagine, we do not wish to propose."

"May you find dung in your beer," growled su-Lal. He poured himself another mug and contemplated it as carefully as if he did expect to find something improper in it.

"I am not particularly surprised at this situation," su-Irzim said. "The Merishi are hiding like boreworms in their holes. Our informants may also fear that Rahbad Sarlin's fate will be theirs, or even that he has given their names—"

"They dishonor his name and that of Special Projects!"

Su-Irzim was not unsympathetic. He also wanted to shriek. But it would accomplish nothing, save to strain a voice he would need to explain to Fleet Commander su-Ankrai why they were as helpless as a snared bogrooter.

"They do. But there has already been so much folly in this business so far that a little more does not surprise me at all. What would surprise me is Colonel Nieg's not ordering his people to burrow deep or allowing them to do so if they wish. He has not been a fool yet, and I do not expect him to become one for our convenience."

"No. But what if one of our people were to go down to Silvermouth? Those who cannot talk to us in orbit might be willing to tell us something in an alley or a beer hall."

"Who?"

"If Su-Ankrai could be persuaded to send you down—"

"That was the first point I raised after we knew that Sarlin had vanished," su-Irzim said testily. "I was refused, and ordered not to ask again."

"Really?"

"You question both my truthfulness and my courage?" Su-Irzim kept his voice low. Death duels had been fought over lesser insults.

"I—no, curse it, I doubt neither. Perhaps I do doubt that your knowledge of the Smallteeth is as great as you said—"

"I am beginning to doubt that myself," su-Irzim replied. "But let us remember that there are more varieties of humans than we will ever know. Also, our friendly Scaleskins seem to have sunk their claws into this prey and are trying to pull it away from everybody else."

"I need another beer," su-Lal said, and provided one for both of them.

Halfway through the mug, su-Lal set it down. "What

about sending F'Mita ihr Sular down to Silvermouth? Most of her trading experience has been among the Scaleskins and Sm—humans."

"Yes, but merchants are an unheroic lot. She might be detected long before she found one with both knowledge and courage. Also, she knows little of Inquirers' work and not much more of Special Projects."

"We could teach her."

"Between now and tomorrow's haltmeal? This is too serious for jesting."

"I suppose so."

"I *know* it is. I also know that we may need *Perfumed Wind* with her commander aboard, not rotting in some cell in Silvermouth. F'Mita has a good crew, but none of them fit to outthink our enemies the way they may have to."

Su-Lal threw up his hands, forgetting that he held a half-filled mug. Beer descended in a shower on su-Irzim. He bared tusks in mock fury.

"Forgive me. But I do not think su-Ankrai will be happy to learn this. I know I am not."

"And I am not happy to be the bearer of such news," su-Irzim finished. He looked with wry sympathy at the Fleet Inquirer.

Su-Lal's lack of rivalry with him was genuine, and his desire to serve the People regardless of who gained the glory was strong. But no Syrodhi of su-Lal's rank and upbringing could entirely ignore a situation in which an ambitious and promising Antahl might break a tusk!

Colonel Chatterje hastily burrowed under the blankets as General Kornilov heaved himself upright and reached for the screen. Sometimes, suddenly waked from sleep, the general forgot to cut off the vision.

This time the screen was safely blank before Commander Franke's voice came on.

"Good morning, sir. I have just received a request from Senator Karras to meet with you. He said he was planning on visiting the wounded from Buschton in the hospital, subject to Colonel Chatterje's permission. So he thought he might have a chance to speak with you, if you would be available."

It was too early in the morning for Kornilov to feel more

than a twinge of suspicion. "I trust you told him that I would not be available, but not why?"

"Yes, sir. He said he would be happy to wait at Fort Stafford for you, if that was acceptable."

"Call him back and say that is all right, but don't imply that I may be a while."

"No, sir." Kornilov saw lights glow as the link switched over to the maximum-security scramble. "I thought of telling him that it would not be useful to wait at Fort Stafford, but that might have given away too much."

"May I ask why?" Kornilov's suspicions were now more than a twinge. Chatterje thrust her neat dark head out from under the blankets to listen.

"He sounded and looked nervous, even apprehensive. He was more flushed than usual and I could see him sweating, although I don't know what the temperature was in his room. Sir, I think Karras is afraid of something."

"Commander Franke, your specialty is intelligence, not psychology. Karras has never heard a shot fired and now he's about to visit five hundred-odd men and women who have survived a fusion explosion. In his situation, I too would be afraid—of vomiting all over some poor burn case when it was all too much for me."

"Yes, sir."

"No harm done, Commander. Just stick to your job, which is delivering Governor-General Gist to Government House in time for the meeting."

"Yes, sir. With your permission, I'd like to rout out one of those naval security teams we have in reserve and add it to Gist's escort. Should I provide one for anyone else?"

"General Parkinson is flying with me."

Even over a secure line, Franke didn't need to know that Glicksohn had agreed to let Prime Minister Fitzpatrick represent her, and Kuwahara had provided an eighteen-page memorandum that covered contingencies Kornilov hadn't even considered. With just enough people for a bridge game and all but one of them military or ex-military, it shouldn't take long to hammer out the approach to the Merishi.

That might not be the "open sesame" that Kuwahara seemed to think it would be. No, *could* be. But at least Victoria Command would be acting against its opponents, instead of reacting to them.

"Yes, sir. With your permission?"

"Certainly, certainly. Start calling, but don't interrupt Gist at breakfast, or you'll be the final course."

"Yes, sir." The link broke, and Kornilov managed to stand without lurching. Not without vagrant drafts reminding him that he had nothing on, and that he really wanted to crawl back into the bed where Indira waited, at least warm and probably willing—

"I hope you're right about Karras," she said.

"Why shouldn't I be?"

"No reason, but—do you want my professional opinion on his state of mind, after I've played hostess all day?"

Kornilov bent down and kissed her. She promptly threw her arms around him, and her light weight but strong grip was enough to pull him off balance. He landed on top of her, a position which he had no great wish to leave, and which led to the logical conclusion.

When Kornilov finally climbed not only out of bed but into his full-dress uniform, he knew that he was going to be late. But he decided that it was lateness in a good cause.

Thirteen

The capital of a dominion with more land than money, Thorntonsburg had sprouted less than a dozen tall buildings in two centuries. Two of these made up Government House.

Commander Franke saw the twin twelve-story towers rising ahead as soon as Gist's lifter cleared the crest of Weber Hill. As they passed over the tube station serving the homes on the hill, Franke scanned around the lifter.

The escorts were still in place, a gunship flying high cover and two armed troop carriers to left and right. To the rear, invisible except to the pilot, was another lifter carrying the Navy security team, with a load of C-cubed gear and (although this was something they didn't mention) EI and ECM gear.

Now they were less than three kloms from Government House. The map display showed no higher buildings between them and Government House, so the pilot lowered the nose. Now they were less than a hundred meters above the tangled streets of Parrville, the poorest part of Thorntonsburg.

As Parrville gave way to the downtown, they passed a ten-story apartment building. At least it must have begun life that way. Now a good half the windows were sealed or showed merchants' signs. Its location on the edge of Parrville must have driven away higher-paying tenants and turned it into a mixed-use building.

Very high-paying, considering that it had a roof landing platform for private lifters. And the platform wasn't empty.

Franke counted three lifters and a liftscooter, all of them civilian as far as he could tell. The men around the vehicles were also civilians.

"Squatter Leader to Squatter Flight. Conform to my

movements." Franke tapped the pilot on the shoulder. "Circle that apartment building we just passed."

"What the hell are you after, Commander?" the governor-general growled. He hadn't been interrupted at breakfast, but sounded as if he hadn't finished digesting it before Franke cajoled him into the lifter.

"I want to check with Lu—with Major Morley—and her local police liaison. See if that's a security team in plainclothes up there."

"And if—" Gist began, then broke off. He'd been a professional soldier on Southern Cross; he knew what unauthorized civilians might mean.

"Max scramble," Franke said. "Squatter Leader to Squatter Talktalk. Interrogative to Thorntonsburg Police, MP Police Liaison, and Athena." That was Lu Morley's well-chosen code name, and Franke prayed that her usual sense of duty had put her in charge of security for the meeting.

"Do you have any security personnel on top of the building at—" he called up the address from the computer, "112 Barron Street? We have three lifters, one scooter, and an indeterminate number of either plainclothes or civilian persons on the roof platform. No, correction. At least twelve but not more than twenty people. No sign of weapons or—"

"Commander Franke," Gist broke in. "I do have to get to the meeting, you know. Can't we just swing wide around Government House and approach from the other side?'

"Your Excellency, that depends on what those people are packing, as well as who they are. I want to make sure there's a meeting for you to get to."

This time Gist saw reason before saying anything. Franke wouldn't have heard it if Gist had said it. He'd spotted three groundtrucks rolling down Barron Street—which led to Melbourne Avenue, and Melbourne Avenue led straight to Government House.

By itself, that wouldn't be suspicious. But trucks loaded with crates, in a part of town where deliveries were made at night—and with men sitting or standing everywhere the crates would let them.

Franke started to dictate a second message, then the radio squealed like a dying rat. "Solar flare, I guess," the copilot said.

Franke's throat was so dry his first words came out like

a croak. This was combat, he was leading in it, and what was worse he might be the man standing between Victoria and chaos.

He swallowed, and this time managed at least an intelligible croak. "Visual signal to Squatter Talktalk. Recommend Security Red Alert for Thorntonsburg. Get that off to our relay, then try to get the recipients of the last message."

The copilot understood the tone and the words, if not the reason for them. She picked up the signal laser and the pilot turned so that she could point it aft at the communications lifter.

"Relay?" Gist asked.

"We've got an attacker about sixty kloms up, beyond visual range. The talktalk crew can shift frequencies faster than the jammers can, and get the alert through."

"Jamming?" Gist said. "Bloody Christ!"

Franke didn't know about Christ. He suspected that the governor-general was right about the blood.

Major Morley had several pieces of luck, as well as her own wits.

She was in the Government House communications center when Franke's message came through. The senior communications operator turned to her, grinning.

"Sounds like your friend has the wind up, or wants to joke. Well, one of the high mucketymucks'll ream him a new arse—"

The operator broke off, because he was staring into the muzzle of Morley's pistol. "No, I'll ream you a new one, also a new bellybutton, if you blink."

With her free hand, Morley motioned two of her MPs in from the door-guard detail. "Search and secure this man. Report anything you find on him."

"Yes, ma'am."

Morley sat down at the console. "Athena to all Government House security personnel. Security Red Alert. Repeat, Security Red Alert. Maximum surveillance for aerial and ground intruders."

Now, if we can just trust the Vic Special Branch people—

The lights went out, the air-conditioning stopped, and somebody screamed. Morley snapped her snooper goggles down over her eyes. The communications center turned from black to a shifting pattern of greens, the brightest the warm consoles and the people at them.

Another scream was answered by two shots from outside. Morley thought she heard more shots and at least one explosion farther off in the building, maybe on a lower floor.

After a real five minutes and an apparent millennium, power returned. Inspector Gehvru, the Special Branch liaison, marched through the door with four of his men behind him.

"They had two people for an inside job on the building systems office," Gehvru said, as usual not wasting words. "We shot one. The other set off a bomb, killed herself and one of my people, but didn't hurt anything else."

"We're going to need—" Morley began, when the communications alarm began screaming.

"Communications Center, Athena."

"Major, what in the name of all the devil's relatives is going on?"

"We think somebody's trying a coup, or at least seizing the building," Morley told Kornilov. "We've had to take out some inside people, and there are too many strangers wandering around for my peace of mind."

Kornilov muttered something in Russian, containing the word *Karras* and what Morley suspected was quite a few obscenities.

"We're checking on all the strangers and bringing in Squatter Flight. Once we have the roof secure, I'll be up with a squad to escort you to the roof and you can lift out."

"And what do we do in the meantime?" That was Fitzpatrick.

"Sit still," Morley said, in a tone she knew majors shouldn't use to prime ministers.

"Now listen—" Fitzpatrick began, before both Kornilov and Parkinson shouted him down. Morley left the VIPs to get on with their arguing, ordered a check of all security-troop positions, and started a situation report.

"Copies to Fort Stafford, COMMAND SECRET and General Langston's eyes only, and another to the armory. Also tell the armory C.O. to secure all the nonlethals. Only Federation personnel around them."

"You have the most extraordinary command voice I've

ever heard," Inspector Gehvru said when Morley was finished.

"I was cadet drillmaster at the Kemali Academy, my last year," Morley replied. "Third woman to hold the post, I think." She drew her pistol again, checked it, then her ammunition supply, gas mask, and body armor.

"Lieutenant Blaise!" she shouted out the door. "First and second squads, load, lock, and mask up. We've got a call to pay on some VIPs."

"Yes, ma'am." Blaise's voice was shaking, but from eagerness rather than fear. Morley knew that her own voice had the same edge. The maggots had finally come out into the light of day, and now maybe, please God, enough of them could be squashed to let the decent Vics live in peace!

"Major Morley seems to have the situation well in hand," Kornilov said.

"At least as far as she knows it," Parkinson amended. "I'll feel better when we all know more, including General Langston."

Kornilov nodded. Marcus Langston, his deputy for Victoria Command, was literally holding the fort—Stafford. If the two Federation brigades had to be reshuffled to meet an internal threat, it would be Mark's job.

If the threat was serious, Kornilov would have preferred to reshuffle the Victorian militia—specifically, get them out of Fort Stafford entirely or clamp them under airtight surveillance. But there was no place to go that could support the whole battalion plus the local civilians "on leave of absence." If they went into the wilderness, they would have no Moses to lead them. While it might not take them forty years to reach their destination they would be useless while they were on the way.

Equally serious objections applied to tighter surveillance. Fort Stafford's cadre and regular battalion were all at full stretch right now, and the battalion might have to head into the field at any moment. If the Vics went with them, it might be no problem. If the regulars went and the Vics stayed . . .

Not to mention that the Vics in general and Alys Parkinson in general would be mightily offended at any further signs of "Feddie paranoia" (a phrase Alys had already used at least once herself). Then either military or political cooperation would be hard to come by, when both were urgently needed.

Bite the bullet, leave the Vics alone, and get back to the subject at hand. This was the legal status of Victoria's Merishi, fled, fleeing, or just lying low and hoping that whoever blew up the Web of Hrar wouldn't find them.

"Does anyone have anything to add to Kuwahara's memorandum that can't wait until Gist arrives?" Kornilov asked.

"I don't see any mention of being careful about coercion," Parkinson said.

"Probably because Kuwahara assumes we're smart enough not to need it," Fitzpatrick said. "Besides, one of our Merishi refugees is the son of a board member of Simejos Associates. That's minor royalty, or the equivalent."

"What does that do for us?" Parkinson asked.

"If he doesn't squall 'coercion,' nobody else will have any credibility," Kornilov put in. He emptied his teacup and poked dubiously with his fork at a cold sausage half-buried in congealed gravy.

"As a matter of fact, if he can persuade his friends to make it official, we'll have a whole new option. We can enter the Freedom Legion AO 'to provide emergency assistance to endangered civilians.' We can turn over every rock in the area, as long as we claim to be looking for Merishi."

"Only in the invaded area?" Fitzpatrick asked.

"My, don't civilians get bloodthirsty when they scent an opportunity," Parkinson said. Her smile didn't quite take the sting out of her words.

"I'm sick of being buggered about by every half-stellar would-be guerrilla with ten men and nine pulsers," Fitzpatrick said. "Yes, I want their blood."

"I think we'll be on the way to getting it, if Kuwahara and Gist approve," Kornilov said. "But we'll have to limit operations to the Freedom Legion AO. The Alliance will protest, if we imply they can't protect Merishi in the territory they control.

"Also, the 96th is on the offensive. I absolutely refuse to risk our 'assistance' running into one of Pak's battalions, fresh from retaking a town and full of vitamins."

"I don't have any problems with that," Parkinson said, and Fitzpatrick nodded slowly.

Parkinson rose. "I don't know about you gentlemen, but I need to get rid of some of this tea." She walked to the rear of the office and turned the corner to the suite's amenities room.

A hundred meters above Government House, Squatter Flight circled, trying to get through the jamming. They had all the communications they needed with the attacker now plunging down to join them, but nothing with Government House.

"Why the bloody hell didn't they put in a military C-cubed rig instead of that pisspot lashup they've got?" Gist asked everyone and no one.

"Economies," Gist's aide said. She said it as most people would have said "child abuse."

Franke was trying to look out of all windows at once, but knew that the gunship would be out of sight below, staying between the flight and any attack from the ground. Now if that attacker would just get down to provide top cover, not to mention an escape route for everybody—

"We're going to land in two minutes, Your Excellency," Franke said. "We can secure the roof against anything short of a fuser. Then the security people in the building can bring the others up and you can all ride to Fort Stafford aboard the attacker."

"If you think Fitz and Alys are going to like hiding behind Feddie skirts—"

"Your Excellency," the aide said. "If I understand Commander Franke, he believes there's no place except the fort that's safe for you and the other—"

"High-priority targets?" Gist finished.

Franke nodded, then stiffened. The three trucks were stopping outside the vehicle entrance to the Government House compound. Two men walked up to the gate and seemed to be asking for admission. Franke stepped up the power of his binoculars.

He promptly spotted two other men in the MP battledress lying on top of the service building that joined the two towers at their base. Snipers, Franke thought. A moment later he knew, as three men climbed the wall. The MPs shifted slightly. Two of the climbers fell back, arms out-

flung. The third jumped down before he could suffer the
same fate.

Lu or somebody else seemed to have things at least not
completely out of control at Government House. Now for
the roof—

"Hey, what the hell are those clowns doing?" the pilot
shouted.

The lifters on the Barron Street roof were airborne, in a
ragged formation with the scooter in the center. Franke
shifted his binoculars. Still no signs of weapons, and no ID
on them from Government House.

The jamming was still on, but maybe Police Headquarters
had a better com rig than Government House. Enough better so that if they reached it they could finish the security
check and know what side those damned lifters were on—

Smoke puffed from the middle of the formation, then
flame streaked out of it. Franke's eyes picked up the first
missile immediately, the second one a moment later. Both
tore into Government House before his brain could absorb
what his eyes had detected.

The two missiles launched by the scooter were unguided,
therefore unstoppable short of destroying them in midflight.

Since they crossed a populated area on their brief journey, the gunship had to maneuver so that guns, lasers, or
its own missiles wouldn't hit any civilians. Long before the
gunship was below the missiles, they struck.

Both the propellants and the warheads had been modified, sacrificing stability for extra power. One of the missiles
exploded as it struck the window of the prime minister's
suite, instead of penetrating. The second one tumbled in
the blast, striking at an angle. But the unstable propellant
detonated from that impact, setting off the warhead.

The combined explosion pulped Prime Minister Fitzpatrick and gutted General Kornilov. In the amenities room,
General Parkinson escaped most of the blast and all the
fragments.

She staggered out, ears ringing and eyes and nose clawed
by the fumes, to see an MP major sitting on the floor. The
major's thigh and one temple were bloody, but she had a
pistol in one hand and was waving her people forward with
the other.

Parkinson looked toward the table, saw what was left of her colleagues, and wanted to be sick. But generals, even militia ones, don't vomit when badly wounded MP majors are still in command of themselves and the situation.

"Where should I go?" Parkinson asked. She might get an answer to that, while "What happened?" was probably something no one knew right now.

Except the people who did it, she thought. *But they are going to die, and before they die, talk. No matter what it takes to make them talk, because they are not going to take Victoria away from us.*

"General Parkinson. Are you all right?"

"Better than you are, Major—ah, Morley, isn't it?"

"Just nicks from flying bits. That's what comes from taking point. Now, I want you on the roof, or at least on the top floor. We've got a lifter flight with Gist on board somewhere around here. You and he are going to be attackered to Fort Stafford as soon as our top cover comes down."

The thump of an explosion made the dust swirl and more loose bits fall from the wall. Morley used her free hand to pick some out of her hair. "So much for the new hairdo I had for this meeting. I—" Her lips tightened as the pain of her thigh wound broke through the shock.

"Medics!" Parkinson shouted. She was proud of herself for not screaming. "Medics, for Major Morley!"

Franke knew that if he added getting Gist killed to letting the missile strike, he would be lucky to escape a court-martial. The only consolation was that with him and Gist in the same lifter, they would probably go together.

Meanwhile, the gunship was down at street level, beating down the attack from the three trucks. Franke couldn't count the figures on the service building's roof because the lifter was maneuvering too violently, but there were a lot more than two. They all seemed to be good guys.

Meanwhile, one lifter and the scooter had headed for the roof of Government House. Both escorts jumped them, chopping the scooter out of the air with 22-millimeter bursts. The lifter staggered as far as the roof, but lost power just as it crossed the edge. It balanced for a moment, then toppled over, plummeting straight down into the frozen pond of the formal gardens.

A second lifter tried to get away, dodging low over roof-tops and sometimes below them. The second escort wanted to go after it but Franke refused. Government House might need reinforcements more than the last lifter needed arresting.

Help came from the sky, in the form of attacker Vermilion Two. It screamed in at just below Mach One, rattling but not breaking windows, overshooting the lifter but also cutting off its escape. The jamming had stopped now, and Franke heard the lifter's end.

"Got him in our sights now—hey, the little son of a Tusker's trying to ram us—hitting him—there!" as 75-millimeter shells blew the lifter apart in midair. From the size of the smoke cloud, it must have been carrying a good part of the rebels' ammunition. Smaller puffs told of time-detonated misses, so that the shells wouldn't fall live and lethal into the town.

More smoke billowed as the gunship touched off the street attackers' load of explosives. The blast finally knocked the gate down, but there was hardly anybody left alive to exploit the opportunity. The few hardy spirits who tried met a wall of fire from the service building and none of them made it more than ten meters inside the gate.

The attacker swung back over Government House, turning sharply to slow down, then hovered over the platform.

"Thanks, Vermilion Two," Franke said. "See anybody on the roof?"

"All clear."

"Good. We're landing to make pickup. Then can you dock and take our passengers back to Fort Stafford?"

"Sure—hey, aren't you Fat Herman?"

"Who the hell are you?"

"Clinging Klinger, from C-17."

"I'll be damned." The attacker's pilot was not only a classmate of Franke's, but a C-1 corridor veteran too.

"Let's save the reunion for later, if you don't mind," Gist said. He sounded uncharacteristically subdued.

Franke nodded. It had just occurred to him that quite in the line of duty, he could now find out what had happened to Lu.

*   *   *

Franke leaped out of Gist's lifter and ran to Morley. His hug nearly knocked her chair over backward.

"Sorry, Lu." He looked at the field dressing on her temple and the bloodstained trousers. "Everything under control here?"

"As far as we can tell," came a voice from behind Morley. Franke snapped to attention and saluted General Parkinson. She looked all right but Morley wondered if delayed shock was lying in wait. Another reason for getting her to Fort Stafford: If she went down, she could stay down without anybody knowing it until she was in shape to face this not-so-brave new world.

Parkinson herself almost came to attention as Gist dismounted from the lifter. Both salutes came at the same time.

Gist laughed. "All right, Alys. Salute me if you want, but right now I'm only a civil member of a government under attack. I think there's going to be martial law, which puts you and Kornilov in charge.

"Kornilov's dead. So's Fitzpatrick."

Gist's massive fist slammed against the lifter hard enough to make the four-ton machine quiver. He rubbed his knuckles and spat.

"All the more reason to declare martial law. Unless—What's the situation in Thortonsburg?"

Morley would have saluted if she could stand. "We're in communication with the armory and with Third/Victoria. The bad guys tried an inside job on the armory, but our people were ready for it. Ten prisoners, one dead, no friendly casualties.

"Several terrorist incidents, with mostly civilian casualties. Also, they tried to take out the Provost Marshal. He's down but not dead."

"And the Third?" Gist's tone asked a dozen wordless questions. It had been a gamble, putting the security of the Associated States' capital in the hands of a largely local Federation battalion. A gamble, with their own lives among the stakes.

"They sent one company to secure the armory. It's done well. The C.O. says he's been ordered by Admiral Kuwahara to place himself under the authority of the Associated States until Thorntonsburg is secure."

"What about Langston?" If something had happened to the deputy for Victoria Command, it could mean rebel penetration of Fort Stafford.

"He's authorized the Navy to handle Thortonsburg. It seems that rebel formations are popping up all over the place, and he's got his hands full."

The radio squawked. "Squatter One here," Franke said.

"Vermilion Leader. I've got the rest of the flight coming in, ETA ten minutes. I've also got a column of ground vehicles and pedestrians over in Parrville. Looks like the head's up near Barron Street and the tail winds off into those alley streets down by the river."

Gist swore. "Those stupid bastards," he said finally. "I'd been suggesting a settlement scheme for them for ten years, but the Labor delegates kept calling it indentured servitude."

He straightened to his full two meters, and it wasn't only his height and massive frame that made him dominate the group. "Alys, we'll limit the declaration of martial law to Thorntonsburg, unless the Federation asks for more. I also think we'll go to Third Battalion instead of Fort Stafford. Commander Franke, can the Navy give us the C-cubed we'll need to run things, if the Third Herd's short?"

Morley hoped that Franke knew this wasn't the time for complete honesty. "Anything we have is yours, Your Excellency."

"Good. Start by giving me—us—those inbound attackers. Alys, what's next?"

Parkinson shook her head. In another moment, Morley knew, it would be obvious to everybody that she was too shaken to command. Then confidence in the jury-rigged government of the Associated States would also be shaken, and maybe the whole lashup would come down with a crash.

Burying hopes of peace and a good many of my people and friends under it.

Morley pronounced a silent but comprehensive curse on amateur generals. Then she said, "If I might make a suggestion, General Parkinson?"

"Of course." At least that sounded right.

"We lay a cordon of nonlethals—gas and tangler mines, mostly—across the major exits to Parrville. We cover them with snipers, using marker or stun rounds mostly. We can watch their rear with the attackers and gunships."

"Pretty passive," Gist said.

"That's exactly what we want," Morley said. "Don't forget, the Parrville people almost certainly aren't hardcore sympathizers with the coup. They may not even know that it's largely failed. They've probably been promised miracles, and when those don't come they'll all go home. If they do, we can let them.

"The one thing we don't want to do is get into a house-to-house fight in Parrville. We'll kill innocent people, lose our own, and maybe generate enough support for the coup to make it really dangerous.

"If the Parrvillers really want to break heads, we'll be glad to cooperate. But let's leave the decision to them."

Gist was smiling by the time Morley was finished, but what the major really wanted was Parkinson's opinion. If Gist had to start answering for her . . .

"I think that's an excellent idea," Parkinson said. "I also think we should order a ban on civilian air movement. That way, we'll know that if it's in the air and not one of ours, it's one of theirs.

"We can use mostly Special Branch SWAT people for the covering snipers. But I'd like to borrow a few of your MPs if we can."

"Be my guest, ma'am."

"All right," Gist said. "I think we can mount up. Major, I'd like you to come with us. As long as the Provost Marshal's out of commission, you're the senior MP in Thortonsburg."

"Well, I could leave Blaise and Gehvru here—"

"You not only can, you will," Parkinson said briskly. "Major, remember that I can now command Federation units in the Thorntonsburg area. If you don't come with us, I'll order one of those attackers to take you to Fort Stafford."

Morley wished that Marcus Langston hadn't been quite so free handing out authority to the Vics. But at least Parkinson was thinking and speaking for herself now, and that was another battle won without a shot being fired.

Fourteen

The supply convoy out to Scout Company brought supplies (extra ammunition, food, and collapsible shelters), Lieutenant Longman with a Navy party to set up aiming beacons, and Major Abelsohn with an intelligence briefing for both Scout Company and the Ranger Team.

Candice Shores welcomed everything, particularly the briefing. The tension around the position had been thick enough to absorb laser beams ever since word of the assassinations and uprising reached the company. Even the well-cured nerves of Scouts and Rangers weren't immune to the stress of sitting on the sidelines, unable to play and not even knowing how the game was going.

She would have welcomed the supply convoy more if she hadn't suspected that it meant Scouts and Rangers would go right on sitting. She told herself that she didn't want a promotion or a medal. Now that the enemy's ass was out in the open, she just wanted her Scouts to have a chance to kick it.

She told herself this several times, while Longman distributed the beacons, a lifter distributed the supplies, and both returned with all of the platoon commanders for the briefing. She was still telling herself that when Abelsohn punched up a map display on the screen in his command lifter.

His briefing was as fluent as ever. It covered the whole situation throughout the affected territory, everything from Silvermouth to Thortonsburg and north to Loch Prima, in fact—in five minutes.

Thorntonsburg was divided between loyal areas and Parrville. The Federation and Victorian forces weren't trying to get into Parrville, and so far the Parrvillers weren't trying to get out. For now, this stalemate gave the edge to the good guys.

Elsewhere, organized rebel forces had appeared in the Blanchard Canyon area and at several points between Fort Stafford and the Vinh River. "Flight Blue didn't see ghosts when they grounded after the Buschton bomb," Abelsohn concluded. "They detected rebel movements. In fact, their landing may have helped precipitate the uprising."

Farther north, the Bushrangers' forces (now rechristened the Second Brigade, Associated Victorian States Forces) were holding Mount Houton and Kellysburg. They were also helping a bit around the edges with the operations of the two militia battalions hitting the Freedom Legion's supplies.

"So far those operations are going fairly well, the Vics are behaving themselves, and there's no sign of organized enemy opposition," Abelsohn continued. "Priorities for air support are going to the places where organized enemy units have appeared, and the south has priority over the north.

"Our guess is that the rising was premature, and that most of the local leadership took part in the assassination of Thortonsburg. Very few of them survived, so the key to the capital now is preventing reinforcements getting to Parrville. The rebels there don't seem to have many weapons or much enthusiasm."

"Why don't we just dump a battalion on each area and be done with it?" Longman asked.

"Dumping a full rifle battalion in shape to fight takes longer than you Navy people think," Sergeant Major Zimmer said. "Begging your pardon, sir."

Shores's eyes told Zimmer not to bait Longman anymore. The lieutenant was scared, but not out of his wits, which were fairly good ones at a time when everyone who had any at all was needed.

"That's part of it," Abelsohn said. "The other part is our friend across the border and overhead. The Alliance is definitely pushing the Freedom Legion back. Langston probably wants to keep at least three battalions in hand in case the 96th jumps the border or the Freedom Legion gets desperate and joins the rebels."

Lieutenant Piccone, the Scout X.O., looked bemused. "I

thought the rebels and the Freedom Party were the same people."

"That's a definite maybe," Abelsohn replied. "Most of the identified rebels with any political affiliation at all seem to be Action for Independence."

Shores wanted to put her head in her hands, and her X.O., Lieutenant Piccone, actually did so. The idea of the fanatical, terrorist Action for Independence putting this many people in the field was upsetting, to say the least.

She heard Piccone muttering, "To paraphrase Freud, 'What do the Victorians want?' "

"To paraphrase Intelligence officers since the days of the Assyrians, 'Damned if I know,' " replied Abelsohn. "But I will throw one more guess at you.

"This is a last desperate gamble, in the hope of establishing a viable military presence that the Baernoi can recognize and support. That's another reason why the brass are playing their reserves very close to their chests. Kuwahara may have to take out the Seventh Force. If the Tuskers don't do something that justifies that, they may still do things like shipping arms to the rebel ground troops.

"Nuclear-dispersal alert remains in effect until further notice. We'll try to give you situation updates at least twice a day, more often if anybody starts moving faster."

"Thank you, Major," Shores said. She took the stack of printouts from Abelsohn's console and handed them to Zimmer. "Sergeant Major, if you can distribute these, I'd like to talk to the major outside."

A wink at Bloch told her to join them. Outside the wind was just strong enough to kick up an occasional puff of snow. For inland Victoria in winter, it was almost comfortable.

"What's the matter, Candy?"

"Not a flaming word on anything in the Roskills, is there?"

"Nothing official."

"So the damned Vic militia's ghosts turn out to be real rebels, and my ghosts are still ghosts. Shamil the Camel's going to love that!"

"If he does, he'll be the only one," Bloch said. "I suppose my Rangers are also supposed to have bumped their heads before they saw unknowns where there was supposed to be nothing?"

Abelsohn looked around, saw nobody in hearing but Longman, and waved him back. "Stop shooting at the bad-news bringer," he said urgently.

"That won't improve the news," Shores said.

"And shooting me won't improve the situation." Abelsohn led them away from the lifter, pulled them into a huddle, then whispered, "I can tell you that you're being kept out here together with an eye to the future. When the situation does improve, you'll be the first people sent into the Roskills on a ghost hunt."

"That another guess?"

"No, that's straight from the top but unofficial and classified about three steps beyond BBA. So let's drink to the situation improving."

"You can drink, if you have anything besides Victorian piss," Bloch said. "We have to stay out here in the cold and fight off hypothermia."

"Tea, coffee, chocolate?"

"All three, if Zimmer's finished handing out the prints," Shores said.

"What do you think I'm running, a refreshment stand?"

Joanna Marder knew from the places that hurt approximately the things that had been done to her. She didn't remember any of them, but was sure this was a blessing. With only a little effort, she could even keep from imagining any of them.

A little effort was about all she was up to now, even mentally. Physically she hadn't felt this bad since the time she was in intensive care after a lifter crash. She was also strapped to the stretcher, with straps that cut into tender places. The mask over her mouth and nose was too tight, so that sweat made itches in some places and stinging in others where her face and neck were rubbed raw.

They'd left her eyes uncovered, and Marder hoped this was because they expected her to be unconscious. Or at least to have no memory of anything she saw. Her knowledge of Intelligence's drug collection was too limited to tell her which. (Not to mention that Intelligence's labs were notorious producers of customized potions and poisons.)

With another enormous mental effort, she reached a decision. She would keep her eyes open and staring, hope this would fool any casual observer, and pray that no other kind came by.

By the time she'd stared at the roof of the lifter for at most ten minutes, her eyes had begun to sting and water. Controlling the blink reflex was taking more out of her than whatever drug they'd given her had left.

She heard only two voices, though, so maybe the lifter had just its two pilots and nobody likely to sneak up on her. She also had the sense of being surrounded by piles of lashed-down supply containers. The insulation on the lifter was gouged and the finish under the insulation chipped and scarred. The cabin was also barely heated, and the cocoon of blankets over the straps didn't make up for being unable to move. Not all the pain in her toes and fingers was missing fingernails; some of it was the early stages of frostbite.

The lifter tilted; Marder heard tie-downs groan and her own stretcher slide a trifle. Then the lifter was descending quickly. Marder risked swallowing, to save her eardrums from the pressure change.

The lifter darted forward and tie-downs groaned again, louder. Marder now hurt in so many places that she almost wished something would break loose and crush her.

She beat the thought back into the dark cave where it began. She was alive and conscious and approaching someplace where her enemies expected her to be neither. If she learned where that place was and remembered it, she'd have something worth all the submarine schedules on Victoria.

The lifter's fans speeded up, and the faint vibration of the lift field died. Then with a clang and a thump they landed on some hard, level surface.

Marder had just time for a final swallow when the rear door swung open. Someone grabbed her stretcher by the head and started to lift it before another someone grabbed it by the foot.

For a moment Marder was half lying, half standing. She saw a bearded face in a cold-weather hood bending over the foot of her stretcher. Beyond the face she saw a narrow slit in the rock, with a segmented door beginning to slide across it.

Beyond the rock slit, before the door cut off her view,

she saw a ravine with a peculiar grayish-red rock at its foot. The rock was shaped uncannily like the helmeted head of a Baernoi Death Commando.

For a moment Marder had a nightmarish fantasy. She'd been kidnapped to the cave of a wizard, who commanded spells that could turn Baernoi to stone. What could he do to mere humans?

Then the door closed, and with a rumble and thump slabs of rock closed in front of it like a fangface's jaws. She felt herself being lifted and carried down the ramp, heard the sound of machinery around her, smelled oil, ozone, and cold damp rock.

She wanted to close her eyes. Voices told her there were too many people around; one of them might not only see her but recognize her act. Her muscles wouldn't obey. Or rather, they obeyed another impulse: to go on seeing everything she could, so that she could remember it until she could pass it on.

Intellectually, she knew that everything she saw would die with her. At every other level she rejected that knowledge.

In the next minute, the choice was taken out of her hands. Another face loomed over her, also bearded but the beard shot with gray.

"That her?"

"Everything they gave us says so."

"All right. I'll give her another dose."

"Better make it a double, unless—"

"Not yet. Is she in that bad shape?"

"Take my word for it, she is." Marder was obscurely glad that the second voice—it sounded like one of the pilots—hadn't described what happened to her. The farther she could push it back into the cave, the better.

"You're not a doctor."

"No, but I have S Clearance. You want to match that?"

The gray-shot beard without an S Clearance—Alliance Field Intelligence's second-highest category—nodded. Marder felt the blankets being pulled down from her throat and saw the man whistle. Then she heard a hiss and felt a spray-injector against the skin of her neck.

She sank into warm darkness. The warmth was so welcome after the long cold that she didn't even want to struggle.

*   *   *

"Control Five, this is Simba Six. We have a hard contact. Repeat hard contact, bearing 45-10."

In today's verbal code, that meant 130 degrees true and six kloms. Elayne Zheng added the contact to the plot in front of her.

"This is Control Five. Describe the contact."

"It looks like a bunch of camouflaged vehicles around a couple of farms. At least I see what looks like camouflage netting over stuff that's the right shape for lifters. There's an organics recycler and a hydroponics greenhouse, and what looks like a private house."

"Signature from the house?"

"Powered up. The vehicles are cold." Zheng was adding the data to her plot when another voice broke in.

"Control Five, this is Simba Leader. We are closing on the Six position. ETA four minutes. Good work, both of you."

"Thanks, Leader. But I've got an oxy system problem. Don't know how long I can stay on station."

"How long can you go and still maintain visual contact?"

"Oh, I can get right down to a thousand, but I'll be in range of all kinds of AD stuff if I do."

"I'll write up a real nice letter for your husband. If you'll pardon the expression, Simba Six—let's get down!"

"On the way."

For the next three minutes Zheng heard nothing except an occasional crackle of static and one report from Simba Six that she'd reached planned altitude. Zheng could sympathize with the unknown pilot. Simba Flight was light attackers, carrying mixed rockets, guns, and cluster bombs. They had neither the armor, the endurance, nor the firepower of the big space-based attackers.

On the other hand, they could stay on station in the face of handicaps that would defeat one of the more sophisticated machines. Like oxygen systems acting up, for example. Open the vents or even crack the canopy, and at low altitude a light pilot could get by on natural air breathed into natural lungs.

At low altitude and at low speed he was also likely to be an easy target for a wide variety of weapons, not all of them specialized AD hardware (which, thank God, the rebels seemed to lack so far). Simba Six's husband had a statistically significant chance of receiving that letter of condolence, if the rebels were there, armed and antsy.

At four minutes, Simba Leader reported the rest of the flight on-station. At seven minutes, Elayne Zheng found General Langston peering over her shoulder at the plot.

The new ground chief of Victoria Command looked better than when she'd last seen him, an hour after he'd acquired the job. Then he'd looked twenty years older. Now he only looked ten.

Langston put on a head set. "Simba Leader, this is Swivel Mount. How long can you remain on station?"

"We're throttled back to the max now, Swivel Mount. You want us to move in, we'll need a drink afterward."

"What about grounding?"

"Where's the nearest secure area?"

Zheng saw Langston frown, but she liked Simba Leader's spirit. It was part of the true faith of those who flew, not to let themselves be pushed around by groundpounders no matter what their rank.

Meanwhile, she was already interrogating the computer and coming up with an answer to the last question. Light attackers, like any other lift vehicle, could ground on any piece of reasonably level and stable ground. But grounded, they were not just easy but helpless targets.

She was about to give a discouraging reply when Langston spoke again. "We'll provide one, with fuel. Can you stay on station for thirty-five minutes with a margin for combat?"

"That's affirmative, Swivel Mount. What shall we look for?"

From Langston's description, Zheng gathered that the rumored Quick Reaction Force was now reality. Eight heavy attackers, four carrying an infantry force, two loaded for ground attack, and two probably loaded with fuel, extra power packs, and anything else to make such an air-ground team independent.

It made sense. After one air strike had chopped a company fine enough for mu shu pork, the rebels were dispersing. They were also trying to look like civilians or at least stay close enough to civilians to discourage the use of heavy firepower. This made the Federation's find-fix-flatten sequence harder to carry out.

So Simba Flight would circle the rebels until either they moved out, they opened fire, or the QRF arrived. In the first two cases, Simba Flight would do its own shooting. In the last case, it would be part of the tac air support for the riflemen, as they went on the ground and tried to draw fire.

After that, there were so many possible combinations and permutations that Zheng was glad she didn't have to work through them. For a moment her sense of the flier's superiority to the ground fighter slipped.

High-tech wasn't the only way to make a battle complicated. It took something special to face those complications with only the weapons in your hands and the organic computer in your head.

At twelve minutes, Zheng put the QRF on the plot. For the next five, she watched its attackers burning sky.

At eighteen minutes, she heard a door squeal and running feet. A lieutenant she knew only by sight ran down between the consoles.

"Everybody get your sidearms and body armor on. Now!"

A chorus that amounted to variations of "What the devil?" drowned out anything else the lieutenant said. She raised her voice nearly to a scream.

"The Vics have infiltrated our sector. They've got sapper and sniper teams on the way now. We have to be ready to defend here!"

Zheng was still staring at the lieutenant as she fumbled her pistol out from under her console. She was rummaging for her helmet and armor as more doors squealed and slammed. Then lights came up on all consoles and messages on all screens.

WARNING. WARNING. WARNING. SECURE ALL POSITIONS FOR GROUND ATTACK, INCLUDING EXPLOSIVE AND CHEMICAL. THIS IS A SECURITY RED-PLUS ALERT FOR FORT STAFFORD. REPEAT, SECURITY RED-PLUS.

The Fort Stafford alert reached *Shenandoah* at the same time as Communications signaled an incoming message from the Seventh Force.

Aren't multiple number-one priorities a stimulating way to spend a morning? was Kuwahara's first thought.

His second was a series of orders.

"Commodore Uehara is OTC until further notice. Fort Stafford security has priority claim on all Navy forces. I want an update from Fort Stafford as soon as they have time, and meanwhile I'll wish them good luck. Now, put that misbegotten Tusker through."

Su-Ankrai was smiling when he came on screen, and Kuwahara's first impulse was to say something to remove the smile. He forced himself into diplomat mode instead, and smiled back.

"I trust that you are as aware as I am of the true and lawful connection of my parents," the Fleet Commander said. Kuwahara winced as he realized his last words had reached su-Ankrai. He had lost face, and the old Syrodhi were as face conscious as the people who'd started the Bad Manners Wars.

"I did not know who might be calling," Kuwahara said. "As little as I knew what connection the People might have with the events of this morning."

"None," su-Ankrai said.

"You are prepared to swear this?" That definitely crossed the borders of diplomacy, but sheer incredulity slowed Kuwahara's thought processes.

"I am prepared to swear all the oaths that it is lawful or appropriate to swear, to one who has twice insulted me."

Kuwahara decided that there was no alternative to an apology. "I ask your forgiveness. That you are not responsible for the events of this morning makes them no less unsettling."

"I would be quite unfit for my post if I thought otherwise," su-Ankrai said. That formula of humility meant that the apology was accepted. Kuwahara felt the tight bands at both temples loosen.

"I would also be unfit for my post if I did not ask you what we can do to assist in a peaceful solution of this latest crisis," su-Ankrai continued. "Our folk have not always had common goals, but I believe that on this unhappy occasion we do."

Quite true, but define "peaceful solution" before I make an offer on what you're selling.

"Have you any specific actions to propose?"

"One action we will refrain from, and that is providing any form of assistance to the rebels. We have not done so in the past, but we will now actively prevent any of the People from procuring weapons and equipment for the rebels."

Kuwahara decided that the offer was genuine. It would also have been more generous if the first part of su-Ankrai's statement had been true. The various rebels and rabbles on Victoria had already acquired from the Baernoi enough weapons and equipment to give the Federation or at least Eleventh Zone major headaches. Lack of any further encouragement might affect of the rebels' morale.

It might also make them even more desperate. Considering what had happened to the Bonsai Squadron, and what was now happening at Fort Stafford, Kuwahara was inclined to the second theory. At least unarmed desperation was better than armed desperation, and su-Ankrai was offering to help in that.

"Before we discuss anything more," Kuwahara said, "may I ask if you have communicated with Admiral Uzel?"

"Yes."

"What did he say?"

"He said that since this rebellion was no threat to the interests of the Alliance, he needed no help in dealing with any aspect of it."

Kuwahara decided to have that checked, if possible, and also provide Uzel with a recording of the discussion with su-Ankrai. "I cannot say that this rebellion is no threat to us, but I am not sure that we need help beyond what you have already offered."

"What about assisting the Merishi and other neutrals?"

Kuwahara was glad that he had enough traditional training to keep his face blank as surprise surged back and forth inside. The Merishi! Was that a lucky guess, or had something—or somebody—leaked?

Kuwahara knew that question had to be settled privately. The job now was to toss su-Ankrai's grenade back before it exploded in his hands.

"We know very little about the situation of the Merishi outside Silvermouth. In fact, we don't even know that there are any. There may be some refugees, but I'm afraid our intelligence sources are rather thin on the ground in Silvermouth at the moment.

"However, I think a joint approach to the territorial government of Seven Rivers would be useful. We will have to consult with them regardless, and they will probably be more receptive to a joint approach."

"Of course, that will also make it harder for either of us to make a separate agreement," su-Ankrai said. He was smiling again, and the smile was the twin of the one he'd worn first.

This time, though, Kuwahara knew why the Baernoi admiral was smiling. He thought he had made it impossible for the humans to establish direct contacts with the Merishi.

He might have, if it wasn't for those Merishi refugees. They were a card Kuwahara hoped was still up his sleeve. While the two naval squadrons were arguing with Hollings, Uzel, Fegeli, and anybody else with the breath to spare, the Federation and Associated States could make an agreement with their own Merishi.

That would open them to accusations of bad faith from the Baernoi. Kuwahara thought that was a fair exchange, if the Baernoi were going to reopen their contacts with the Merishi in Seven Rivers, who were a good part of their intelligence assets.

Best of all, nothing had been said about Merishi outside Silvermouth. With reasonable luck, nothing would be said, until the Federation was ready to act on behalf of those Merishi—defining *act* to suit its own interests.

That action would carry some weight, if it saved Merishi merchants from the consequences of their warriors' plots. Unless the Merishi had gone from a mercentile to a warrior culture while the human race's back was turned, the weight might be decisive.

"I propose that we communicate this proposal to Admiral Uzel," Kuwahara said. "I doubt that we need to consider details until we have his approval."

"Or at least know his true opinion," su-Ankrai said.

The two admirals nodded in unison. On the subject of their Alliance counterpart, they were entirely in agreement.

Fifteen

Brian Mahoney crouched behind the boulder as the lifter settled in front of the cave. Much more of this crouching, and his limbs and joints would be as stiff as they'd been when he woke this morning. Then he'd felt as if he was made of glass, and would shatter if he moved, let alone hurried.

It all came from the shortage of lift, which kept the 3rd Platoon and its advisers in the cave overnight. That, and the fact that Mahoney didn't quite trust the Vics. So he ordered that the advisers sleep separately, not in their sleeping bags (which could be hard to get out of), and with two of the five on watch at all times.

Like a good C.O., Mahoney took his share of the hardships and duty. So he woke up with most of the warmth leached out of his body, unable to fight the fatigue toxins that lack of sleep had pumped into his system.

Hot tea was just beginning to thaw him when word of the Thorntonsburg assassinations and the new rebellion reached the camp. Between garbling, panic, and the usual Victorian poor reception in rough terrain, it was hard to tell exactly what had happened and impossible to guess what might come next.

To do them justice, none of the Vics looked happy. (They may have taken one look at Brigitte Tachin's face and decided that if they did, they'd be dead on the spot.) Most of them looked apprehensive. Their discipline, which had impressed Mahoney the night before, now seemed to desert them. It was as much as Langwell could do to get sentries posted and their area of the cave policed up.

After that he came over to Mahoney, lit an aromatic, and sat down without an invitation. "I'd guess a hard core of about ten, twelve loyalists, who think this rebellion's crazy," he said. "The next group's the ones who are afraid of Federation retaliation. Not anything you five'll do, mind you, but the others. Rumors are all over, about those two brigades being on the way."

"Just because we have the muscle for a brute-force solution, does that mean we'll do it?" Brigitte asked indignantly. "They know the Federation's record."

"Yeah, and they also know that anybody's patience can run out. They're afraid you Feddies may be at that point. Honestly, Lieutenant, you scared *me* an hour ago."

"Sorry," Brigitte said.

"Then there's the ones who basically support the rebellion, mostly Action for Independence people. The problem is, they know they're way out at the back of beyond if they start anything. They're afraid to commit suicide by starting something. They're also afraid that if the rebels win, those self-appointed A.I. commissars will kill them for not getting killed."

"*Merde,*" Brigitte said. She looked hard at Langwell. "And what side are you on, Lieutenant?"

"I'm on the side of keeping the platoon together. If we don't, people on all sides will be killed and *all* the deaths will be stupid. I didn't sign on with the militia for that."

"We didn't sign up with the Navy for that, either," Mahoney said. He put out a hand for one of Langwell's aromatics.

Before he could light up, the radio operator reported the lifter flight inbound, ETA seven minutes. Then she reported that Fort Stafford had declared a Security Red-Plus Alert and gone off the air. Before anybody could raise an eyebrow over that, let alone a weapon, a sentry shouted that they had an incoming lifter flight.

"Five minutes too early," Mahoney said. "Lieutenant Langwell, we'd better assume hostiles."

Langwell saluted. Mahoney decided that his command presence must be improving, if his advice could draw a salute.

Certainly the platoon's discipline was back on line. They trooped out fast enough to be concealed all around the cave mouth with a minute to spare.

The only people left in the cave were three Vics and Brigitte Tachin, volunteers to defend the supplies from inside. They had the best protective gear, and Mahoney knew without being told that Brigitte had a deadman switch that would detonate the ammunition rather than let it fall into rebel hands.

He told himself that her sense of duty would allow nothing less, and that he would almost certainly be dead himself before she blasted the cave. Both were true; neither consoled.

At thirty seconds to the ETA three lifters entered the valley, flying raggedly two hundred meters up. They were all civilian models with improvised armament and carried a weird mixture of camouflage and civilian finishes. Their insignia mixed the Bushranger hat and the gold crown of the Associated States, and altogether they made very little sense.

They certainly didn't seem to expect a fight. They hovered, then grounded as raggedly as they'd flown, fifty meters downhill from the cave mouth. The top gunners manned their weapons and swung them around so enthusiastically that Mahoney wanted to duck.

Then the rear door of one lifter opened and two men climbed out, one short and dark, the other taller and blond. The blond man cupped his hands, and shouted in a familiar stentorian roar:

"Hey, anybody home?"

"The doorbell's not working," Mahoney shouted as he rose from cover and waved.

There were a number of impossible things, even on a world gone mad like Victoria. Two of them were that Dr. Somtow Nosavan and Lucco DiVries could be on the side of this latest rebellion. Correction: Colonel Somtow Nosavan and Captain Lucco DiVries, Associated States Medical Corps.

"How can you get anything done with such lousy maintenance?" DiVries shouted. Then he was running toward Mahoney, and around Mahoney the militia were rising from hiding, gaping at the new arrivals.

"You're going to need more than this," Mahoney said when he got his breath back after DiVries pounded him on the back. "You wouldn't believe what's in there."

"Oh, yes, we would," Nosavan said. "We were supposed to get a second flight, but I don't know what will happen to that with the Fort Stafford situation. They're still off the air," he added.

Mahoney felt so light-headed at seeing friends at his back that he only shrugged. "Ready for the two-stellar tour?"

"Bloody hell!" Governor-General Gist swore. "I tell them we need a new Provost Marshal for Thorntonsburg. They promise to send one from 215 Brigade but can't promise when he'd be here. I ask what about using an attacker, and they say they can't promise Navy assets until control is shifted completely to *Shenandoah*."

Gist slumped into his chair, which creaked under his weight. "I didn't bother to ask when that would be, or tell them what to do with themselves. Wasn't I being nice, Major Morley?"

"Under the circumstances, yes, sir," Morley said.

"When you start being tactful to your superior officers, I start to worry. I thought the regulars could shift C-cubed instantly. At least that's what my tactics liaison always said."

"So did my instructors," Morley said. "I suppose they both read the same manuals."

"Manuals!" Gist made the word sound like a particularly revolting sexual deviation. "I'd like to trade places with one of those manual writers. Just for an hour, please God!"

Morley would have gladly done the same, for considerably longer. Freezing her thigh wound had done no more than force her to work sitting down, but the scalp wound and the aftermath of shock had left her dizzy, nauseated, and generally a great deal less interested in the world than she ought to be if she was acting Provost Marshal of Thorntonsburg.

From Gist's last conversation, she not only was, she would have to stay that way for a few more hours at least—while the only Federation force around Victoria that didn't already have too much on their plates already was the Navy heavy ships. The heavy ships, twenty thousand kilometers overhead and as useless to Thorntonsburg as if it had been twenty thousand light-years.

General Parkinson stirred in her corner of the office. It held a desk and chair, a terminal with displays, and a second chair that now held Commander Franke. The commander

was now acting as a combination of chief of staff, aide, and
secretary to this highly improvised command group, so he
hadn't spent much time sitting down.

"If you're not fit for duty, Major, I can appoint someone
from the JAG's department or even the Ministry of Justice," Parkinson said. "My powers of appointment extend
that far in an emergency."

"Your choice would have to be approved by Admiral
Kuwahara, if they were to have any authority over Federation personnel," Morley said. Unspoken and unspeakable
was everybody's question: Would Kuwahara approve? Or
did his suspicion of Parkinson because of her lucky escape
extend too far?

Morley had heard the suspicion in Kuwahara's voice the
last two times he called, and knew the admiral had explanation if not excuse. She was more worried about delayed
reactions setting in with Parkinson, starting with survivor
guilt.

Loaning Franke to Parkinson, to give her a massage and a
stiff drink, might work. Franke had a wonderfully soothing
presence when you could persuade him to stop talking or
at least use short sentences.

*But she is a two-star general, even if she's a Vic. There is
such a thing as* lèse-majesté, *even in an emergency*. Morley
decided that the idea was her own delayed reactions setting
in.

"I can manage for a few more hours," Morley said. "In
fact, if you can set up another terminal I can take some of
the phone-answering work off Herman's shoulders. There
won't be too many orders to give until we decide about
moving into Parrville."

The Thorntonsburg MPs were divided among security
teams for VIPs and major installations, the *cordon sanitaire*
around Parrville, and a handful deployed with the Third
Battalion to handle any prisoners it took. Morley had no
reserves and in fact work for twice as many people as she
had under her. She knew enough not to trouble her subordinates with unnecessary calls just because she felt nervous
and sore.

"You can use mine," Parkinson said. "I think I'm going
to lie down for a few minutes. If I don't feel better after
that, Jere, I will see the doctor. Word of honor."

Gist gave Parkinson a not-quite-brotherly pat on the rear and pushed Morley's chair over. It was a good thing she was in place, because calls started pouring in.

Inspector Gehvru and Lieutenant Blaise reported that Government House was secure and all prisoners and casualties were being dealt with appropriately.

The Minister of Defense, who'd survived an assassination attempt in his house, reported from Port Harriet. All was orderly, except for a few posters and one inflammatory speech that died under heckling from the audience.

"I think most of the hotheads went north with the Fourth Battalion last year or joined the spearhead in Thorntonsburg," he added. "If we can slip a few more regulars in here, we should do fine."

Morley didn't remember what she said. On even the most secure line, she didn't want to discuss troop dispositions, particularly when they would be pure bad news to somebody in the minister's position.

President Glicksohn wanted to report to the armory and complain about the Special Branch people interrogating her staff without her knowledge. Morley promised to provide secure transport as soon as possible and inform the chief of Special Branch about the complaint.

Father Brothertongue, who'd been missing since last night, reappeared at his parish church. He said he had six hundred and fifty refugees from Parrville with him, most of them needing food. Could the provisional government assist him?

"I wish Brothertongue could make up his mind whether he's a priest or a politician," Gist muttered. He cut the sound off Brothertongue's call and turned to the others.

"If he's been in and around Parrville since last night, I'm damned sure he knew more about those bloody twits of rebels than he told us. I'm also damned sure he did his best to talk them out of it. I'm for giving him what he wants."

Franke nodded. Morley had discovered that nodding made her head feel like a low-order grenade explosion, so she only raised her eyebrows.

"I'd suggest that he give the refugees half an hour to dispose of any weapons, no questions asked," she added. "That should keep any hothead from causing an incident."

"That also implies an amnesty for the Parrvillers," Franke pointed out.

"What alternative is there?" Morley asked. "There are thirty thousand people in the cordoned area. We don't have the resources to do anything to any of them unless they're caught armed and resisting."

Gist turned to the screen with the expression of a man with acute diarrhea and cut in the sound. Morley saw Brothertongue grin.

"—calling us a provisional government," Gist concluded, "so why don't you come in and help us proclaim it. Judy will be over here by the time you've fed your strayed sheep, so all we'll need is Karras."

"He may find it hard to get back south until the shooting stops at Fort Stafford," the priest said.

"How the hell—" Gist began.

"I'm afraid I've been eavesdropping on the military frequencies," the priest said. "Not decoding anything, but there's been enough traffic in clear to let me draw my own conclusions."

Again Morley heard something in a man's voice that she didn't want to put into words. Again Gist seemed to hear the same, and he had no such inhibitions.

"Father Brothertongue. If you know something about Senator Karras that you're not telling us, I want to know what it is and how you learned it. *Now!*"

"Are you asking me to break the seal of the confessional?"

Gist looked ready to ask much more than that, but only snarled wordlessly. "Is it under that seal?"

"Not all of it—" Brothertongue began.

An alarm shrilled, making Morley start and jar her head. Through surging waves of pain and nausea, she realized that it was only an emergency call coming in. She saw Franke switch on the audio and heard a frantic voice say:

"Fort Stafford to all Federation units. Fort Stafford to all Federation units. Rebels led by Senator Karras have seized the base hospital and are holding hostages. I repeat, rebels have seized the base hospital." A deep breath that was almost a sob. "Communications are expected to be impaired within a few minutes. The rebels' demands are on the way here by messenger and may include a communications blackdown.

"Repeating: the Fort Stafford hospital has been seized by rebels under Senator Karras. They are holding hostages. Victoria Command is now under a Red-Plus Security Alert. Victoria Command is now under a Red-Plus Security Alert."

Gist's mouth worked silently, and Morley looked at the screen. Father Brothertongue had both hands over his face, and tears were trickling out between his fingers.

Two minutes before Senator Karras entered her office, Colonel Chatterje was sitting at her desk. That was in fact precisely where she was supposed to be during a Red-Plus Security Alert, unless she was actually performing surgery.

She hadn't been on the roster for this morning, and if she had she would have taken herself off. The first shock of Mikhail's death had worn off; the aftershocks were yet to come. Right now she felt a hollow place somewhere inside, where Mikhail had been. Around the edges of that place burned raw pain that made her hands shake and her nose run.

She had told herself several times what she'd told the staff when the bomb victims from Buschton came in. "Take care of yourself, or you can't take care of anybody else."

Part of taking care of yourself, for her or any doctor, was to accept that you weren't omnipotent, that even the death of someone you loved wasn't a professional failure, that there would always be some people you couldn't have saved any more than you could have saved Alexander the Great. (The speech ran through her mind like an endlessly replayed holodrama, and by now it produced boredom edged with nausea.)

She opened the desk drawer, eased the printed chart of the Alert Stations out from under her sidearm, shut the drawer, and unfolded the chart. The display on the far wall matched the chart impressively well; her hospital people seemed to be taking this emergency in their stride.

Part of it was the good news coming in, half of it maybe rumors or exaggerations but much more than half of it good. The sappers and snipers had been stopped well short of anything vital, let alone the hospital. The Victorian mili-

tia hadn't contributed many people to the rebels; most of
the weapons they'd given had been taken at gunpoint. The
hard core of the rebels in Fort Stafford was less than a
hundred people with small-arms at most, and a battalion of
regulars could take care of that even without a plan.

They had a plan, though—Mikhail's doing, even if Langston was executing it—and plenty of time to execute it
before nightfall. She only hoped there wouldn't be too many
more casualties. The hospital was at full stretch already, the
trauma center beyond it, intensive care approaching that
point, and Federation casualties from the fighting in the out-
back and Thorntonsburg hadn't even started coming in yet.

It was time to start considering if they could shift some
of the less serious Buschton cases over to secure civilian
facilities—

The door chime sounded.

"Come in."

Major Barkuss, the chief of administration, entered, followed by an orderly. Barkuss was sweating and pale. Surely
escorting Senator Karras couldn't be that hard—

Then the orderly stepped out from behind Barkuss, showing the pistol aimed at Barkuss's stomach and the grenade
in his hand. Behind him Karras loomed up, and behind
Karras three of the senator's staff and a mixed collection of
staff, ambulatory patients, and civilians.

By the time they were all in Chatterje's office, it was
packed to the walls and nearly to the ceiling. The colonel
kept her hands in plain sight on her desk; she could not
keep them from shaking.

This was clearly a hostage situation, but who was behind
it?

"Well?"

"Action for Independence," someone said harshly. The
orderly signaled for silence and stepped forward. Now his
weapon was pointed at the colonel.

"We have you and about twenty of your staff and patients
under our guns. We can add more any time we please. We
want you to send a message to the fort's com center, and
have it broadcast. The message will give our terms.

"If they are met, nobody will be hurt. If they are not,
two hours from now we start shooting hostages."

Chatterje couldn't keep the contempt out of her voice.

"You know Federation doctrine on hostages as well as I do. You've destroyed your own basis for negotiation."

"How would you like to be raped on a planetwide broadcast?" the same harsh voice came again.

Chatterje's voice grew colder. "What a disgusting idea, even if you could get it—"

The orderly slapped her hard across the face. "Enough!"

"Please, Colonel, don't provoke them any further," Karras said. He was paler than Barkuss and looked about ready to faint. His eyes refused to focus on Chatterje.

"I suppose this—"

Another slap, this time hard enough to make her ears ring and drive teeth into her upper lip. Chatterje sucked at the blood, wishing she dared spit it in the leader's face.

"Write the message, right away, and only what I dictate. Otherwise we kill a hostage now."

Chatterje forced her voice to be both steady and mild. "I still think you're making a mistake."

"Are we, Colonel?" one of Karras's staff said. "I know Federation doctrine and tactics. But some of the hostages aren't Federation personnel. What's the law on them?

"And what's the law about doctors who endanger their patients? Five hundred Buschton bomb victims down there, all ready for a lungful of sleep gas when the Feddies come in. How many of them will wake up?"

Chatterje decided that if she ever had a chance she would castrate Karras and his too-bright staffer before she worked on the others. The pig was right. Lung-damaged patients wouldn't survive. Neither would those on untended life-support equipment in the trauma and intensive-care sections.

Call it forty or fifty dead at a minimum. Forty or fifty dead Victorians, already innocent victims of their world's madness but still with a chance to live that she would be taking away if she went by the rules. She and the troopers.

Federation personnel weren't the main hostages here. The main hostages were her patients, and regulations, Hippocratic Oath, and common humanity bound her hands as far as endangering them. For now.

Chatterje took a deep breath. "I commend you on your sound reasoning. I have no intention of doing or leaving undone anything that would endanger your fellow Victorians." She opened her notepad and pulled it toward her. "What do you want me to write?"

The leader cleared his throat. "We, the people of Victoria, as represented by Action for Independence, make the following nonnegotiable demands—"

Colonel Nosavan's arrival boosted morale for several hours.

"Permission to address the men?" he asked Mahoney.

Mahoney looked around for Nosavan's Federation adviser, until he saw DiVries beginning to fidget, then glower. Presumably full colonels in the Associated States Medical Corps were trusted to wander around without Federation keepers.

Finally Nosavan nodded. "Show him our orders, Lucco."

The orders passed every authentication Mahoney was in a position to give them. If he wanted to cover his ass completely, he could wait until both atmospheric and tactical conditions let him get a confirmation from a higher headquarters. If he wanted to get anything done, he would stop worrying about his ass.

Mahoney saluted. "Go ahead, sir."

Nosavan waited until the demo team from the cave arrived, then spoke briefly. Orders had been changed, he said. This supply dump was still going to be confiscated, but it would be turned over to the Second Brigade, Associated States Forces.

Most of the platoon favored Victorian independence and thought kindly of the Bushrangers for leading the way. Knowing that the supplies were now going straight to fellow Victorians instead of to Federation dumps where they might sit until "Feddie clerks" divided them up was pure good news.

Everyone promptly turned to, unloading and assembling the lift pallets and shoehorning them into the cave. With no hands-on work and little supervising to do, Mahoney had time for a chat with DiVries.

"You didn't make a lot of points, wondering if the colonel could be trusted," DiVries began.

"I wasn't after points. I was after doing my job, which is not necessarily to hand confiscated supplies over to any and every high-ranking Vic who wanders through."

He pointed at DiVries's carbine and ammunition pouches. "Speaking of points, you won't score many with some of our hardheads, going armed."

"Nosavan's packing too. We have the feeling that this—" he tapped his MedCorps arm band, "means 'cheap kill' to some of the people out there." He waved his hand at the grim hills.

"I see. So, you're going armed on doctor's orders?"

"Ugh. I see your sense of humor hasn't improved."

"Lucco, has anything happened on this godforsaken— sorry, on Victoria—lately, to improve anybody's sense of humor?"

"You have a point. And if you get *La Tachin* to give you a good haircut, nobody will be able to see it."

They stood for a moment, the wind whistling between them. Then Mahoney held out his hand.

"Sorry. And sorry about Ray."

Lucco shrugged. "I wish I could say he wasn't asking for it, but he was. Ray couldn't have been the man who raised me, to tie up with those damned fools. He couldn't have been the man 'Reesa married, either."

"Hey, you guys going to play landmark or pitch in?" somebody shouted. Mahoney saw that the first pallet, loaded high with crates, was already wobbling out of the cave. Even at this distance, he could see the Baernoi design of some of the containers.

"Coming," he replied, and led DiVries uphill to the grounded lifter.

The scheduled flight came in only a little later. With four lifters shuttling back and forth to the base, the cave was emptied quickly. More than the containers were Baernoi, Mahoney noticed, and some of the human-applied markings suggested AD weaponry or at least sensors.

Three more lifters arrived at the same time as the news of the hostages at Fort Stafford. At least that was what Mahoney *thought* he heard; the transmission was fragmentary to begin with and garbled the rest of the way.

Each of the new lifters had a four-man crew, two Vics and two advisers. Mahoney noted that the advisers all looked like seasoned groundpounders, and one of them was a master sergeant even if she didn't look old enough to vote.

"I suggest that if we offload half the crew of these lifters, they'll be able to carry more cargo," Mahoney announced. "One adviser and one Vic apiece, if that will leave them a full crew."

"It will," the sergeant said. Her look dared anyone, regardless of rank, planet, or species, to argue with her. Langwell looked wounded and motioned for Mahoney to step aside.

"You don't trust my people," he said petulantly.

Mahoney tried to hold on to both his temper and his good opinion of Langwell. "I swear by all the saints you've ever heard of and the rest as well, I trust your people. None of them are vicious or mad, and the—" epithets failed him, "individuals at Fort Stafford are both.

"What I don't trust is whoever may be out there. I have a nasty feeling we'll be out here another night, what with priority going to settling the hostage situation. If the people out there wander in, wanting their supplies—well, all the infantry-trained people we could get might not be too much."

Langwell sounded acquiescent rather than enthusiastic, but didn't protest or let anyone in his platoon do so. The three lifters filled quickly, and in twenty minutes the hillside was empty except for Nosavan's machine and a few Vics taking a smoke break.

Two minutes after that, they saw a liftscooter approaching up the valley. One look from the sergeant gathered up her troops and they seemed to sink into the ground while Mahoney blinked.

The scooter was an old one and barely made the climb up to the cave. Two men dismounted, while a third tried to handle an SSW with one hand and the controls with the other. His struggles might have been humorous, except for the look in his friends' eyes as they approached Nosavan's lifter.

"Good morning," the colonel said. He didn't take his eyes off the men, but shook his head when Mahoney rested a hand on his pistol. Mahoney relaxed, remembering the sergeant.

"Good morning," the taller man said. "All this belongs to Action for Independence. Hand it over peacefully, and we won't arrest you."

In spite of the situation and the tone, Mahoney wanted to laugh. Again Nosavan shook his head.

"I would like to oblige you," he said, as if commenting on the weather. "But I have no authority to turn over the property of the Associated States Forces to Action for Independence. Particularly not now, when your name has been mentioned in connection with the hostage-taking at Fort Stafford."

"Slim, show him our authority." The liftscooter pilot grounded his machine and hoisted the SSW.

Nosavan smiled. "That requisition is not in proper form, I'm afraid." Then both face and tone turned sober, even grim. "I warn you. The hostage-taking threatens to make Action for Independence total outlaws, even in the eyes of your fellow Victorians. The best course of action for you is to stop worrying about these supplies."

"Surrender and be bounced around by the Feddies?" the pilot shouted.

"Yes, except that I'm sure some sort of amnesty will be negotiated, once the hostages are free. If you surrender now, we can testify that—"

The SSW man raised his weapon a few centimeters and shot Dr. Nosavan in the chest.

Sixteen

The playback of Colonel Chatterje's broadcast of the Action for Independence demands faded into a dark screen and a silent room.

Gist was the first to break the silence. As Major Morley expected, it was with an oath.

Then he seemed to get himself under control. "Of all the bloody cheek! A free lift for all their people up to the Baernoi squadron, and political asylum! I suppose it didn't occur to one of those towering intellects that the Tuskers might not have room for them? Or be willing to take them, if they had room?"

"I would estimate that the Baernoi will consider it, maybe—" Franke began.

"Who asked you?" Gist muttered.

Franke continued. "The Baernoi may even offer at least temporary asylum, while they pressure us to negotiate with the A.I. Apart from the political value of being seen to help their friends, the A.I. people would be a mine of intelligence about Victoria. I doubt if the Baernoi have abandoned hopes of influencing an independent Victoria."

That, Morley decided, was an understatement even for Franke.

"Well, we can fry their circuits one way right now," Gist said. "We can offer an amnesty if the hostages are given up within a specific time."

"Sir—Your Excellency—anyway, you can't do that," Morley said. "You are still legally an appointee of the Federation authorities. That means you cannot violate Federation policy in hostage situations."

"I can resign."

"You can resign, of course," Franke put in. "But if you resign as governor-general, you hold no authority that

Major Morley and I can recognize, unless we are ordered to do so by Admiral Kuwahara. I doubt if he will give us those orders. In fact, I am sure he will order us to leave at once if you proclaim an amnesty."

"Then leave and be damned!"

"If they leave, I'm leaving with them," General Parkinson said.

"Alys!"

"That is a nonnegotiable demand, to quote someone or other," Parkinson said.

"Jere, are your ambitions running away with you?" President Glicksohn added. "I agree with Alys."

"Christ!" Gist said. "What's this business of my ambitions all of a sudden, Judy? Do they run into yours?"

"I don't have any ambitions," Glicksohn said, and Morley heard real anger in her voice for the first time. "I just have a few ideas about what kind of planet I want this to be after the shooting starts. One where the Federation is hostile, the Baernoi are overhead, and those A.I. bastards think they can get away with murder isn't my homeworld. Or it won't be."

"All right," Gist said heavily. "I was thinking out loud, anyway."

And the Pope keeps a harem, Morley thought.

"So scratch the amnesty, at least until we've freed the hostages," Gist went on. "Now, does anybody have any suggestions other than nailing my hide to the wall?"

Lu, you're the closest thing to an expert here, even if you don't have a business case and aren't from off-planet.

"I'm going by Colonel Chatterje's face and tone when she used that phrase about 'a gallant handful of men.' I think she intended that as a message. The A.I. people at Fort Stafford *are* a handful."

"So?" Gist said. "A handful with the guns are still a menace to an army without them."

"Our army isn't exactly without guns, and neither is yours," Morley said. "The problem is winning back the freedom to use them. That means eliminating the danger to the hostages.

"If they are a handful, we could mount a penetration effort," Parkinson said. "It would have to be hasty, and we'd have to pick people with an eye to secrecy rather than skill—"

"I'm volunteering anyway," Morley said. "So there's one skilled member."

"Lu!" Franke exploded.

"Down, Herman," Morley said. "Consider what a perfect disguise I have, being on crutches—no, better yet. On a stretcher. I've collapsed suddenly, you see."

"Yes, and if you're covered in blankets, so nobody can see—"

"Herman, you're even more devious than I am. Does the Institute know that?"

"Confidentiality rules—" Franke began, when Gist erupted again.

"Hold it! Just hold it there a bloody minute! You're about four light-years ahead of me and I'm trying to catch up." He took a deep breath.

"It sounds like you're planning some sort of penetration stunt, to take out the command group. Fine, if we can come up with the right people on a hasty basis. But what about the others?"

"My estimate is that there won't be enough others to do major damage," Morley said. "Colonel Chatterje was giving us that clue."

"That's more of a guess than an estimate," Gist said. "Your best guess?"

Morley nodded. Her throat was suddenly too dry for speech. Knowing that she would be among the dead if she'd guessed wrong really didn't help as much as she'd expected.

"This also assumes that the A.I. people will let us anywhere near their leaders," Glicksohn pointed out.

"Judy, look at the logistics," Parkinson said. "Even if the Baernoi say yes in the next ten minutes, it will take days to get the people and the transport together. A lot of the details will have to be negotiated face-to-face. If we send a negotiating team, the A.I.s will think we're meeting them at least halfway."

"That's violating Federation doctrine all over again," Gist said. "Or is it?"

"We will need Admiral Kuwahara's permission," Franke said judiciously. "But we don't need to describe the real nature of the operation. Sending a team in to see if the people have lost their nerve is acceptable. He'll probably think we're planning that."

"We certainly don't tell him otherwise," Morley added. "The Baernoi are undoubtedly monitoring all channels—"

"I know something about basic communications security," Gist said. "I will even observe it. But what I want to know is, what if Kuwahara says no?"

Morley and Franke exchanged looks. "Then we'll have to go without his permission."

Gist slapped his forehead. "Bloody hell! First you're ready to slit my throat if Kuwahara says so. Then you'll risk a court-martial to obey me instead of him. Do you people have any respect for senior officers at all?"

"Yes, sir," Morley said. "We have great respect for their ability to clear obstacles out of the path of the people who actually have to do the work."

Gist turned red, started another round of cursing, then collapsed over his desk, choking with laughter. Parkinson joined him, then Glicksohn, then, discreetly, Franke.

Morley didn't laugh. For one thing, it made her head hurt. For another, she had to get started, finding out who was in the armory or going to be coming there in the next hour or two, that she could grab for the team.

Dr. Nosavan's death produced immediate and near universal paralysis among those who watched it.

Fortunately one of the people who wasn't paralyzed was Brian Mahoney. Even more fortunately, he was only half a meter from the corner of the lifter. He lunged for that corner, dragging one companion and pushing another.

That gave one of the other unparalyzed watchers a clear shot at the scooter rider. A pulser droned and a burst of solid slugs flipped the rider one way and the SSW the other.

That exchange of fire unfroze everyone, which did not help the killers. The leader stood his ground and died firing a chem carbine from the hip; the last tried to run, found no cover on the open slope, and died when Mahoney among others got his range and sent him sprawling in a patch of bloody gravel.

"What the devil did they do that for?" Mahoney asked the empty air.

From her hiding place up the hill the sergeant shouted, "They probably thought the rest of the platoon would come over if they killed the doc."

"Dumb—"

"No, you're a bunch of goddamned traitors!" a man screamed. "Now we—"

Three people jumped on the man at once, the only thing that saved him from being shot down on the spot. Mahoney's and the sergeant's shots both flew over the tangle on the ground. A moment later the tangle sorted itself out, as two of the militia stood up and let Lieutenant Langwell pound the man's head on the ground until it was bloody and he was quiet.

Langwell stood up, shaking and holding red-smeared hands out in front of him. "Sorry, I got carried—"

His apology ended as the ridgeline above them sprouted running figures. Mahoney was raising his binoculars when he heard the ridgeline sentries opening fire. Too late for them, maybe, but not too late to warn their friends below.

Everybody who hadn't found something to get behind found one in the next moment. One of the regulars popped out of his hiding place and snatched up the fallen SSW. While this happened, the attackers overran the two sentries and committed themselves to a rush down the open hillside.

They had more than two hundred meters ahead of them, bare rock with a few patches of snow and at least one of ice that sent three people sprawling. Two of them got up again, just in time to be knocked back down by the fire from below.

Half of the Vics were good shots but none of them needed to be. The marksmen simply speeded up the inevitable. By the time the ridge assault was reduced to a dozen limp forms on the hillside, Mahoney's wits had recovered.

"Ah, Lieutenant Langwell. I think we should replace the sentries on top of the ridge. Also, do you have anyone who can take the lifter up for a recon?"

"I can," DiVries said. His tone didn't allow argument. Mahoney nodded.

"Just play observer, not gunship."

DiVries and Nosavan's other bodyguard scrambled into the lifter. Its fans wound up, then the field came on and it lurched into the air. As the whine of the fans faded, Mahoney heard the sergeant cursing, cajoling, and threatening a squad or so of militia up toward the ridge.

Between Mahoney's suggestions and the sergeant's more

forceful methods, the platoon got itself organized. Brigitte and a work party vanished into the cave, to reappear with a pallet hastily loaded with a job lot of supplies. The platoon's medic started collecting and treating the wounded. By the time DiVries landed, even Lieutenant Langwell was giving orders in an almost firm voice.

"Back of the hill's clear, as far as I could see," DiVries reported. "There's a bunch of people around the second bend in the valley, about two kloms away. They don't look friendly."

"Any heavy weapons?"

"Couldn't see any, but you said not to get too close."

Mahoney hadn't said that, but he wasn't going to argue interpretation of orders now. Not when DiVries had another order coming that he was going to like even less than the first one.

"Okay, Lucco. This is as close to an order as I can make it. Load the wounded and one medic on that lifter and haul out of here."

"I have another score to settle with those bastards now," DiVries said. He didn't seem to trust himself to say more.

Mahoney gripped DiVries by both shoulders. "Lucco, by everything you want me to swear by, I'll swear to let you join us for the next fight. Right now, we need to get the wounded and a report out. You're the best man for both."

"Can you swear there's going to be a next fight?" DiVries's face was now harsher than his voice.

"We've found organized rebels where we didn't expect any. I doubt that the ones we've seen are the only ones."

"My thinking exactly. So take care, Brian. There might not be enough rebels to pay for a *third* friend."

Two of the wounded turned out to be able to ride shotgun, so the lifter took off with four crew, six casualties, and three friendly KIA. Mahoney watched it fly out of sight, then turned to what he supposed had to be called his "command group"—Langwell, Brigitte Tachin, and Sergeant Stuck. (At least that was the name on her battledress.)

"I think we want to cover both the ridge and the cave entrance," Mahoney said.

"That's spreading us pretty thin," Stuck said.

"Yeah, but we don't want to just give the cave to the rebs or blow it now."

"Why don't I set up the cave for three modes—booby trap, command-detonated, and time-fused?" Brigitte said. "That way if we have to pull in our horns, we'll still be pretty sure the rebels won't get the supplies."

"Maybe the supplies will even get the rebels," Langwell said.

They all laughed much longer than the joke really needed.

The subdued conversation between Gist and Admiral Kuwahara suddenly erupted in a blast that raised echoes.

"If you had any balls, Kuwahara, I'd tell you to cut them off and eat them!" Gist thundered. "Franke's the best man for the job that we can get. Do you want to piss around until the Baernoi stick their thumbs into our pie?"

Franke couldn't hear the admiral's reply, but started to cross the office. He was halfway from the hostage-rescue side of the office to the strategy side when he realized he shouldn't let Kuwahara know he was even here.

If he wasn't officially present, Franke could pretend never to have received Kuwahara's most likely order—not to accompany the negotiating team. Otherwise he'd be guilty of direct disobedience to a lawful order, something the Shogun could hardly ignore.

He also couldn't be sure that his reasons for going weren't a rationalization for a desire to impress Lu Morley—and if it came to that, to die at her side. He did know that he'd reached the point where angst had to give way to action if anything needed doing.

"Excuse me, Jere," Father Brothertongue said. He pushed gently past Franke, positioned himself to block Kuwahara's view of the rest of the room, and signaled Franke to sit down.

"I appreciate your concern for Commander Franke's safety. But the Baernoi would be committing an act of war by kidnapping a Federation officer, or even interrogating him on any matters covered by his oaths. Action for Independence knows that if they act against the negotiating team, General Langston will order his strike force into the hospital according to doctrine.

"I think Commander Franke will be a valuable asset to

the negotiating team. Furthermore, if either of the opposing parties do threaten him, I will offer to go in his place."

Franke saw both the admiral on the screen and the governor-general at the terminal staring gape-jawed at Brothertongue. He smiled. "One of our opponents may feel that they need a high-ranking hostage. I think my rank is sufficient and I am probably the most expendable."

Gist's mouth worked silently. Kuwahara stared impassively, giving Franke the impression that he could see around corners. Finally his head jerked.

"Very well. Tell Commander Franke that if all goes well I will expect a complete report from him. If it doesn't, I swear that I will urinate on whatever the Baernoi leave of him. Is this understood?"

Gist saluted and cut the connection. Franke mouthed a silent thank-you to Brothertongue and left him with the other politicians. There was plenty of work still to be done on the operational-planning side of the room, starting with how to discreetly warn Langston to use pepper gas (QV) instead of sleep gas (SK).

QV was more violent in its effects than SK, but nonpersistent and less dangerous to the patients, if the antidote was applied in time. The antidote, eye lotion and antihistamines, could be applied by anyone with a free hand and two brain cells to guide it—which meant that the whole strike force could be turned into practical nurses if they knew in advance.

How to tell them in advance, without any A.I. sympathizers listening in? Franke wished they had a communications expert on hand, and knew of several who would be glad to come over. But all of them were people whose movements would be noticed, and even asking them leading questions might give clues to the wrong people.

He turned to Lu, to ask if she had any ideas, and saw that she was asleep. Lucky as well as tough, if she could sleep with two throbbing wounds and facing a life-or-death confrontation before sunset.

Brokeh su-Irzim had been expecting su-Lal's visit for nearly a quarter-watch before the Fleet Inquirer actually knocked on his cabin door.

"I thought we should consult and prepare a joint recommendation to the Fleet Commander," su-Lal said. He kicked the door shut and unloaded a shoulder bag full of files and jugs of beer.

"Bless you," su-Irzim said.

"For what?" su-Lal replied, looking up from his sorting. "The cooperation, the files, or the beer?"

"All of them."

"The High Lords know we'll need all three," su-Lal said, unrolling a printed chart and anchoring its corners with notepads and beer mugs. "Have you come to any conclusions?"

"About the questions we should ask, yes. Can we accommodate two thousand or more humans? If we can accommodate them, how will we transport them to orbit and feed them once we have them on board?"

"You're opposed to offering them asylum?"

"I beg you not to put words in my mouth. On the contrary. I think it would be dishonorable not to give people who have sought to serve us some chance of safety."

"It is also foolish when many of them may know what we would like to learn, or what we hope our enemies will *not* learn."

Su-Irzim hesitated. After days of cooperating with su-Lal, he still was not sure what the Fleet Inquirer had done in the early planning for the operation on Victoria. He also did not know what su-Lal would say to his own opinion, more firmly held with each passing day.

The operation on Victoria had been dangerous from the beginning. It had been foolish to discount the risk of the humans gaining control of the sunbombs, and criminal to continue the operation once it was suspected they had done so.

It would not, however, heal matters if any of the humans or Merishi who knew the deadliest secrets became desperate enough to tell all. Saving them from that desperation was now the greatest service anyone could render the People.

"I suggest we compromise," su-Irzim said. "Bring them up to orbit, but don't promise that we'll take all of them to some world out of reach of the Federation. We can certainly squeeze them in for a few days, but not for any kind of Passage voyage."

"I agree. But that only delays matters."

" 'Trouble delayed may be trouble prevented, for each trouble has its proper time.' "

"If you are going to begin quoting the Great Khudr, I am going to call the Healers."

Su-Irzim poured himself a beer. "Delay may be all we need." He called up a chart of the human dispositions. "Consider that the rebels are certainly going to lose, hostages or no hostages. They have nowhere to turn but us. Also, consider that the Associated States is going to end up ruling two-thirds of Victoria at once, and the rest as soon as the Alliance comes to its senses."

"If the Alliance is depending on Hollings, that may be a long journey."

"I doubt that Hollings is at peace with his military chiefs. I also doubt that Kuwahara is at peace with the Associated States, which is going to have to form a provisional government of some sort."

"Do I smell opportunity there?"

"The wind is blowing the right way, certainly. Suppose that we take up the rebels, then offer to recognize the provisional government in return for their giving the rebels an amnesty. Not all the rebels, of course—the foot soldiers, who would be too many to carry on Passage."

"Kuwahara might forbid that."

"Then he would be very foolishly starting a quarrel with the Victorians. His superiors would probably forbid him to do any such thing, if not relieve him outright. I hope they do not, by the way. He is a worthy opponent as well as someone whose strengths we already know.

"Besides, we have a bribe for Kuwahara and his superiors. Suppose we persuade su-Ankrai to recognize the Associated States' claim to Seven Rivers?"

Su-Lal nearly dropped his beer mug. "Persuade him to declare war on the Alliance? You have been very free with calling others mad, and now you propose this?"

"I said 'recognize a claim,' not 'assist in conquering.' The Alliance is going to give up Seven Rivers sooner or later. We simply will be telling the Federation and the Victorians that we know this, agree with it, and will befriend them in bringing it about."

Su-Lal absently ran his right thumb along his left tusk. "Very bold. That still leaves us with a few dozen or even a

few hundred human passengers, but I am sure we can find
a starship for them. Besides, not all of them need reach
their promised destination.''

That thought had been in Su-Irzim's mind as well. "Leave
that for later," he said. "Now we need to present a plan
for lifting this mob of rebels into orbit. I doubt if the
humans will let armed ships of the People land on Victoria.
I also doubt that they have enough unarmed shuttles to lift
the mob quickly enough."

"Let me have the display," su-Lal said, swinging the table
so that he could reach the controls. Rattling fingers and a
barking voice called up lists of ships and shuttles, while su-
Irzim lay back and sipped a fresh beer.

They had been torturing their wits to find a way of going
to the Smallteeth. Now perhaps they had a way of making
the Smallteeth come to them.

Who says the High Lords have no sense of humor?

The deck lurched, then swayed slightly. Major Morley
felt the rising vibration of a lift field on full power. On the
screen the armory shrank until she could have covered it
with her thumbnail. Around it the gray streets of
Thorntonsburg stretched into a hazy distance.

Some of the haze was smoke from fires started by the
rebels, but not as much as she'd feared. Even the hard core
rebels among the Parrvillers seemed to be waiting to see
what would happen at Fort Stafford. The less determined
ones or those with families were leaking across the cordon
by twos and threes and half dozens. Sometimes an entire
company would march up to a police or Third Battalion
post, turn in a collection of handguns, knives, and home-
made grenades, and drift off to one of the emergency shelters in search of a hot meal.

Hot food was turning out to be a more potent weapon
than riot-control gasses or other nonlethals in the battle for
Thorntonsburg. In fact, that battle was already as good as
won, unless something went horribly wrong at Fort Stafford.

Which put the ball back to her.

"Hospital schematic, please," she told the computer. The
display swirled and flickered for a moment. She knew a
stab of fear that everything was going to fall apart because

someone hadn't loaded the hospital data into the attacker's computer—

SCHEMATIC DISPLAY OF CENTRAL OFFICE BLOCK, FORT STAFFORD BASE HOSPITAL.

scrolled past and vanished. Morley sighed.

"Gather 'round, people."

The penetration team obeyed—Franke, Brothertongue, her two hand-picked MPs who would turn from stretcher-bearers into fighters, and Inspector Gehvru with his four hand-picked Special Branch men. All five were experts at unarmed combat and concealed weapons, and two really were trained negotiators.

"If we find the whole crew together in the offices, it will be bloody but comparatively feasible. If they've split up, we will have to do the same, essentially on the spot. The most likely split will be me and my bearers in the office, Gehvru and up to three of his team to eliminate outposts, and one man for security for Brothertongue and Franke."

"We're neither of us entirely helpless, Lu," Franke said. "Besides, I thought being bait was part of our job."

"Yes, but once the fish sees you I want it harpooned before it bites," Morley said. "Nothing personal, I'm just too much of a coward to want to explain to both Gist and Kuwahara how you got killed." For the first time today, Brothertongue laughed.

"Now—display and describe your weapons."

The team began running through their individual arsenals, as Morley felt the vibration in the deck change pitch. Now the attacker was running north on both lift and drive, keeping low but hitting Mach 2 or better. They would have to hurry with the final review.

At least she didn't need to review her equipment. The stretcher was lashed in one corner, and from one of the poles the snub carbine hung by its strap.

"Anybody on the other side?" Mahoney asked the radio.

Sergeant Stuck's voice replied. "I've had a couple of movement reports, but I can't see anything myself."

"Don't forget that some of our militia know this country. They can tell a bush from a bushwhacker."

Stuck laughed briefly. "I'd like to see a bush, any kind."

"Where are you from?"

"Sierras Verdes. My family were Hive War refugees, and the Old Starworlds—"

"Ah, people, I hate to interrupt, but could we have a little less chatter on the radio?" Lieutenant Langwell broke in.

Beside Mahoney, Brigitte Tachin stifled a giggle. Langwell still sounded as if he were apologizing for having to give orders, but he was giving them. Most of the time they even made sense. Mahoney remembered how he'd handled his own first try for the Order of the Reluctant Infantryman (a yellow duck, sitting, over two crossed shovels) and was inclined to charity.

The day was far enough along so that the valley downhill was sinking into shadow. The upper slopes were still sunlit, so that Mahoney's eyes had to adjust when he shifted them from hill to valley.

As they finished adjusting, he saw movement, like a swarm of ants with a snake following behind them—or chasing them. He tapped Brigitte on the shoulder and they both raised binoculars. Langwell joined them.

"If that's all bad guys, we're in trouble," he said. He looked up toward the crest. Mahoney knew what he was looking at—the two hundred-meter stretch where the only cover was the dead bodies of the first rebel attack.

Protecting the cave mouth, the platoon really wasn't in a single perimeter. It was in two almost entirely separate ones. If they'd found a second SSW in that pile of stuff Brigitte hauled out of the cave, instead of ammo for the one they had, it might not make any difference.

Mahoney raised his binoculars again. "Bad guys, all right. The bugs are their scouts. The snake's the main column. Looks like about a company. I still can't see any heavy weapons, but they'll be in SSW and shoulder-launch range pretty soon."

Langwell looked and double-checked the ranges before nodding. "You're right. I hate to lose the cave, though."

"In your position, I'd hate to lose the platoon even more," Mahoney said. "I don't know what your orders are—"

"Let's not waste time playing games," Langwell said

sharply. "Boss to 3rd Platoon. We are withdrawing to a position on the ridge. Leapfrog by squads, and take appropriate action on the cave."

"I'd better do the time-fuse by hand," Brigitte said, and dashed off down the slope. Mahoney watched her go, reminded himself that the enemy was still out of range, and looked at the harsh and empty sky.

"Where the Hades is everybody?" Langwell echoed Mahoney's thoughts. "We know Captain DiVries made it in. I thought we'd have someone out here by now."

He whispered, "Could the rebels have demanded that we stop offensive operations against them?"

"No," Mahoney said. "If they did that, Langston would move into the hospital five minutes later, and let the patients take their chances. If he didn't, Kuwahara would fire him and go down the chain of command until he found somebody who would move.

"I'll bet they have found that larger rebel force out there. They're making it their priority target and won't come for us until they've got it on the run."

Langwell didn't ask the obvious question: Then why haven't we heard the air strikes? He seemed content to be consoled by a half-truth.

The whole truth was that with everything happening at once, Victoria Command might have forgotten about an isolated platoon of militia and their advisers. A platoon was small enough to slip through the cracks in any command system.

Seventeen

Colonel Chatterje sneaked a look at her watch. Twenty-two minutes before the terrorists' next deadline expired. Possibly twenty-two minutes more of life for her, followed by a slow, excruciating death.

Only possibly, not certainly. The deadline for killing hostages had been extended twice already. A third extension wasn't impossible.

But the first two times, the terrorists had made long, disgustingly boring speeches about how this delay showed their moderation. Chatterje suspected they would consider that a third delay would make them appear weak.

Which would they prefer to face: appearing weak, or outlawry and immediate Federation action? When the hostages started dying, Langston would no longer have a choice. Regulars, Rangers, and probably SWAT experts from the Special Branch would move in and end the situation.

They would also end a good many lives, not all of them terrorists'. Chatterje's training as a Federation officer and her training as a doctor had been arguing politely for some time over what she should prefer. So far they had come to no conclusion.

Neither, apparently, had the terrorists. Of the ten she'd counted (including Senator Karras and two staffers), nine were openly nervous about what they'd got themselves into out of desperation. Chatterje wasn't sure that twenty professionals would have been less threat than the small number of amateurs her hospital faced.

The professionals might fight better if it came to that. But they would also consider other options and not start a massacre simply to ease overstrained nerves!

Senator Karras appeared in the doorway. He was half a meter taller than the colonel even when she was seated, but she did her best to look down on him. His tunic was stained with sweat and the ashes of the aromatics he'd been smoking until their pleasant herbal odor turned into a stale stench.

"Some good news. Victoria Command HQ has sent word that a negotiating team is on the way. We don't have an ETA for them yet." He looked at the four guards and one staffer holding the terrorists' CP. "So please—don't do anything drastic, at least until we have the ETA."

Even watching him crawl to the A.I. thugs, Chatterje felt no sympathy for Karras. He was more frightened than she was, and with good reason. She might die slowly today, but she would leave a good name behind.

Karras, on the other hand, would be remembered as one step above an assassin worm, if that. People would spit when they mentioned his name. No reward would be worth that—and Karras's likely reward was in any case death, as soon as the Baernoi or the Alliance had sucked him dry. If his friends didn't terminate him, the Federation and loyal Victorians would be on his trail for the rest of his life.

The leader of the guards, a middle-aged woman with a Madrassi accent, frowned. "You don't give orders here, Karras."

"That wasn't an order," Karras said. "It was just a suggestion, based on my—"

"Having wet your pants already at the idea of anybody getting killed," the would-be rapist muttered. The woman frowned but did not correct him.

Karras slumped into a chair and fumbled for a sodden handkerchief. Chatterje cautiously stood up. Two guns swung toward her. She held her hands out in front of her.

"Can someone provide me with an escort? I need to use the bathroom."

The would-be rapist stood up, and the woman nodded. *More amateurism*, Chatterje thought. *I can ignore worse than a man watching me on the toilet. If they don't realize that, they're even bigger fools than I thought.*

Chatterje stepped out from behind her desk. It was the first time she'd done that since the terrorists arrived. Her gun was still in her desk drawer. A couple of hairs judiciously placed would warn her if anybody got into the drawer while she was gone.

"Ready for your thrill?" she said to her escort.

"Colonel, please—" Karras began, then wilted under three glares—two terrorists' and Chatterje's.

Ramdur met three other people as he roamed the recesses of the base, looking for Commander Marder or someone who knew where she was. He hoped he would find Marder herself.

The people he'd met had been as casual as he'd expected. Ever since he'd reached the base, no one questioned his right to be where he was, as long as it wasn't one of the few secure areas such as the computer center where he worked. It also helped that now he could saunter along as casually as if he had business wherever he was.

He'd some time ago drawn what he feared was the correct conclusion about this lack of security consciousness. He also knew that it made no difference until he had carried out his mission with Commander Marder. (Or gone back to the other, riskier methods he'd considered for carrying out the mission, before Marder arrived—but he had never in his life felt so strongly that God did answer prayers as when Marder arrived.)

Three-quarters of an hour into his search, Ramdur was beginning to worry. Sooner or later someone would question his presence in these increasingly remote corners of the complex. The alternative was asking about Marder, likely to make even the least security conscious mercenary or even supply clerk suspicious.

It was just short of an hour when he found the commander, dumped in a corner with an intravenous life-support pack tied to one arm. She was also tied to the stretcher, and at first glance she looked comatose, even dying.

Ramdur crept close. He had only rumors to rely on, that she would be sent out as part of a *maskirovka* (the Russian word had been specifically used). But having gone this far, and with the microslip in its gelatin capsule ready in his pouch, why not go all the way?

Closer up, Marder looked both worse than he had expected and better. Worse, because clearly there'd been no orders about leaving marks. Better, because she was murmuring softly to herself and working her mouth.

Was her swallowing reflex intact? Ramdur wished he'd

brought some water, then noticed a pool of condensation a few meters from the stretcher. It was dirty and he had nothing but his cupped hands to bring it, but it was enough. As he dribbled the water in, Marder's mouth opened, her throat worked, and her tongue crept out to lick her lips.

Quickly, Ramdur placed the capsule on Marder's tongue. Then he pinched her nostrils shut—reluctantly, because he could see that her nose had been broken.

He almost undid everything with that gesture. Marder's mouth opened to suck in air, and the capsule went down. She also opened her eyes, and for a moment looked ready to cry out or vomit.

Then her eyes drifted shut, and the faint murmuring began again. Ramdur caught one or two words: "—Tusker with a helmet" seemed to be a complete phrase. Nothing that made sense, though, and he'd hardly expected anything else. She had to be loaded to the limits with amnesiacs; it must be an idiosyncratic reaction to them that she was conscious at all.

Again Ramdur thanked God for a blessing. If Marder's clothes were changed, anything hidden in them might not leave the complex with her. Using the other body orifices would have meant a long, distasteful job that could leave traces, not to mention a more easily detectable microslip. Now, nothing except a full medscan or an autopsy would turn up the message.

As he turned his back on Marder, Ramdur prayed it would be a medscan. He knew that God blessed the warrior who died in a good cause, although he doubted the traditional description of Paradise. It would have little appeal for a woman. He also knew that it was a great blessing to live to enjoy the fruits of one's courage.

General Langston himself led the negotiation team into his office. There Colonel Vesey poured out coffee, tea, or chocolate and passed around a plate of doughnuts and stuffed grape leaves.

Major Morley managed not to fidget during the formalities. She tried to send a telepathic message to Franke and Inspector Gehvru to do the same, but they didn't seem to be receiving. Only Father Brothertongue seemed to match the general's calm. The two men might have been carved out of the same dark brown stone.

Finally, just before Morley herself started screaming from more than the throb of her wounds, Langston nodded. Colonel Vesey closed the door, slapped switches that produced a brief light show, then nodded.

Langston's mask broke into a thin smile. "We are now in the most secure room on Victoria. Nothing said here must go outside it." He nodded at Vesey.

She switched on a situation display on the wall behind Langston's desk. It showed most of Fort Stafford solid blue, except for the red patch over the hospital and a pink wedge in one sector.

"Except for the hospital, we're back in control," Langston said. "Those pink areas are a courtesy to the uncertain loyalty of our Vics. We've got the civilians in one hangar and the militia companies in another."

"Are the militia still armed?" Brothertongue asked.

"Yes, but both hangars are guarded. We've also arranged to sleep-gas the whole bunch if they make any more trouble."

"Have you warned them about that?" Brothertongue asked.

"No. We haven't—"

"Then you might be accused of trying to provoke them into a move that gives you the excuse—"

Langston said a rude word and slammed both hands down on his desk. "I don't have enough respect for either Victorians or priests to eat that kind of garbage. Not now."

"Excuse me," Father Brothertongue said. "I was not implying that you had done any such thing, or accusing you of it myself. I believe you innocent of any such intention. But—"

"Get to the point!"

"The point is politics. There will be people in both Houses who wish to embarrass the Federation, no matter how this current situation is settled. I was calling your attention to a detail that might make it harder for them to do so."

Langston's thin smile was back. "Never yet met a politician who didn't talk too long, but you do talk sense. Milla, take care of it."

The general continued the briefing. The sappers and snipers had apparently been as much of a diversion as a serious attempt to neutralize Fort Stafford. They were all dead, prisoners, or in hiding now, and they'd failed to do any critical damage to the fort's vital installations. They hadn't failed to inflict a fair number of casualties on the garrison battalion.

"Enough so that I'm keeping the Vics on ice for their own protection as much as ours," Langston concluded. "Our people are extensively pissed, and I don't blame them."

The brown mask was back. "Major Morley, what's your plan for your team?"

Morley managed to compress it into five minutes, in spite of contingency plans and feeling muzzy-headed from painkillers. Langston was almost grinning when she finished.

"Good. You won't need to make any changes, except in timing, to coordinate with our plan."

By now Colonel Vesey had finished her messages and took over the briefing. The plan was to hit the hospital from both top and bottom. Top would be through the front door, the office windows, and the landing pad on the roof. Bottom would be up through the contaminated-waste outlet.

"We'd use something cleaner, except that it's the one closest to the stairs," Vesey said. "The big problem is getting between the terrs and their potential victims. Once that's solved, we can do the rest by brute force if necessary.

"Your negotiating team will be a big help. It will certainly keep the command group busy, maybe cut down their numbers. Once you've done that, don't try to play Sam Briggs at the Waskow farm. Hole up and wait for rescue, which will be hitting both top and bottom about two minutes after you start shooting."

Signals, security, and other details took less than ten more minutes. Morley wanted to meet with the C.O. of the main assault force, but Langston turned thumbs-down.

"We can't pull her out of her position without somebody noticing, or be sure our communications with her are completely secure. I think you'll admit that without complete surprise we're all in very thick compost, starting with you people."

Vesey produced another tray of refreshments. Morley felt

bloated from both medication and the first round, but
thought of the saying, "The condemned ate a hearty meal."
She made a polite gesture with a cupcake and herb tea.

"Now, before we start setting up your entrance, there are
a couple of matters I wanted to ask you about," Langston
added. "Admiral Kuwahara was on my back just before you
arrived. Without his naming them, I gather he was concerned about the Merishi refugees."

Morley wondered if the people in Thorntonsburg had
been too lazy, fearful of eavesdroppers, or something less
pleasant to contemplate, not to pass the word. At least she
could be the good-news bearer.

"Your predecessor"—she couldn't quite say "General
Kornilov"—"left strict orders with the Provost Marshal. Any
sign of civil disorder, they would go under an airtight guard.
The last we heard of them, they were alive, guarded, and
even grateful."

"Good," Langston said. "Admiral Kuwahara was being
even more reticent than usual about the Merishi. He wasn't
being so polite about General Parkinson."

Morley heard enough throat-clearings to brace herself for
an explosion. "Why not?" Brothertongue asked.

"She wanted to come up here and take command of the
militia. Try to make them a force we could trust and use,
apparently. Kuwahara said she wasn't to be furnished Federation transport for the purpose, or allowed into Fort Stafford if she used her own."

Brothertongue's face looked as close to rage as Morley
had ever seen it. Fortunately he was so furious he was
speechless long enough to let Franke cut in.

"I think doubts about General Parkinson's loyalty are
unjustified. Major Morley is satisfied that it was just luck
that she was out of the office when the rockets hit."

"Has this been confirmed by a truth-test?" Vesey asked.

Franke glared in all directions except that of the two
senior officers. Brothertongue used several unpriestly phrases.
If the matter hadn't been so serious, Morley would have
laughed.

"No, sir," she said. "We didn't feel called on to insult
the Victorians that way. Nor will we do it, without a direct
order."

Langston looked at the display, Morley suspected mostly

to avoid meeting the others' eyes. "I won't give that order," he said finally. "I do question General Parkinson's judgment. She needs to be closer to the central authority, such as it is. Leading from in front is no good, if it cuts off your communications."

"No, sir," Morley said.

Langston's gaze turned to Franke. "Commander, I think I will recommend against a truth-scan of General Parkinson. I will even consider letting you go with the negotiating team.

"But there's one condition. A confidential briefing, on what Kuwahara and Kornilov were planning that involved the Merishi."

"He didn't—" Franke began, then closed his mouth.

"As you just realized, I would not have asked you if Mikhail had briefed me. Or if Admiral Kuwahara was speaking freely."

"Communications—" Franke began.

Muscular brown hands slammed the desk again. "Bounce communications! Victoria Squadron seems to think that the Army sits around with its thumb up its arse while the Navy does all the work! I think there's been enough of that."

"Sir, I think you are under a misapprehension—"

"So correct it, Commander," Langston snapped. "Starting as soon as we clear the room." He glared around him. "If this is really hot, I may not let even Commander Franke go where he can be captured. I'll be damned if I let anybody else!"

"Upsy-daisy, Lu," Franke said, holding out his arm. She gripped its solidity and realized for the first time how much the thought of its being cold and dead within a few hours bothered her.

"Still nothing on the other side?" Lieutenant Langwell asked. Mahoney shook his head. "I wonder if they're trying to surround us, staying out of sight and out of range."

Before Mahoney could raise an eyebrow at this defeatism, Langwell added, "I wish we had another platoon and a few heavy weapons. Even an armed scooter would help. Then we could probe those bastards down there"—he pointed downhill into the gathering shadows—"instead of sitting up here with our arses hanging out to be kicked."

Somewhat to Mahoney's surprise, the Victorians had been doing anything but sitting. On top of the ridge, they'd laid in fighting positions as well as lots of hard rock and a shortage of tools allowed. A little advice from the Federation regulars had given the fighting positions good fields of fire. For amateur soldiers, the Victorians were singularly unafraid of hard work. But then, Victoria was no place for the lazy.

"Oh, well," Langwell said. "Even that mob probably has enough snipers with night sights to make trouble for anyone coming downhill."

"Speaking of night sights," Sergeant Stuck said, "do the people up there have their share?"

"One per squad all 'round," Langwell said. "Or at least that's what the sergeant said."

"Mind if I check?"

"It'd be better if you did it through the advisers up there, rather than confront—"

Langwell's advice on tact ended abruptly as Stuck stiffened, with a hiss of breath. "There's a whole Hades of a lot of movement down there all of a sudden. Permission to illuminate?"

Langwell nodded. Stuck rolled over, aimed her pulser downhill, jacked a flare into the grenade launcher under the barrel, and fired.

Pop. White light blazed over the hillside. A long straggling line of rebels was creeping out of the valley, mostly individuals but with a few clumps like beads on a string.

"Peste!" Brigitte Tachin said, in Mahoney's ear. He bit back shock and concern that she was down here rather than up on the ridge as he'd thought.

"What is it?"

"I thought they would not be moving until after dark. So the time fuse will not go off until 1930."

"Bloody hell!" Langwell said. "That gives them time to overrun the cave, find the fuses—"

"Remember the booby traps. Also, there is a command-detonated setting on the fuse, if I can signal it before they reach the antenna."

"Then for God's sake signal it!" Langwell said, licking his lips. "If they get the rest of the load in the cave, they'll take weeks to hunt down."

It was good to hear Lieutenant Langwell thinking of lost opportunity instead of present danger. Or maybe he was just learning that acting is part of an officer's job. If anybody didn't realize that the rebels would start by hunting down the impudent platoon on the hill, they wouldn't learn from Langwell. Or Mahoney.

Brigitte pulled her own night sight down over her face. It hid everything above her lips, which were curved in an impish smile. *Like a small girl who's worked out the perfect trick to play on a teacher she hates,* Mahoney thought.

"Now, come on, *mes vieux*, put another of those squads or whatever they are in line—ah, yes—*magnifique!*"

Brigitte squeezed the switch and became a prophet. The hill shivered like a giant rolling over under thick blankets. Then a jet of flame spewed out of the cave, shooting a hundred meters down the slope through the advancing line of men. A second, smaller jet vented through a natural fault fifty meters upslope from the cave.

Both flames carried with them a load of flying debris and rock fragments. They scoured the hillside below like a shotgun blast. Watching the IR picture of the enemy's positions, Mahoney saw the bright glowing green of hot fragments and the gentler green of human bodies. Some of them were still, others blurred as they crawled or writhed. Most of the ones moving quickly were retreating.

"Come on!" Langwell yelled. "We *can* push them right off the hill." He jumped to his feet. "Follow me!"

Given a choice between ignoring a direct order and committing suicide, Mahoney jumped up and followed Langwell. *If nothing else, that may keep Brigitte from thinking she's needed. Besides, I am senior adviser to this mob!*

Langwell survived the first minute of the counterattack. Then a rebel sniper unaffected by the blast shot him through the head. He'd barely hit the ground when another rebel had the good luck to land a grenade to the right of the counterattack. Mahoney was on the right, and the blast knocked him off his feet. Fragments jabbed hard even through the armor, and one gouged his hand open right through his gloves.

He'd gotten back on hands and knees when he saw the Victorians scrambling back uphill as fast as they could go. Mahoney turned to look downhill; he was damned if he'd

die without firing at least one shot or with wounds in his
back—

Before he'd completed the turn, the rout ended as quickly
as it began. Brigitte seemed to sprout from the ground,
waving her carbine. Behind her Sergeant Stuck was running
up, carrying the SSW, which still looked two sizes too large
for her.

"Stop!" Brigitte shouted, and Stuck let fly. The SSW
burst was obviously aimed downhill, at the rebels. Just as
obviously, another burst could chop the Vics off their feet
where they stood.

The fleeing Victorians halted so abruptly that the first
half dozen fell over each other's feet. They sprawled on the
ground in an ignominious tangle, and the people behind
them burst out laughing. Stuck and Brigitte turned away,
so they wouldn't join the laughter.

The fallen Victorians got up, looking ready to fight the
whole world starting with their own comrades. Their own
NCOs and Stuck prodded them into forming a base of fire
that raked the lower slope of the hill. One more grenade
came uphill, and a few stray small-arms rounds, then
silence.

Keeping his head below the level of both friendly and
hostile fire, Mahoney crawled to Langwell's body. Bruises
and his gouged hand protested as he heaved the lieutenant's
body on to his back in a fireman's carry. They protested
more as he lurched uphill, too winded to call out until one
of the Vics saw him.

The Vic—Mahoney thought it was a woman—raised her
pulser, but someone struck the barrel down. Then two other
Vics and Brigitte were coming down to help him, the Vics
lifting Langwell and Brigitte grabbing his arm as if she
wanted to pull it out of its socket.

"Easy, Bridey," Mahoney grunted. "I'm not badly hurt.
Yet."

"Thank God. Can you make it to the top of the ridge?"

"Depends on how much we have to hurry."

They didn't have to hurry. Some of the rebels driven
off by Brigitte's giant improvised anti-personnel mine kept
running until they vanished into the valley. Others rallied,
at a discreet distance from any possible Federation positions.

Only a few hardy souls remained in any sort of fighting stance. Even these kept their heads down and their weapons silent as the militia and advisers retreated to the ridge.

"Probably don't know what else we've got up our sleeves," Stuck said. "Or maybe that counterattack made 'em think we're more'n a platoon. That wasn't such a bad job Langwell was doing, when you get right down to it."

"No," was all Mahoney had the breath to say. He suspected that he'd cracked a couple of ribs when he went down. He hoped they were only cracked. The first aid likely to be available on the ridge was hopeless for dealing with a punctured lung.

Stuck stepped closer and put her arm through Mahoney's, until she could whisper in his ear. "Lieutenant, I got to say this.The Vic's sergeant may not be quite up to taking over the platoon."

"May not be, or isn't?"

"Well, if you ask me—"

"I am."

"Isn't."

"Which makes me the Old Man?"

"Until I find somebody who can be moved up without the sergeant's throwing a fit or maybe a grenade. I'll look, but it may take a while."

The way Mahoney felt now, five minutes would be too long and half an hour would seem like an eon. But when you were standing under the pipe and the stuff came down, there was nothing to do but catch it the best you could.

Eighteen

The three A.I. guards on the hospital roof looked long and hard at the negotiating team. They looked the longest at Lucretia Morley, swathed in blankets on her stretcher.

"What's wrong with her?" one of them asked.

"She was hit in the fighting in Thorntonsburg after she'd volunteered for the team," Brothertongue said. "It was only a flesh wound, but the medics advised her not to stand."

The chief guard looked at his comrades, then nodded jerkily. "All right. I'll warn them about this."

Commander Franke tried to study the rooftop without being obvious about it. The three guards with them were the walking dead; they would stop walking any time the Federation chose. But it wasn't the easy targets that were the problem in this hostage situation. It never was.

Just how difficult the crucial target was, Franke quickly learned. Their guide—one of Karras's staffers, Franke recalled from the pictures—led them through a maze of corridors and down at least four different staircases. It took ten minutes to reach Colonel Chatterje's office and the command group.

By then Franke was beginning to feel rather like a Theseus asked to penetrate the Labyrinth and bring back the Minotaur's head without Ariadne's thread to guide him. It didn't help that he was rather less of a warrior than Theseus, even if Lu Morley was better in a fight than your average Minoan princess.

It helped even less that there were terrorists instead of minotaurs waiting in the heart of this labyrinth. They were much less mythical, much more numerous, and far more dangerous.

At least he understood why the computer had said that the negotiating team's presence tripled the safety factor of the rescue operation. Enemies who had already passed all the choke points would give the enemy's command group an immediate and possibly fatal distraction.

A medium-sized woman with a Madrassi accent and another of Karras's staffers met them at the door of the office. She looked the team over much more intently than the guards on the roof.

"I hope that's all."

"It is the number agreed on," Brothertongue said.

"Yes, and I think it's too many."

Franke and Brothertongue exchanged glances. A split in the leadership they might exploit? Brothertongue nodded. "Ah—we agreed that some of your less—some of your more zealous members—might think of kidnapping us and taking us up to turn over to the Baernoi," Brothertongue said. "This would immediately lead to a bloody confrontation and a great many innocent people dead.

"We are trying to open negotiations among reasonable beings. The extra security is intended to help with that, nothing more."

Franke decided that if he ever learned to tell that big a lie with a straight face, he might try politics himself.

The woman frowned. "I won't send anybody back. But half your security is going to wait outside. We don't want a mob scene in the office."

Franke wanted to grin idiotically, the way General Langston had done when Franke had finished explaining Kuwahara's plan for the Merishi. This was part of the victory handed to them on a platter. Now the team's maneuver squad would already be outside when the shooting started, instead of having to fight its way through doors probably held by armed and alert terrorists.

They had to pretend to protest, though. The protests took up another five minutes, with the terrorists all joining in at one time or another. Franke thought of a flock of geese and reminded himself that these geese carried guns.

After all the protests were beaten down, it took another ten minutes of feigned argument to divide up the security people. Inspector Gehvru wound up out in the hall, which Franke didn't care for, but Lu was a professional even if she did have to take this situation lying down. The people in the office would not be fatally short of leadership.

That fifteen-minute holdup would also make sure that the other rescue teams would be completely deployed. In fact, if the holdup had lasted much longer, Franke would have started worrying about someone outside pushing the panic button.

Franke and one MP lugged the stretcher inside and the rest of the team followed, with the woman bringing up the rear. Without moving his head, Franke counted the A.I. command group.

Good. Five, six at most, allowing for somebody being out of sight or in the bathroom. They had Franke, an MP, two Special Branch officers, and Lu to contend with. (Brothertongue, Franke hoped, would have the sense to hit the floor the moment the shooting started and not get up until it stopped.)

Colonel Chatterje was seated behind her desk, looking as if she'd been planted there. Her face was thinner than Franke remembered it, seemingly reduced to two enormous dark eyes. He hoped she would also hit the floor, but wasn't optimistic; the colonel had too many debts to pay, doctor or no doctor.

"All right," the woman said. "Now, before we start serious discussion, I want everyone strip-searched in the bathroom." Franke nodded, to keep his jaw from dropping.

"Any problems with that? I hope not, because the alternative is no negotiations at all. We'll put things right back on a take-it-or-leave-it basis."

"I think you should appreciate the concession the Federation is making in negotiating at all," Brothertongue said with elaborate gravity. "If you throw that concession back in their faces—"

"Why are you pimping for the bloody Feddies?" a small man standing beside Chatterje's desk said. "We thought you had your head screwed on right."

"I did, and I do. That is why I am *cooperating with* the Federation in this matter. When a situation has come to be dominated by the two extremes, a moderate voice—"

"Is going on too cursed long," the woman said sharply. "Joel, pick a partner and start the searches. Her first," with a wave toward Morley.

"I appeal—" Brothertongue began. The woman drew her pistol.

"I appeal to your sense of self-preservation not to interfere with what we have to do." She sounded almost pleading, which decided Franke to kill her quickly if the job fell
to him. "We won't search you."

"I insist on being—"

"We insist on getting on with it," the small man snapped.
The prospect of strip-searching a crippled woman seemed
to delight him. Franke decided that if there was time, the
little son of a pitsnapper was going to die slowly.

Brothertongue stepped close to the woman. "I will not
lend my countenance to this barbaric—"

"Joel, grab him!" the woman shouted. She clutched one
of Brothertongue's arms. The small man stepped forward
to grab the other. Franke saw that the other terrorists in
the room were all watching the confrontation.

Franke did not see Lu fling off the blankets and come up
with her snub carbine. He did hear the *rrrrrummmmm* of a
quick burst and see the woman's head disintegrate. Lu was
following her own orders: head shots if possible, to get
quick kills and avoid body armor.

Franke's mind and senses went on tight focus, trying to
pick out the immediately dangerous opponents from the
rest. If he guessed wrong he might be dead; if he tried to
keep track of everyone he certainly would be.

The small man tried to shield himself behind Brothertongue, but the priest flung him away. The small terrorist
went down but came up rolling, a gun in his hand. Franke
shot at him; missed, shot at one of the guards by the door
at the same time Lu hit him, then hurled himself backward
against the wall.

Meanwhile the Special Branch man was down on the
floor, bloody but grappling with another terrorist. The MP
was just drawing his darter when two more guards ran in.
He snap-fired, hitting one. The other got off enough shots
to hit the MP but not enough to hit Franke, who finally
scored on a lucrative target.

The small man got up just as the bathroom door burst
open. Franke shot through the door, then into the head and
torso that lurched into the open. Colonel Chatterje was on
her feet now, holding a Steurmann darter and squeezing the
trigger frantically without results.

The small man had his gun out now and was drawing

down on Colonel Chatterje. Brothertongue blocked Morley's shot, and Franke knew it was up to him.

The next moment Brothertongue's foot shot up, catching the small man between the legs. He bent double, and Colonel Chatterje lunged over her desk to grab his gun arm and heave. Leverage and vigor made up for her lack of weight; Franke heard the terrorist's elbow shatter. Everybody on the floor must have heard his scream.

Sliding off her desk, Colonel Chatterje reversed her pistol and walked over to the grappling of terrorist and Special Branch man. The *craaak* as the butt came down on the terrorist's skull was loud in the sudden silence.

Outside Franke heard an uproar, more shouting than shooting, and what he thought was an explosion. That should be two MPs, blowing the nearest window that gave access to the office complex. If they could hold the window or even if they couldn't, a team of Rangers was supposed to swing in from a hovering lifter and sanitize the rest of the complex.

Inspector Gehvru and the rest of his maneuver squad should now be maneuvering. With luck, they'd stay between the remaining terrorists and the hospitalful of hostages. With somewhat less luck, they'd have to follow the terrorists around and try keeping them too busy ducking to kill anybody.

Even with no luck at all for Gehvru and company, the situation would still be better than if the negotiating team hadn't come in. On the whole, Franke was reasonably happy with the situation.

Colonel Chatterje rose from beside the MP and shook her head. "He's gone, I'm afraid." She knelt beside the bloody Special Branch man. "Commander, could you hand me my kit from the bottom left-hand drawer of my desk?"

It took five minutes for the colonel to finish doctoring the Special Branch man, who looked worse than he was. By then the shooting had died out and the shouting sounded more curious than angry or frightened. As Colonel Chatterje stood up again, a black-clad figure seemed to float into the doorway.

"Taco."

"Bean," Franke and Morley countersigned together.

The man pulled off his mask and shouted a string of numbers down the hall. Then he held out a hand.

"Sergeant Muoc, Rangers."

Franke did the introductions while Muoc looked at the bodies on the floor. "Any live ones?"

"Two, I think. We lost one."

"Your people outside lost that Special Branch inspector"—a muttered "Damn!" from Morley—"but otherwise did for practically everybody except Karras and one of the terrs." Muoc slung his carbine and grinned. "Oh, well, he can't go up, and the drain-crawlers will get him if he goes down."

Muoc stationed himself by the door while Chatterje turned to Brothertongue. The priest tried to smile.

"Don't worry about me. The blood isn't mine. Major Morley had to shoot the leader a little too close for comfort."

"Better that than the comfort of the grave," Chatterje said briskly. "That was a well-delivered kick, by the way. Soccer?"

"Oh, yes. I had quite a kick when I was at school. My nickname, though, was 'Own Goal.' I'm afraid I didn't have such a good sense of direction."

At this point Brothertongue staggered and started to topple. Franke lunged forward and reached the priest in time to keep him from cracking his head on the edge of Chatterje's desk. Then the colonel slipped under Brothertongue and lowered him to the floor.

"I hope that none of the rest of you are planning to faint," Chatterje said firmly. "I have enough patients—enough—" She swayed, and Franke stepped forward to catch her in his arms.

She didn't quite go down. She simply let him hold her while she took several deep breaths, then murmured what sounded like a prayer in her native Hindi. Behind him, Franke heard Lu giggle.

"Herman, if you must fiddle around with other women—"

Franke stiffened, indignant that Lu could joke at a time like this, then saw understanding in Chatterje's eyes. Doctors and policemen—both had their own special brands of black humor, to cope with life-and-death situations and their aftermath.

*   *   *

"Attention, attention," the intercom boomed. "All hands announcement. The Red-Plus Security Alert for Fort Stafford is canceled. The Red-Plus Security Alert for Fort Stafford is canceled. All duty personnel remain at your posts until further notice. All off-duty personnel report to your posts immediately."

As if it were addressing a convention of the mentally limited, the speaker repeated the message twice more before signing off. Elayne Zheng adjusted all the garments she could without stripping and swore she'd do that at the first opportunity. Possibly in Rafael's company, so that he could rub not only her back but her bottom, which after a double watch in this plague-rotted chair felt like a lump of armorplast—

"Hey," the controller at the next console said. "Heard what happened to Karras?"

"No." Nor did Zheng particularly care, but why not be polite?

"They cornered him in the basement. He wouldn't disarm, wouldn't surrender, wouldn't shoot back. They finally closed on him and he blew his brains out."

"I didn't know he had any," Zheng said in a tone that discouraged further conversation.

Another score for the good guys, and with no headaches about shooting a politician. Not that half of them don't deserve it, but they've got such a strong union—

"Control Five, this is Arrak Leader. Understand you've got the bad guys out of your hair. Hope *Shen* turns us loose pretty soon."

"Control Five to Arrak Leader. Stop insulting my ship and don't go in your pants. Believe me, we'll take over again as soon as we have com security restored."

"Can't be soon enough for us, Control Five."

Zheng let the second insult to *Shenandoah* pass. Proud as she was of her ship, she had to admit that *Shen* might have been less than the ideal tac air controller for the whole Associated States AO. Far out, maneuvering to avoid being an easy target for rebels, Alliance, or Baernoi, and with her own communications none too secure, the battlecruiser must have left a lot of frustrated birdpeople flying or squatting around today.

But those were details. For once the big picture was really more important, and the big picture was the good guys winning. Zheng tugged at her slacks again, leaned back in her chair, and asked for an update of her situation display.

Nineteen

Admiral Kuwahara lifted his gaze from the paper in front of him to Commander Franke's face. The commander had lost most of his military posture and even some of his cherubic look.

"Commander, I want it clearly understood. If you ever stick your neck out this far again while you are under my command, you are in serious trouble."

"Aye-aye, sir."

"I will not even bother with a court-martial. I will personally tear you into so many pieces it will need a microscope to detect them and a computer to count them. Is this clearly understood?"

"Aye-aye, sir."

Kuwahara tried to think of something else to say that wouldn't sound jealous. He knew he was jealous, that a born staff officer like Franke had managed to find his way to the sharp end, while a combat leader like his admiral had found his way to a large desk where he looked at displays, papers, and the faces of his staff.

He also knew that admirals had to think of their dignity— and their subordinates' self-respect.

"Beyond that—well done, all of you." He motioned to a chair. Franke's movement was more collapse than deliberate sitting.

Kuwahara held up the paper in front of him so that Franke could read the title: PROPOSED AGREEMENT BETWEEN VICTORIA COMMAND OF THE UNITED FEDERATION OF STARWORLDS FORCES AND THE PROVISIONAL GOVERNMENT OF THE ASSOCIATED STATES OF VICTORIA.

"Any idea why you were chosen to play messenger for this?"

"Yes. I think they felt my perspective would be useful. I

know the Navy and the Federation, I'm reasonably familiar with the situation on Victoria, and I'm connected with the Kishi Institute."

"Meaning?"

"The Institute tries to look not just beyond the next year, but even beyond the next century. At least that's the image we try to project. The Victorians may think I can come up with a long-term assessment that nobody else can."

"They may even be right," Kuwahara said. He put the agreement back in his IN tray. "How soon does the provisional government want our reply?"

"As soon as Parliament authorizes the provisional government to sign agreements," Franke replied.

"How soon will that be?"

"They want a quorum of both Houses of Parliament to ratify the proclamation of the provisional government before they start dealing with us officially. That could take as little as one Victoria day, if we give some of the politicos a lift."

"And if we don't?"

"Sir, I would strongly suggest that we—"

"Commander, I wasn't asking for suggestions. An estimate, please."

"Three days, at least. But the Victorians may suspect us of trying to—"

"Commander, I am as aware as you are that the Victorians are feeling a trifle paranoid. So am I. This proposal does not help. It also does not help that virtually all our attackers and shuttles will be committed to supporting the Army for the next eight to twelve hours. Suppressing the rest of this mite-ridden rebellion is also in the interests of the Victorians, in case either you or they have forgotten it."

"No, sir."

Kuwahara sighed. "I'll request a list of politicians who may need to hitchhike and see what will be available when. We'll cooperate, but they shouldn't expect miracles."

"I'm sure they won't, sir."

"Then how do you account for this provision for a complete amnesty to the whole Freedom Legion, if it participates in suppressing the rebellion? No mention of withdrawal from Alliance territory, either. I think anyone who proposes that does expect a miracle, from both us and the Alliance."

"Sir, if I'm allowed to make suggestions now—"

"Under the circumstances, I doubt if it would be wise to stop you. Go ahead."

"The Freedom Legion will have to withdraw from Seven Rivers and come under Associated States command if it is to effectively join in against Action for Independence. It will also be in territory where we can keep it under closer surveillance.

"Sir, I think Gov—ah, Mr. Gist is trying to give the Legion and the Alliance a way to save face."

Shrewd, if true. "You sound like you've come to respect Gist."

"I have. I think he's both ambitious and loyal. He sees Victoria as his home, and he wants independence, union, and peace for the planet. I also think he'll be a better wartime leader than Glicksohn, if peace doesn't break out."

That agreed with Kuwahara's staff assessment and instincts alike. "I suppose we can live with the Freedom Legion, if we aren't going to be allowed to live without them. But I wish he hadn't mentioned the Merishi."

"This isn't a public document, sir."

"It had damned well better not be!" Kuwahara massaged his temples and cheeks. It didn't help. He swallowed one of Dr. Mori's mystery pills dry, then nodded.

"Get some sleep, Commander. Staff conference tomorrow morning, as soon as everybody has a chance to read this." He slipped the report into the secretary slot of his console. The console began to hum as it scanned, recorded, and duplicated the document.

"Oh, by the way. How is Major Morley?"

"The last I saw of her, she was dictating letters of condolence to the next of kin of our dead teammates."

"Definitely a nocturnal life-form," Kuwahara muttered. "That will be all."

By the time Franke left, the magic pill was working as usual. The incipient migraine was going and slight nausea was taking its place. Mori had been adamant about meditation or yoga being better than this particular remedy; Kuwahara had been just as adamant about not having the time.

Time. They'd bought some, all the people who'd stood against the rebels and sometimes died where they stood. If the Merishi cooperated, the survivors might be able to do something with that time.

Kuwahara wished he could use a stronger word than *might*. But this was war, the province (or world, or sometimes whole universe) of uncertainty.

"Carlotta?"

"Yes, sir?" The chief of staff sounded half asleep herself.

"There's a stack of all-staff documents coming up in about ten minutes. See that everybody gets copies and reads them before the conference tomorrow."

"What time?

"Ah—0830. And I want Captain Liddell at the conference."

"Aye-aye, sir."

"Brian, wake up. I think we have company."

Brigitte Tachin's words penetrated half-numbed ears into Mahoney's chilled brain. As consciousness returned, he realized he'd never slept this cold before. Not even that winter at the seminary, when the heating system died and Father Ogburn thought it would be good discipline not to fix it until summer.

At least he wasn't frostbitten. Mahoney satisfied himself on that, running the standard extremity tests. Federation cold-weather gear was supposed to cope with worse than a Victorian winter night; so far it seemed to be doing its job.

By the time he was finished, he was also fully awake, and Tachin sounded impatient. "Brian, look over to the west. Air traffic!"

She was right. Several miniature constellations were moving against the more distant stars. As Mahoney watched, one of them started growing larger, rapidly.

As Mahoney opened his mouth to call the alert, Sergeant Stuck did it for him. Her yell woke everyone and would have started avalanches if there'd been enough snow on the slopes.

The platoon had just finished stumbling and scrambling to their fighting positions when the leading star in the approaching constellation started flashing lights. Mahoney raised his binoculars, set them to decode, and looked at the lights.

"Fed attacker, and she's giving the right recognition."

"Thank God!" Stuck picked up one of the night scopes, flipped it to visible light/transmit, and began flashing the response.

By the time the exchange of messages was done, the attacker was almost directly over the ridge. The lights died and a squad of soldiers seemed to drop from the sky. Mahoney groped to his feet, wincing at the pain in his ribs, and let Brigitte guide him uphill to meet the soldiers until his night vision returned.

"Lieutenant Stroessner, Fourth/215," the leader said. "We're more an SFO team than anything else, but we've brought a couple of SSWs. Meanwhile—"

The rumble of disturbed air interrupted him. Mahoney saw a dark shape flash over the head of the valley. Smaller shapes fell from it as it passed, some of them bursting with angry *craacks*.

"—the rest of the flight's going to lay a mine and sensor net across your front. That should keep the rebels down there from coming at you again. If they try to go around to your right, there's twenty kloms of rugged terrain on the way. We can pick up the survivors sometime next year.

"If they try to go around your left, they have about five kloms of open ground to cover. Flat as a pool table, and we've got two more attackers with anti-personnel loads on call."

Mahoney found a convenient rock and sat down. He watched in silence as the mine-laying attacker made a second pass, thickening the barrier. He hardly heard Lieutenant Stroessner's going on about how they'd forced a whole rebel battalion to deploy and kept it busy and out of the fighting. He had the vague feeling that he ought to be proud of this, and he was proud of how the Vics had held up.

Mostly he felt cold, tired, and relieved. Maybe the relief did have a little pride in it, though. He might be a reluctant infantryman, but it seemed he wasn't an incompetent one.

Charles Longman studied the lifter's rearview screen. It showed the beacon they'd just dropped, swaying down toward the ground under its transparent parachute. A puff of sand and snow rose as it touched down.

Longman checked the wind data. Good. The chute should blow clear, but not pull the beacon over if the release failed.

A toppled beacon lost much of its capabilities, and a chute-draped one lost some, even if the chutes were supposed to be sensor-transparent.

"How long to the next drop?"

The pilot tapped the printed card on the control panel. Hamilton held up ten fingers. The pilot nodded.

"Time for a final check."

Longman took a final look into the darkness, hoping to catch a glimpse of the Roskills. But here the valley was wide enough to hide them on a moonless night, even without the haze in the valley.

He didn't mind the haze. It meant little or no wind, and easier navigation of the tricky passes through the Krainiks. Much easier, when the lifter and its mates were flying in blackdown mode, navigating strictly by passive sensors and inertial systems.

He walked aft to the next beacon on the launch rail, loaded his computer with the right diagnostics, and plugged it in. Everything came up nominal, which left him with nine minutes to sit on his hands, except that even that didn't keep them warm.

Longman was nominally in command of the lifter, but the two pilots had made it quite clear that they regarded him as excess baggage. Fortunately his computer and talent for hands-on work with machinery let him make the final checks on the beacons before they dropped. That earned him a certain grudging respect and kept him from sitting with his teeth chattering with more than the cold.

At Camp Aounda, he'd managed to get used to being a sitting target for long-range weaponry. Now he had to get used to the prospect of being a moving target for shorter-range stuff.

The orders to the beacon layers were strict: Cover both slopes of the Krainiks. The fact that the northern slope of the range was well into disputed territory didn't seem to bother the order-givers.

It would have bothered Longman less if he'd known the reason for it. He suspected it had something to do with those "ghosts" that Major Shores and others had turned up over the past few weeks. He'd gone right on suspecting it, even after a few polite questions got rude put-downs. The "ghosts," apparently, were on a strict need-to-know basis.

So he'd come out into the darkness to freeze in ignorance. Blackdown this close to hostile territory meant cutting off the cabin heat to reduce the lifter's IR signature. Cold-weather clothing over heated battledress only helped somewhat.

"Coming up on the next drop," the pilot called. "Stand clear of the track. Beacon Eight ready and counting."

The pilot counted down from ten to one. At "Mark," the drogue chute flared, pulling the beacon out. Longman watched it fall. As it plunged toward the rock he suddenly realized that the main chute hadn't deployed.

He winced as the beacon augured in, throwing up a fountain of dust. Without waiting for orders, the pilot began a sharp turn. Longman hung on, watching for the IR display to show if the beacon had survived. It just might—

"Got it," the copilot said. "Looks like we won't have to make another drop after all. . . ." His voice trailed off. "Wait a minute. That's not on the beacon position."

"Refine the scan," Longman said. He didn't realize that he'd snapped out an order until the pilot looked at him.

"Refine the scan, and let's keep our minds on the job," Longman said. *Also keep them off what a mysterious IR trace might mean.*

The computer-generated refinement of the mystery trace came up in seconds. "Bioform?" the pilot said. The copilot nodded.

Longman looked at the display. The trace did look like something living, but just barely, and not very large. A few people, or maybe only one, and either trying to hide or—

"Let's check it out."

"Sir?"

"It could be somebody airwrecked. If they've passed through this area, they could have seen something useful. In fact, that could be why they were airwrecked. They got too close to whoever's been making the ghosts around here, and the ghosts turned solid and bit them."

Longman realized that he was babbling, but as long as he talked he wouldn't be afraid. He hoped he was also making sense.

Apparently he was. The pilot got a firm position on the trace and homed in on it. A hundred meters directly above the position, Longman saw it. A light lifter, on its side, looking as if it had crashed while low and slow, and the bioform IR trace too strong to be denied.

"Take her down," Longman said. "There's somebody alive in there. Copilot, come with me when we land. Got the survival kit?"

If I keep giving orders fast enough, maybe they'll think I know what I'm doing.

The lifter grounded with enough lateral movement to grate, squeal, and throw Longman against a beacon. He shook a tingling hand, then ran aft as the pilot dropped the rear hatch.

The light lifter was precariously balanced on its side, but the figure in the pilot's seat looked to be well strapped in. Longman and the copilot pushed at the lifter until they began to sweat, but its balance turned out to be too precarious for human muscles to correct.

Longman waved the pilot forward. "Give it a nudge," he shouted. For a moment he thought the pilot would refuse. Then the Navy lifter slid up and forward, and *thunnggged* into the wreck. The wreck toppled over into normal position.

Longman was the first into the cabin. There was only one person inside, the pilot. The faceplate was down and frosted over. Hamilton groped for a patch of bare wrist to feel for a pulse, while the copilot stood ready with the first aid gear.

"Alive, but barely. Stim, and then let's get him back and warm him up. We— Good God!"

As the copilot rolled up the unconscious pilot's sleeve, a forearm covered with bruises and scabs appeared. Even in the dim light, it was apparent that these weren't crash injuries.

"Hold off on the stim," Longman said. "I want to get the helmet off." Some of the side effects of stims could be dangerous for head injuries.

"Careful, his neck might be—" the copilot began.

"Well, I'll be damned!" Longman said, and nearly dropped the helmet.

The face above the collar belonged to that Alliance commander who'd come through the Armistice Base around the time of the first rebellion. Jeanne—no, Joanne, and what was that last name?

Marder. Joanna Marder. Now he had the *who*.
But *why*?

"The last shuttle is under way" came over the circuit from
the bridge. Brokeh su-Irzim recognized the First Guidance's
growly voice, now sounding both relieved and irritated.

"He's been in a bad temper ever since the shuttles
englobed us," F'Mita ihr Sular said. "He doesn't trust Navy
Guidance."

"Well, su-Ankrai didn't trust our various opponents not
to take a shot at *Perfumed Wind* if they could hit her without hitting a Fleet vessel. If that was made an act of war,
we could probably trust the Alliance and the Federation.
Anything the Victorians could launch, our cruisers would
be able to stop."

Ihr Sular looked as sour as if she'd bitten a rotted nut.
"Or don't you trust Fleet Detection?" su-Irzim asked.

The woman looked even sourer. Su-Irzim decided that
she was in no mood for jokes. In truth, neither was he.

The rescue at the Fort Stafford hospital had cost the People both an embarrassment and an opportunity. Many of
the Fleet commanders saw only the lost opportunity and
made *Night Warrior*'s corridors ring with their anger and
frustration. Some stopped just short of denouncing the
Inquirers in duel-worthy terms, and a few even muttered
against su-Ankrai himself.

Meanwhile, the Federation warriors were spreading across
Victoria, striking at the rebels wherever they found them.
The People would have no chance to slip a shuttle down
and rescue rebels in the hope of gratitude or even useful
information. A *bird* would have a hard time entering the
rebel-held areas unless it walked.

Rahbad Sarlin was still missing. If he had somehow
remained alive until now, he would do well to leave Silvermouth, even if that meant exposure. The city seemed
divided between areas held by the army and areas held by a
polite, largely unarmed, but generally determined resistance
movement.

And what could the People's Fleet do about any of these
situations? All the answers and all their combinations and
permutations came to the same sum: zero.

Su-Irzim had asked for permission to brief ihr Sular partly

for security reasons. Mostly it was a desire to get away from *Night Warrior* for even as little as a single watch, to put his thoughts in order and share his frustration with someone who would not judge him.

"I was looking up the term *civil disobedience* when you arrived," the woman said. "The Smalltooth Inquirer Josephine ihr Atwood has been using it about the situation in Silvermouth."

"I don't think ihr Atwood is an Inquirer," su-Irzim said. "Or if she is, she is a privately employed one, not with their Fleet."

"Private Inquirers? The Smallteeth are indeed strange."

Su-Irzim laughed. "Come, F'Mita. Even you know better than that."

"Well, consider how many meanings of the word *civil* there are." She pushed a sheet across the table at him.

"I think they are using it in the sense of 'not criminal,' " su-Irzim finally said. "Certainly they are not using it in the sense of 'polite.' "

"With half the city refusing the orders of its own government? I doubt it." She looked at the clock and wrinkled her snout. "I will have to be a poor host in another quarter-watch, but that does leave us time for a meal. Will you throw your stomach to my cook's mercy?"

F'Mita had allegedly abducted *Wind*'s cook from a luxury café on Kithroes. He certainly cooked like a mad genius: Nothing was usual but everything was delicious.

"I think it can survive the experience," su-Irzim said. "Unsettled stomach, unsettled mind."

"I don't remember the Great Khudr—"

"That was the Great Brokeh su-Irzim, respected host and friend."

Ground reinforcements reached Mahoney's position during an auroral display so bright the lifters turned off their lights. The wavering streams of blue, green, and iridescent silver lit up Federation insignia on some lifters and Victoria markings on others.

Part of a company from the Fourth/215 and a platoon of Victorian militia unloaded and went into position on the hill. Mahoney had nothing to do with that except to stay out of their way; Federation officers senior to him were now not only present but in command.

The aurora was fading by the time two more Victorian lifters appeared. The hatch light of one showed Lucco DiVries dismounting, at the head of a squad of medics loaded with stretchers and supplies.

"Captain DiVries, Associated States Forces Medical Corps," he said, saluting Stroessner. "Permission to go down and retrieve enemy wounded?"

Stroessner stared for a moment, then shook his head. "Captain Meluch's senior, but don't bother her. She'll just tell you the same thing I will. The whole area downhill's loaded with mines and sensors. Anybody wandering around there's going to be dead meat in ten minutes."

"I'm damned if I'll leave Victorians down there to freeze or bleed out!"

"You'll be dead if you don't," Stroessner snapped. "Why the sudden charity, anyway? You want to keep the rebels out of Intelligence hands, maybe?"

DiVries's arm muscles locked as he refused to reach for his sidearm. Mahoney stepped between the two officers.

"That was uncalled for, Lieutenant. Apologize."

"Why the—"

"Either apologize to Captain DiVries or explain yourself to Meluch, and if she doesn't listen I'm taking it as high as I need to go to hang your ass!"

Stroessner backed away from Mahoney's glare and tone. More quietly, Mahoney went on. "Captain DiVries has lost a fiancée, a brother, and a good friend to the rebels. Right now I'd trust him more than you!"

"All right, Captain," Stroessner said. "I guess I was out of line." The two men shook hands, then DiVries turned and led Mahoney away from the lifter.

"I wish you hadn't mentioned Sophie," he said. "Now they'll be watching me even more closely. Probably decide I've gone terminally weird right when we're about to lift off with a load of wounded."

"Lucco, I was wondering about you myself. Why the sudden passion to pick up rebels?"

DiVries turned away. "I'll tell you if you tell me one thing. Why weren't the mines under command? Was it because the Feds didn't trust the Vics close to the controls?"

"That might be it," Mahoney said. "But I didn't hear the orders. Anyway, they'd have gone to the Navy, not here."

In the darkness, he heard something very much like a sob from DiVries. Then DiVries swung around so fast that Mahoney backed away.

"Damn them! Do you know what we've been picking up, when rebels surrender? Kids not much older than BoJo Johnson, if that, boys and girls both, some of them gut-shot, some of them frostbitten. . . .

"And the goddamned Navy wants this to go on? That's why I changed sides, Brian. I couldn't be part of messing up my own planet and then walking away from it."

Mahoney's temper flared again. If it hadn't been for the aching ribs he might have punched DiVries. As it was, he gripped the man's hood with both hands.

"Listen," he said, from two centimeters away. "We are *not* making a mess and walking away from it. We are doing our damnedest to clean up the mess before we leave. Some of us are getting killed doing so. Maybe we're mercenaries saving the sum of things for pay, not fifteen-Standard kids. But don't go spitting on us. Not after Fort Stafford, not after a lot of other garbage with more to come!"

Gently, DiVries removed Mahoney's hands from his hood. "I'm sorry, Brian. I guess I'm still looking for some-body to be mad at, if I can't hate the rebels anymore." He held out his hand.

Mahoney winced as DiVries's shake nearly pulled him off balance. "Brian, are your ribs hurting?"

"Only when I wrestle."

"Right. And I'm having an affair with Baba Lopatina. Get your ribs and the rest of you over to our op-room lifter. I want those ribs scanned."

Mahoney wanted to pull away, but when he tried, the pain in his ribs really was worse than before. He nodded and allowed DiVries to lead him up the slope.

Ramdur watched a batch of routine data feed into the computer and looked at his watch. At the present feed rate, he would have nothing to do for another five minutes. He didn't want to leave his console—the shift supervisor was that daughter of six mangy dogs who thought this was a

wholesale distribution center with twenty operators instead
of a secret intelligence operation with six.

At least she would die along with the rest of them, or at
least her memory would, if her skills were too valuable.
How would they die? Gas in the ventilation system? Poison
in the food? An explosion?

Probably the last, Ramdur decided. He had seen no
charges being placed, but that proved nothing. Those who
placed the charges would be the handpicked Field Intelligence operatives destined to leave Victoria alive.

Or might they be arranging something with the power
plant? Ramdur suspected that the underground facility used
geothermal heat, since a major pile could give a detectable
radiation signature even though many meters of rock.

But he did not know how far down the caves went; quite
possibly they went far enough to shield a full-sized pile. Or
a small one might have been brought in in pieces, for the
sole purpose of being detonated at the right time, to make
an "accidental" end to the facility and everybody in it.

Yes. That seemed to be the most likely course of action.
An "accident" that would wipe out all evidence that might
prove it was something else than, say, sabotage in a "rebel"
ammunition dump. Wipe out all the people capable of giving the evidence, too.

Ramdur looked around the room. He could not call any
of the people here his friends, but he regretted their coming
deaths more than his own. In God's good time every man
and woman met their end, but so many, by such sudden
treachery?

Did any of them realize what their masters' carelessness
with security might mean? *Had* to mean? Were they as
fatalistic as one sworn to a jihad? Or were they so desperate
that they denied the evidence because they could not accept
that the people who had rescued them would also kill them?

Some of the mercenaries were certainly that desperate.
Or so hinted the stories they told when they were drunk
and boasting loud enough to be overheard. Only desperate
people could have done some of the things they described.
And there were enough planets where a man could become
that desperate, Ramdur knew too well.

At least Colonel Pak would see that Ramdur's death was
proved and his insurance and everything else he had left

behind went where he had intended. His sister would try to take it all and leave none for his wife and daughter if she had a chance. But Pak was a just man—too just for his own good, except that he probably defined *good* in another way than most—

"Hola! Ramdur! Keep your head up and your brain powered! Three glitches and a black hole could have gone by while you were stargazing."

Ramdur forced himself to look at his console rather than glare at the supervisor. It would be foolish to attract notice now and be singled out for special punishment.

Twenty

Mahoney woke twice during the night, once when Brigitte Tachin put her hand on his cheek, once when two mines exploded downhill. The second time, he awoke to see Sergeant Stuck looking down at him.

"Theirs or ours?" he asked.

"Ours, but damned if I can see what set them off. Could be the wind."

Mahoney couldn't feel a breath of air stirring. Stuck was probably trying to spare his feelings. For a moment he was annoyed, then realized that after seventeen years' service she was probably cautious with inexperienced junior officers.

The third time Mahoney woke, dawn was flooding across the hills and he stayed awake. He was drinking tea in the shelter spread between the two medical lifters when the first air strike came in.

Six light attackers came first, each with a swollen football shape under its belly. They dove toward a part of the valley out of Mahoney's line of vision, dropping their footballs as they dove.

A tremendous ragged explosion thundered up the valley, hurling smoke, sand, dust, snow, and rock fragments higher than any hilltop. When the shock wave reached the hill, the shelter cover flapped wildly and Mahoney had to grip the edge of the nearest hatch to stay on his feet. Dust flew into his eyes, and he was still blinking when the second wave arrived.

The FAE bombs had blocked the valley behind the rebels and possibly dumped part of it on their rear. Now two heavy attackers with guns took position, one above the minefield, one above the spreading cloud. Even from a distance the snarl of their rotary cannon was vicious.

"What happens if the rebels aren't under all that fire-power?" Mahoney asked.

"I thought you Navy people had enough to answer any question—" Stroessner began.

Mahoney was too tired and too sore to argue with any-body, let alone Stroessner. He stood up and nearly collided with Lucco DiVries.

"What's going to happen, I suspect, is that the attackers will pump shells into the valley," DiVries said. "If the rebels are there, they'll either surrender or charge us. If they're not, we'll have to round them up like stray dogs over the next few days. We can't be sure of that until we've gone down into the valley on foot."

"What about the mines?" Mahoney asked.

"They'll deactivate the controlling sensors," DiVries said, glaring at Stroessner. "They could have done that last night, from the air, when I wanted to go down."

Stroessner looked at the two men, decided against repeating last night's argument, and left the shelter. Mahoney sat down and gulped the cold remnants of his tea. "I guess I'd better start pulling things together to go with—"

DiVries handed him another cup of tea. "Brian, you are pulling nothing together except yourself and going nowhere except the hospital. We have a medevac flight laid on for you and five other walking wounded."

"If we can still walk, we can—"

"Go on until you fall over? In theory, yes. In practice, that won't earn you another medal. Easy, easy. I'm not calling you a glory-hound. Just remember that if you collapse and need emergency care, all the dirtside hospitals are crammed. If you let us medevac you properly, you can be lying in a nice warm bed in *Shen*'s sick bay by lunchtime."

"Lucco, you could talk a man into deserting under fire."

"I may get that chance, with a few rebels. But seriously, Brian. This order's like the one about the mine controls—it came from a lot higher up than either of us. So there's no point in arguing."

DiVries unhooked a flask from his hip and unscrewed the top. " 'Reesa calls it *grappa*, but I think it's really intended for cleaning fluid. Cut it with tea and it's not so bad." He started pouring. "Say when."

*   *   *

Rose Liddell quickly saw that the staff's minds, bodies, and uniforms were in much better shape than they'd been last night. She was glad that she was in full undress uniform herself, but wouldn't have minded a couple more hours' sleep and a leisurely breakfast.

At least those deficiencies weren't Kuwahara's fault. Officer's Call and Morning Quarters took a certain amount of a captain's time, and they weren't needed just to keep *Shen* up to Kuwahara's standard of discipline, either. A battlecruiser with a crew of five hundred took the Hades of a lot of routine housekeeping, and every so often the captain had to check on the housekeepers.

The main display saved Yague a good deal of talking. Fort Stafford was clear, and so was Port Harriet. Most of the Thorntonsburg (really Parrville) rebels had disbanded, although Victorian and Federation forces were staying clear of the area to avoid incidents.

In the field the rebels were surrendering or running. When they ran, they were pursued and attacked as vigorously as possible, with nonlethals where these would be effective, otherwise with any appropriate weapon.

"This policy has not been protested by the Victorians so far," Yague added. "I doubt if they will. They know that any rebel bands who survive will be a bandit and terrorist problem for months. If we can't bring them in alive, we'll bring them in some other way."

The 96th Regiment's offensive had cleared about half the Freedom Legion's "liberated" towns, with the invaders usually evacuating themselves and their sympathizers. If the Legion recrossed the border with all its supporters, it might end the campaign more numerous than before, Buschton bomb and all.

"A good many of these 'recruits' will be rank civilians, even noncombatants. But their armed strength may still run over two thousand."

In Silvermouth an uneasy peace prevailed, with both sides avoiding confrontations and casualties. The Third/96th held key installations and government buildings. The rest of the city was mostly quiet, although absenteeism was high and there were reports of panic buying.

The Alliance Navy was supporting Pak's offensive as effectively as its strength and the situation allowed. The

Baernoi Training Force had reembarked the force of shuttles they had intended for lifting rebels to safety. Otherwise
they were doing nothing except sending routine reports of
equally routine ship movements.

"This may mean they have a few aces up their sleeve,"
Yague added. "It may also mean that they're about to
throw in their hand. With the Tuskers, your guess will be
as good as mine." Liddell saw both Intelligence officers
nodding.

All available Federation transport was being used to
assemble Parliament for an emergency session. That might
begin as early as tonight; if it did, the provisional government could be formally in power tomorrow.

"It could also take a week or more," Yague said. "We've
already heard of opposition to Gist himself, the amnesty for
the Freedom Legion, dealings with the Merishi, and quite
a few other things. My estimate is that we will have to make
our own policy in areas critical for the safe operation of
Federation forces, without waiting for the Victorians."

Making up that list took nearly half an hour. Everybody
seemed to have one area where they wanted to impose a
solution on the Victorians, except the admiral himself and
Commander Franke.

Liddell kept quiet. She disliked talking for the record.
She also disliked the assumption that the Victorians had
proved themselves fundamentally untrustworthy. (A couple
of officers had gone as far as suggesting independence for
Victoria only at the price of a Federation base.)

Liddell was able to hold her peace for exactly ten minutes
after the meeting ended. She was just sitting down to a
belated breakfast in her cabin when her steward announced
the admiral and Commander Franke.

"Two more places, Jensen," she said, and poured herself
another cup of tea.

"Let's not stand on protocol," Kuwahara said, entering
and pushing a chair toward Franke. He apparently preferred
to stand. "You have some private reservations, Captain?"

"I don't like the idea of another day's silence on the
amnesty. I think we need a set of guidelines, worked out
with the Army and distributed confidentially.

"We and the Victorians have small units scattered all the
way from the Krainiks to Loch Prima. If the Vics are really

going to garrison individual farms, we'll soon have even more.

"That means peace on Victoria could depend on any sergeant's whim. I don't like that. I don't think the Victorians will like it any more when they understand the situation.

"Commander Franke?"

"I agree, sir. I think we should at least have a policy on disarming Freedom Legion units. We might disarm all the ones with nonstandard weapons or no ammunition and turn them into supporting units. Then we could pair up Freedom Legion and militia units and assign each pair a Federation counterpart unit. I haven't checked out the logistics of this, but—"

"Fine. Then go and do it now, and have a report for me by noon. I'll tell the supply people to expect you."

Alone with Liddell, Kuwahara poured more tea into a cup already full. Liddell sacrificed her napkin to the resulting spill and fixed the admiral with a disrespectfully intent look.

"Sir, do you disapprove of the amnesty?"

"In principle, yes. In practice, the Victorians have made it fairly clear that most of them don't think fighting the Alliance is a serious crime. If we treat it as such, we'll have the Victorians being uncooperative.

"But if we don't, we'll have the Alliance on a hair trigger. When their reinforcements show up, they may do so with orders to shoot. The local forces may shoot sooner—at their own citizens, if our people aren't in range."

"I agree, sir, but—do you have something in mind, that involves keeping the Alliance off guard? Something involving the Merishi, perhaps?"

Kuwahara's cup tilted in his hand. The already damp napkin turned completely sodden. "Captain Liddell, I trust your talent for mind reading is not public knowledge?"

"Not yet, sir."

"Then keep it that way. I would rather not discuss the plans for the Merishi until they're a little farther along. But I'd like to arrange a meeting to discuss your ship's capabilities for another low-altitude maneuver."

That would mean Bogdanov, Fujita, and Charbon at least—the shiphandler, the engineer, and the officer-of-all-work. "How low, sir?"

"Lower than last time. And in more rugged terrain." Liddell frowned. "Problems, Captain?"

"Not likely, unless—how fast will we have to move?"

"Somewhere between dead slow and not at all."

Liddell's mind whirled even as she nodded. She couldn't ask Kuwahara for information he might not even have. But—

"I just have to remind you, sir. A capital ship at low altitude is a superb weapons platform. She is also a superb target."

"I haven't forgotten, Captain. Now, could I have some more tea? This time, I'll try not to spill any."

In civilian clothes with a hooded parka, Colonel Pak went unnoticed as he ate a late breakfast in the coffee shop on Meng Promenade. He lingered over a second cup of tea, so that by the time he left, the gray clouds overhead were keeping their promise of snow.

The taxi stand at the corner held four taxis but only one would-be fare. He was a large man, not dressed for the weather and with his face turning even redder as one taxi door after another refused to open.

The man had started hammering on one of the taxi windows when Pak came up.

"What's the matter, Citizen?"

The man turned on Pak with a "What business is it of yours?" glare. Pak pulled his hood back, and the man's glare turned into an almost obsequious grin.

"Well, thank you, sir. Couldn't have come at a better time."

Pak nodded. The local media had shown his face often enough. Almost too often, he suspected, for the privacy he always preferred and might soon desperately need.

"So what is the problem?"

"These damned cabs—I stick a government credit slip in their slots and they spit it out! It's a conspiracy to keep government workers away from their jobs!"

"Where's your job?"

"I was attached to the Agricultural Division of the Border Prefecture."

Pak nodded. Another refugee, which explained his gratitude to the man who was getting the credit for driving out the Freedom Legion. "No, I mean where are you working now?"

"I'm at a temporary office in the Gunston Hotel."

Pak nodded. The man was probably telling the truth. So were those who said that the Gunston Hotel was a Field Intelligence safe house.

"You've tried all four?"

"Want me to show you?" the man grumbled.

Pak shook his head and studied the taxis. They belonged to three different companies.

"Better have your card checked at your bank and take a bus this morning."

"Now, dammit, whose side are you on? Mine or those rebels who're marooning loyal citizens?"

"I am not on the side of making a spectacle of yourself in public and throwing around accusations of disloyalty. We have enough—"

The man raised his fist and Pak stepped back, ready to defend himself. Instead the man started wrenching at one of the cab doors. The cab rocked on its wheels, then sounded its alarm.

As if the alarm had conjured her out of thin air, a police officer came up behind the two men. "Enough, Citizen," she said sternly. "Much more and you'll be guilty of malicious damage."

"And I'll be a witness," Pak said.

The man collected enough breath to explain his situation. Pak recognized the police officer, but said nothing as she listened, then shook her head.

"Frozen slots aren't evidence of anything except that it's a cold winter—"

"God almighty! You too! I've heard stories about the police joining the rebels, but—" He made an angry gobbling sound. "I'll have your badge for that!"

"You can try," the officer said. "I'll even save you time." She handed a plastic slip with her name and badge number to the man. "Right now, though, I suggest that you try to get a bus while they're still running. I think the street crews will be out plowing, but I wouldn't bet *my* job on it."

For a moment Pak wondered what the legal complications would be if the man had a stroke and dropped dead at their feet. Instead he whirled, nearly poking the colonel in the eye with an elbow, and stamped off.

"Hello, Anna," Pak said when the man had vanished. "When was the promotion?" He pointed to the sergeant's stripe on the sleeve of her blue jacket.

Anna Chung grinned. "Last month. Bureaucracy will go on, even when the skies are falling."

"Or maybe they think that when the skies are falling, people who stay on the job are worth promoting. Still breaking up bar fights?"

As a senior patroller, Chung had been assigned to the strip outside the Silvermouth army base. She'd been a recognized expert at breaking up brawls with a minimum of unnecessary casualties.

"Not unless they get political," Chung said. "But that covers quite a lot of territory."

Pak looked around. "I've heard rumors that would make it seem our friend was telling the truth. About policemen who look the other way."

Chung's face worked. "They're not all lies. A lot of us on the force either can't or won't emigrate if Victoria goes independent. We have to walk a very fine line."

Pak nodded. It was a dilemma that had faced armies and police forces a thousand times. Enforce the law, when that means offending people who may have the power of life or death over you and your family in a year? Or look the other way and unleash Hobbes's war of all against all?

"I can see about the 96th contributing something to the Police Benevolent Fund, to help people move. But it would have to be on a voluntary basis. A good many Army people blame the police for the Border Counties trouble."

"They'd be right, too," Chung said. "The prefects were hiring any warm body and not caring if they knew squat about the border. Searching people's water stills, for God's sake! Do you have any idea how much damage a hamfisted search can do? And what happens to a border farm when the still won't come back on line and there's no credit or cash to get it fixed?"

Pak didn't, but suspected that Chung did. Her family were originally border farmers, but lost their farm and moved to Silvermouth when she was five.

"Sorry, sir," Chung said, brushing snow off her cheeks. "I got carried away."

"You have something to be carried away about," Pak said. He looked at his watch. "I have to run. If that clown goes to the Investigative Office, call me."

Chung saluted and Pak strode off. After the man's experience, he didn't want to try an Army card on one of the taxis.

Besides, the snow was coming down hard enough to interfere with anyone trailing him, but not hard enough keep him from reaching the hospital before Brigadier Fegeli. He might not need to brief his partner before they went upstairs, but he'd be damned if he'd let the man see Admiral Lopatina alone.

Joanna Marder knew that she hadn't escaped. She was back where they'd tortured her before, where they were going to torture her again.

It was the only thing she knew, because her brain now had room for only one thought at a time. She'd tried to hold two thoughts at once several times. One of them always slipped away.

Brain damage? That wasn't a thought, it was a cold dark presence that made her writhe, her limbs and her mind and her stomach—

"Restraints!" she heard someone shout. It sounded like one of those *things* in the cave. She wouldn't call them men, even if they were male. Oh, God, she knew how male they had been. All the hurting told her that—

"Hey, she's not a prisoner!"

What was that voice doing here? She knew it, but it hadn't been here in the cave the last time she heard it.

"I can't up the dosage—"

"I won't let you shackle her, damn you! Look at her!"

"The scan—"

"Oh, shove your bloody scan—"

"Lieutenant Longman, you are—"

Longman. The name floated in Marder's mind, then sank like a balloon losing gas, to settle on top of her memory of the voice. Somehow they merged into a single entity.

Sounds of footsteps and curses without words. Then a face appearing—no body, just a face. But a face that seemed to match the voice and name. A thin face, topped with tangled blond hair, ending in a much neater blond beard. An earring in one ear, and large blue eyes that stared at her with—she groped for an image, a word, anything that would define what was in those eyes.

"Commander, please. You're not back in that bloody torture chamber. You're among friends. Relax, and let the doctors work on you."

"Ah—" Her mouth was dry and sore and her lips were cracked; a sound was all she could make.

"You can hear me? Good. I'm Lieutenant Longman. I brought you in after your lifter crashed. I'm off duty for now, so I can stay with you. But you have to promise to lie still. Otherwise the doctors will have to strap you down."

She felt as weak as a baby, so maybe it made sense for him to be talking to her that way. And that was holding two thoughts in her mind at once!

She was alive. She was going to stay alive. She might even have a friend here, because she heard something in Longman's voice that she hadn't heard in a long time. She heard sympathy.

"Ah—eh—" It was too much effort to speak. But she'd moved arms and legs before, in spasms. Maybe she could control one arm—there it was, moving, a centimeter at a time—

Yes.

Long fingers, thin and hard but gentle, gripped her hand. She tried to return the grip and saw Longman smile.

"Just relax, Com—Joanna. Just relax. I won't go away." Another smile. "You look pretty good, even when you look pretty awful."

Marder thought she ought to smile back and discovered that her lips weren't as badly cracked as she'd thought. The pain wasn't bad, and even more important, it wasn't futile.

Admiral Lopatina's round cheeks were sunken, showing the high cheekbones, and the thick gray hair showed more white. The visible part of the mouth and both gray eyes were just as hard to read as ever.

Leading Hand—no, he wore a Third Class Petty Officer's stripes now—Cantacazune had warned them that the admiral tired easily. Pak nodded absently; how could it be other-wise, when she'd only been allowed visitors two days ago?

Then Pak had remembered that Cantacazune had been Joanna Marder's . . . *gopher* seemed as appropriate a term as any. Something to distract the man. . . .

"We haven't found Commander Marder yet. But that's one reason we're calling on Admiral Lopatina. She may have some ideas we've overlooked."

Cantacazune had been grinning as he let the two officers into the admiral's room. That was more than the admiral was doing. Fegeli was so nervous that Pak wanted to call a doctor and have the brigadier sedated. Hospital rooms had never improved Pak's mood, either.

"Good afternoon, I believe," Lopatina said. "You gentle-men have taken your time in coming by, I must say. Could you start by explaining why?"

"Ah, well, you were only allowed visitors—" Fegeli began.

Lopatina raised a hand. The hand was thinner and the gesture a mere ghost of her former imperious wave, but enough to silence Fegeli.

"I'm aware that I am not in command, nor do I intend to argue that point. Yet. But a little less delay would have shown a little more courtesy. Please note that for any future occasions."

The gray eyes shifted to the bedside table. One of her cherished pieces of antique enamel stood there, its brass filigree frame scraped and twisted."

"Could you hand that enamel to me? Uzel keeps promis-ing to send down the rest of what they salvaged from my cabin. So far that's all I've seen.

Pak handed Lopatina the enamel. She twisted several lengths of wire back into shape, the visible part of her face twisted in concentration. Then she put the enamel down on the blanket.

"Sit close to the bed and be brief. Without an external power source, this scrambler doesn't have the range it used to. But it should still give us a safe fifteen minutes."

Fegeli looked as if he were going to spend some of those minutes gaping at the disguised scrambler. Lopatina smiled benignly, looking like her nickname of "Baba" (Grand-mother) for the first time.

"Colonel?"

Pak summarized the situation, condensing nearly three weeks of events into less than seven minutes of briefing. His instructors at the Staff School would have been proud.

So was the Baba, it seemed. The smile was even more benign, with a touch of triumph.

"Mordecai hinted that I might need protecting from you gentlemen. That's why so many of those orderlies you may have overlooked are grounded Navy people. I will take a modest pleasure in proving him wrong."

Pak shrugged. "I'm sorry if our guards gave that impression. Were there any incidents?"

Lopatina shook her head, then looked at Fegeli. "Brigadier, some German once said that the best commanders are the brilliant but lazy. So far you're proving that he was right. Only don't carry the laziness so far the next time."

Pak thought he heard a note of dismissal, but the hand came up again. "Wait. I think you people have our side of things under as much control as we can hope for. We can't do anything about the Federation, and we don't want to do anything about the local opposition."

Fegeli stared. "Absolutely not," Lopatina said sharply. "The more Hollings and Field Stupidity worry about local dissidents, the less time they'll have to worry about us."

"Unless Hollings worries himself into some radical move," Fegeli pointed out. "Or into listening to suggestions from the Field people."

"True. But some things are always in the realm of chance. Our governor's mental stability—such as it is—may be one of them.

"The Baernoi are also a matter of chance. But su-Irzim is no bloodytusked bombthrower, and the Federation outguns him considerably.

"No, it is a case of 'Deliver me from my friends, I can take care of my enemies.' When naval reinforcements appear, they will have somebody outranking Uzel in command. We can hope that the commander will have the sense to consult with us, or at least me."

"What if the commander outranks you?" Fegeli said.

"There are only nine admirals senior to me in the whole Navy," the Baba said. "The last time I looked at the list, all of them were in positions where they could not be spared. But that is something else we have to leave to chance.

"One thing I suggest we not leave to chance is what is to be done if either one of you is arrested or shot. I will have reliable Navy people help with any—ah, arrangements—you may need to make."

"That's been taken care of," Pak said. Even in reach of the scrambler, he didn't want to give details.

"Good. Then I'll suggest—no, make it a request. Put me on the list of people whose death or arrest will—ah, trigger your response."

This time it was Pak who stared and Fegeli who nodded. "Yes, ma'am. But—do you have any reason—"

"Only the normal paranoia about our self-appointed watchdogs of loyalty. Also, if I am going to become involved in what is technically a treasonable conspiracy, I would like to know that my death will not be wasted."

The Baba settled down into the pillows and adjusted her bed. She looked almost cozy, and her tone matched the look.

"Now, can we talk about something pleasant for a change? You are the first visitors I've had who have the wits to be good company." She grunted as she reached for the scrambler and turned it off.

"Domenic, have you seen Estelle Wojik's version of *Tosca* . . . ?"

Brigitte Tachin spent a dull morning after Mahoney was medevacked, inspecting weapons that were all as good as they were going to be on this miserable frozen pimple of rock. She ate an even duller lunch of lukewarm field rations, then took a nap out of sheer boredom. She had no advice to give her Victorian charges except "Stay clear of the Federation regulars," and they were already doing that without her saying a word.

The afternoon was considerably more interesting than the morning, in the Chinese sense of the word for *interesting*.

Tachin awoke to find that she, Lieutenant Stroessner, and Captain DiVries were the only officers left on the hill. All the others had piled into a lifter along with a security squad and flown off in a northerly direction on an unspecified mission with no ETA for their return.

Ten minutes after that, she was having a wake-up tea in the medical lifter when Sergeant Stuck put her head into the compartment.

"Lieutenant Stroessner's compliments, ma'am, and he'd like to see you at the CP."

Stroessner was glaring as if she'd deserted under fire when Tachin arrived. She learned quickly that the glare wasn't for her.

"Some Vics coming in to surrender," he said. "Can we trust your people?"

"They aren't my people. What they do depends on what kind of 'Vics' are coming in. Freedom Legion or Action for Independence?"

"Messkit Flight reports three civilian-model lifters about forty kloms out, low and slow. Freedom Legion insignia on one side, white triangles on the other."

Tachin nodded. That was one of the standard visual signals for surrender. "Did they say how many they were?"

"No. Just an ETA and a request for medical assistance."

"Fine. I'll alert Captain DiVries—"

"Lieutenant. I'd rather DiVries didn't know about this until we've moved the regulars into position."

The implications of that remark struck Tachin like a fist in the stomach. Her voice died, but she wished that Brian Mahoney was still on hand. He outranked that *espèce de chameau* and might have some alternative besides obeying and kicking him in the balls.

"Is that an order, sir?"

"Yes."

That could sign the death warrant of any critical cases with the Freedom Legion.

"Sir, it's an illegal order. It involves the potential of mistreating prisoners of war."

"You still have to obey it before protesting. Also, 'potential mistreatment' isn't a crime—and don't play barracks lawyer with me, you damned Navy socket!

"Yes, sir."

"Look, a fight with the Vics will do a lot more damage than a five-minute delay in alerting the medics."

"If there was any danger of such a fight, I would agree with you."

"But you don't?"

*I wonder if he transferred from Graves Registration in
order to drum up some more business.*

"No, sir."

"All right. But I hope you'll find some way to stay out of
the line of fire between us and your—the militia platoon."

"Is that an order?"

"No, but I'm tempted to make it one. I wouldn't want
Lieutenant Mahoney to learn I didn't take care of you."

Tachin hurried outside. She was halfway to the Victorian
positions before she had her gear fully sealed.

The three platoons had plenty of time to go on alert and
even time to start being bored. "Low and slow" was an
understatement for the Freedom Legion lifters. They barely
cleared the southern side of the valley, and they drifted up
to the open hillside no faster than a man could run.

All three grounded safely, although one slewed and
started to tilt before the pilot caught it with the fans. The
people who climbed out looked more like a collection of
newly landed indenturees than any sort of military force.

Standing beside Stroessner, Tachin noticed him sneering.
Then she noticed something else. About thirty of the new
arrivals were armed. Seven were not, and a closer look
showed that they had their hands tied behind their backs.

A pinch-faced redheaded young man stepped forward and
saluted. "Sergeant Lewis of Six Company, Second Battalion, Victorian Freedom Legion, reporting with his platoon.
We wish to turn over seven prisoners of war from Action
for Independence."

Stroessner and Tachin returned the salutes, unable to
think of anything else to do. The Army officer recovered
his voice first. Orders barked into his radio brought a squad
down at a run, to cut the prisoners out of the Freedom
Legion ranks and march them out of the way.

"Now, I must inform you that you yourselves, as members of an illegal military organization, are under arrest. By
the powers vested in me—"

Tachin studied the faces of the Freedom Legionnaires as
Stroessner finished his proclamation. If she was any judge
of this sort of thing, they would not be disarmed peacefully.

She looked back over her shoulder and saw some of the
militia quietly shifting position, weapons in hand. The sergeant looked as if he wanted to crawl under a rock. She

shook her head, then reinforced the gesture with a double-handed thumbs-down.

"Lieutenant, what—" Stroessner began.

DiVries hurried up, scanned the Freedom Legionnaires, and pointed at Lewis. "Sergeant. Do you have any casualties?"

"We've got six walking ones out here, sir. Two stretcher cases and a couple of bodies back in the second lifter." He looked toward the Action for Independence prisoners. "We thought Gwen and Cao were going to make it, but those bastards grenaded the aid post when they tried to overrun it."

"You fought the rebels?" If Stroessner was talking in order not to appear stupid, he was not succeeding.

"There's about ten bodies back there—" the sergeant began.

DiVries interrupted again. "Sergeant, get your wounded over to our MedCorps station. I'll call in a medevac while you're doing that."

"These people have not surrendered!" Stroessner yelled.

"If they haven't surrendered, they're allies and entitled to medical assistance," DiVries said. "If they have surrendered, they're POWs and also entitled to medical assistance."

"Captain, I order you—"

DiVries made an obscene gesture, brushed past Stroessner, and headed for his lifter. Tachin saw the lieutenant's hand dart toward his holster, and she unslung her own carbine.

Behind her she heard a slithering hiss as Sergeant Stuck did the same with her pulser. Tachin shook her head. She was the officer; it was her duty to be executed for shooting Stroessner, if it came to that—

Stroessner folded his arms across his chest and glared at everybody impartially. Tachin stepped forward, glad to be able to trust her legs and hoping her voice would also do its job.

"Now, while we're dealing with your casualties and prisoners, Sergeant Stuck and I will hold weapons inspection." She raised a hand at the protests. "No, we're not disarming you. Just seeing what you have.

"It may be just propaganda. But we've heard that many of you have substandard weapons, or defective ones, or ones for which ammunition is hard to find. Since you're the first Freedom Legion unit to sur—to come in, your cooperation will be important."

She thought she heard a strangled curse from Stroessner and she knew she heard a strangled laugh from Stuck. "Sergeant, if I can start with you . . ."

Sergeant Lewis swallowed, then unslung what looked like a medium-bore scattergun and a bandolier of shells, and handed them both to Tachin.

Twenty-one

Madeleine Bloch hugged Candice Shores, then climbed into her lifter. Shores stepped back as the lifter's fans kicked up dust and snow, then waved as the lifter climbed up from Pad 2. As it joined the other Ranger lifters orbiting over Camp Aounda, the whole formation swung ninety degrees and sailed away to the west.

Glory be, Maddie's hug didn't last too long this time! What next—Captain Liddell having an affair?

Scout Company and Bloch's attached Rangers had come into camp this morning, replaced on outpost duty by a company of Associated States forces. Shores wished the Vics luck in fighting boredom, sinus inflammations, and the occasional Action for Independence diehard.

She also hoped her Scouts hadn't done anything outrageous in pursuit of liquor, entertainment, or congenial partners. She'd given them the rest of the day off, and if any senior officer wanted to countermand that order he'd damned well have to do his own dirty work. The Scouts had come in after a week of hard training and ridge-running, fit, finely honed, and frustrated at spending that week on the sidelines while the newlies and the Vics did most of the rebel-chasing.

She could use a drink herself, Shores decided. So first stop was Major Abelsohn's, and after the drink he could tell her who the real SOP was. The camp was still the base for Task Force Borha, but half its officers were usually in the field and the SOP more often than not was some visiting fireman. However, any visitor who brought orders sending the Scouts into action would have his or her feet kissed, regardless of rank, sex, or previous acquaintance.

Sergeant Esteva met her at the door to Abelsohn's office.

"The major expected you'd be over here and told me to offer you anything in his cabinet on one condition."

If it's a proposition, I might actually accept it.

"Yes?"

"That you drink up, then get over to the hospital. Colonel Nieg's over there and he wants to see you."

"Nieg? In the hospital?"

"Not *in*, Major. *At.* He's got into a brawl with the chief surgeon over interrogating a prisoner who came in last night. Or maybe you should call her a defector."

"She?"

"Commander Marder."

"I thought she'd been killed by terrorists."

Esteva looked very sober. "Major, from what I've heard of the shape she's in, she might wish she had been."

Shores turned and sprinted for the door. She could always raid the hospital's liquor supply instead of Abelsohn's.

The masked man leaned forward. Rahbad Sarlin concluded that his interrogator was either pretending to be eager or else so careless that he did not care how much his body language betrayed.

Carelessness seemed more likely, considering what else the Special Projects agent had seen and heard since he awoke in this underground prison. For much of it, Sarlin would have dismissed any of his subordinates, if not indeed had them tried by Special Projects Justice.

But carelessness by inferiors did not always mean that the superior was contemptible. Best not assume what would be most convenient—a dangerous error in Special Projects, even when you were not a prisoner of the people about whom you were making the assumptions!

Sarlin did his best to project total indifference, allowing for physiological differences and the fact that he was not using his native language. He ended by shrugging, a gesture that surprised the human out of either his eagerness or his act.

"You don't care what happens to you?" the masked man asked. Sarlin was almost sure it was a man; the configuration of chest and hips differed more between male and female in humans than among the People, and the interrogator was narrow-hipped and flat-chested.

"I do. But not enough to turn traitor."

"Ah. But what about suffering the fate of traitors among your own people, without any reward from us?"

"You speak in riddles. It is your right, but is it wisdom?"

The man started so that he nearly fell off his stool. It rattled; Sarlin saw a guard's face appear at the small window in the door of his cell.

"Your guards are efficient. But there is no need for them."

The man rose, waved furiously to the guard, then sat down again. He took a deep breath.

"Very well. Plain speaking you wish. Plain speaking you shall have. We know that death, torture, or drugs mean nothing to you. You would—"

"End up a corpse, past suffering, useless to you, and a subject for endless inquiry and possible vengeance from the People."

"If you wish to spend the whole day putting words in my mouth, I cannot stop you. But I do not need to endure it. I will leave the next time I am interrupted."

He apparently thought that was a significant threat. Sarlin decided that he could not be sure it was not and should hold his tongue.

"We will release you," the man said. "But if you do not cooperate, we will also release . . . call them rumors—that you are now working for us. Think of what that could do."

Sarlin thought, and found his conclusions neither pleasant nor trivial. He might end his career spattered with dung, and while it had been a long career it was not one he wished to end yet, or dishonorably at any time.

Even if he was cleared, it would take much work by Special Projects to do so. Work by agents who had better things to do. Indirectly, this diversion of effort might do as much damage as he could do by actual treason.

Above all, it would weaken confidence in Special Projects, one place among the People where there was neither Antahl nor Syrodh. Either one was Special Projects or one was not.

The duel between the two great folk among the People was a weakness. It might yet lay them naked to their enemies. Anything that might make that duel worse or more durable should not be done.

"I think it could do much harm, which I would rather not see happen," Sarlin said. "*If* you had any way of making the rumors convincing. I have to wonder if you could."

"You may wonder all you wish. But would you care to wager your career or anyone else's on it?"

Sarlin would not, and said so. Under the mask, the man seemed to be smiling.

"Good. Then I am sure you can think of matters on which you have information that we would find valuable. When you have done so, give the guards the code word *rowboat*. Everything you need will be provided."

Sarlin feigned disappointment. "Nothing today?"

"We have no way of returning you to your own people safely now. Do not, however, think that we are giving you time to make up fancy stories. If you lie, our bargain ends."

"I would expect nothing less."

The man rose and bowed himself out.

Actually Sarlin had expected much less information and much more threatening behavior. The man had virtually confirmed the agent's suspicion, that his captors' military situation was poor. Something they had put much hope in— apparently a rebellion against the Victorian government— had failed.

So givi~ ~im time was making a free gift of what he would have gladly paid for. With time, the enemies of his captors might find where he was held—for their own reasons, but he would gain regardless. It was even possible that his captors might face division in their own ranks.

Meanwhile, what should he tell? Perhaps it was indeed for the best that he had been given some time to think this over. He knew that he should not give anything that might let the humans make the story of his treason convincing. Humans had already been given dangerous weapons once on Victoria, and thousands of ghosts bore witness to what might come of that. It occurred to Sarlin that it might be worth revealing more than he would otherwise, if it helped win one of two victories.

The greater victory would be that the Alliance Navy never knew who had provided the sunbombs that destroyed the Bonsai Squadron. The lesser victory would be that the People learned how their access codes had been bypassed, so that they could exercise more control the next time they chose to make such a dangerous gift.

Candice Shores found Nieg and the chief surgeon, Major Huth, in the surgeon's office and looking daggers at each other. To keep the looking from turning to throwing, she stepped between them before saluting.

"Major Shores reporting, sir."

Nieg waved her to a chair. "Thank you, Major. Dr. Huth, I'll trust you with the briefing."

Huth was prolix and if he'd gone on five minutes longer would have required surgery himself. From his flow of words Shores did extract the substance of the situation.

Commander Marder had turned up, after escaping from her terrorist kidnappers. She'd been brutally treated as a prisoner and added exposure and minor fractures during her escape.

She might be an intelligence windfall. She might also be a plant, by Field Intelligence or somebody equally hostile to the Federation. She needed to be interrogated as soon as possible, to decide which. If she had any valuable intelligence, about her captors or anything else, every hour—every minute, for that matter—counted.

But she had been heavily loaded with drugs and hypnotically implanted false memories. This had been handled incompetently as well as brutally. No one seemed to have done a metabolic analysis to determine the effects of her alcoholism.

She could not safely be either restrained or drugged again. The only thing that seemed to make her cooperative was the presence of Lieutenant Longman—

"Him?" Shores thought she'd managed not to sound incredulous. Nieg and Huth both laughed. She flushed.

"Well, apart from his being a man, and most women who've been mistreated not liking men around—Charles Longman *comforting* somebody?"

"I've seen stranger things happen, in people loaded with amnesiacs," Huth said. "Apparently she has some sort of residual memory of Longman in a benign role. Do you happen to know if they were ever intimate?"

"I'd put a large bet against it," Shores said. "So what do you want me to do?"

"Talk Longman into leaving, and substitute yourself for him if Marder needs a friendly face," Nieg said. "You're cleared for the material we'll be discussing. Longman isn't."

"Why not get him a clearance?"

"That would take too long."

Shores decided that she didn't really *have* to end her career as a general and faced Nieg.

"From what Dr. Huth said, it will be quite a while before Marder is in any shape to talk. If we start processing Longman's clearance now, why shouldn't it be ready before Marder is?"

Huth made a noise halfway between a laugh and a cheer. Nieg glared at him. Huth glared back.

"Doctor, if you—"

"If Major Shores is going to help us, she needs all the facts. Ah—Colonel Nieg asked me not to mention this. But there is . . . an implant . . . in Commander Marder's stomach. It shows up on several scan modes, and is definitely synthetic and recent. It was probably administered orally—"

"Never mind the medical terminology," Nieg said wearily. "The problem is, we can't tell what it is without going in and pulling it out. It could be a time-release poison. It could be a bomb."

"It could also carry data that someone among the terrorists was trying to send out," Shores said.

Nieg looked at her. "Have you thought of transferring to Intelligence?"

"I promise to think of anything you ask, if you'll let me go in and talk to Longman now. Oh, one thing more. Major Huth, what's the problem with operating?"

"Invasive procedures might render Marder catatonic. Many of the anesthetics might kill her, or do major brain damage."

Which was explanation, if not excuse, for Nieg climbing the walls. He could appeal Huth's opinion all the way up to Colonel Chatterje, but the doctors would probably all say the same about endangering a patient by premature surgery, and he couldn't appeal to anyone in his own chain of command.

They were all under doctor's orders, as unlikely as it

seemed. Charlie Longman was an odd key to any situation, but here he seemed the only one.

"Did you see Sergeant Stuck assume firing position?"

"I saw her after she had assumed it. I can't say exactly when she did so."

The Federation colonel frowned. "But it was after Lieutenant Stroessner appeared ready to use a weapon?"

Brigitte Tachin shook her head. "I am not an infantryman. I could not be sure if he was preparing to actually use his weapon, or merely to be able to draw it quickly if the need arose."

"I know you're not an infantryman," Peter Bissell said. He now wore the badges of a full colonel in the Associated States Forces. "But you are a major witness to the threat presented by the Victorians and other parties in this situation. So I have to ask you: Is there any previous connection between you and Lieutenant Stroessner?"

Tachin flushed, and the colonel let out a hungry growl. "No."

"Remember, you are under oath—" Bissell began.

The Federation colonel let out an obscenity in Italian and General Langston slapped his hands down on the table. "Colonel Bissell! Your privileges as a member of this investigative body do not extend to insulting witnesses by implying that they are either promiscuous, untruthful, or mentally limited. Is this understood?"

"Yes, sir," Bissell said blandly. "So you have no reason to defend Lieutenant Stroessner?"

Tachin decided that an affair with Bissell would have been an even bigger mistake than she'd previously thought. Unless he was behaving like this on orders from somebody higher up in the Associated States Forces.

"Could you answer the question, please, Lieutenant Tachin?"

"No. I never saw or heard of him before last night. My only concern is that this investigation distinguish crimes from mistakes."

Langston smiled. "We share that concern, believe it or not. Continue with your testimony, Lieutenant."

Tachin went on describing the Freedom Legion's arrival for another ten minutes, with fewer interruptions. By the time she was done, her skin was slimy and her uniform damp with sweat. She wished they would turn down the heat in the command module. Then she decided that under the circumstances she would be sweating if she were stark naked!

The investigators finally let her go, with a warning not to leave the camp. Since she had nowhere to go and no means of getting there if she did, Tachin thought the last was superfluous.

In fact, she thought a good many of the high-ranking officers who'd descended on the camp were superfluous. Victoria Command's brass had been caught with their pants down by the incoming Freedom Legion; maybe they were just demonstrating how quickly they could pull them up again.

Anyway, four attackers brought General Langston and six other officers out to the camp. The company officers hastily returned from their personal reconnaissance, just in time to be superseded by an entire company of Third/215 with a light colonel for overall command of the area.

Now the worry was how to accommodate all the newlies. Fortunately a heavy transport came rumbling in from Camp Aounda, with modules, supplies, and shelters dripping from every hatch. At the price of turning virtually everybody except one security platoon into a labor gang, the expanded camp was ready to do business by midafternoon.

The first item of business was investigating the behavior of the Freedom Legion walk-ins, and apparently also of their reception committee. This involved five of the six officers besides Langston, and the only one Tachin had ever heard of besides the general was Peter Bissell, who behaved like a prosecuting attorney!

Tachin was sure of one thing: If all this was because the Army needed good relations with the Vics, it was a good argument for *never* transferring to the Army. She would leave the diplomacy to Brian; she could take over with brute force when the talktalk didn't produce—

"Hello, Lieutenant. Need a warm-up?"

It was Sergeant Stuck, holding two steaming cups. Tachin practically snatched one, then choked on her first gulp. It was nearly half brandy, and not local liquor either.

"Where did you—"

Stuck looked at the ceiling and gave a brief explanation that mentioned generals' private stocks, militia supply clerks, and Freedom Legion equipment useless except as souvenirs. Tachin decided that if she understood what she heard, she would probably have to reprimand Stuck. Ignorance clearly was bliss in this case.

She took another, smaller swallow and began to feel some of the bliss. Stuck sat down and sipped her own drink.

"Don't sweat Stroessner, Lieutenant."

"Did I ask for your advice?"

"No, but I think you need it."

When a sergeant decided that a junior officer needed advice, that junior officer was damned well going to listen. Either that or be written up in the sergeant's bad books for the rest of their respective careers. Tachin decided she didn't have the energy to argue. Besides, Stuck might be right.

"Go ahead."

"Just this. You were doing your job. Peter Bissell is doing his. Stroessner wasn't. Christ knows I don't like this frozen dustball, but I've got sense not to bully the people when they're carrying guns.

"Stroessner doesn't. You won't convince the board that he does. He'll spend his next couple of tours as recycling projects coordinator in Lower Fungoolistan and then be told his services aren't required."

"You've got a lot of faith in military justice."

"When it comes to weeding out the terminally dumb, it's not bad. We've got an incentive that some people don't. The dumb get us killed, and administrative action's less tricky than fragging the bastards."

Stuck drained her cup. "Dividend?"

"No, thanks."

"Okay. But I'd recommend getting your kit together. Rumor's come down that all Navy advisers are going home."

"Home?" Warmth, liquor, and release of tension were making Tachin muzzy-headed.

"Back to your ships."

"I'm not supposed to leave—"

"Orders can be changed. Will be changed, if it's about to

hit the fan upstairs. Want me to send someone to help you pack?"

Tachin shook her head, emptied her cup, and got to her feet without any help.

Shores recognized a maximum-security hospital room even without the two guards posted outside. Nieg had already sent her authorization; her ID let her in.

She didn't recognize Charles Longman. He looked ten years older, which in him was an improvement. He was sitting beside a barely recognizable Commander Marder and holding one bandaged hand as lightly as if it were a newly hatched bird.

He was also talking to her, which was something of a relief. Shores would have expected the Last Judgment to be at hand the day Charles Longman didn't babble.

"—wild when she was my age, or so the story goes. I know she posed for quite a few artists, and not all of them the respectable kind either. The story also goes that she bought up all the copies of the pictures when she hit four stripes. Wouldn't do to have nudes of a future admiral all over Zone Six."

"Lieutenant Longman."

"Not that the problem really existed, except in my dad's mind. I guess he must have practiced on Aunt Di, for the way he sat on me."

"Charlie," Shores said. He noticed her enough to make a shushing gesture and went right on talking.

Shores refrained from assault when she saw that Marder was apparently listening, and sometimes even smiling. In another ten minutes Longman had run through the entire history of his family and all its branches, regular and irregular, and Marder was asleep. Not smiling, and sometimes twitching and twisting with pain or nightmares, but sleeping almost normally.

"Charlie," Shores said when she had his attention. "You know what happened to Marder?"

"Didn't Huth tell you?" the lieutenant snapped. He began reciting Marder's injuries and abuses until Shores's stomach was ready to turn over. She held up a hand.

"All right. But then why—"

"Did I talk about my relatives' sex life? Look, Major, you're not a therapist. You're here to twist my arm about letting Jo be talked at, ripped open, what have you. Let me finish, and you can lobby until you turn blue, for all I care."

"Will you listen if I do?"

Longman nodded, then started talking. "It doesn't seem to matter what I say. As long as it's me saying it, and holding her hand seems to help even more. Damned if I know why I got stuck in her memory, either. But I'm there, and if I can help . . ."

He went on for another ten minutes, his words slower and quieter with each minute. Halfway along, Shores sat down on the other side of Marder's bed. She'd never seen Longman like this. If both Nate Abelsohn and Brian Mahoney hadn't told her about similar cases they'd seen, she'd have suspected it was an act.

As it was, Longman seemed genuinely humble at the role fate had assigned him in Joanna Marder's life. Humble, and determined that she'd be mistreated (as he saw it) only over his dead body.

That determination might not reflect ideally on his judgment and ethics. But it was firm, and Shores was damned if she was going to add to either Marder's or Hamilton's troubles so that Nieg could chase some intelligence will-o'-the-wisp.

Marder had been through enough hell already, and as for Charlie—Shores began to realize that there were things just as bad as too little parenting. One of them was too much, all of it aimed at molding you into something you couldn't be.

Somewhere toward the end of Charlie's recital, Marder began talking in her sleep. Longman went on for a couple of minutes, breaking off at intervals to reassure Marder.

He finally stopped when they both realized that the commander was saying one thing over and over again. "Across the valley from the door—a rock like a Death Commando's head. Across the valley from the door—a rock like a Death Commando's head. Across the valley—"

"Oh, Christ," Longman said. "Jo, I'm sorry. If I started off—"

Shores held up one hand and gripped Marder's bandaged

left hand with the other. The commander winced, twisted her head on a long, elegant, and dreadfully bruised neck, and went right on muttering the phrase.

Shores eased her grip. "Charlie," she said. "I don't think you've done anything. Or at least nothing wrong. It sounds like a location, or some way of recognizing a location."

"I follow you that far. But the location of—oh, Christ," he concluded, in a very different tone.

Shores nodded. "It could be where they held her. If it's got a distinctive rock outside the 'door'—sounds like a cave—"

"Scan the map and photo files." Longman leaped up, not letting go of Marder's hand and nearly pulling her up with him. Shores grabbed his arm and untangled first him, then Marder's blankets and tubing.

"Charlie, we can put this to Nieg, and he can have the scan done faster than we can. Meanwhile—Charlie, will you submit to the procedures for a security clearance, if we let you sit in on Jo's surgery?"

"I don't see why she needs—"

Shores wanted to turn Longman upside down, to see if that would improve the blood flow to his brain. She settled for gripping his shoulders.

"Charlie, Huth's right. It could be a bomb, or it could tell us exactly what's inside that cave."

"All right. Provided he uses a spinal block, so she doesn't go under again and knows I'm there."

"You don't have a license, Charlie. Where do you come from, prescribing treatment?"

"For that matter, Major, where do you come from, help-ing rather than hurting? I thought Scouts—"

"Scouts sometimes decide it's better to help keep people from doing what they'd otherwise have to be hurt for." She stopped as she realized that she was nearly quoting Nieg.

Then she looked at the commander, now silent, her blan-kets slipped down to expose one shoulder that looked as if it had been branded with acid. "But there's going to be hurting, Charlie. Don't worry. Some people are going to get hurt very badly over this, and you've helped."

She stopped as Longman winced and she realized she was gripping his shoulders hard enough to break the skin. She flexed her fingers, then took a deep breath.

"Let's get on the horn, Charlie."

The attacker passed over the edge of a storm front, and the gray desert and grayer mountains of Victoria vanished from the screen. A familiar voice came on the intercom.

"This is your cabin attendant for Navy Flight 19, to *Shenandoah, Baikhal, Valhalla,* and other scenic Victoria Task Force destinations. The smoking lamp is now lit in all authorized spaces. Self-service food and beverage will be available for the next thirty minutes. We will give you our ETA for *Shenandoah* as soon as possible. Thank you."

Brigitte Tachin had just unstrapped and put her finally thawed feet on the deck when Elayne Zheng popped through the hatch at the forward end of the cabin. "Hi, Brigitte."

"Hello yourself, Elayne. What are you doing on a flight crew?"

"It's a long story, but to make it short, they've got an Emergence report."

"An Emergence?" somebody said from another bunk.

"Multiship and unidentified," Zheng said with relish. "So the Navy's taking no chances of having people it may need down picking mites out of their pubic hairs. That meant getting everybody back upstairs fast, which meant attackers, which meant every attacker-qualified body finally had to be plugged in.

"Speaking of plugging in, Brian sends his love—"

"Elayne!" Tachin didn't waste time blushing. "You've been up to *Shen* already?"

"Hauling a batch of lifter-carriers borrowed from Candy Shores's Scouts."

Zheng conjured up a flask; several people replied by conjuring up cups. Tachin shook her head. The half-brandy tea was still fuming in her brain.

"Poor Candy," Zheng went on. "If they don't get her into action pretty soon they'll have to chain her up to keep her from biting generals. Oh, well—"

To stem the flood of words, Tachin said, "How is Brian?"

"He'll be in sick bay tonight, but only for observation. Of course, if you don't want any observation in Mori's Pain Palace—"

This time blushing was a pure reflex. "What's the matter?" Zheng asked. "Never heard of a sick bay without beds yet."

"Elayne, you have a one-gutter mind."

Twenty-two

"We have it?" Shores said, as Lieutenant Colonel Nieg entered the secured computer room.

Nieg silently held out a shiny gray plastic capsule, about the size of a mite-nest cocoon. A second look showed writing on it. A third look turned the writing into chemical formulae.

"If that's the access code, fine," Nieg said. "If that's what detonates it—are you through with your review of the 'ghost' data?"

Shores handed an all-modes file to the Intelligence officer. "I had to rush it a bit toward the last, but I don't find any holes big enough to notice, let alone worry about."

"No. Shamil wasn't twisted enough to actually destroy data. So we're left with normal human error, which the Lord knows can be quite enough."

Shores rested her hands lightly on the colonel's shoulders. She needed the touch, after four hours in the company of a computer, and Nieg looked as if he would welcome human contact.

He didn't move or smile, but at least he didn't frown. Then he reached up to her hands and put both of his over them.

"Thank you, Major. Now I would like you to leave. If it is a bomb—"

"Permission to get drunk at your funeral, sir?"

"Permission to get drunk at all the funerals, both military and family. I've left a message requesting my family to invite you to the service. It may be rather wild, but you'll be there as a warrior, not a woman."

Considering the colonel's ancestry, this might be useful. "Thank you, sir."

"I also left in your quarters a thumbprint-coded autoerase

briefing on what we're planning, if we wind up with a reasonable amount of data. That will go ahead no matter what happens to me, but I thought you should know before General Langston descends on you."

Nieg called up the communications log. "Any word on the survey-data scan?"

"No. The squadron seems to be a bit busy with that Emergence. Either I'm not on the need-to-know list for a straight answer or they don't have one."

Nieg shook his head. "I should have put your name in for need-to-know. But I suppose it won't matter, until Kuwahara gets back.

"Anyway, my last word from upstairs was that the Emergence is multiship, unidentified, and probably more than five days from Victoria. Almost certainly, I would say, unless they were cutting the Jump very fine indeed."

Shores nodded. If the incoming visitors had Jumped into Victoria's system close to the safe limit of its star's gravity well, they were in a hurry. But then, anybody coming to Victoria now would be, and the laws of physics bound Baernoi, Merishi, and human alike.

"So we have about a week to do whatever it is you're cooking up?"

"What makes you think anybody is cooking anything?"

"I don't *think* it, sir. I *know* it. Right here."

Nieg's eyes followed Shores's hand. She flushed as she realized that she'd patted herself about twelve centimeters lower than she'd intended.

The colonel's eyebrows rose. Shores saluted.

"See you in the morning, sir, and . . . good luck."

Kuwahara knew that biologically the Merishi really *were* a nocturnal life-form and that personally he was not. Personal preferences, however, were quite irrelevant. Councillor Payaral Na'an wanted to discuss the status of Victoria's Merishi tonight. Nothing short of the primary going nova was going to put him off. A mere unidentified Emergence was less serious than a heating-system failure.

Kuwahara ran a finger around the inside of his collar and briefly wished that the heating system *would* fail. Evolved from reptilians on a hotter planet than Earth, the Merishi had a comfort range about ten degrees higher than humans.

It would have weakened Kuwahara's position to insist that Na'an or his aides wear heated coveralls; it would have also weakened it for the humans to appear in less than complete uniform.

There was nothing to do but literally sweat out the negotiations and be thankful that the translation was computerized. Kuwahara wouldn't have trusted a Merishi translator, and a human one might have been affected by the heat.

"I trust all is well with your ships," Na'an said, making a basket of his long clawed fingers, four on each square hand. "If these visitors represent an immediate threat—"

Kuwahara shrugged, the human equivalent of Na'an's gesture. "They cannot represent an immediate threat. Indeed, the only question about them is their identity, and they may not seek to conceal it."

"And if they do?"

"Then Commodore Uehara can respond to that situation as well as I could. Possibly better, indeed, having spent more time on courier and survey duty. I will not say that we can continue our negotiations as if these newcomers did not exist. I will say that we have no reason to let them divert our attention."

"Certainly. But if I might suggest a small drink?"

"Juice?"

"Of course."

The Merishi could metabolize alcohol but not well; they were limited to beer among human or Baernoi drinks. The most mutually acceptable beverage for human and Merishi had turned out to be apricot juice. Na'an moved to fill glasses from a jug in the refrigerator under the table.

Kuwahara watched the Merishi merchant's graceful movements. The Merishi didn't have the exquisite feline quality of the Ptercha'a, but they were certainly a contrast with the Baernoi. The Tuskers gave the impression of rugged, durable, versatile machinery with no aesthetic merits whatever. The Merishi could at least be elegant.

Na'an was a little too stout to be elegant, which suggested he was either older or more self-indulgent than his file said. In fact, he reminded Kuwahara of Commander Franke, who was sitting behind him at a small table.

Na'an not only poured but served the apricot juice. That meant that either he was accepting an inferior position to

Kuwahara or he had some reason to ignore formal etiquette. Merishi of Na'an's rank seldom did the first, and he could have fifty reasons for the second, some of them entirely trivial.

Kuwahara drank his juice and reviewed Uehara's plans for identifying the Emergent newcomers. Light cruisers on listening watch several million kloms out would give a reasonable base for fixing the newcomers' position. Ionization from particle contact with either their hulls or their shields would permit a rough guess of their speed, and *Baikhal* was as well equipped for that as the Nicola Chennault Observatory (which had been warned, a warning unacknowledged because it was still on the way).

Scouts flying close formation on the Baernoi and Alliance squadrons might be in a position to intercept even tight-beam signals. Kuwahara hoped the commodore wouldn't interpret *close* too aggressively.

He also admitted that if Uehara was hoping for an excuse to clear the space around Victoria of non-Federation ships, he wasn't the only one. The Victoria Task Force had a battleship-sized chip on its shoulder after the Action for Independence uprising.

Na'an finally set down his empty glass and signaled his aide to tidy up. As the aide set to work, Na'an again made a cradle of his fingers.

"The only matter that seems to stand between us and agreement on the terms you proposed is a small one. I hardly wish to dignify it by the term *matter*, but perhaps you can suggest a better one after you have heard it."

"If it is solid, liquid, gas, or plasma, then it is matter," Kuwahara said. He could play word games as long as any Merishi merchant prince and ten sentences longer.

"I would not imply that Mr. Gist is gaseous. He seems a rather solid object to me."

Kuwahara's mental displays flashed warnings. "So I have found him. Let us call this matter, then, and proceed to analyze it."

"It is simple enough. We endorse the proposed amnesty for the Freedom Legion. If it is accepted, we of Merish in turn will accept whatever legal position the Federation wishes—short of indenture or slavery, of course."

"Those would not be in the interests of the Federation to

propose, let alone in yours to accept," Kuwahara said, simply for the sake of keeping his mouth moving.

"I was jesting. Forgive me. I know this is a serious matter."

Kuwahara nodded. "You are aware that the Alliance is likely to oppose that amnesty and that not everyone in the Associated States favors it?"

"We are. We also hope that you have not suddenly become solicitous of the interests of the Alliance on Victoria, which will not survive a Standard year except by military force. That, I presume, you would resist."

"May earthquakes crush my young if I endure it." The Merishi phrasing would not conceal Kuwahara's distaste for the Alliance.

In fact, he felt considerably more distaste for the Alliance than he now felt for Gist's proposal. He could understand why the ex-governor-general and aspiring prime minister wanted to push the matter, to obtain Merishi and Federation endorsement of it before parliament convened. It would encourage his friends and present his enemies with a fait accompli.

It would also pull most of the citizens of the Associated States into a common front, in favor of a united and independent planet but against Action for Independence. If the Freedom Legionnaires could be kept out of the armed forces, at least as organized units . . .

The alternative was the Federation appearing to reject a political goal supported by most Victorians. That would feed the fanatics, until they had won back all their potential to make trouble—and to ally themselves with any of the Federation's enemies who wanted to use them to divert Federation resources.

It was a long and winding road, and right now they were all staggering along a fog-shrouded path. But somewhere in the fog lay a fork in the path. One way lay endless trouble and bloodshed, the other way lay a respectable chance of peace.

The other way also led to cooperation with the Merishi corporate interests, against the young bloods of their fleet. Neither was a united faction, but more often than not the merchants favored peace or at least subtlety; the fleet saw advancement for both themselves and their race in risking war.

"I think your young are in no danger, if I know anything of human faces," Na'an said.

"One does not know the Highest Will, but I do know my own," Kuwahara said. "Now, I must ask you a question you may choose not to answer. Why have you endorsed the amnesty?"

"How did Gist buy us, in other words?"

"You put the phrases of a boor in my mouth—"

Na'an shook his head. "In this case, they would be the phrases of a man zealous for the safety of the folk under him. I can endure much, from such a one."

"Can you endure the question?"

"I can even answer it. My association will have a monopoly of Merishi trade with Victoria, if amnesty is included in the independence agreement."

"I trust you will not take that as an invitation to sell weapons to all comers?"

"Indeed, it was because we have not been among the arms sellers that Gist approached us."

Kuwahara doubted that Na'an's claim of innocence would pass a truth-scan. "Has Gist put anything in writing?" the admiral asked.

Na'an thrust out a hand at his aide. The aide put an envelope in the hand. "Mr. Gist did not wish us to delay or have to guess."

"He also did not expect me to refuse," Kuwahara said as he tore open the envelope.

"He said not, but he meant that as praise, I think," Na'an said.

Kuwahara scanned the two sheets inside. The phrasing was so tactful and moderate that without Gist's handwriting the admiral would have suspected fraud. Gist being tactful seemed to involve a suspension of natural law.

Then he came to the closing:

I'm putting this to both you and the Merishi because we have to make common cause against the Christless bloody Alliance. If you don't see this, then you've spent too much time in vacuum without EVA gear,

and I won't waste any more time kissing Federation
bums.

> Yours faithfully,
> Jeremiah Gist

The signature was as large and florid as the signer himself. Kuwahara put the two sheets on the table.

"I presume you have read this?"

"Yes."

"Then perhaps we could begin discussing the details of
implementing these general suggestions."

Candice Shores started on the file without even taking off
her coat. Halfway through she decided to get her coat and
boots off. By the time she finished, she'd decided this called
for a drink. One strong one, a shower, then bed. She would
not be getting much sleep for a while if the plan in the file
came off.

The plan was simple enough. On the strength of Merishi
permission to safeguard Merishi interests outside Seven Rivers Territory, the Federation would mount "rescue missions" as far as the Roskills. Sooner or later, one of those
rescue missions would smoke out the secret base the Alliance or their terrorist allies were using.

Maddie Bloch's Rangers were already moving out, to be
ground reconnaissance, continually linked to *Shenandoah* by
an attacker relay. When they found what they were looking
for, Scout Company would move in on the target, remove
everything that wasn't nailed down (including Merishi), neutralize everything that shot back (it was hoped *not* including
Merishi), and leave.

What happened after that depended very much on the
haul from the rescue mission, in both prisoners and other
sources of intelligence, on Alliance and Baernoi reaction,
and on the possibility of cooperation with civilian and military authorities in Seven Rivers Territory.

Shores's eyebrows went up at the last phrase. Nieg was
going to have to explain that one, even if he was giving
Scout Company the chance to end its career in a blaze of
glory. She'd been dreaming of that, and now it seemed that
the dream might come true. But there was a difference

between a glorious end and blindly committing suicide, and if Nieg had forgotten it he was going to be reminded.

After they both got a good night's sleep. Shores emptied her drink and decided to heat water in her room for a sponge bath. The kettle had just started whistling when someone knocked.

"Who is it?" Shores said, grabbing for a robe and turning off the kettle.

"May I come in?" She recognized Nieg and slapped the lock switch.

Nieg did not actually float in a meter off the floor, but he looked like he might defy gravity at any moment. Shores sat down, suddenly sure that her knees wouldn't stand this kind of news.

The colonel stood in silence, his smile slowly widening. The silence dragged on until Shores was tempted to yank off her robe just to get his attention.

"Well, don't keep all the good news to yourself," she said finally.

Nieg collapsed into a chair and held out a hand. Shores thrust a filled glass into it. "The bottle's getting short, so—"

"Don't worry. We'll never be short again, and we can celebrate until Independence, and then start celebrating all over again."

"Can I translate that as good news?" Shores decided that another drink was more useful than the truth, retrieved the bottle, and refilled her own glass.

Nieg stretched like a cat. "Oh, yes. Very good. We have data on the underground base, data on its activities and people, even a partial layout diagram. Whoever did this was well chosen. But that's only what I would have expected of Colonel Pak."

"Is he one of those cooperative military authorities?"

"I wondered if you were going to ask. Yes. We've known for some time that he had agents of his own, working with or against Field Intelligence as his judgment suggested. One of those agents, code-named Lionheart, disappeared recently. Now we know where he is. Or was." Nieg waved a hand toward the north wall.

"I see. The code name makes the whole thing authentic?"

"Highly probable, let us say. Also, Marder seems to be

recovering faster than we expected. We have graphic simulations of four natural features that fit her description ready for her when she wakes up tomorrow. We should be able to start the interrogation—"

"Debriefing."

"What? Oh, yes. Longman used the same word. He said that you interrogate an enemy, but debrief a friend. Marder is a friend, or at least someone with the same enemies."

"Damned right!" Shores said. She sat down on the bed. Nieg pulled his chair closer. Shores realized that with her on the lower bed and him in the taller chair, they were almost the same height. At least he wouldn't have to pull her head down or make her stoop.

Nieg rose, tipped Shores's head back, and kissed her firmly on the forehead. She had just enough time to be annoyed that the kiss wasn't on the lips when he kissed both eyes.

She closed them, and kept them closed as his hands slid under her robe and tightened on her shoulders. She ran one hand up his thigh while she undid the robe with the other. His lips were now on hers, and his hands were pulling the robe down from her shoulders, her breasts—

Out of tact, she let him take the lead. His birth culture was conservative; a woman as aggressive as she felt might spoil things. If he was the kind of man she thought he was, he'd reach a point where he didn't care. If they were lucky, they'd reach it together.

They were lucky. Also agile, in managing to strip and get into bed without losing touch or Shores having to stand up. Lying back and waiting those last few seconds was about the hardest thing she'd done in bed, but she managed, and after that the results were entirely worthwhile. When they finally slept, it would have taken a computer to figure out who was holding whom.

The printer *beeped* and spat out four copies of the agreement governing Federation efforts to "rescue" Merishi. Admiral Kuwahara and Payaral Na'an each picked up two, signed them, exchanged them, then handed the stack of copies to their aides as witnesses.

Commander Franke had just finished signing the last copy when his pager gave a more subdued *beep*. He rose.

"With your permission, sir, that's the message center."

Kuwahara waved him out the door and turned back to Councillor Na'an. The Merishi had weighted down the stack of agreements with an empty juice glass and was rummaging in the refrigerator for another jug.

"By the way," Kuwahara said. "I trust you are aware that a government can extend an amnesty only to its own citizens. The Seven Rivers citizens who joined the Legion will not be covered if they cross the border into the Associated States."

"They will not, and Gist has no intention of usurping the rights of the Alliance authorities. He feels that would be needlessly provocative."

"I quite agree. Also, it is my understanding that no more than a few hundred of the Seven Rivers recruits crossed the border. A good many civilian dependents have come across, but Gist plans to treat them as ordinary refugees."

"Wise of him."

Kuwahara wondered if Gist was wise enough to know that a good many of the Seven Rivers recruits had stayed behind to go underground or even take to the bush as guerrillas. He hoped the guerrillas wouldn't team up with the Alliance for Independence survivors; if they did, their present military and future legal prospects would be dismal.

"The Seven Rivers recruits cannot be returned without danger to them and to Gist," Na'an added. "We would gladly take custody of them, if we had the resources. The Associated States have the resources, but are their troops reliable? You would be a better judge than I."

Kuwahara doubted the superiority of his judgment in this matter, but knew that Na'an was right. Some of the Associated States troops would fraternize with the Legion; others might mistreat them. Incidents would be certain, and after enough incidents, high-order trouble.

"I think Mr. Gist can be assured that Federation units will take custody of any Seven Rivers members of the Freedom Legion until some other arrangement is developed."

Kuwahara decided to assign that job to Major Morley, whether or not she was back on her feet. It would keep her from trying to join Operation Mikhail, the search-and-destroy operation against the Field Intelligence base. (Nobody had protested the name; it might be the only monument Kornilov had, whether or not he deserved more.)

"What makes you think I will bear messages to Gist?" Na'an said.

"The fact that you were willing to bear messages from him to me," Kuwahara said, grinning.

Na'an was smiling back when Franke entered. Franke wasn't smiling; his face looked so grim that Kuwahara felt his stomach turn over.

"Admiral, if I may . . ."

Kuwahara followed Franke outside. "Bad news?" he asked the moment the door closed.

Franke's ceramic grimness cracked in favor of his more normal cherubic smile. "Read this, sir."

Kuwahara read the message from Colonel Nieg. By the time he'd finished he was not only smiling, he had to look down to see that his feet were still on the floor.

Euphoria vanished as he noticed the time on the message. "Why didn't I see this at once?"

"The colonel was waiting for further data. Also, sir, with all due respect—"

"Commander, if you're going to try justifying your usual insubordinate attitude, could you at least do so briefly?"

"Aye-aye, sir. You were at a delicate stage of the negotiations. I thought you should finish them without distractions."

Kuwahara's resentment at being managed lost out to knowing that Franke was right. Na'an would have suspected something, and what the merchant prince suspected he would inquire about until he learned the truth. The time would come for Na'an to learn the truth, as representative of the Merishi Kuwahara was setting out to rescue, but it wasn't tonight.

"Very good, Commander. Now you are going to take an attacker to Camp Aounda and pick up Nieg's full report. Then you are going to meet me aboard *Shenandoah*."

Franke looked dubiously at his watch. "Now, sir?"

"Now. Remember, Commander, the paths of insubordination lead but to late hours."

"Aye-aye sir."

*   *   *

"Excellent," Colonel Nieg said.

Candice Shores wasn't quite sure what he was referring to. That was one of the problems with giving a briefing to a superior officer when you and he were both naked in bed together and his hand was on your breast. Was he referring to the state of your unit, the clarity of your report, or the tactile qualities of your breast?

"What, sir?"

Nieg spread the fingers of the hand. Shores felt a soft-edged warmth where the hand lay. "Everything," Nieg said.

"Thank you. Now, you'll note that nine Scouts have some physical limitation. That includes Sergeant Major Zimmer, unfortunately. I would really rather not break anybody's heart by leaving them out, his least of all."

"I doubt if there's any danger of that," Nieg said. "If we have a firm fix on the base's location as I expect we shall, the nine limited people can be assigned to vehicle security."

"And if we don't?"

"I'll think of something, don't worry."

They passed on, or rather back, to reviewing the rough plan of attack. When they had the problem of finding the base, it was: Rangers find, Navy fix, Scouts fight, and everybody pitch in to finish.

Now the finding was done. The rest would go Rangers fix, Scouts fight with some help from the Rangers, and Navy finish.

"Two platoons in through the front door, one mounted to hold the back door when we find it, and two in reserve," Shores said. "That still holds. So does going in with full unarmored kit and lift-pallets for the extra supplies."

"I don't like that any better than I did the first time."

"The reasons are still as good, sir." *Was taking me to bed a bribe, to get me to go for armor or even leave the job to 215's Scouts?* "Armor gives protection, carrying capacity, long-range sensors, and mobility," she added. "The only thing we might come up short on is the first. It adds weight, target value, signature, and time to requalify my people.

"We can afford the first three, but I don't see how we can afford the last. Not with those ships inbound."

"No." It still sounded dragged out of Nieg, but she didn't doubt his honesty.

"Sir, we have to commit one Scout company or the other

to training tomorrow—excuse me, later today." Her watch showed 0330. "We don't have to commit on armor for another forty-eight hours. It'll take that long to collect, brief, check out, and memoryload my people.

"After that we'll need at least one day of live training. If it turns out armor's a good idea, we can warm up the suits during the first day, then requalify during the next . . . oh, two or three days at most. If we have them. If we don't . . ." She shrugged.

"All right. But you'll still be fighting underground, which means falling rocks, natural or otherwise. Since your naval support will have virtually unlimited payload capacity—"

"*Shenandoah*, right?"

"I think if you commanded the first Scout company to have its own private battlecruiser as close support, you would become totally insufferable."

"But it is *Shen*, isn't it?"

"Barring accidents, yes. Which means virtually unlimited power and payload, which in turn means we can have a great deal of engineering equipment at the objective. The sort of thing that can be very useful for dealing with rocks, falling and otherwise."

Shores slid out of bed and sat down at the terminal without bothering to dress. She was able to ignore the gooseflesh until she'd finished reviewing Victoria Command's engineering assets.

Nieg draped a robe over her shoulders while she assembled a list of what the raiders might need. He read it over her shoulder and nodded.

"You're planning to be ready to blow one of those bubble caves, if necessary."

"Yes. Some of them are so thin-walled you could practically do it with a mining drill. If we load up on geoprobes, the people on the surface can look for one while we keep the people inside busy. Then the Navy can go to work, and we'll have an extra back door."

Nieg rested his hands on her shoulders. "Major, you realize I am going to have to beat this equipment out of Captain Steckler and Commander Fujita, probably but not certainly with Admiral Kuwahara's cooperation?"

"Of course. The sooner the better too. We'd like to have

the engineers going in with us do the last day's training,
maybe more."

She stood up and shrugged the robe off her shoulders.
"Do you have to leave now?"

They found a height at which they could both touch
everything that needed touching. Kissing one ear, Nieg murmured, "Is this a bribe for my cooperation?"

Shores ran a hand down his chest and across his belly and
heard him laugh softly. "No," she said. "It's just another
attack of lust."

"Ah."

She drew the line at carrying him to the bed, but they
got there fast enough anyway, although this time Shores
woke up alone.

Twenty-three

Last night, the fourth since it started training for the "rescue mission," Scout Company camped in its main training site. The cave complex was nameless and not much like their objective. It was also roomy, warmer than the outside (hot-springs somewhere out of sight, Shores suspected), and completely secure. Nobody could get in or out without passing a squad of Nieg's handpicked Intelligence operatives.

Scout Company was now under security lockdown. It would leave these caves when the alert order came through. Meanwhile, it went on training. Anyone who wasn't practicing hands-on rock climbing or orientation in darkness was working with the simulators and hypnoteachers, which had somehow followed the company from Camp Aounda, or checking weapons and equipment. Anyone who wasn't doing one of these things was either giving briefbacks or working with the engineers.

Shores's watch said that it would be twilight outside. A good night's sleep would do everybody a lot of good. She thought of triggering the implanted Scout sleep commands, but she decided to save that for a last resort. Her people knew they were no more than days from being committed. Even the lustiest lovers would bounce themselves into exhaustion fast enough.

She had no temptations to resist there; Nieg had stayed at Camp Aounda. He'd hinted that he would not be aboard *Shenandoah*, but that was no shame to either Nieg or the Shogun. The moment always came, when the down-and-dirty fighting was just too much of a distraction from commanding or analyzing the flow of data.

Shores checked her water jug and decided that she had enough to heat for a sponge bath. She was wearing a wash-

299

cloth and a fine collection of gooseflesh when she heard a
cough outside her alcove.

"Major?"

Field modesty, she decided. "Come on in."

Esteva had the right spirit; he nodded appreciatively, then
sat down while Shores toweled herself back to something
resembling warmth. Then he reached into his shoulder pack
and pulled out a box.

"It's from Colonel Nieg. It gurgles, if that helps."

Shores confirmed this. She also noticed an envelope taped
to the outside of the box. Inside was a message:

Dear Major,

  This is a translation of a message I am sending to
my family, in the event we do not meet again. It guar-
antees you a place in the family rites for as long as
they continue. Since our family has been in continuous
recorded existence since the 20th century, you face
more immortality than you may want, but not more
than you deserve.

                              Respectfully,
                    Liew Nieg, Lieutenant Colonel
                              Intelligence Corps

What he'd translated was a poem, praising her as both
warrior and woman. The second part of the praise was
highly erotic. Shores felt blood flowing warmer under her
skin as she read it.

"Thanks, Sergeant," she said. "Incidentally, I'm putting
you in for a merit promotion to First Class."

"Thank you, ma'am. But that needs the colonel's approval.
He may not give it, when he learns I'm pulling out of
Intelligence."

"Taking your bonus?"

"No, just getting back to being part of line outfits instead
of spying on them."

"Well, I don't think you need to worry about Nieg's being
petty."

"Yes, ma'am. You know him better than I do."

Shores couldn't hold a glare for more than a few seconds.

Esteva knew about her and Nieg and was behaving a bit like a brother whose older sister can probably look after herself. But if she was wrong, his help was available.

Shores pulled on her underwear. "Anything else, Sergeant? I'm going to do a final equipment check."

"Well, ma'am, I wanted to tell you that Zimmer and I did it for you. Everything's signed, sealed, and set up."

"If you've neglected your own gear, you'll both be on vehicle guard!"

Someone cleared his throat outside. Shores recognized Sergeant Major Zimmer. "Come in."

He was already in battledress, with a message stuck in his belt.

"We go on fifteen-minute alert, effective immediately?" The Top nodded. "Any hints which mode?" The Top shook his head. "All right. Any guesses?"

"Mode Two."

That meant riding in the attackers themselves instead of in troop lifters docked to the attackers. It was faster, more crowded, and left them with no lifter-mounted fire support until they joined up with the lifters aboard their supporting ship. Except that enough attackers to haul the whole Scout Company could do some fair shooting themselves, and a battlecruiser—

A battlecruiser like *Shenandoah* could reduce a medium-sized mountain to smoking slag in minutes. Lack of firepower was not going to be one of Scout Company's problems.

"Jump or airland?" she added. Zimmer made a coin-flipping gesture. "We'll have everybody chute up," Shores said. "Easier to change, if we're packed into attackers."

"Just as long as those Navy pukes give the chutes back," Zimmer said. "Damned if they haven't found a lot of things you can buy with one."

"Top, I'll trust you with any arm twisting we may need. Now go and spread the word."

The rocket had a flat trajectory, so Madeleine Bloch could lie on her back and watch it trail flame overhead. It also had no target-seeker or else a faulty one. It kept right on going straight, clearing the top of the next ridge and hitting the higher one beyond.

"Abdul! Data on that blast!"

Her partner, keeping watch, turned his suit's sensors on the missile's explosion. A moment later danced on to Bloch's own heads-up display.

"A biggie, for those bastards."

"We could have stumbled on a band defending another dump."

"How many dumps can those *sacré* Action for Independence rebels have? Never mind, I know the answer." *Too damned many for the peace of mind of honest Rangers.*

"Prophet One to Balthazar Four. Any acknowledgment for your Seven?"

The location of the long-sought enemy base had been known for two hours; it had been transmitted upstairs half an hour ago. But had it reached the people who could order Operation Mikhail into execution?

"Balthazar Four to—"

Static interference that sounded unpleasantly like jamming drowned out the message. Then four more rockets came in. Abdul read the bursts, even though fragments of warhead and rock tinkled and pinged off his armor.

"Truly, I begin to believe in that dump," Abdul said when he'd transmitted the data. "They are flinging them about as if there were no tomorrow."

"For those *croutônards*, there will not be," Bloch said. She sounded more confident than she felt. The rockets didn't bother her as much as the interference. Sixteen well-dispersed, fully armored Rangers were a hard target in every sense of the term. But the jamming might not be the rebels. It might be the Alliance base, alert, ready to defend itself, ready to turn Operation Mikhail into a bloody, compromising battle.

Bloch shifted frequencies as fast as her com gear would allow, and heard Balthazar Four doing the same. One of the virtues of armor: Its com gear was nearly the equivalent of a light attacker's.

"Balthazar Four to Prophet," finally came through. "Seven message has purple acknowledge." Purple, the royal color, meant it had gone all the way up to Kuwahara and Langston.

"Good work, Balthazar. Now, record all data on the jamming and send it upstairs. It won't hurt if—"

This time it was squeals instead of static. But Bloch trusted Balthazar Four to know what came next. From orbit, it would be easy to pinpoint the source of the jamming. If it was the rebels or whoever else was out here in the hills, Operation Mikhail had a green light.

If the source coincided with the location of the underground base, Operation Mikhail would need an extensively modified plan and set of objectives.

Picking them wasn't Bloch's problem. Hers was to redeploy her sixteen Rangers to fit in with *any* plan coming down from upstairs, whether they told her about it or not. The Rangers' reputation and Candy's life hung on that redeployment.

Bloch turned her heads-up display into a map. She wouldn't need all sixteen of her people to maintain contact with the rebels. Eight would be enough for that. Twelve would be enough to keep the rebels too busy to close on the base, even if they were ordered to.

That left only four Rangers to mark the objective. Four Rangers who would be busier than one-armed men in a crotch-scratching contest, but who should be enough. *Shen* had the rest of Bloch's Rangers aboard, plus her own LI detachment, and it was not as if Candy's Scouts needed their hands held.

Bloch studied the map while four more rocket salvos burst across the landscape. Elijah Two had just reported ground movement when she finished her plan. Coding it for visual transmission took another minute, then Bloch scrambled up to the ridge top and turned on her helmet laser.

Using squirt, she was still exposed for thirty seconds. Abdul's dark face was paler and sheened with sweat by the time Bloch climbed down, five seconds ahead of a well-aimed rocket.

When the fragments stopped clattering up and down the ravine and off their armor, she put her helmet against Abdul's. "Nervous, *mon vieux*?"

"Captains like you are not to be picked off trees like figs."

"In another, I would imagine you hoped to flatter me into bed."

Abdul looked horrified. "Insults I can forgive, Captain. Madness, however—"

She slapped his armored shoulder. "*Pardon*. Now, I see no fig trees, but perhaps we can pick a few rebels." She checked her fuel readings, decided she could use an unboosted jump to the bottom of the ravine, and went soaring downhill.

"Now hear this, now hear this. Alert One. Repeat, Alert One."

Brian Mahoney was swinging his legs out of bed when the intercom blared. As his feet touched the floor, the alarm went for battle stations.

This was sick bay; nobody ran or shouted for a mere Alert One. A dying patient would be another matter, or so Mahoney had heard. No one had presented that kind of emergency since they admitted him, not even some of the casualties from Fort Stafford. Most of them had been stable when they arrived; the rest had been stabilized quickly. Then all vanished one night while Mahoney was sleeping, to *Baikhal* or *Valhalla* or the Dockyard or even back down to Victoria, depending on which rumor you believed.

Mahoney didn't believe in rumors. He saved his belief for God, Brigitte, and right now the need to be back on duty. He pulled off his hospital gown and was cautiously testing the bracing of his ribs when the ward nurse walked in.

"Lieutenant—" the nurse began.

"I'm checking myself out," Mahoney replied, reaching for his pants. The bracing wasn't perfect; he winced as he reached and the nurse noticed it.

"Your ribs aren't in any shape—"

"For running around this ship? Quite right. But I'm not going to be running. Remember, my job is done sitting down."

"We still ought to scan—"

"Will it be enough if I sign a waiver? I note I'm not on the mandatory bed list."

The nurse muttered something about patients who got too damned good at reading medical charts. "Well?" Mahoney prodded.

"All right. Remember, though, a waiver may affect your disability rights."

"So talk to me about that if I get disabled. Meanwhile get me that waiver."

The nurse produced a yellow pad from his shoulder bag. Mahoney grinned. "You've been carrying that around for a while, right?"

"Nobody seems to want to sit this one out, unless they're too sick to know what's going on." The nurse shrugged. "Hell, I wouldn't mind having something to do besides sit and wait until the casualties start coming in."

"Then I wish you a very boring battle," Mahoney said. He signed his name with a flourish that sent more twinges through his torso. "Now, can you help me on with my shirt?"

They hadn't sounded an alert in the caves, but Ramdur wondered who they were fooling. Certainly not anyone who was coming on duty now. He couldn't be the only one who saw the mercenaries moving on the double, the pallets loaded with shrouded piles of supplies, the taut looks and sweating faces.

By the time he reached the computer complex, he was sure he heard the sound of lifter fans winding up. He'd already been hearing orders, delivered in tension-cracked voices in several human languages and even Commercial Merishi.

The silence as the door slid shut behind him was a relief. He'd been bombarded with clues; now he could think about what they were telling him.

His hands automatically opened his console as his mind sorted clues. The mercenaries were clearly moving out, armed and equipped to respond to some sort of threat to the base. A threat either so distant that revealing the base's location was no worry, or so great that they were being lifted into action at the risk of compromising the location.

That would reduce the base's already limited internal security to a negligible level. It was a pity, Ramdur decided, that he was on duty at this of all times. He already had the codes he hoped would block any attempt to erase main system's data. He thought he knew the location of the demolition charges—although if he was very lucky, he might dump some of the critical data into undestroyed segments of the network before the charges went.

But if he could wander around—

If was an obscenity, in Intelligence work or computers.

He repeated the old wisdom, and it kept his body and face from betraying him.

It didn't help the frustration. An observant man who could roam the corridors at will with the usual guards absent might learn something valuable. He might even learn how to prevent the destruction of the base. More probably, he would get himself killed to no purpose, or even to the loss of the cause he served if all he had learned died with him.

God does not produce miracles on demand, Ramdur, so do not ask Him for them. The family tutor never wearied of saying that. Ramdur wearied of hearing it, but it was the teacher and not the student who was right.

The door opened to admit a pallet of food and drink containers and also the sound of more lifter fans. Several lifters at once, Ramdur thought—and since it wasn't any mealtime, why the pallet? How long were they supposed to be here? And what might be in the food and drink?

"We have a confirmed location for the jamming," came the voice in Candice Shores's ears. Even scrambled, it was recognizably Langston's and exultant.

"Ready to record," Shores said, punching up the map display on her console. As Langston read off the coordinates, she would have jumped out of her seat if it hadn't been an attacker's.

Whoever was jamming and engaging Maddie Bloch's Rangers were doing so a good hundred kloms east of the objective. By now all the shouting and shooting must have alerted the base to *that* battle. It was no better than even odds that they were alerted to anything like Operation Mikhail.

"Looks like Maddie just stumbled over the rebs and they bit, like a springer snake," Shores said finally.

"Our guess too," Langston said. "Now, we do have a second major objective, and maybe Captain Bloch has too many opponents. So we are modifying the plan. You will drop off one platoon and two attackers to support Captain Bloch against her opponents. Otherwise, we go with a basic Mode Two."

Airlanding was better than jumping, other things being equal. But four platoons was *not* equal to five, even if the fifth was going to be saving Maddie's ass—

"You object?"

Something in Langston's tone said this was not the time to exercise the operational commander's prerogative of questioning weird orders. Anyway, this wasn't weird enough to come under that clause. A gamble, maybe, but what part of Operation Mikhail wasn't?

"Practical problem. We're supposed to rendezvous with lifters from our support. The platoon we drop off will be on foot and a long way from the support."

"Captain Bloch will give us an update before we deploy the platoon. They can either airland or deploy by jumping. We'll also get docked lifters in to them with the next flight of tac air attackers."

Shores could do that simple a set of calculations in her head. The results fell short of being exhilarating.

"That's cutting it fine, sir."

"That's also hitting the largest remaining organized body of rebels before it can fade back across the border. I trust you agree that's a major objective."

Since it wasn't a question, Shores didn't answer. With no visual, she couldn't salute, and maybe it was just as well that Langston couldn't see her face.

If the general got Maddie or the Scouts or both blown away through the classic error of pursuing too many objectives at once, Shores might not survive the process. If she did, she was going to carve her opinion of Langston across his record and possibly his anatomy.

She cut over to the all-hands circuit. "Huntress to Safari. Safari Three is detached for an alternate objective, effective immediately." None of the platoons had any real weak spots for working under her, but 3rd Platoon was the best candidate for a semi-independent role. Shores switched back. "Huntress reporting. I have detached 3rd Platoon pursuant to your orders. Permission to proceed?"

This time she could hear a triumphant grin. "Permission granted. Execute Operation Mikhail."

"Command Simulation Mode ready," came from the intercom. Captain Liddell thought she recognized Lieutenant Mahoney's voice. She knew he'd been in sick bay half an hour ago, because she'd been going over the roster of nonduty personnel to keep herself from fidgeting.

"Stand by, Communications," Commander Charbon said. She looked at her captain. "Permission to start the act?"

"Hold for authorization," Liddell said. Four days and lots of people contributing their acting ability had left *Shenandoah* with enough recordings, codes, and holos to simulate Admiral Kuwahara's presence aboard for several hours. After that repetition might lead to suspicion and suspicion to itchy trigger fingers, if not actual shooting.

"We heard the groundcrawlers' 'execute' a week ago," Charbon snapped.

"Pray for patience," Bogdanov said over the open command circuit.

"I won't be answered," Charbon said.

"Oh, ye of little—" Bogdanov began.

An incoming signal interrupted Bogdanov's homily before Charbon could lose her temper.

"Lazarus to High Card. Execute. Repeat, execute."

"High Card to Lazarus. Acknowledge."

Shenandoah had been doing the main job of ground monitoring, then relaying her results impartially to *Baikhal, Valhalla*, three cruiser flagships, and Dockyard. No one could tell who was listening at any of those destinations. No one except Wolfgang Steckler and his volunteer crew of communications experts, playing host to Kuwahara and most of his staff.

"Pavel," Liddell said.

"Ma'am?"

"You have the con."

"Aye-aye, ma'am." A moment of silence, then, "All hands, prepare for atmospheric entry and maneuvering. Ground-operations personnel, make your final equipment check.

"Counting down for maneuvering. Five—four—three—two—one—departing orbit!"

On the display in front of Captain Liddell, both a number and a label changed. Where she had previously read the duration of *Shenandoah*'s orbit around Victoria, now she read ETA in Victoria's atmosphere.

Eleven minutes when she first saw it, it had already changed to ten minutes forty seconds.

Twenty-four

Mount Baijan flashed by on the right, or so the display told Candice Shores. The ETA figure was now six minutes.

The altimeter showed the ground falling away below. They were through the last of the Krainiks, closing toward the Roskills. They would be visible on the objective's radar, if it wasn't jammed or its operators hadn't panicked.

"If the bad guys have an AD zone, we're in it now," the pilot said. She scanned displays. "Our jammers are hitting them for six, though. Not to worry."

At well over Mach Two, the attackers thundered across the valley. Anyone below was going to have to worry about shattered windows, cracked roofs and walls, and maybe hearing damage. Shores would cheerfully pay their medical bills and repair their houses herself rather than lose Scouts through losing time.

"Radar contact, bearing one seventy, altitude sixty thousand meters and coming down fast," the EWO said. "Diffuse contact, but it's a biggie."

"Oh *Shenandoah*, at last you're coming—" the copilot warbled, until the pilot glared him into silence.

"Major contact has slowed its rate of descent. One, no two, smaller ones still coming down fast." Shores looked at the bulkheads, wanting magic sight or X-ray vision to pierce them and see *Shenandoah* deploying for action.

"Visual lock on radar contact," the pilot ordered.

The screens came to life, showing four attackers englobing a bumpy ovoid. The combat-engineer lifter had an attacker's power plant and could reach orbit, but gave up other attacker capabilities for a load of exotic landscape-rearrangers.

Beyond the engineers, Shores saw a row of lights gleaming. *Shenandoah* was descending as fast as a ship a third of a kilometer long could safely maneuver at this height over this kind of terrain. She was also coming down with all her lights on, as if she really was engaged in a rescue mission.

On most missions, even the largest ship was better off undetected. This time, the more people who saw *Shenandoah*, the better. If everyone knew where she was, what she was, and that killing her would be an act of war, the minority of fanatics with fingers on the triggers of shipkillers might find their fingers pulled away in time.

"Parsifal One to Huntress. We are ready to mark the target."

"Huntress to Parsifal One. Are the rockmovers in position? We have visual contact but no messages."

"They've given us the thumbs-up, Huntress. Any problems with that?"

"May you break something vital in a moment of ecstasy, Parsifal One." Shores looked at the pilot, who nodded. "I have an all-clear from the flyboys. Let 'em rip."

For the next minute the nine attackers carrying the four platoons of Scouts would have given an air-traffic controller a stroke. They all zoomed to cut speed without cutting power, then looped and came out of their loops in four different directions. More loops, then they leveled out and cut internal gravity.

By then the four attackers carrying the reserve and backdoor platoons were in stable hover over the ridgeline. The other five went to drift-and-squat, then punched out ground anchors.

Cold air puffed up into the cabin as the lower hatch opened. Shores was already locking her faceplate and chambering a round into her pulser when the pilot gave her another thumbs-up.

"See you around," she said.

"Or a square, if that's the best I can do."

Shores slid down to the lower deck, dashed aft to the hatch, and flung herself at the unfolded ladder. For a moment she had to force herself downward, then she cleared the lift field. She jumped off the ladder a meter above the ground, landed spring-legged, closed her helmet, and pumped her pulser up and down over her head.

At her double-time signal, the two main assault platoons began closing on her, as she led them out from under the attackers. Two minutes and they were safe from anything that happened to the attackers, short of a fuser. Shores finally had a chance to turn and look at their objective.

As she turned, a solid bar of light lunged down from the sky. Only her faceplate filters saved her night vision. The combat-engineer lifter was eating out the initial laser-bore with its rotary cannon. A ton of heavy-compound slugs did wonders for enlarging a hole, if you didn't have to worry about innocent bystanders. Even through the helmet, the scream and snarl of the gun-boring made Shores's ears ring.

The engineers' attacker escort flashed overhead in a bomb-burst maneuver taking them out to the four points of the compass. Silver-glittering ovoids popped out of each attacker, fired braking rockets, then plummeted toward the mountainside. Shores saw one of them land squarely on top of the rock shaped like the helmeted head of a Baernoi Death Commando.

A moment later the geoprobe's implanting charge went off. The rock dissolved into dust and debris. Scratch one landmark, but the geoprobes were deployed now. In ten minutes or maybe less they'd be giving a real-time update on underground activity, maybe even refining the Scouts' maps.

Shores wondered if she should ground the reserve platoon to protect the probes. Right now the probes were nearly as critical as the main assault, more so than the back door. Not to mention that eyeball readings on the geoprobes saved time, particularly in the usual overcrowded electronic environment of a battlefield.

"High Card to Huntress. High Card to Huntress. Come in, Huntress."

"Huntress here. What—"

"We have an unidentified air contact, bearing 145, course 110, low and slow."

"Are you warning Captain Bloch too? That's heading out toward her."

"Don't teach your grandmother to suck eggs, Huntress." Shores recognized Brian Mahoney's voice and thought she heard a chuckle. "They've already been warned."

"Thanks." That scratched grounding the reserve platoon. They needed attacker mobility and protection if the bad guys had something wandering around loose.

"Thank us by hustling," came a voice Shores thought was Captain Liddell's. "The engineers—"

Ground shock slammed up through Shores's boots and blast-driven air punched her in the ears. The engineers must have inserted and tamped their main charge while she was yattering with Brian.

Flame, dust, smoke, and rock fragments vomited out of the hillside. Along with them went pieces of twisted metal and at least one unmistakable human figure.

"Parsifal One to Huntress. We're doing a temperature check now—okay. Hustle your people through, and you can get them in fine. The rock-movers are unloading the portable fuse dampers. You can pick them up on the way in."

The temperature readings transmitted to Shores's heads-up display showed that was the usual Ranger optimism, but what the Hades! The enemy's front door was open, and when you came calling like this you didn't send in a card first. You went right in and made yourself at home, whether your host liked it or not.

"Huntress to Safaris One and Two. On the count of three, head for the door. One, two, three—on the double!"

"What in the name of all lawful gods—" Admiral Kuwahara began.

Before he could finish, the screen beside the map display lit up. General Langston stared out of it.

"If you've just detected the Second/Victoria's movements, I won't waste your time."

"You won't be wasting my time if you can explain *why* they're moving." Kuwahara looked at the map display again. It wasn't as crisp as the one aboard *Shenandoah*, but cheap computer capacity and Wolfgang Steckler's ingenious technicians had given Dockyard an adequate flag plot in less than sixty hours.

The map was certainly clear enough to show what was going on, including the things Kuwahara didn't understand. One was the large formation of fast lifters heading west from the militia base on the border, toward the Operation Mikhail AO.

"Alys Parkinson is with them, and they're blacked down in all modes," Langston said.

"I said I wanted an explanation," Kuwahara said. Either he or Langston was going to get a migraine out of this—unless they could join forces and pound on the Vics until *they* got one—

"They acquired several heavy liftliners by irregular methods of requisition," Langston said primly.

"In other words, hijacking?"

"You might call it that."

"I do. Why didn't you stop it?"

"Because by the time we knew it had happened, the Second was loaded up and on the way. Up to that time, we were a trifle busy dealing with the sudden emergence of a short battalion of rebels where we hadn't expected any at all. A well-armed outfit, too, with enough firepower to put the fear of God even into a half team of Rangers and a platoon of Scouts!"

"Don't jump down my throat, Marcus. I'm not accusing anybody of anything. Yet. But I'm going to send down a flight of attackers to fly wing on Parkinson's Pets. They can provide AD suppression, IFF, and progress reports if nothing else."

"Thanks, Admiral. I'll see what we can do about them too. Back in ten minutes?"

"Try for less."

It was actually six minutes before Langston came back on-screen, but that was enough time for Kuwahara to skim an update on Operation Mikhail and confer with Commander Franke. Operation Mikhail so far looked like a success: Two platoons of Scouts were inside the objective, the geoprobe network was up and running, and *Shenandoah* was unloading all the racked and ready lifters and their contents as fast as her launchers could work at essentially zero altitude and velocity.

Talking with Franke had been a little more complicated. So was the situation they were talking about.

"There's no question of the Victorians trying to interfere with Operation Mikhail, is there?" Franke asked.

"I thought you were the Intelligence expert. Sorry. Half of one percent, maybe."

"At most. Then what they're probably doing is trying to

join the fight against the last rebel holdouts. Maybe they think they'll be in time to save the Rangers and Scouts."

"Our communications security must have sprung leaks."

"Maybe, or the Vics have EI capabilities they haven't talked about. Anyway, I can't see why we shouldn't let the Victorians have a share in the last battle. It may improve their negotiating position in the planetary-union conference."

"It will also improve their negotiating position toward the Federation," Kuwahara said.

"I know. But can we afford to play dog in the manger, if we can't do it without lethal force?"

"You can give me advice without insulting my intelligence, Commander."

"Aye-aye, sir. Does that mean you concur in letting the Victorians join in?"

"It means—" which was as far as the admiral got before Langston returned to the screen.

"We're sending in two Scout platoons and a company from Task Force Borha, also some light attackers," Langston said. "Can you refuel the lights, or at least provide security while we do?"

"With only a couple of small miracles, yes."

"Fine. You may gather we're not planning on fighting the Vics. Just holding their coats, and rabbit-punching the rebels if they turn their backs on us."

"Very good. But all prisoners are to be turned over to the Federation forces. We'll release native Victorians to the Associated States Forces as soon as we sort them out from the off-planet types. That is a nonnegotiable condition. Otherwise we withdraw all our units from the area and the Vics can stand or fall on their own."

Who or what might come out of the base was still unknown. Off-planet prisoners from the rebel battalion could be an invaluable intelligence windfall that the Victorians could not be allowed to have.

"Ramdur, what the devil are you doing?"

The technician started violently, and not because he had a guilty conscience. He had inserted the erase-blocker into the system ten minutes ago, and nobody had noticed. Now, when he was simply waiting for orders about what to do next, somebody was playing policeman.

"Nothing, ma'am—ah, sir," he amended his reply, as he saw the battledressed figures in the doorway. Mercenaries, four of them, and he knew two but that didn't seem likely to help in the mood they were in.

"We're evacuating the whole lower complex upstairs into Sector F," the man said. "Close down in one minute."

"Can we get our personal gear?" someone asked.

The mercenary gaped, then laughed. Ramdur was quite sure he would not have found the joke funny if he had known what it was.

"The Feddies are already in Sectors A and B. We have ways of dealing with them, but we need to be out of the way first."

"Well, I'm not leaving without my—" the supervisor began.

One of the mercenaries shoved a pistol into her stomach. She put a hand on his shoulder. "Excuse me, soldier, but I—"

Blood sprayed over the wall behind the supervisor as the soldier shot her in the stomach. She stood, swaying and groping for the wound with both hands for a moment. Her face was twisted in outrage.

Then it twisted in agony, and she began to scream. Another mercenary pushed her hard, and she fell, still screaming. The one who'd shot her pointed his pistol in Ramdur's general direction.

"Any of the rest of you going to argue?

Words were pointless, and not only because the supervisor was still screaming. The mercenaries herded the comuter operators out into the hall, leaving her on the floor in a spreading pool of blood.

By the time they reached the main corridor, the supervisor's screams had died; Ramdur hoped she had also. No one deserved such a death, possibly not even those who took pleasure in inflicting it. Were the expendable people in the base going to die of something as quick and merciful as gas or an explosion?

He stopped wondering when they reached the main corridor and he counted the mercenaries. Nine, no, ten, and a couple of armed civilians, to handle more than forty unarmed civilians. Pilots, technicians, supply people—half the base seemed to be here.

Half the base, and maybe too many to guard effectively, let alone execute. Ramdur realized that his chances of living beyond the next hour had just increased. He might increase them still further if he was ready to act when he found the chance.

"Seismic event!" shouted the petty officer at the geo-probe console.

"What have I always said about shouting?" Liddell asked without taking her eyes from her own display.

"Sorry, ma'am. Shifting over."

The seismic-event data came up on Liddell's displays. She cursed. That was a big one. Was it artificial, or had the mountain chosen this of all times to have the hiccups?

"Analysis," Liddell asked.

Computers, she had long since discovered, could hem and haw as well as human beings, even if their techniques differed. She was left with a mass of raw data and probabilities, an impulse to strangle the software designer, and an urgent need to guess.

"Engineering," she said.

"All systems nominal for now, Captain," Fujita reported. "Estimate that we can hold for another two hours—"

"Good. We may have to. Break out all the mining equipment and land it half an hour ago. Something just blew underground."

"On the way."

Fujita was silent for five minutes, long enough for the smell of sweat and tension in the Combat Center to thicken noticeably. Then:

"Parsifal Two to High Card. Parsifal Two to High Card. For God's sake come in, High Card, somebody—"

"High Card here. Is this everybody's day to panic?"

"I—ah—ma'am, there's been a hell of a big bang in the base. Parsifal One doesn't answer. Neither does Huntress. I'm going in to see—"

"Parsifal Two. We're sending down all our mining equipment. I want the remaining Rangers to provide security for it and the crews. Who's taken over for Huntress?"

"Ah, Safari Five Leader to High Card, that would probably be me."

"Okay, Safari Five. Back up the Rangers in providing security for the mining crew. But your main job is to eyeball monitoring of the geoprobes. I want any sound louder than a sneeze reported immediately. In fact, I want to hear about sneezes too."

"Got it, High Card. Only—hurry those rock-movers, will you?"

"Don't flash, we're loading as fast as we can. High Card out."

Liddell wished she had a sweat band, or even better, a helmet to hide not only her sweating forehead but her ravaged hair. Then thoughts of what might have happened to the Scouts underground broke in. Preserving a captain's dignity wouldn't help salvage Operation Mikhail.

"Captain, we have the first mining load ready to launch," Fujita said. "It includes two light borers. All the people have drawn sidearms."

"Good work, and keep at it," Liddell said. She called Swan One, the leader of *Shen*'s embarked Rangers.

"Do you have a secure LZ?"

"There's a little more cover around than I'd like, but—"

"We can do something about that, Swan One. Prepare for close supporting fires." She punched up Weapons and the coordinates of Swan One's LZ.

"I want everything within three hundred meters of this perimeter flat as a golf green. Can do?"

"On the way," Commander Zhubova said. "Only tell those hairy-eared engineers to stay out of the line of fire while we're making their life easier."

The data on Liddell's display now superimposed itself on a visual of the hillside where the engineering equipment was going to come down. The rocks looked close enough to reach out and touch. Liddell had to remind herself that this was a real-time display and only slightly magnified. *Shenandoah* was considerably less than her own length from the ground.

Flash! Liddell's night vision vanished. By the time she'd finished blinking, so had most of the rocks. A switch to IR showed glowing green spots where they'd been beamed out of existence. Softer green spots showed the Scouts and

Rangers, and a big green blob falling on to the screen was
a load of engineering equipment on its way down.

Liddell wiped her forehead with the back of her hand.
Short of going down there and heaving rocks with her bare
hands, she'd done everything she could.

When the blast came, something slammed into Candice
Shores so hard that she went down. She cut her lip and
panic clawed at her mind so that she thrashed wildly. Then
she recognized the glove on a hand gripping her arm. It was
Sergeant Esteva, who'd flung himself on top of her to shield
her from the blast and fragments.

"Thanks, Sergeant." *Good. My voice sounds like the Old
Lady's ought to.* "Casualty report!"

One squad was gone completely, caught in the collapsed
portion of tunnel. Some of them might survive; all of them
were out of the fight.

Other casualties were major from flying rocks and being
hurled against the walls, minor from blast and noise. Even
unarmored Scout gear improved survival chances; except
for one private with a crushed chest it looked like all the
unburied Scout casualties would survive.

There were still too damned many of them, including 2nd
Platoon's leader and 1st Platoon's sergeant. One fuse
damper was buried with the missing squad, one was erratic,
one was still functioning nominally. Shores grimaced at the
thought of how many more old-fashioned powder-train fuses
might be lurking in their path, against which even functioning fuse dampers were useless.

Meanwhile, she had thirty-five able-bodied people and a
shortage of leaders. She had some decisions to make.

"All right, people. We're going to combine the two platoons from here on in. Lunt, your squad provides security
for the medics and the wounded. Romero, you take your
squad and the best damper up the tunnel and establish an
advanced OP."

"How far up?"

Here comes what no books tell you how to do, really.
"Far enough up so that if they send down drones or infantry
attacks, you can engage them in time to give the alarm."

*Which could be out of supporting distance, so I may have
just sentenced Romero to death.*

She could see the thoughts scroll across the sergeant's thin dark face. The Army had given him twelve years of a good life. He'd been Light Infantry, one of the chosen. Now the Army was asking payment, in the one coin every infantryman always had available.

Romero saluted. "Check your radios, everybody," he said. Four thumbs rose. He slung the damper. "All right. Move out." The squad broke into a trot as they rounded the bend. Shores watched them vanish into the dust haze before turning back to her main force.

"Higgins. Punch our geoprobe into a handy piece of rock and turn it on. Passive mode only."

"But that won't—"

"Tell any bad guys' probes where we are. Or if they know where we are, that we're alive and kicking."

Higgins started unpacking the probe while his partner started tapping sections of wall. By the time they were scraping insulation off the rock, Shores had finished her dispositions.

Main body under her command, advancing cautiously up the tunnel, holding interval with Romero's point squad. The point squad ahead, security squad, probe, and casualties behind. Flankers? The diagram showed a possible air shaft off to the left that might help with a lot of things, starting with Romero's survival.

But any recon of it would have to be made without a reliable fuse damper, which meant the smallest possible force.

"Ito. Take two men and—"

Pulsers droned up the tunnel, the enclosed space magnifying the sound. One of the wounded cried out, half hysterical. Rounds sprayed sparks from bare wall and gouged shreds of plastic where they struck insulation.

"Fléchettes!" Shores shouted, so loud Romero probably didn't need the fuse-damper-jammed radio to hear her. Then a disheveled figure staggered out of the haze, holding out both hands in front of him. It looked like a man, with a high forehead and dark skin under the dust.

"Please, mercy. I surrender. I surrender."

"Who the Hades—" Shores began. The man stopped and raised his hands, then stared at her.

"Captain Shores—"

"How the Hades—" Shores began, then realized she was repeating herself. She stepped forward.

"Position!"

The man almost grinned as he splayed his legs and pressed his hands against the wall. Shores patted him down and found nothing except a package of microslips.

"You in the computer section?"

"Are you Captain Shores?" the man repeated.

"What difference—" several Scouts said in chorus.

"Please." The man sounded ready to beg. "If you are Captain Shores—"

"All right. I'm Major Candice Shores. Who are you?"

"Lionheart."

Before Shores could react to meeting Pak's agent, Higgins shouted from under the probe. "I'm picking up Fed codes. They've got a light borer loaded and ready to go. Can I give them the go-ahead?"

Shores nodded. "Up the tunnel, everybody. We don't want the borer punching through right on top of us."

Corporal Ito and his people started off first. Shores grabbed Lionheart and practically dragged him up to Ito.

"If you know this complex, tell us about the ventilation shaft." Fortunately Shores's portable computer was made to survive more than demolition charges or fuse dampers. The schematic of the complex came up promptly, blurred only by dust on the screen.

Lionheart wiped the screen with an even dustier sleeve, giggled, then pointed at the green line tracing the shaft. "Yes, yes. I know it. I escaped down it when I got away from the mercenaries."

"Back up. What mercenaries?"

"The security guards in this complex. I mentioned them in what I sent out. You must have seen it or you would no be here."

Shores took a deep breath, which overloaded her helme filters and left her gasping. When Esteva had finished slap ping her on the back, she could see Lionheart trying not t laugh.

"Assume that I can't discuss why I'm here and that m intel on the mercs needs an update. Give it."

Somewhere during Shores's coughing fit, the agent ha patched up his wits. He explained about the mercenaries how they had rounded up the civilian staff, their blood-thirsty streak, and their small numbers.

"How small?"

"I only saw twelve armed people before I escaped. There may be more, but far fewer than normal."

Normal, by the report, was sixty to ninety. So figuring twenty to thirty left behind, half the security was somewhere else. Probably aboard that unidentified air contact, heading out to engage Maddie.

Well, any of those bastards the Navy left, Maddie could roast with a clear conscience. If the last of the rebel rabble wasn't keeping her too busy—

Meanwhile, the Scouts had an edge in numbers overall. But they were divided, their opponents weren't, and their opponents also held the choke points and controls for heaven only knew how many more nasties. Which brought them back to the ventilation shaft.

"Oh, yes," Lionheart said. "It goes as you have it, and it is wide enough for your people."

"Looks like a great place for an ambush or a gas attack, too," Ito said.

"Oh, no. I fixed one of the hatches. It blocks the shaft from above, but it can be opened without anyone detecting it. At least, if I open it."

"Want to go with—" Shores began, on a question she was sure was rhetorical.

"Hey, they've got the borer coming down!" Higgins yelled. "We'd better move it."

The assault force turned into a chaos of running figures, carrying or dragging equipment and casualties. It turned back into an orderly military unit fifty meters up the tunnel.

Shores was just about to repeat her question to Lionheart when another explosion thundered in her ears. No mistaking the direction of that one, either. It came from up the tunnel, where she'd sent Romero's squad.

"Keep your head down," she told Lionheart as she signaled her people to deploy as best they could. Alcoves and doorways were better protection than nothing, but that was about all you could say for them.

The complex's defenders might have lost half their strength to a stupid order. They hadn't lost their arsenal, apparently, or their will to use it.

Twenty-five

Candice Shores was just about to order a recon up the tunnel when the first borer broke through behind her people. The scream of metal ripping through solid rock tore at ears. So did screams from up the tunnel as Romero's wounded found their voices.

Dust rode blast waves in all directions, swirling, eddying, choking, and reducing visibility to arm's length. Shores desperately wanted a brilliant solution to the tactical situation, if only for her self-respect.

Unfortunately, the situation's basic characteristics were poor visibility and sensory overload. Shores decided that for ten seconds, keeping her head down would also protect her ass, both literally and figuratively.

She'd counted to nine when a mass of coolant foam shot out of the borehole, adding steam to the dust. Now that the hole was cooled enough for insulated equipment, a com rig and cable followed. Several standard field containers were next, crashing down like more falling rocks. The same wounded trooper cried out again, and screams from up the tunnel echoed him.

Shores scrambled back to the com rig, ignored the blast of heat from the bore (still hot enough to flay an unprotected human), and punched the rig to life. As she waited for a reply, she noted that three of the containers were ammunition, one medical supplies, and another a portable fuse damper.

"High Card to Huntress. Come in, Huntress. We need your tactical situation." The com rig sounded importunate.

"Huntress calling. Our tactical situation is more fun than a barrel of monkeys." Shores summarized the last ten minutes, then added, "Unless you object, we're going to move up the ventilation shaft and the main tunnel simulta neously. I want to make pickup on Ito's people and try to take the mercs in the rear."

"High Card to Huntress. Is Lionheart reliable?"

"So far, I think so. If we get blown away, so does he."

"Understood, Huntress. Report when you are in a position to move against Sector F. We have the heavy borer and nonlethals ready for a coordinated attack."

"We'll move as fast as we can, High Card, but don't hold your breath. Try to get somebody in through the rockfall behind us too. They can at least pick up the bodies."

It was important with all regulars and sacred with the Light Infantry not to leave your dead behind. But sometimes you had to do the next best thing, which was turning the retrieval over to the people coming up behind you.

"High Card to Huntress. We have people in the cave now. We'll start them digging as soon as they've checked for booby traps."

"Thanks, High Card. Huntress out."

Splitting her force was making the best of a bad job and putting part of it at Lionheart's mercy to boot, but the tactical situation had defined itself. Shores could no longer sit still without giving the initiative to the enemy and letting the Navy hog the rest of the fighting.

The ventilation shaft turned out to be loaded with the usual mess of equipment and supplies stuck there for lack of space anywhere else. Getting around some of the bends was a stiff job for battledressed troopers; it would have been impossible in armor. Lionheart kept up, even though he was dripping sweat, and Higgins brought up the rear, carrying their damper and snapping pictures of everything interesting.

They came to the doctored hatch two-thirds of the way up. Lionheart pulled out one of his microslips, stuck it into the control, then punched a four-digit code on the manual board. Silently the hatch slid aside.

"I'm beginning to believe you know what you're doing," Esteva whispered.

"I begin to believe that I may see the sun rise tomorrow," the agent replied. "If the sky is clear."

Keyed-up troopers laughed longer than the joke deserved and louder than safety allowed. Once everyone had quieted down, they took the rest of the shaft in a rush. In the last ten meters, Shores and Esteva moved up to share point with Ito.

The head of the shaft opened in a semi-cylindrical cave, with tunnels leading down from the farther end and up from the nearer one. In the middle of the cave were eight armed men in Alliance battledress without insignia, an SSW, and a liftscooter. One of the men was fiddling with the scooter's controls, while another strapped packages to its seats.

Shores realized she was looking at another bomb carrier. An improvised one, too. Did that mean the people in charge weren't giving the high-powered triggers to the hired help?

Since the high-powered triggers were probably connected to fusers, this seemed likely. However, disgruntled hired help could produce useful intelligence, if they survived in shape to talk.

Shores passed a description of the situation down the shaft. Everybody had a riot pistol and grenades as well as issue and personal weapons; firepower would be no problem. Keeping the mercs distracted while the firepower was brought to bear, though . . .

Shores drew her flare pistol. She aimed at the farther tunnel, thumbed off the safety, and let fly. The flare smoked across the cave, just as the liftscooter started for the same tunnel. The flare hit the scooter, making it wobble, then lodged under one of the seats. Most of the mercs looked around wildly. Two ran after the scooter, and one had kept his eye on the smoke trail.

The last one was drawing down on the head of the shaft when Esteva, Ito, and Shores all shot him at once. They sprayed the cave with fléchette rounds, painful but not lethal to men in battledress, while the rest of the team piled out of the shaft behind them.

Six mercs got off shots, three of them died along with one trooper, but when the shooting was done Shores had five live prisoners who looked like they wanted to stay that way. She was seeing to getting them trank injections when the liftscooter's load went off with another ear-torturing roar. Blast and fragments flew back up the tunnel and flattened several Scouts who were too slow getting down. They got back up, though, and were picking fragments out of their battledress when the other team came up the tunnel.

"Romero?" Shores asked.

Sergeant Lunt turned one thumb down and held up all five fingers of the other hand.

"Damn." Scout Company had taken more casualties in the last half hour than in all the previous fights put together, including the capture of a whole platoon in the first rebellion. They were getting killed doing an important job, but it was amazing how little that thought helped.

"Any word from High Card?" Lunt asked.

"Yes. We're supposed to move up to a position just outside Sector F. Then we rush the main cave when they blast through and have the gas going."

Lionheart swallowed. "I think you should know that beyond Sector F are tunnels to—I suppose it is a sector, but I have never heard it named. I think it is the arsenal."

Where the fusers would be, with desperate men between them and the Scouts, and nothing but those fusers between the desperate men and death or disgraceful capture.

"This is not my idea of an entertaining evening, people," Shores said. "But we've spoiled the bad guys' fun even more thoroughly. Lunt, you take over point. Higgins, stay back. Lionheart, you stick close to Esteva if I get busy.

"Standard formation. Move out!"

As Governor Hollings's face came up on the screen, Fegeli winked at Colonel Pak. The colonel tiptoed to the corner of the room. Now he was off-screen but could hear everything without any detectable eavesdropping. Unless Fegeli's scrubbing of his office and the implanted scramblers had both failed, and if either had why hadn't Hollings moved already?

"Good evening, Governor. I assume you wish a briefing on the situation in the Roskill Mountains?"

Pak heard a choking noise that sounded like an affirmative.

"Good."

Fegeli delivered his report so precisely that Pak began to be afraid it would sound rehearsed. Would Hollings be flattered or suspicious? At least the reasons for his not acting on his suspicions remained; in fact tonight's events made them even stronger, to a thinking man.

At some point, though, Hollings might cease to be a

thinking man. It was a race between his reaching that point
and *Shenandoah* completing her mission.

"Then you aren't proposing *any* action?" Hollings said.

"The Federation is acting under authority given them by
representatives of the local Merishi community. They are
acting in an area where this authority allows them to act.
They are also acting in a manner sanctioned by most of the
interstellar conventions and agreements on terrorism.

"Finally, they are acting in territory that has been in dispute, so they theoretically don't even need Merishi permission."

"They're also acting with a capital ship and a mob of
Scouts," Hollings snapped. "Is that your idea of a rescue
mission?"

"If I wasn't sure what I would be facing, I would ask for
at least that much myself. Admiral Kuwahara and the Merishi both know what happened to the Bonsai Squadron.
They know that our local terrorists may have more shipkillers."

"They can't—I mean—" Hollings began to gobble.

*That's right, Your Excellency. Please go right ahead and
hang yourself.*

Hollings seemed to retrieve some shards of sense. "I will
have to consult with Admiral Uzel on this."

"We have already done so, Your Excellency. He says that
even if the Federation action was not entirely legal, he
would not be able to prevent it without using lethal force.
Not without Baernoi help, at any rate, and they have indi-
cated they will not act outside their authorized area."

Hollings made a sound like a machine tool overloading
its drive. "I am going to consult with Admiral Uzel, regardless of what he has said to you. I hope I can convince him
that the Merishi may only be a pretext for action against
Alliance interests."

"Your Excellency, we have obviously come to radically
different conclusions in this case. But we cannot object to
your discussing the matter with Admiral Uzel."

"You're damned right you can't." Governor and connection both fizzed into silence.

Fegeli popped out of his chair like a spring toy. "Colonel,
get over to the hospital and take command of Baba Lopatina's security personally. I'll supply you with C-cubed for

running the 96th. I want to get on the horn to Uzel and make sure he doesn't change his mind."

"What does the Baba have to do with this?" It seemed to Pak that Fegeli had gone from apathetic acquiescence to shooting from the hip too fast and too thoroughly.

"Do I have to teach my teacher in intrigue? If Uzel changes his mind, the only way we can avoid being ordered to fight *Shenandoah* is if the Baba resumes command now. Hollings may realize that. If he does, do you want to bet he won't try arresting the Baba? Or letting his Field Intelligence bedmates do worse?"

For one of the few times in his life, Pak was caught standing with his mouth open. By the time he'd closed it, he realized that Fegeli was right.

He also realized that mistresses might have their uses. If danger to one could move someone like Fegeli into a frenzy of constructive action, maybe mistresses could be made issue equipment.

It took Shores's force half an hour to advance a distance they could have jogged in five. It wasn't enemy resistance that slowed them either. No living opponents appeared and the fuse dampers now seemed to be doing their job.

They were also doing their usual job on radio communications, but Scouts were trained to work in a situation like this on visual signals only. It wasn't as convenient to be out of radio contact with the surface, and Shores would have given a good deal for a secure fiber-optic link.

She would have given even more for the certainty of seeing the stars once more. Just once, and after that she would face a soldier's end without too much fuss. Rocks under her were one thing; she would never have been on the mountain with Maddie Bloch otherwise. Rocks all around her and even overhead, threatening to squeeze her like a grape in a wine press, weren't the same.

What slowed them was the need for twenty soldiers to avoid ambushes in front and leaving enemies, hostages, or useful intelligence material behind. Everything had to be searched while point and rear tried to cover their compass. It had to be done silently too. Not just electronic silence, either, but as much physical silence as they could manage. The remaining enemies might be few, demoralized, or busy guarding their prisoners, hostages, or whatever they were called. They could still wreck Shores's company if they knew where to find it.

That knowledge escaped the surviving mercs and their leaders, until Shores was lying on the floor of a ventilation duct, looking through fan blades into what had to be Sector F. It matched both the old and updated descriptions, except that statistics hadn't translated into the sheer visual impact of the cave.

Seventy-five meters from floor to ceiling, at least, Shores thought. *The rock overhead could be damned thin.*

She counted four other tunnels leading out of the cave. With the one where her people waited, that made the five Lionheart had described. Also as he'd described it, one of the four tunnels was noticeably larger than the others, large enough for small carriers.

Shores rolled over on her back, set her binoculars to maximum IR sensitivity, and began studying the ceiling of the cave. In five minutes she found a rectangular patch of ceiling distinctly cooler than the rock around it. The patch, like the largest tunnel, could take small lift-carriers.

She'd found at least one of the back doors. Did it have a detectable surface entrance that could save the people upstairs a whole bunch of time?

Probably, but it was an even-handed deal. It wouldn't be easily found; looking for it could consume all the time saved by not drilling and blasting.

Shores motioned the SSW team behind her to take her place behind the fans. "If they start shooting the prisoners, hit them hard. Unless they make a break for the largest tunnel. Then block that one." The gunner's face twisted at the idea of letting civilians *and* intelligence sources be slaughtered.

Shores grinned with more confidence than she felt. "You won't have to hold the fort long. The minute they start moving, we dump all our incendiaries into the mouth of that tunnel too. You only have to shoot if they're willing to burn."

The team didn't look much consoled. Shores backed down the duct, trying to crawl silently in a metal tube that kept wanting to turn into an echo chamber every time her elbow hit the wall. She had an entire new layer of sweat under her clothes by the time she rejoined the rest of her people.

A messenger took off running, with an escort and the fuse damper. Shores held her breath as the damper field weakened around her people, but nothing blew. This close to their own last-stand point, she doubted the bad guys would be suicidal enough to use anything too heavy, but less plausible hypotheses had killed good soldiers.

In ten minutes the damper team was back. In the cave where they'd had the first firefight, they'd cut the damper and squirt-signaled the rear guard to expect the messenger. Once the messenger had covered the last safe stretch to the com link, the people upstairs would know everything they needed in minutes. *Or at least everything they're damned well going to get.*

Shores crept forward to get another look at the sixty-odd prisoners and their twenty guards, roughly an equal number of mercs and armed civilians. So far only the prisoners looked desperate. They knew or suspected what was going to happen to them. Memory-wipe at best, death more likely, possibly death slow and horrible like Joanna Marder had been supposed to receive.

The guards didn't look desperate. Alert, aggressive, and at least some of them thoroughly professional, but not yet desperate. Shores would take aggressiveness over desperation any day. Aggressive people could still react as professionals. Desperate ones could turn berserker.

Day-long minutes crawled by. Shores was quite certain spring must have come to the Roskills, with snowbird lichen giving its brief color show. This mountain wasn't a Field Intelligence base, it was really the Venusberg, where you spent a few days and came out to a world years older—

The back-door rectangle blew out. Chunks of rock and shards of metal rained down into the cave in a cloud of dust and smoke. After them fell several bright green cylinders, already spewing revoltingly green gas.

It's not the chemicals in UC gas that make you sick, Shores had once heard. *It's the color.*

The upstairs people had taken a partial shortcut, boring through into the bottom end of the escape tunnel. Now it was up to Shores and her people to react faster than the guards.

The guards were reacting fast enough, but the first thing they had to do was mask up. Some of them were running as they masked up; one tripped over a chunk of rock and dropped his mask. He was trying to retrieve it when the gas started working. He writhed and held his stomach as it convulsively emptied itself.

Nobody got to the large tunnel. The SSW and the fire of half the Scouts took care of that. Fallen rock blocked off another of the tunnels. Shores heard a lot of screaming and shouting as well as vomiting, but it sounded more like panic than pain.

Dumping borehole rock into an inhabited cave always risked casualties and was never done except when speed was critical. So far it looked as if the Federation had the speed without the civilians taking the casualties.

Shores signaled for the snipers to move out, taking position around the walls to hit any guards who'd masked in time for a last stand. She herself scanned the civilians for the body-temperature signatures of either Merishi or Baernoi. She'd just about decided that one of the masked guards was Merishi when she heard Ito squall like a mating tomcat.

"Oh, Spirits! Look at the ceiling!"

Cracks were zigzagging across the rock, beginning at the gaping hole at the end of the escape tunnel. Then they stopped lengthening and started growing wider. An immense section of the ceiling shivered, tilted, and peeled loose from the rock around it.

In thunder and sparks, trailing dust and gravel, it fell into the cave. It hit like a bomb, and people who weren't pulped under it went down from the shock wave and flying fragments.

Shores and most of her troopers were far enough from the impact area to be reasonably safe. A good many of the civilians were almost as lucky. The ones who survived lurched to their feet and ran wildly toward the Scouts, ignoring their tortured stomachs, ignoring the armed people ahead, ignoring everything except the urge to flee from the inferno.

Most of the guards had no luck at all. They were in the lethal area of the rockfall. The main slab or its cohorts reduced them to molecular thickness.

Shores waved one of her squads to take a blocking position down the main tunnel in order to stop the fleeing civilians. No time to worry about fuse dampers, assuming the ground shock had left any fuses functional.

She led the other three squads forward to mop up before any surviving guards or reinforcements from the unblocked tunnels could rally. For the first twenty meters she moved catfooted, to avoid tripping over rock fragments. Then the dust swirled away from around her, and she looked up.

Through the hole in the ceiling, the stars were shining. The stars, and every light aboard *Shenandoah*. No, not every light—the battlecruiser was so low that Shores could see only part of her.

Shores's first thought was that she had seen the stars again before her death. Her second was that the hole was big enough for a troop lifter. Hades, it was damned near big enough for an attacker!

She ran to the fallen rock slab and scrambled up onto it. It was hot enough to scorch her through her clothes and she made a fine target, but she had to communicate with the people upstairs.

She fired a flare as she reached the top of the rock. The golden assault signal soared up through the hole and burst, almost lost in the glare from the battlecruiser's lights.

But they would see it up there, they had to, and if they didn't see the flare she still had her radio and her signal laser and—

A grenade burst on the far side of the rock. The fragments and blast together swept her off the rock, just as another grenade exploded where she'd been standing. She felt muscles twist and joints strain in ways nature never intended as she slid head-first and arse-uppermost down the rock, but it was better than being gutted.

Shores was on hands and knees when she heard the hiss and rumble of armor-suit jets. She sprang up and waved frantically as a squad of Rangers rode their suits down into the hole.

"Sergeant Eggert," the first one to land shouted.

"Fuse dampers?" Shores called. Eggert didn't seem to hear, until she realized she hadn't switched on her radio. "Fuse dampers?" she repeated.

"One each."

"Good. You armored people start clearing the tunnels

you can get at. We're not going to do any rock moving until—"

Another quartet of Rangers flamed down into the cave. Then a Navy-marked lifter followed, banging alarmingly against one edge of the hole. Shores saw a wiry figure standing up in the unbuttoned turret, pounding a fist on the hull. Raoul Zimmer was coming into action at last, with the other two platoons of Scout Company.

The lifter grounded, rocking as it settled down among the rock fragments. Shores prayed the pilots had done their best to avoid any bodies that might not be quite dead. Zimmer scrambled out of the turret, slid down the hull, caught an SSW that someone tossed him from the cockpit, and ran up to Shores.

"Sergeant Major Zimmer reporting, Major."

"What's the matter, Raoul? Still don't trust me to go out by myself?"

"Ma'am, you're only a temporary field-grade. Captains still need a chaperone." Then he dropped the SSW and hugged Shores, nearly lifting her off her feet.

By the time the second lifter had grounded, Shores had updated Zimmer and Lieutenant Piccone on the tactical situation. They didn't know anything about the battle against the rebels to the east, but the lower tunnel of the base was being cleared out.

"They've even got three of the last squad people out still breathing," Zimmer said. He looked at the rock-littered cave. "I don't think the people under that are going to be so lucky."

"They were mostly bad guys, and anyway, it wasn't your fault," Shores said.

"No, it was the mountain's fault," Lionheart said earnestly. "You just hit it the wrong way."

Shores could not believe that the man had just said what she'd heard with a straight face. She glared.

"Look, Li—what *is* your real name?"

"Ah—you may call me Ramdur."

"Look, Ramdur. You are going out on the first lifter from this cave. Partly because you are a priceless intelligence source, and partly because if you make one more joke like that I will forget the intelligence and strangle you with my bare hands."

"I must give you the access codes to the computer system first," he said.

"The—" Shores said, then glared. "Why didn't you give them before?"

"You did not ask. Also, I was afraid it might set off demolition charges. That would not only destroy data, it might make you think I was treacherous. You would be unhappy about that."

"Unhappy," Shores said, shaking her head. Then she held out her hand. "The codes. Ah, thank you. Raoul, find this man a terminal and a portable data carrier for what he can access. Don't let any of them out of your sight until he's done."

"Yes, ma'am!"

Ramdur smiled and bowed. Shores turned back to her leaders. "The armor people are doing a recon on the accessible tunnels, and they'll be laying fiber-optic com lines. So let's plan our follow-up on that basis."

Twenty-six

"Move it, move it, move it!" someone shouted. He sounded both angry and self-important.

Lucco DiVries decided to move now and argue later. "Follow me, people," he called, and led his MedCorps platoon out of the lifter at a trot.

They kept trotting straight ahead behind DiVries, while he looked around, trying to pick the most probable or least improbable destination. *Improvised* could describe this advanced base from which the rebels were being fought. *Cobbled together* would be more accurate, and DiVries thought it was hasty cobbling even if Federation regulars had done it.

A hundred meters later, the self-important man barking orders realized that the newlies might need guidance as well as prodding. "Hey, you MedCorps Vics. The ASP is over to your left, about a quarter klom. Look for the POW holding lifter, and it's just beyond that."

Left covered quite a lot of territory, since the base was not only improvised but dispersed, in case somebody retaliated for any of the Federation's actions tonight. It didn't cover too much to prevent DiVries from finding a large cargo lifter, with its rear hatch open and a crowd of scruffy-looking people sitting or standing in the cargo hold. A Scout with a bandaged ear sat behind an SSW, aimed at the hold.

The ASP was impossible to miss, a square of four of the largest field shelters plus outlying containers and tents. The medical red lozenge flew from one shelter.

"Unload but don't get too comfortable," DiVries ordered. "I'm going to see where they want us."

"What if the rebels attack?" someone asked. He seemed to be voicing a popular fear.

DiVries mentally cursed the self-important voice who'd

earlier done half the job of scaring his people. Then he jerked a thumb toward three miniature constellations of lights riding low over the camp.

"We've got gunships or attackers right overhead. Nobody and nothing's going to get through them without a lot more warning than you people should need. Remember you're all veterans and you can damned well behave like it where the Feddies are watching!"

He hoped none of them had seen the lights flaring to the west and flickering to the north. In the west *Shenandoah* and the Scouts were hopefully chopping one band of enemies to bits. To the north, Rangers, Scouts, and Fed rifle companies were already tied into the rebel diehards, with more attackers overhead.

In another hour, the full strength of a battalion of Associated States troops would be loaded into the scales against the rebels. Then their morale should crack. If it didn't, their bodies would, under the sheer weight of numbers piling on top of them.

Before that hour was up, though, the rebels might be able to counterattack if they were desperate enough. No, they had to be that desperate already. DiVries just prayed that they didn't have anything to counterattack with.

For ten minutes after he entered the ASP's command shelter, DiVries wasn't sure if the Feds wanted his people anywhere except on a lifter going back the way they'd come. Nobody was flat-out rude, but everybody passed him on to somebody else, and every somebody else had to consult with a third party.

DiVries finally found a Major Huth who had just come from surgery and looked as if he'd been the patient rather than the surgeon. As he stripped off his gown and washed, he told DiVries that he honestly didn't know where to put the Victorian medical people where they wouldn't be in the way.

"You came in your own lifter, right?"

"Yes, but it's one of the ones we—ah—"

"Hijacked?"

"That seems to be a popular word with you . . . ah, Federation people."

"I'm a surgeon, not a lawyer. What I'd suggest is that

you use your lifter as quarters until your own casualties start coming in. When will that be?"

"Don't know. We haven't even heard that our people are deployed, let alone engaged. If we don't have access to the Fed com net, it may be a while before I find out."

Huth wiped his hands on a sanitowel and tossed it in a contaminated-waste can. "It'll be a while, I suspect. But if you use the lifter, nobody's going to yank it away from you. I'll get on the horn to Borha as soon as I finish rounds, and maybe he can get something moving."

"Can I come with you? We have some paramedics along with the administrative cadre. They could lend a hand with your patients until our own start coming in."

Huth shrugged. "It can't do any harm."

One ward shelter was already filled, thanks to a handful of wounded rebel prisoners. Most of them wore hand and ankle restraints, but DiVries noticed a couple of armed troopers at either end of the aisle.

Huth stopped between a stretcher with an unrestrained prisoner and one with a complete life-support cocoon filling it. All DiVries could see besides the cocoon was a round dark face and a Ranger badge on the ID.

Huth bent over the display on the cocoon. He was shaking his head as he straightened up. "Captain Bloch's not going to be happy by morning. Abdul won't last the night."

"Partner?"

"Four years, now. Not bedfriends, though. They each go the other way."

DiVries turned away. Mortality seemed a little too close, when Rangers could die.

Then he felt something fumbling at his slung carbine. He whirled as the fumble turned into a jerk, and turned the wrong way. The sling flew off his shoulder and now the carbine rose, in the hands of the unrestrained rebel.

DiVries's reflexes took over. He kicked upward, tilting the stretcher. The prisoner grabbed the edge with one hand, leaving only one to hold the carbine. He got off a burst as the stretcher flipped completely over, but the burst went into the ceiling.

Plastic showered down, lights flared and went out, and DiVries flung himself on the stretcher. It landed on top of the prisoner, jamming the carbine against his chest. His head struck the floor with a sharp crack. To finish the job DiVries grabbed the man by his thinning brown hair and began banging his head against the floor even harder, three, four, five times—

Huth and one of the troopers finally had to pull him off the prisoner. They both looked at him as if they were ready to put restraints on him.

"Sorry," DiVries said, which sounded lame but was the best he could manage. "I thought I had that sort of garbage out of my system."

"You weren't thinking at all," Huth snapped. "Or maybe you were thinking of taking out one of our intelligence sources. You Vics stick together—"

"Now just a damned minute—"

"Not one second, Citizen DiVries. Get the hell out of here, or do you want to leave under arrest?"

It might make a useful point if he forced the Feddies to arrest him, but useful to his platoon? Or to the Victorian wounded, who would be counting on his platoon to have things ready for them?

No. He gently pulled his arms free of the others' grip and walked down the corridor. As he reached the end, he saw Huth look at Abdul's display, then cut the power to the cocoon.

Dead. And how much better off was Lucco DiVries, with his life blowing across his homeworld like a sandstorm? Were Sophie's arms the only place where nobody would tell him to get the hell out?

No. His platoon wouldn't. He would go back to them, give them what they needed from him, and go on giving it. Even if it was only going through the motions.

Rahbad Sarlin knew that the ventilation in his tunnel was gone, and only the emergency lighting remained. He wondered if the electronic elements of his cell's lock worked off the emergency or main power, or if they had their own source.

The answer came minutes after he'd asked the question. A sturdy figure in coveralls appeared outside the door, wearing a mask pushed up over his bald head, a bulging shoulder bag, and a wad gun held at waist level.

"Rahbad Sarlin?" the man asked. Sarlin studied the man

before replying. It was not the same one who'd interrogated him before and who had not returned for a further bargaining session. Allowing for a more pallid complexion and some loss of weight, the man most resembled General Liu, the Federation traitor.

Sarlin willed every controllable function of his body to maximum alert. Then he nodded. "I am Rahbad Sarlin. Who are you?"

"A friend."

"Prove it."

"If you will stand clear of your door—" The wad gun swung.

Sarlin deferred dignity to a later moment and obeyed. The wad gun thumped, and its charge of gelatinous explosive slammed into the lock. It solidified, until the chemical changes from exposure to the air set it off. The lock flew into pieces and the door flew open.

Liu reappeared, bleeding from a cut forehead. He'd been standing too close to the blast. *Useful to know that he may have become careless.*

Sarlin stepped toward the door, hands empty and held out, lips drawn over his tusks. "Where are we going?"

"Somewhere out of here, to start with," the man said. He gestured to the left with his free hand. *Those wad guns are not easy to control with one hand. More signs of stress-induced carelessness.*

"Let me bring—"

"We haven't time. We can find some warm clothes on the way."

"And a weapon for me."

"Of course." Even one of the People less trained than Sarlin in reading Smalltooth voices and body language could have recognized a lie.

The man allowed Sarlin to get behind him, but kept a two-body interval between them. Normally that would have been enough for safety. One of the short-legged People could not have closed the distance before Liu turned and fired, with either the wad gun or the pistol at his hip.

Rahbad Sarlin was not one of the normal People, and a professional soldier like Liu should have at least admitted that possibility. But then, if Liu had done half of what h probably had, clarity of thought was not one of his most conspicuous qualities.

Sarlin knew they could not have covered a quarter of the distance it seemed in the tenth-watch he followed Liu through a maze of tunnels. Sometimes the battle sounds were loud and behind them, at other times quiet and ahead of them. They never ceased completely, and Sarlin knew that the base would be captured or destroyed or both within another tenth-watch. He decided, however, to wait until the attackers were close enough to further confuse Liu before taking any action, if he had the choice.

In considerably less than a tenth-watch, he knew that the confrontation with the attackers was approaching quickly. He heard the sound of armor-suit jets and heavy weapons, lifter fans, and shouted orders. From the amount of shouting, he judged that the humans were extensively using fuse dampers. It was a trade he would have made in their place—no radio, but fewer risks from bombs.

As the noise grew, Sarlin saw Liu sweating in spite of the chill. He also saw Liu opening the distance between them. Another half body, and Sarlin's exceptional swiftness would not be enough. Sarlin began studying the tunnel walls, looking for possible hiding places. He also looked for weapons, but with less hope of finding anything.

Sarlin had just pocketed a couple of loose stones when Liu stopped and turned. The wad gun was now held in both hands and pointed at Sarlin's stomach.

"All right, Citizen Sarlin. In about two minutes, we'll reach an emergency com station. I want you to contact your Fleet Commander. Tell him that he can have you back if he'll take me with you."

"I suppose I could waste our time asking," Sarlin said. "You should know, however, that the People have the same view of hostage-taking as the Federation and Alliance. My death might be more honorable if I said nothing."

"I doubt that," Liu said. "I very much doubt it. You see, you will not die if you refuse to call. You will simply be turned over to the Federation. They may be grateful enough for that gift to let me—"

While Liu outlined his strategy, Sarlin had been willing himself to full alert again. Now he dove for the floor, flinging one of the stones as he went down.

It struck Liu high on the chest, knocking him backward and jerking up the muzzle of the wad gun. It also forced his tense finger to close on the trigger. The wad roared up to the ceiling. Liu started to run, to get clear of the blast area before the explosive reached critical state.

But wad explosive could be detonated before that by a sharp mechanical impact. Sarlin provided that with the second stone. The blast flattened Liu and would have flattened Sarlin, except that he was both People and trained.

Another human was considerably closer than Sarlin to the blast, judging from how fast he came around the corridor. But he was wearing an armored suit, with Ranger badges and the name EGGERT on the helmet.

Sarlin stood up, unable to hear much except a whining in his ears. Instinct bared his tusks; reason spread out empty hands. The armored figure backed away so that he could cover both Sarlin and Liu with his pulser.

Then two unarmored figures appeared behind the Ranger. The taller of the two was a woman, and Sarlin thought he recognized the famous Major Shores. The shorter male turned Liu over and started violently.

"Translation gear!" Shores called back down the tunnel.

"I speak Anglic," Sarlin said. At least he thought the part of his brain that controlled language had survived the last watch. "I would rather you left the fuse dampers on."

That drew a thin smile. "So speak. What are you doing here with General Liu?" The short man finished examining the body and turned thumbs-down. "The late General Liu?" the woman corrected herself.

For once, the honorable, prudent, and pleasurable things were all the same—telling the truth. When he'd finished, Sarlin saw the two unarmored soldiers—Scouts, he now recognized—looking at each other. His hearing was returning, so he heard what they said more clearly than he might have wished.

"From what I know about Liu, it sounds just like him," the short man said. "I wish he'd survived, but I don't suppose we could have asked Sarlin to get himself killed so we could pump Liu."

"No. That would be asking a lot of anybody—"

Sarlin coughed. "Could I ask the courtesy of not discussing me as though I were a child or one of faulty wits?"

This time the woman's smile was not so thin. "We can do better than that. Come with us, and we'll have you aboard *Shenandoah* in a tenth-watch."

The man nodded, but as he did he pulled out an injector. "Now, we're going to have to ask you to—"

Sarlin made every Smalltooth negative gesture he remembered, then started on those of the People. By the time he'd started on those of the Ptercha'a, Shores was holding in laughter.

The man—his name seemed to be Esteva—remained grim. "Major, he may see a good deal—"

"I will," Sarlin said. "But I have not been drugged or restrained, except for being locked up, nor blindfolded, nor tortured all my time here. Not since my capture, in any case, and my captors were enemies to both of us and far less honorable than I am sure Federation Scouts wish to be considered."

He hoped that speech would convince them. If not, his life might end and his voice certainly would.

"We'll do it his way," Shores finally said. Esteva opened his mouth, but she held up a hand. "I'll take the responsibility, Sergeant. Coming, Commander Sarlin?"

Sarlin nodded. He wanted to save his strength for legs that seemed about to desert him.

He didn't find his voice again until the humans led him into a vast cave, a ragged hole gaping in its roof. Through that hole, Sarlin saw bits of night sky, but no stars. Their distant glow was lost in the blaze of lights from a huge ship riding just above the hole.

"That *is Shenandoah*!" Sarlin exclaimed.

"It sure as Hades isn't an all-night pad restaurant," Esteva said.

Brigitte Tachin had finally achieved the ideal weapons-panel officer's total concentration. Nothing except the Tulwar missile that she was checking out prior to loading existed. She knew that Commander Zhubova had returned from Combat Center, but Zhubova was still only a voice that might have been computer or human or K'thressh.

Finally her own displays all read as they should, and she could spare a glance for the repeater displays covering the general situation. Her breath caught as she read their story:

The rebel base captured, cleared, and evacuated, including Federation personnel, POWs, and refugees.

Substantial quantities of electronic, hard-print, and physical intelligence obtained.

Most vehicles aboard *Shenandoah* or clearing the area.

Moderate friendly casualties, heavy hostile ones, no friendlies left behind.

Zhubova slapped switches, and the display showed one more piece of data:

Both Federation and Associated States forces fully deployed and in action against the rebels. Rebels suffering heavy casualties and not expected to be effective past midnight.

Past midnight? Tachin looked at the clock. It was still only 2210. She ran a finger around the inside of a sweat-sodden collar. Had she drained herself this much in just three hours?

"Hard work," came Sumo Nakamura's voice from behind her. "But then, you have no problem with that."

Tachin felt a quick surge of energy, probably adrenaline. Nakamura seldom used that traditional salutation, and then only to people he thought met his high standards.

Zhubova rose and came over to Tachin's console. "Our bird ready?"

Bird, for a missile with a fifty-kiloton fuser aboard, somehow didn't seem the right term. "The missile is nominal."

"Fine. Then when we get the word—" Zhubova handed Tachin a red plastic card. Tachin reached for it, but it needed an effort of will to make her fingers close on the card.

It was a weapons-release card. Tachin would be one of the five officers aboard *Shenandoah* inserting the red cards, to start the warhead on the road to being armed and lethal.

She told herself that there would be no one alive where the bomb hit, and few alive near it, friends or enemies. She reminded herself that there might be dangerous weapons or compromising evidence left in the inaccessible tunnels of the base that had to be completely destroyed.

She also knew that Commander Zhubova had given her the classic weapons officers' test much earlier than usual. That was a vote of confidence she could not fail. Not and live with herself.

"Problems, Brigitte?" Zhubova could sound amazingly

motherly for somebody who made her living off fusion bombs and gigawatt lasers. Although since she was a mother—three children, Tachin recalled—maybe this wasn't so amazing after all.

"I hope all the fuse dampers are turned off."

"Sorry. I should have told you. The bomb's been specially fitted with a mechanical impact fuse and a mechanical time fuse. We can even back those up from orbit if we have to."

"I'd rather get it right the first time."

"Good philosophy, when you're tossing fusers." Then the intercom whistled.

"Now hear this, now hear this. All hands to stations for getting under way. Missile-release and preparatory nudet alert in effect in one minute."

The petty officer's face on the screen vanished; the scarred and smoking mountain took its place. It began to slide toward the right side of the screen and shrink as Tachin watched. Then the lights over the bomb-status displays came on, five in a line, all red.

Zhubova leaped for her seat, pulling out her own card. Tachin thrust hers into the slot, Zhubova did the same, two lights turned green, then three more, then:

"Launch!"

Tachin's hand was millimeters from the manual plate, but Launcher Two worked perfectly. *Shenandoah* seemed to leap as the missile fell free, blazing across the screen in an eyeblink. Tachin knew the missile couldn't be the cause; Liddell must have the power wide open.

The next moment Tachin was sure. The mountain vanished, and rugged snow-patched terrain began unrolling below, faster and dimmer with each moment. *Shenandoah* climbed up through a level of haze, and now the ground was only something glimpsed at intervals, then something imagined—

Shenandoah was well past Mach Two, above three thousand meters, and fifty kloms down the valley toward the sea when the bomb went off. Tachin watched the screen flood with the searing fusion glare, dazzling even with the filters up.

Then the intercom was playing an exuberantly bouncy march, with an antique flavor to it.

"Isn't it a little soon to celebrate?" Tachin asked.

Zhubova grinned, waving one hand in time to the beat. "Who's celebrating? That's what we're sending out on every Alliance and rebel tactical frequency. It's known as jamming."

Brian always said that Captain Rosie had class. After a moment, Tachin thought she recognized the march. One of the Old Lady's favorites, and associated with something called the Royal Marines. Which kingdom, Tachin couldn't recall, but probably something European. It certainly had to be antique, too. Something called "A Life on the Ocean Wave" might go back to sailing ships!

"What was that?" Joanna Marder asked. She spoke almost normally, but Charles Longman could hear the pain and doubt in her voice.

"Nowhere near here, unless I miss my guess," he said. "The main raid was going to be on the place where—Field Intelligence, I suspect—had you. I mean, held you . . ."

Longman tried to speculate soothingly for a good ten minutes. He hadn't been cleared for a good deal of what was going to be done with the intelligence Jo brought. Neither had a lot of other people, but they'd been guessing out loud where Longman could hear them. Adding their guesses to his, he had plenty of material.

Too much. Marder finally forced a smile, even though mouth and teeth still must be hurting. "Charlie—Lieutenant—which do you prefer?"

"Whatever makes you—"

"No. You have to decide."

"Really. Either one will do. But not Charles. That's Aunt Di, mostly."

"The one who posed nude?"

"Yeah. Anyway, let's flip a coin. Heads it's Lieutenant, tails it's Charlie."

The coin was actually a Dominion credit slug, but it came up Charlie well enough.

"All right, Charlie. You're babbling, trying to keep me calm when you're scared yourself. Why not go and find out what really happened?"

"You sure—"

"Don't even *think* 'Can she be left alone?' "

As unmistakable an order as Longman had ever received. He almost saluted as he backed away from the bed.

The guards didn't know much except the thump and that some of the outdoor people had seen what looked like a fuser burst way off to the west. Longman started down the hall toward the nurse's station, and halfway there met Colonel Nieg coming toward him.

"Good evening, Lieutenant," Nieg said, almost airily. "How is Commander Marder?"

"Giving me orders," Longman said.

"About time too—" Nieg began.

"She wants to know what happened. So do I."

Nieg did not give Longman the familiar "Who is this presumptuous worm?" look. Instead he gave a jerky nod.

"*Shenandoah* and the Scouts took out the base. They loaded up people and material, then fused the rest."

"Like arson to cover robbery."

"Lieutenant, I hope you're not planning a career in Intelligence."

"Christ, no!"

"You don't have to be so positive about it. The last report is that the base is slagged down and *Shenandoah* is on her way back to orbit with the loot. The Alliance hasn't done or said anything and it's too late now.

"I'm heading for orbit myself in ten minutes, but I wanted to drop by and say thank you to Marder. Thanks to you, too, for taking care of her."

The thanks to Marder would have to wait; she was asleep when Nieg catfooted up to her bed. Longman sat down, ready for another night's vigil, although he hoped it would be the last.

As the door closed behind Nieg, Marder opened her eyes.

"Charlie. I heard that bit about taking care of me. I don't want that. I mean, after I get out of the hospital, I can't afford to—somebody trying to take care of me always winds up—oh, damn. . . ."

She started to cry, from weakness and at weakness that wouldn't let the words come out right. The message was clear enough for Longman. He pulled his chair close, but didn't even take her hand. (It would still be sore from pulled fingernails and intravenous tubing anyway.)

"Commander—Jo—I promise I won't give a damn about you. Fair enough?"

A half sob, half laugh. "That wasn't what I was asking."

"Then maybe—no. Look, it really *can* wait until you're feeling better. I only have the *reputation* of a selfish idiot. Deep within I'm a golden-hearted altruist."

Considerably to his surprise, Marder took his hand. "Charlie, that's not as funny as you think."

Then she really was asleep. Longman resigned himself to spending his vigil knowing that the good guys had won but not what Jo Marder was talking about.

Twenty-seven

The wind blowing through the hole in the roof changed
pitch, then volume. It had been a low moan; now it was a
loud shriek.

Pak had too much self-control to wince. He could not
help asking Colonel Nieg, "Did you choose this meeting
place to remind me of my responsibilities?"

Behind the faceplate, Nieg's features only twitched.
"Hardly. If I thought you needed something this drastic to
remind you, I would be considering a termination mission
instead."

Nieg gestured toward the broken window, which showed
a view of half-ruined and wholly abandoned Buschton. "It
was much simpler than that. Who would suspect anything
from an inspection tour to Buschton? Radiation hazards
would be the perfect excuse for a small escort. It might
even improve morale by hinting that you felt matters were
under control in Silvermouth."

Pak did not like having his thoughts read back to him
with such precision, and his face must have showed it. Nieg
actually looked contrite, or at least simulated it con-
vincingly.

"I have the complete data here. I assume you have read
the summary?"

"Yes. I suppose authentication of any doubtful pieces is
available?"

"Yes, although I don't recommend asking for too much.
We can hardly afford delay."

"If Lopatina or Uzel remain skeptical, there will be more
delay than any number of authentications could produce."

"I have taken a precaution against that," Nieg said.
'Admiral Lopatina has already received her own copy of
the material."

347

Pak decided that he had exhausted his quota of bemused looks. "I was not aware you had the facilities for such a delivery."

"We do."

It was even odds whether Nieg was using a previously secret channel or one he had acquired since the amnesty for the Freedom Legion. Certainly most of the pro-independence people in Silvermouth were closer to the now legal Freedom Party than to the fanatics of Action for Independence.

"In that case, I should return to Silvermouth as quickly as possible. But I think we need to discuss the fate of at least three people caught up in this affair."

"What makes you think we have anything to discuss?"

"Perhaps the phrase was not well chosen. Would you care to inform me which three people you are thinking of?"

"Commander Marder, Rahbad Sarlin, and Lionheart."

"We agree in that much, at least."

"I hope we will agree on more. Commander Marder and Ramdur Lionheart wish political asylum. Ramdur has requested a memory-wipe, as he wishes to leave intelligence work entirely. You may arrange for a reliable witness to the operation. However, it will be performed entirely by Federation personnel.

"Commander Marder may receive a memory-wipe for medical reasons, if she wishes it. She seems to be making an acceptable recovery, however.

"If *anything* suspicious happens to either of them, there will be terminations in retaliation. In Commander Marder's case, I will carry out the retaliation regardless of orders."

Pak had no trouble believing the warning. The Federation had no shortage of people as ruthless as any in Field Intelligence; many of them added discipline and imagination to the ruthlessness.

"And Rahbad Sarlin?"

"He has returned to *Night Warrior*. We refrained from interrogating him, but he did volunteer some useful information that he felt would not compromise the interests of the People."

Pak wanted to flee, even into the heart of the contaminated zone, to get away from this arrogance of victory—a

victory so complete that Nieg felt he could throw crumbs to
the Baernoi.

He also knew that Nieg had a right to at least some of
the arrogance. Part of the Federation's victory had been
handed to it, by Field Intelligence bungling. Much of it had
been won fairly, by shrewdness and courage.

Much of it had also been a victory for the whole human
race (indeed, the sensible members of all races) over the
senseless or at least the shortsighted. That was a victory in
a war that had no end.

Pak held out his hand. Nieg put the package in it and
saluted. Pak returned the salute and held it until Nieg had
backed out of the ruined house. He didn't leave the room
until he heard the distant whine of Nieg's lifter taking off.

Candice Shores looked at the brandy bottle on the table
in the center of the triangle of chairs. Colonel Nieg looked
at her, then at the clock.

"Pak should be in Silvermouth by now," he said. "If
things go the way we want them, Admiral Pritkin will take
no action when he arrives tomorrow, and Silvermouth will
remain quiet."

Shores decided against asking if Nieg had contingency
plans for making Silvermouth noisy. She knew the answer.

She also decided against another drink. She had cleaned
up, debriefed, taken a physical, visited Scout Company's
wounded in the hospital, and caught up on sleep and food.
She'd made love to Nieg, let Maddie cry on her shoulder
over Abdul's death, and written up a stack of com-
mendations.

In short, she had done everything that needed to be done
before she could get royally drunk, except for one thing.
She hadn't arranged the universe or even Victoria so that
she would not be needed to lead Scout Company (minus its
fourteen dead and thirty-one wounded) into action again.

Maddie Bloch had no such problems. The Rangers were
standing down, temporarily noneffective from their battles
at the base and against the A.I. holdouts. That they'd won
both battles didn't affect the limits of flesh and blood.

Maddie had accounted for most of the missing half of the
bottle and now was looking belligerently at Nieg. "If you're

going to ask Candy to go out and get killed again, could I ask a favor?"

"You can ask."

"What the devil happened, to make this . . . *tasse de merde* . . . in the first place?"

"You can't wait for the full report?"

"Are we going to get one?" Shores asked.

"Yes. Partly because you've both earned it. Partly, too, because there are some things about the situation where I'd like both of you to stay involved."

"I'm not transferring to Intelligence, Colonel," Shores said.

Nieg poured himself a surprisingly large drink. "I'm not asking you to. By the time we've reached the bottom of this business, a great deal more than Intelligence may be involved."

"Are you going to add mystery or reduce it?" Bloch said.

"Reduce it," Nieg said, doing the same with his drink.

Baldly told and greatly oversimplified, the scenario was still chilling. The Victorians had wanted union and independence. They approached the Baernoi Special Projects people, who provided them with weapons, including the fusers.

At this point Alliance Field Intelligence got wind of the business, but decided that it would do more harm to the Federation than to the Alliance (first clanger). Also, the Victorians did not have the codes necessary for arming the bombs.

"As we suspected, Hollings was crucial. Field Intelligence had a free hand for all their clangers because they were leading him by the nose. They'd convinced him that if he gave them their free hand, they would get him reinstated, even promoted, in the Army."

Shores had never seen Maddie Bloch so completely speechless.

Enter the Merishi militants, who had been in contact with, or possibly leaked to from, Field Intelligence. They came with more weapons, ships, and their contacts with both Khudrigate's Special Projects and General Liu. (The general had been selling the Merishi a modest quota of secrets, in the hope of a retirement in the style to which he wished to become accustomed.)

Field Intelligence did not realize that Liu knew how to break the bomb-arming codes (second clanger). Neither did the Baernoi. So both went on stirring things up, either directly or by arming the determined and the desperate among the Victorians.

As Field Intelligence saw it, things began beautifully and went on that way for quite a while. They were caught completely unawares by the fact that Action for Independence decided the Alliance had betrayed the first Bushranger Rebellion. Thus the bombing of the Bonsai Squadron.

After that, Field Intelligence and their puppet Hollings were in a frantic race to cover their tracks—a race which at the moment they seemed to have lost. (Nieg made several gestures of aversion.) They faced not only the wrath of the Federation and the Victorians, but a lack of cooperation from both their erstwhile allies the Baernoi and Merishi and from their own armed forces.

"So what about the bomb on Buschton?" Shores asked. "Was that to keep the Freedom Legion from winning? Or was it to keep Pak from beating them and making his position stronger?"

"They probably thought it would cover both contingencies," Nieg said.

Shores decided she did want that drink after all. She wasn't surprised when Bloch held out her glass, too, but when Nieg's turned out to be empty she almost reconsidered her own refill.

She had not drunk enough to be suffering from hallucinations.

"Have you asked for any of the authentications?" Admiral Lopatina said. She was wearing a dressing gown that could have served for a witch's robe and was sitting on the edge of the bed. Cautiously, as if her head or limbs might part company with her torso if she moved too vigorously, but definitely sitting.

"Nieg names too many places, dates, and names," Pak said. Fegeli nodded.

"I agree," Lopatina said. "So what do we want to do with this trail of piss Field Intelligence has left?"

The two Army men looked at each other. "Present it to Uzel, I think," Fegeli said.

"You think. You aren't sure?"

"Ma'am, you're talking as if you had some other course of action in mind," Pak said.

"No, I don't," Lopatina said. "But I point out that I am only senior Alliance officer here. As of tomorrow, I will no longer control the only forces capable of defending Seven Rivers. If Hollings declares that I am under arrest and Pritkin is in command, then we have to start a civil war or let Pritkin take over."

"In either case, Nieg will release all the data," Pak pointed out. That would start a civil war if one hadn't already begun, the more so because Pritkin's reinforcements included the 53rd Independent Regiment and a pair of brigadiers senior to Fegeli.

"We don't want that," Lopatina said. "Field Intelligence will never recover from it. There will be too many people in the Navy who will see to that."

"Good luck to them," Fegeli said. "Who needs the F.I.O. bastards anyway?"

"The Alliance does," Lopatina said. "As long as we have three times the frontier and a quarter the resources of the Federation, we need all the frontier guards we can get. The Navy and F.I. are the two most important. If they're too busy fighting each other to keep a lookout, who's going to gain?

"I can live with losing to people like Kuwahara or Kornilov. Even Gist. But the Federation has plenty who want to roll the clock back two centuries and wipe out the Alliance entirely. Then there's the Tuskers and the Merishi and Lord alone knows who else waiting in the wings."

"Nieg implied some similar reasoning," Pak said. "He wants to give Field Intelligence a reprieve, so it can put its own house in order."

"So do I, God forgive me, and I hope the ghosts of the Bonsai Squadron do the same." With a firm grip on Pak's hand and the bed railing, Lopatina stood. "So we have to do more than persuade Uzel that Field Intelligence has stepped on its equipment. We have to persuade him to face all the implications we've just been discussing."

"Lopatina, Fegeli, and Pak; Miracles on Demand, Limited," Fegeli said.

"Colonel Pak should be senior partner," Lopatina said. She cautiously moved down to the end of the bed. "Now gentlemen, I am a little too old for field modesty. If you will retire while I get on my walking harness and uniform, we can be off."

Fegeli was fidgeting noticeably by the time the Baba called them in. She was sweating and pale, and her hair was a ruin, but in uniform she no longer looked so much like her own ghost.

"I've called my shuttle. Would one of you gentlemen be handy with a hairbrush?"

Fegeli took the brush and comb from the side table, sat down behind the admiral, and began a struggle with the gray tangles.

"You do this very well," Lopatina said as Fegeli brushed away. "Practice on your daughters?"

"Ah—well, it's Sharon. She likes me to brush her hair out before we—ah—"

Lopatina nodded. "That makes something else Sharon's good for, besides scaring you into sense."

Brokeh su-Irzim felt that the silence in Fleet Commander su-Ankrai's cabin was sacred. It would offend the High Lords to break it.

Of course, if everyone else felt as he did, they would be sitting there in silence tomorrow, when the Alliance reinforcements arrived, and the day after that, when something had to happen, and possibly even through the time when the Federation released all that they had learned in their raid on the base—

That was carrying reverence too far. Su-Irzim cleared his throat.

"Yes, Inquirer?" su-Ankrai said.

"Do you have anything more, Commander Sarlin?"

Sarlin shook his head. "Nothing that would change my recommendation."

"Which was not requested," Zhapso su-Lal said.

"Duty does not wait upon requests," Sarlin said piously, "and if the Great Khudr didn't say that—"

"Well, I say that your recommendation is for us to pull lips, lower ears, and all but go on our bellies as we scuttle off into the safety of a Passage out of the Victoria system!" Su-Ankrai's bellow shattered the silence into powder.

"Yes," Rahbad Sarlin said.

If su-Ankrai had not started laughing two heartbeats later, su-Irzim would have disgraced himself by being the first to laugh. As it was, he contented himself with a smile until the Fleet Commander ran out of breath and summoned a robot with beer for all of them.

Silence returned, as no one dared to ask the Fleet Commander what he was going to do about the recommendation. Or perhaps they were all too busy wetting their throats to sharpen their wits.

It was a good hundredth-watch after the beer arrived before su-Ankrai spoke. "It appears that the wisest thing to do is in fact to declare that our objectives have been gained and the mission of the Seventh Training Force is completed. So we are leaving the Victoria system in the hope that all parties will respect—and so on and so on and so on," he finished airily. "Su-Lal, composing our farewell message is your task."

"Yes, lord."

"You sound dubious."

Su-Lal had learned by now that one did not lie to su-Ankrai, even when the truth might be embarrassing. "I fail to see why we must assume that the Federation really has so many secrets. Particularly when they did not interrogate Rahbad Sarlin."

"I saw and overheard enough to make it reasonable that they can do as they say," Sarlin snapped. "Unless you wish to question my wits?"

Su-Lal did not wish it. Probably it was common sense. Possibly it was fear of what he saw not only in Sarlin's face but in su-Irzim's. After a long and degrading captivity, custom would entitle Sarlin to a champion in any duel with su-Lal. Su-Irzim intended to be that champion.

"I agree with Commander Sarlin," su-Ankrai said. "I also caution you against gambling with more than the People can afford. If the Federation has the data and carries out its threat to release it, then the Alliance may join them against us. They may do this at the exact moment their strength on Victoria increases.

"We would then face approximately twice our own force. We would also face the choice between humiliation or destruction if we opposed anything the humans proposed.

"If we are Passage-bound when Pritkin's task force

arrives, on the other hand, we face no risk of destruction and only a lesser humiliation. We did our best to keep the secret of the sunbombs' origins out of hostile hands.

"We also failed. We will not make anyone believe otherwise by sitting at Victoria flapping our ears. We may kill good warriors and destroy ships that the People will need."

"There is also something else worth investigating," su-Irzim said. "I have analyzed some of the data from Rahbad Sarlin's report. I suggest that we may have discovered where the mercenaries came from."

"A dozen different planets, judging from the accents," Sarlin said testily. "Or are you now thinking I was struck on the head?"

"Please, Commander. You also overheard them describing living or training or both on a planet with certain life-forms, gravity about Smalltooth standard, and a double primary, one yellow and one red dwarf."

"They babbled like children," Sarlin growled. "Do these babblings tell you anything?"

"The computer tells me that they could have all come from or at least through Linak'h."

Su-Lal nodded. "The Ptercha'a colony in this sector."

"Actually it's an independent planet, even if the Merishi control most of its trade," Sarlin said. "But it has no human population, except a small, strictly regulated enclave. Unless . . ." He stared at su-Irzim. "It could be."

"Could be what?" Su-Ankrai sounded irritable.

"An outlaw human colony on a Ptercha'a planet to which the Merishi control access," su-Irzim said. "An outlaw colony from which the Scaleskins can recruit mercenaries—or anything else that they may need."

"Humans would have to be fairly desperate to serve the Merishi," su-Lal said.

"When did the High Lords say they could not become so?" su-Ankrai asked. "If it were otherwise, we would not have spent so much time to so little purpose around Victoria."

Su-Irzim could see the course that both the Fleet Commander and the Special Projects expert were steering. A new subject for investigation could lead to a new assignment for both of them. Success at this investigation could make both Fleet and Inquiry forget Victoria.

Success at investigating it would also be a good deal more likely if one Brokeh su-Irzim put his hand to the rope. If nothing else, he could make sure nobody handed out sun-bombs to people who might be driven to use them!

"If Commander Sarlin will not mind a suggestion—" su-Irzim began.

"I throw myself at your mercy, lord," Sarlin said. "If I had—"

"Not been a prisoner in the hands of dishonorable captors now justly punished, you might have performed miracles," su-Ankrai finished. "Now, let us assume that forgiveness has been craved and granted, and we can go on."

It took another round of beer for a line of investigation to be sketched out. It would take most of the time to Passage for the sketch to be turned into the finished plan, and only if both Inquirers and Rahbad Sarlin worked their tusks down to nubs. But they would be leaving a place of defeat, with the hope of winning victory elsewhere.

"I think I'm going to take that position in the Gan Eleazar Citrus Cooperative," Admiral Uzel said.

For once Colonel Pak didn't know what to do, which would be awkward if Fegeli overreacted to this non sequitur. Fortunately, Baba Lopatina seemed to have the key to her former chief of staff's programming.

"I thought your wife was connected with Gan David," she said.

"Ruth was born there, but she never had a mother on the board. Rachel's mother always thought her daughter was a fool for leaving me. She would give me her board seat just for the pleasure of seeing Rachel throw a screaming fit."

The former Rachel Uzel was not going to be the only one throwing a screaming fit if Uzel didn't stop talking in riddles. Fegeli would be the first.

"Well, I wish you a prosperous retirement," the Baba said. "But we have a few details to get over first. You've read it?"

Uzel made a face. "Yes."

"So?"

"Are you asking me what I'm going to do?"

"Yes."

"Nothing—"

Pak hadn't realized how taut his nerves were stretched until he found his hand diving for his sidearm. He was prepared to stun Uzel if necessary, to let Lopatina take command, but—

"Nothing, until the Army people either put their guns out on the table or at least engage the safeties. A shootout at this point won't help discipline."

That was an order, and a cough behind Pak told him that the Baba endorsed it. Pak put his sleep-wad-loaded pistol on the table in front of him and after a moment so did Fegeli. The Baba spread her hands out in front of her. Looking closely, Pak saw that they were trembling.

"Thank you," Uzel said. He drew a two-shot holdout pistol from a breast pocket and laid it beside the other two weapons.

"Of course I'm going to support you. I can't do—"

"Wait," the Baba said. "It's not so simple as 'of course.' What if Hollings resists arrest?"

"Were you thinking of going straight for an arrest?" Uzel asked.

"Yes," the Baba said.

Uzel shook his head. "We don't have any charges that we can bring against him, without making this"—he tapped the file—"public ourselves. You've said yourself that we don't want to cut the throat of Field Intelligence."

"I didn't say we don't *want* to," Lopatina snapped. "I said we can't afford to. Mordecai, don't go back to your old habit of putting words in my mouth. That's why I never trusted you with a major memorandum."

"Sorry, ma'am," Uzel said. "What I suggest is that we ask Hollings to resign, explain why, *then* threaten him with arrest if he won't go."

"If we give him time to organize resistance—" Fegeli began.

"If we arrest him without a valid charge, we'll look just as bad as he will. Then Pritkin might decide on his own to supersede you, whether he restores Hollings or not.

"Even if he does, he still won't be able to win more than mutual destruction against the Federation without Baernoi help. The minute he calls up the Baernoi, the Feds release the file, everything is known, and Pritkin either breaks with the Baernoi or faces mutiny."

Uzel glared at Fegeli. "Brigadier, nobody bought me. So either accuse me out loud or stop muttering." Fegeli stopped muttering. The little admiral shrugged.

"I want to try settling this by using the law, not burying it deeper under the dunes of this godforsaken planet!"

"I thought Bar Kochba had a whole bunch of sand," Fegeli grumbled.

"Our dunes come in a fine selection of decorator colors, not just one shade of dismal gray," Uzel said. "Now, Admiral Lopatina. I will recognize your assumption of command and provide all the naval support you need for any contingency, on one condition. Ask Hollings to resign before you ask me to blow him up!"

Pak didn't want to be the first to nod, but he had to admit Uzel's point. He had been so close to the dirt for so long that perhaps it had blocked his vision—and so close to the people of Bonsai Squadron who'd died or suffered.

Uzel had a different perspective. It wasn't impossible that he saw more clearly.

"Now hear this, now hear this. The admiral will address the Victoria Task Force. Repeat, Admiral Kuwahara will address all hands of the Victoria Task Force."

The camera shifted from the petty-officer announcer to Admiral Kuwahara, who thought of at least twenty things that might be wrong with his appearance. He found he really didn't care about any of them.

"I have an important announcement. Governor Martin Hollings of the Alliance Seven Rivers Territory has resigned from office as of 1545. He has appointed as his temporary successor Brigadier Domenic Fegeli. Colonel Sun Ji Pak has assumed command of Alliance ground forces on Victoria, under the overall command of Admiral Marya Lopatina, who has returned to active duty.

"At 1900, Acting Governor Fegeli met with leaders of the civil disobedience campaign in Silvermouth. At 2030, they announced a cessation of the campaign in return for recognition of the Freedom Party in Seven Rivers Territory. They also proposed a conference concerning the future union of the planet of Victoria.

"At 2100, ten minutes ago, we were informed that the Associated States of Victoria are sending a delegation to that conference, headed by Father Elijah Brothertongue."

Kuwahara hesitated, because he could already hear the cheering from outside the flag suite. He also had the vague feeling that the minute he stopped talking, something else would turn up desperately needing to be announced.

"This is victory. Our victory. A victory for peace and for the future of Victoria. I can't say anything more or less than a phrase that's old but hasn't lost its weight for all that.

"Well done, Victoria Command."

Kuwahara was telling the truth about not being able to go on. He wasn't crying like Rose Liddell or on his knees praying like Pavel Bogdanov, but his voice was gone and his wits were about to join it.

He swallowed and kept looking sternly into the camera until the operator had the wits to shift back to the petty officer. It was a relief to Kuwahara to hear that seasoned public speaker's voice also shaking slightly.

Epilogue

Three months had brought spring to Victoria. Spring brought mites, flash floods, food shortages in the refugee camps and isolated towns, and drunken brawls between Associated States and Federation troopers.

Spring also brought a peace conference. It began to look as if Victoria would be independent and united before midsummer.

Candice Shores wasn't going to be around for any more of Victoria's troubles or achievements. The man who walked down the road from the Fort Stafford gate beside her would be. Raoul Zimmer wore fatigues, with the shoulder patch that declared him a Federation regular seconded to the Associated States (eventually, Planetary Republic) Forces.

"They need good NCOs," he'd said when announcing his application for the staff of the Associated States' NCO School. "I know the job. I've even taught it. So why not me?"

Nobody had any arguments, particularly since Scout Company and its parent Victoria Brigade were going out of existence. Had gone out of existence, in fact, a week ago, and now Fort Stafford was waiting for its new tenants. Most of them were still down in Thorntonsburg or up north, at Kellysburg, Mount Houton, or Fort Kornilov (which had been Camp Aounda, and it cut back on the brawls quite a lot when its new name was announced).

Most of the shops and eateries along the road were closed, some of them shuttered, with one or two being torn down or at least cannibalized for parts. One had a sign so new that it was blank, an open door, with someone out in front planting flowers.

"I feel like a drink," Zimmer said. "Mind if I treat you over there?"

"Lead on."

The gardener looked up as the two soldiers approached. "Hey," he said. "We're not open, particularly not for Feddie troops and their bouncies—oh, sorry, Major Shores and—unh, Top Zimmer?"

Recognition came just in time to keep the boy from being stuffed headfirst into his own fertilizer bag. Shores grinned. "I'm back to being a captain for the time being. And you're BoJo Johnson."

"Hope so," the boy said. "After this last winter, I'm not sure of much. But Kate'll have something for you, no matter what."

"Kate?"

"This is the new branch of Hennessey's. Kate's in to help set up. I'd be painting the sign, but she wanted me to get the landscaping in while the weather held."

"Good luck," Zimmer said. They walked up the path toward the door.

"You don't sound surprised," Shores said.

"I'm not. This is a planet of people hard to put down for good. I've seen refugees on other planets. A lot of them looked like they didn't know what hit them, or how to hit back. Not the Vics. Even the A.I. bastards knew that if the universe punches you, punch it right back."

"You sound like you're planning to stay."

Zimmer looked horror-struck. "Me, stay on this frozen dustball? It's a good thing they took back those leaves, even if they did give you seniority. You're not thinking clear enough for field-grade yet.

"No, I'm going to put in two years here. That'll put me up to thirty-six. Then I can take my bonus, go back to Pied Noir, marry somebody young enough to have kids with, and start a little peach orchard on the side.

"You can't soldier forever, but when it's like our Scouts, or helping people like the Vics, you sort of wish you could."

Shores couldn't find the right reply to that before they stepped inside, and didn't want to give the wrong one. Kate Hennessey saved her the trouble.

Hennessey was standing behind the bar, wearing an apron

over coveralls that were so filthy that the apron seemed pointless. She had three drinks set out on the bar.

"Heard you talking with BoJo," she said. "Then it came on the radio that they're starting pickups on all Fed personnel who aren't staying. Apparently the Shogun wants to be on his way home by tonight."

"Where's the nearest pickup?"

"Right here. I dropped a wee word in the right ear. Hennessey's is the rendezvous for the Fort Stafford area."

Shores suspected that Kate Hennessey had also dropped a not-so-wee bribe in the right pocket. Having Federation people waiting for pickup in her bar would add a nice chunk to her credit balance.

Shores reached for her card. Hennessey shook her head, picked up one drink, and shoved the other two across the bar.

"On the house. I'm not sorry the Federation's going, but I'd be a damned sight sorrier if it hadn't stayed until the job was done."

Shores struggled for a reply and this time gave up. Her eyes were stinging, and it wasn't entirely the raw whiskey or the faulty dust filters in the ventilation system.

Rose Liddell had pulled rank for one of the few times in her career to borrow a massage table from Sick Bay. The surgeon had sworn on the honor of all her ancestors that nobody needed it today, but Liddell had gone on feeling slightly guilty until the table put her to sleep.

She awoke, feeling much too refreshed to even think about guilt, but also hearing the intercom chiming insistently.

"Captain here."

It was the exec. "Our last shuttle just docked. They'll be secured in about ten minutes."

"What else does the squadron still have out?"

"Only a couple of attackers. They'll be staying out to record the departure, then docking on the fly."

"Fine. Then pass the word to start securing for getting under way, and . . . Pavel, how many flares did we use? Up to our allowance?"

"No, Captain. Remember, we had an unlimited allowance, and Commander Charbon drew extras for Operation Mikhail."

"Do we still have them?"

"I'll check."

Liddell had barely finished dressing when Bogdanov came back. "About sixty left."

"Good. Have them ready to launch when we get under way, and fix the accounts accordingly. Also—remember our final jamming effort?"

"Yes, but the security—"

Liddell adopted her most elegant diction. "Bugger the security, Pavel. Unless Kuwahara orders otherwise, I want it for our getting-under-way music."

"Aye-aye, ma'am." She could have sworn he was trying not to laugh. That wasn't as extraordinary for her executive officer as it would have been when *Shenandoah* was commissioned.

In fact, after *Shenandoah*'s first mission, Rose Liddell wondered what would seem extraordinary. She also had to admit that she wasn't entirely eager to find out.

"Warehouse inspection seems a reasonable compromise," Prime Minister Gist said. "I know many of your merchant captains wouldn't let our inspectors aboard. Inspection after issuing makes concealment or unauthorized alteration too tempting."

"I agree," Payaral Na'an said. "I think we can draft a plan for inspection and present it to Colonel Nieg for his approval." Na'an spoke Anglic quite well enough to dispense with a translator when he wanted to relax or didn't want a recording of the conversation.

Gist stared at the Merishi, who had not in fact grown a second head or started projecting telepathic erotica. "Nieg?"

"Why not? He is the real chief of the Security Advisory Committee, with all due respect to Major Morley and Commander Franke. If arms shipments are not a matter of security, what is?"

"Yes, but you've—" Gist broke off as General Parkinson slid open the door to the balcony.

"The task force is forming up for departure," she said. "I've sent my aide for an extra telescope."

Gist looked at his watch. It was 1925 of a soft spring evening, the kind when even Victoria's harshest outlines were blurred by spring flowers and haze. Toward the zenith, though, visibility was perfect, and the squadron was scheduled to get under way at 1930.

"We'll be right out, Alys," Gist said.

"I have what?" the Merishi said when Parkinson had gone.

"No bloody hope of bribing Nieg into talking about why he's on the trail of those mercenaries."

"Why would I be so foolish as to expect Colonel Nieg to take a bribe?"

"Because you and I think a good deal alike. Both of us want to find out why Nieg's got that particular hair up his arse."

Na'an grinned after Gist explained the idiom. "I see. Suppose we offered to help him with the search if he told us the reason for it."

"Trust a Merishi to know how to bargain," Gist said. "But what do you mean by *we*? I really have no information—or at least none that I could acquire without stepping on toes."

"I do not know that I have any information either," the Merishi said. "But I have more . . . contacts, is the word?— in what may be the right places. It would have to be done very discreetly, of course, because already my association has enemies over this monopoly of our trade with Victoria. But it may be that this matter of the mercenaries is so important that knowing about it is worth making enemies."

Gist frowned. "I sometimes wonder if we don't underestimate your people's military skills."

"Of course you do," Na'an said, positively grinning. "Otherwise, the young folk of our Navy who have taken to the way of the warrior would not surprise you nearly so much."

Gist was still trying to sort that out when Parkinson called. "People, the telescopes are here and I think *Shenandoah*'s started signaling."

The five-minute warning had just sounded when Candice Shores slipped into bunkroom D-4 and sat down on the bunk opposite Brigitte Tachin. She promptly slid off the bunk onto the floor, because the bunk was completely packed with personal gear and spares. It had been Charlie Longman's, but Longman was staying behind on Victoria, and it was only two hours ago that D-4 learned it would have a fourth for the return trip.

"Sorry, Candy," Tachin said. "You can take either Brian's or Elayne's bunks for getting under way. He's Communications O.O.W. and she's riding one of the photo attackers. Then we can sort things out when we're all here."

Shores stretched out her long legs and began pulling off her boots. "Thanks for letting me bunk down. You would not believe the mob scene aboard the transports. Even the people pods are elbows in the ear and feet in the crotch."

"Thank Charlie Longman," Tachin said. "If he hadn't used his award of seniority to get out, we wouldn't have a spare bunk."

"Even if you did, I wouldn't bunk with him."

"Oh, Charlie's not as impossible as he was. Besides, I am sure that you and Elayne could wear him to a nub in the course of the trip back to Riftwell."

Even in her bare feet Shores loomed over Tachin. "Brigitte, do you want to spend the trip in sick bay?"

"That would spoil your friendship with Brian even more than your seducing him."

"Then don't insult my taste in men like that again. Please." Shores's severe look dissolved into a hoot of laughter.

She strapped her carry-on to the central console, put her hands on the upper bunk, and vaulted lightly into it. She had just finished strapping herself in when the two-minute warning sounded and the intercom screen lit up.

It showed *Shenandoah* riding against a starscape, what might have been an attacker glinting off to one side. Just barely visible beyond her was Dockyard, now dark and likely to remain so until Victoria had enough of a navy to make it worth reactivating.

"One minute," Brian Mahoney's voice said. Then it was thirty seconds, and finally the countdown of the last ten, to "three—two—one—getting under way."

The sky caught fire, and an ancient march roared out over all the radios tuned to catch *Shenandoah*'s departure.

* * *

The sky burned as long as *Shenandoah*'s flares lasted. By the time they were gone, the rest of the squadron was following the flagship's lead.

Blazing like the head of a comet, trailing her squadron and her flares like the comet's tail, *Shenandoah* rode out of Victoria orbit. Her course took her almost straight out from the latitude of what had once been the Dominion of Victoria. It was a long time before she dropped below the horizon, and then it was as much the result of the planet's turning as of the outward surge of the battlecruiser toward her Jump point.

By the time *Shenandoah* and her squadron were only moving stars fading into the fixed ones, Lucco DiVries had finished dinner and come out on the terrace of the house. *His* house now, or at least "our house," as Teresa suggested calling it, when she threatened to break his head for calling it "the house."

Coming back to the farm and plant had been family loyalty at first, with elements of "making the best of a bad job." With the amnesty, 'Reesa was in no danger of losing the property over Ray's political antics, but she was short of customers, cash, and labor. Several neighbors who were inclined to settle scores over Ray's politics had offered to buy her out. Their offers hadn't been generous, and their threats pretty open.

So Lucco decided that the best thing to do was go back and take over, before 'Reesa had to swallow her pride and ask him. For a while, everything but trying to be a father to the kids was more going through the motions. But he'd spent too many years here for mind or body to forget as much as he'd thought they had. The old routine came back easily, and with it a new pleasure.

The shortage of labor remained, though, until DiVries heard through Brian Mahoney that Charles Longman was resigning from the Navy to stay on Victoria. He'd been awarded enough seniority to fulfill his legal obligation, but his bonus was petty cash, particularly in Victoria's postwar inflation. He also had some sort of working partnership with Joanna Marder.

One thing led to another, and that to a third, which was inviting Karl Pocher to join the farm crew too. Pocher had grown up on a farm and planned to return to one when he and Mahmoud Sa'id both left space. Pocher looked like he was the loneliest but the most useful of the three.

'Reesa had her reservations about hosting what she was convinced was going to be a two-way three-match and expressed them as sharply as usual. It was the first time DiVries felt that he had to stand up to her, and not just because she was discussing his friends' sexual habits loud enough for the children or even the neighbors to hear.

The result was a quarrel that so nearly matched one of 'Reesa's bouts with Ray that she nearly tripped him into bed to make up. Nearly wasn't quite, thank God, and he'd won a little more time to settle the new people and the old memories of Sophie before he had to come to terms with 'Reesa on that point. After all, she was well short of forty, and nobody with eyes in their head could call her bad-looking—

A light blinked on the horizon—no, moonlight reflected off metal. The reflection grew into a lifter, riding low and slow. DiVries waited until it grounded, then squinted against the dust until the fans died and the rear hatch slammed down.

"Hurry up, I've got three more stops!" the pilot shouted. Charlie Longman was the first out, almost tripping as he came and fumbling to do up his coat. Marder followed him, caught him by the arm, turned him around, and gently put his coat in order.

Then she put her arms around him and held him, so that their dusty cheeks met. DiVries grinned. He'd hoped that the farm would provide Marder and Longman with neutral territory where they could decide on their relationship without pressure in either direction. He wondered if he should instead see about finding a double bed.

Karl Pocher came out last, with a benign grin for the couple blocking his way. It was a remarkable grin for someone loaded with most of three people's baggage, and it settled DiVries's last fears. Whatever agreement Longman and Marder had reached, it was all right with Pocher.

"Welcome to Deal Farm," DiVries said, stepping forward to relieve Pocher of his load.

"We should plant a few trees," Longman said. "Then we could call it Shady Deal Farm."

"Fine, if you can provide the fertilizer."

"This is an organics plant, isn't it?"

"Charlie, the only way you can fertilize a tree around here is to bury a large mass of fresh animal tissue and then put the seedling in it. Were you thinking of volunteering to be the tissue?"

Longman stared, while Pocher and Marder laughed. Then he mimed pulling his foot out of his mouth. DiVries swung one bag up on his shoulder and shouted, " 'Reesa! Get the kids washed and put something up to heat. Our new crew's here."

ABOUT THE AUTHOR

Roland J. Green is an active SFWA member, and the author of the PEACE COMPANY series, as well as co-author (with Jerry Pournelle) of two military SF novels in the JANISSARIES series. *The Sum of Things* is the third book in his STAR-CRUISER *SHENANDOAH* trilogy. He lives in Chicago.

SENSATIONAL SCIENCE FICTION